Rising Calm

Haley Fisher

Silver Tongue Press

Published by Silver Tongue Press

Milwaukee, Wisconsin, USA

www.silvertonguepress.com

Haley Fisher

Copyright © 2013 Haley Fisher

All rights reserved.

ISBN: 0615765246

ISBN-13: 978-0-615-76524-2

This is a work of fiction. All characters are from the authors imagination. Any similarities to real people, places, or events is entirely coincidental.

No part of this book is to be reproduced without the publisher's permission.

DEDICATION

To my Mum, whose beautiful fight inspires me every day.

ACKNOWLEDGMENTS

Thanks to my family, my parents and siblings especially, who were my fans long before there was even a story to become fans of, and who took it in stride when I told them rather out of the blue I had decided to write a book. Thank you to Christa, who was the first to fall in love with what I had written, and whose support gave me the courage to share my story with other people. A special thanks to Taylor, my very first editor. Your continued excitement for the story I was writing and all the tips and suggestions you gave before anyone else was even allowed to see the pages helped make this story what it is. Thanks to Natasha, *Rising Calm*'s number one fan. Your unshakable faith in my writing and your love of my characters helps me believe that these stories of mine may be the kind to find other true fans. To my mom and Ali, thank you for always being excited to receive the next pages of my book. Thank you to all my friends and family who could never wait to ask how my book was coming along, and to all of whom I've promised signed copies. Another important thank you to Silver Tongue Press for believing in and being excited by my story. Thanks to my editor Lisa and my publisher Rebecca, both of whom never missed a chance to boost my confidence in my story and my writing, and thank you to Beth for being as excited about all this as I am. Last but certainly not least, I'd like to thank my Lord and Savior, who has given me an incredibly blessed life and the ability—and love—to read and write.

Haley Fisher

PROLOGUE

Thaddeus gazed down into the eager face of the young girl in front of him. Her long brown hair was curling out of its two braids, and her cheeks were rosy from the excitement of the day. It was her seventh birthday and, as far as she knew, no day would ever be bigger.

Her brown eyes were wide as she stared at the ring he'd just placed in the palm of her hand. "What's it for?" she asked in wonder, unable to tear her eyes away from the diamond-surrounded emerald.

Thaddeus chuckled. "It's for you, my dear."

"How come?" she asked curiously.

"Because it's your birthday," he told her.

That was the perfect answer for her seven-year-old mind. What other possible reason could she need to accept a present?

Amos could only assure that her parents were engaged in other conversations for so long, so Thaddeus knew he had to make this quick. Quicker than he'd like. Quicker than the situation truly called for.

The child in front of him was running a hesitant finger over the gemstones that were set in the golden band. He smiled, knowing she would not be able to read the sadness in the expression. "Those are real, you know," he said, causing her to look back up and match his smile with one of her own. "That emerald, those diamonds, they're very real."

She blinked a few times in disbelief before trying to slide the ring on her finger. It was at least two sizes too big, and he chuckled at her confused face.

"You will grow into it, dear one. Sooner than you think."

She left it on her finger anyway and held her hand up between them to examine the way the ring caught the light. He repositioned his body so the ring was hidden from her parents.

"Your mommy and daddy probably wouldn't like it if they knew I was giving this to you. Let's keep it a secret, okay?" he said. He needed her to agree. He was a stranger to their daughter, giving her an elaborate gift; no parent would be quite comfortable with that.

That's all the young girl really needed to hear to be convinced to keep quiet. She nodded vigorously, but he needed to be sure. When her gaze was drawn to her new ring once more, Thaddeus took a chance and murmured a small cast under his breath as he stepped away from her. Her eyes grew cloudy for a single moment, and the light bulb in the lamp next to her popped quietly. Not a soul in the room noticed.

Thaddeus made his way across the room, toward the front door to stand next to Amos. "It's done," he said softly.

Amos did no more than nod. The two of them shook hands with Mr. and Mrs. Weaver who were thanking the guests as they left, and then Thaddeus took one long, last look at the brown-eyed birthday girl. The ring was gone from her hand, hidden away in a pocket, no doubt.

Thaddeus dipped his head to her. "Goodbye, Cara," he said under his breath. "I wish your life would take you down a different path." Then he and Amos were out the door and away.

They walked for a time without speaking, as Thaddeus was uncomfortable with Earth's modes of transportation. Amos finally looked over at his companion. "My *niece*, Thaddeus?"

This was not the first time Amos had asked the question. "I cannot help the way things are, or the way they are going to be. You know that by now."

He did, but Thaddeus knew Amos hoped for a different answer. "My niece," he murmured. It was not a question this time.

"Someday her destiny will make sense," Thaddeus promised. "She does have magic in her; it is strong, even now. And it will only grow stronger in time. She will have plenty of people to help her along the way. She will never be alone, Amos."

"You can't promise that," Amos said sharply.

"I've seen it," Thaddeus answered calmly.

After everything, Amos was still skeptical of magic. The powers Thaddeus claimed were beyond Amos' understanding sometimes, but he didn't refute Thaddeus' claim. He simply sighed heavily.

"When do you go back?" Amos asked instead.

"Where do you think we're walking? I've done what I came to do. And I must return before questions arise," Thaddeus told him. "Amos, watch over the girl. She has great things in store, and she won't know what to do with all she learns. Do not leave her to discover it all alone."

Thaddeus waited until Amos agreed before he drew to a halt. "Your help was indispensable, my friend. None of this could have been done without you. You've played an integral part in the future of my world. And for that I can never thank you enough."

Amos didn't have the time to form a response before Thaddeus had bowed to him, backed up two swift steps, and disappeared.

Book One

"We must be willing to let go of the life we planned so as to have the life that is waiting for us."

- Joseph Campbell

Haley Fisher

1

"Cara!"

"Cara, honey!" My father echoes my mom.

"School starts today!"

"You should be getting ready!"

I groan and pull my covers over my head as the voices of my parents float up the stairs. I peek out of the nest of warm blankets I've created overnight to see my clock. It says 6:20. The alarm isn't set to go off for another thirty minutes. I call out something unintelligible and promptly slide down to the middle of my bed to go back to sleep.

I succeed too, for about ten minutes, before my mother realizes I haven't moved. She enters my room with a loud "Up, up, up!", whips the covers off me, and turns on my light. I don't budge.

"Isn't Jade coming at 7:15 to get you?" mom asks.

I crack an eye open to look at her. "When has it ever taken me"—I check the clock again quickly—"forty-five minutes to get ready? For anything?"

She smiles and pats my arm. "We just don't want you to be late. See you downstairs!" She whirls away, calling out for my younger sister.

Now I'm awake and I'm cold. I have a blanket that was pushed nearly off the bed last night due to my tossing and turning. Without sitting up I drag it over myself and curl up to close my eyes again.

Soon Sophie nestles her way under my blanket. I open my arms, and she slides into them. I kiss the top of her head, which smells like her strawberry shampoo, and the two of us fall asleep together with the sound of pots and pans banging downstairs.

Sophie, at the age of nine, doesn't have to be at school until about 8:00. When I finally have to get up she looks at me sleepily, soft brown hair forming a staticky halo around her head.

"Do we have to go today?" she yawns.

"I'm afraid so, little girl," I say. Unable to see well in the darkness, I stub my toe, hard, on one of the half-empty cardboard boxes lying around my room. I bite my lip to keep from cursing.

"Don't swear, Cara," Sophie tells me sternly, watching from my bed.

"I didn't swear!"

"You were though. In your head."

Affronted, I look over at her as I rub my injured toe. "Okay smarty pants, you walk through this minefield without running into anything."

I should know better. Sophie's had this house memorized since we moved in. Just because it's dark in here and I've shifted some of the boxes doesn't mean she doesn't know where they all are.

She gives me her are-you-serious look—a look she perfected long ago—and daintily makes her way to the door, smirks at me. Then she dashes out of the room giggling. I give chase, knocking over some more boxes sitting in the hallway. She squeals and tries to close her door before I reach it.

"Too late!" I tell her, and she shrieks when I pick her up and toss her onto her own bed, tickling her. She fights back, laughing hard.

Eventually I fall back onto her pillow. "Okay, okay, I surrender!" I laugh. "We need to pick you out some clothes anyway."

Sophie sticks out her tongue. "What if I wore my jammies?" she asks me, still breathless.

"Then all the people at school would be jealous that their parents didn't let them wear *their* jammies, and you'd never make any friends," I reply. She's been trying to wear her pajamas to school for months now.

"Maybe I don't want any friends here." Her big, brown eyes are suddenly serious.

The joyful mood evaporates. I hug her close. "Oh, honey," I say sadly, "yes, you do. You may not know it now, but yes, you do."

She wraps her little arms around me, and we sit there for a minute not saying anything. Then, "Can I wear my Pokémon shirt?" she asks in a small voice.

I smile down at her. "I don't think there's a kid in that school who won't want to be your friend if you wear your Pokémon shirt. Good choice."

She grins and hops over to her closet. "I can't find it," she tells me over her shoulder after a moment of searching through the pile of clothes sitting on the floor. I glance around her room at the stacks of boxes and piles of toys and clothing.

Grimacing, I say, "Yeah, we should probably do something about your room when you get home today kid."

"And then we should probably do something about yours," she shoots back.

"And then the hallway."

"Then the kitchen."

"And the dining room."

"Bathroom?" she suggests. And then she sings out "Found it!" and drags a long-sleeved t-shirt from the pile.

I stare at it critically. "Maybe we should at least iron it first." She tosses it to me. "Find some jeans," I say as I leave the room. "Some clean ones."

I make it down the stairs just in time to hear our front door shut, and I can see my parents getting into their cars through the front window. They didn't even bother to see if we were actually awake after all that fuss. Now I have to find the iron myself.

After digging through a few boxes in the kitchen I finally find it, the cord tangled in some dishtowels. I can't find the board, so I just use the countertop.

I'm not surprised that my parents are already gone, or that they didn't wish us good luck at school, or even that they couldn't be bothered to find Sophie clothes to wear before they left. Just because I'm not surprised doesn't mean it isn't frustrating though. The least they could do is act like they're sorry for up-ending our lives again.

This is our fifth house in four years. All in different states, and we always pack up and move the moment my father needs to be somewhere new, no matter how or what we're doing.

When I finish I unplug the iron, leave it on the counter, and go back upstairs. Sophie is still in her pajamas when I enter her room.

"What have you been doing?" I ask.

"Waiting for you," she answers, snatching the shirt from my hands. Then she grabs her pants and socks from her bed and trots into my room with me trailing behind.

"Do you know what you're going to wear today?" she asks me parentally.

"Yes ma'am, I do. I picked it out last night." In truth I have only unpacked a few of my clothes, so my choices are severely limited. I pull a purple v-neck and dark boot-cut jeans from the suitcase by my bed. Sophie nods in approval, earning a grin from me, and begins changing as I walk across the hall to the small bathroom.

"Hair up or down?" I ask her on my way out.

"Down," she decides. "Will your hair even stay in a ponytail?"

I feel the ends of my dark brown hair, cut just above my shoulders. "I think so," I say uncertainly.

"Still down," Sophie tells me.

Last, I slip on the ring I've had ever since I can remember. It's a bit ostentatious, an emerald surrounded by a few diamonds. I've been told they are real but I have a hard time believing it. So, as I always do, I twist it around so only the gold band shows and the gems are hidden on the inside of my hand.

Finally Sophie and I both make it downstairs so I can throw together breakfast before I leave. By then it's already 7:10.

"Dang," I mutter, scrambling eggs.

"Cara," Sophie says, "can you pull my hair back before you leave?"

"Of course," I say. "Go get a hair tie and a brush."

She rushes off while I scrape the eggs onto our plates.

Before she comes back down, I hear Jade at the door. "It's open!" I yell.

She comes sauntering in, dropping her bag by the door and collapsing at the table, head down.

"Hard day?" I ask.

She grins ruefully up at me, a glint in her pretty hazel eyes. Jade has an elegant face and tanned skin, and, although she's too modest to admit it, she's strikingly beautiful. "Have I ever told you I hate school?" she answers my question with one of her own.

"Hate is a strong word," I say, offering her some eggs, which she accepts.

"So is love. At least I didn't say that."

"So is elephant, but people say that all the time," says Sophie, bounding back down the stairs and sending Jade and me into fits of laughter.

Sophie holds out the brush to me when she's done eating, but Jade says, "Here, let me do that." I nod at her gratefully and stack up the plates in the sink, running water over them and making a note to clean them when I get back from school.

Now Sophie dashes back upstairs to get her backpack, so Jade tosses her heavy, dark hair over her shoulder to gaze at me shrewdly. "You alright?"

I take a minute before I respond. "I think so. A little stressed, kind of anxious. But I think I'm alright."

"Good. Soph, let's go!" she hollers up the stairs. I raise my eyebrows at her. "What?" she asks. "I love being that little girl's third mom."

Jade and I met only a week and a half ago, when we first moved in, but she's already stepped up and been more helpful to me than anyone I've ever met, in any state. I never told her I was overwhelmed, but she noticed anyway. She saw how often my parents are gone and that Sophie is under my care most of the time, so she didn't waste a moment in taking Sophie under her wing. She's the one who asked around and found Mrs. Finch, a mom nearby who has a little boy Sophie's age and can give Sophie a ride to school. And Jade willingly takes on whatever she can to lighten my load. Needless to say, we quickly became good friends.

We're leaving later than planned, but Jade says she doesn't mind. "It's not like I want to spend extra time at school," she tells me as we pile into her car.

Soon I'm hugging Sophie goodbye as we drop her off at the Finch's. Then Jade and I are once again comparing our schedules, deciding where and when we can meet during the day, and then, too quickly, we've arrived at Shawnee Mission East, the latest in my long list of high schools.

"Seniors get the best parking," Jade explains, pulling into a side lot, "but this is way better than where the sophomores have to park." She shuts off the car and turns to examine me carefully.

"What's the verdict?" I ask without meeting her eyes.

"You look a little green," she replies.

I sigh before I explain. "Would it kill my parents to move at the beginning of a school year, just once?" It's the end of February, and by now every high schooler in the building is comfortably settled in. Except for lucky me. I get to come in and screw it up for everyone.

Jade looks exasperated, like she knows exactly what I'm thinking. "You really think anyone here is going to care? There are about four hundred kids in our junior class alone. No one is going to mind one more. Especially a cute one like you," she promises, patting the top of my head. "Now come on. I know Ms. Shepherd: no assigned seats and she only cares about the students that sit in the front, so we want nice seats in the very back row."

That gets a weak laugh out of me. I brace myself, then Jade and I step out of the car into the throng of students making their way through the door. A few call out greetings to Jade, and a few more ask about me. Soon I've met a handful of people, all of whose names I have forgotten by the time we reach the fourth floor.

When we walk into our first class, which I thankfully have with Jade, only about five kids are there. Jade places us in seats in the back corner and slings her backpack into the seat next to her. A few minutes later, I see why. A gangly boy with waves of honey-colored hair and headphones in his ears strolls into the room and makes for the seat Jade has saved. With a glance, he takes in my new student demeanor.

"Cara Weaver?" he guesses, removing an earbud.

"Max Fedderman?" I ask in reply. I've heard about Max, though I've never met him. According to Jade they have been friends forever. I've been told he's a little geeky sometimes (the proof is in the graphic tee he's wearing under his dark blazer), but if he's as great as Jade says he is, I'm sure we'll get along fine.

He nods and flashes me an easy grin. "Nice to finally meet you." Then he shoots Jade a meaningful look.

"What?" she asks. "It's not like it's my fault you all haven't met before."

"Yeah," Max says, sliding into the seat. "Yeah, it kind of is. I've been at your house, what, five times since she moved here? And you never walked me down the street to say hi?"

"You never asked me to!"

"Well that might have been a little weird. 'So, Jade, I hear you have a new friend. I must meet her, so though we've never talked before and she probably has no idea who I am, take me to her house immediately.'"

"Oh, I hope that's not how you would have worded it," I break in, earning a grin from Max. "What were you listening too?" I gesture to the iPod he's stowing into his backpack.

"Snow Patrol," Max answers. "You know them?"

"I love them!" I exclaim. "They're my favorite!"

"You too? They just sound so..."

"Oh, I know! And that new song they just released? I couldn't stop listen—"

"Okay, okay, break it up ladies," Jade interjects, smiling.

"She's just jealous," Max whispers to me as the bell rings. "She has no idea who Snow Patrol is."

I laugh quietly.

"And by the way," he smiles when the teacher's back is turned, "welcome to East."

****

I have my next few classes on my own, so when English ends I wave goodbye to Max and Jade and head off down the hall.

History is my next class, but as I tend to find history uninteresting, it passes quickly. However, when I get to chemistry, a subject I've been dreading, my teacher makes me wait in the front of class while everyone else takes their seats. I shuffle my feet uncomfortably, twist my ring around my finger, and try to look anywhere but at my classmates.

"Class!" he calls as soon as the bell rings. "We have a new student with us today. Cara Weaver, from Minnesota. Cara? Would you like to say anything?"

Not really, I think. Aloud I say: "Umm...I'm actually from New York. We moved when I was seven. To Alabama. Minnesota was just where we lived before Kansas." I look to my teacher in hopes that he will let me sit down, but he just gives me a nod of encouragement so I fumble for something else to say. "Okay. I'm a junior. I've lived in eight different states, but I'd never been to Kansas before we moved here. I..." I stop, unsure what else to tell them, but Mr. Marks claps his hands so I stay silent.

"Well, we're glad to have you!" he tells me.

Some of the class is looking at me curiously, but some are clearly uninterested and two are asleep. Not wanting to get them caught, I hold back a laugh.

"Why don't you sit...there?" Mr. Marks points to a lab table. There's a boy with loose curls of sandy-blonde hair sitting there fiddling idly with a pencil. His books are strewn across the table. Not even looking up when I approach, he just sweeps his books over to clear half the table for me.

I notice some of the girls (most of them, actually) watching me walk to the table with interest, but I realize they're watching the boy, not me. And I soon know why. When I take the time to look at him, I see that he's much better looking than I thought. Incredibly good-looking, actually, with defined muscles showing through his fitted blue shirt and bright eyes.

I must not be a very standard teenage girl, because my first thought is that I'd rather not be paired up with someone who is so unapproachably attractive. I take my seat anyway.

Since my new partner doesn't speak, I don't either. I get out a pen to take notes. Even though I'm trying to follow what Mr. Marks says carefully, within five minutes I'm completely lost. Planning to catch up on my own time, I stop paying attention and doodle on the corner of my page. After a while, I notice the boy next to me watching me with interest.

I raise my eyebrows questioningly at him. Not speaking, he continues to look at me with his piercing, dark green eyes.

"I've never taken chemistry before," I inform him.

"I didn't ask," he replies quietly.

"Maybe not out loud," I mutter, falling silent as Mr. Marks looks up to see who's talking. He doesn't seem to suspect me and turns back to the board.

When I peek over at him, the boy is trying to conceal a grin. He catches my eye and gestures to my half-empty notebook page with a hand that's covered in rings. Almost every one of his fingers has a gold or silver band on it, and some have more than one. I eye them for a moment—I've never seen a boy wear that much jewelry. Then I realize I don't know what he wants. So he slides my spiral out from under my hand himself to write something.

When he hands it back, I point to his equally empty page of notes and wonder why he didn't just use that. He appears to know exactly what I'm asking, because like it was his plan all along, he just smiles and busily begins taking notes on the blank page. I roll my eyes.

I'm Crispin Calaway, the note reads. *I'm new here too.*

After how kept to himself he's been so far, I wonder briefly why he's telling me. Then again, I suppose it doesn't really matter.

Hi Crispin. When did you get here? I scrawl back.

He seems pleased when I hand the page back to him. *Last week*, is his reply.

After I read it, he takes it back and writes again. *You've never taken chemistry before?*

Ha! I knew you were wondering! I show him, and then continue writing. *It wasn't required in Minnesota. Or Arizona. You could choose if you wanted physics or chemistry.*

When Crispin reads that, his eyes widen a fraction. He looks at me, a question on his lips, then remembers we can't talk now and hurriedly starts to write again, pencil flying across the page. Before he finishes, Mr. Marks turns to face the class and begins a demonstration, so Crispin slows his writing to a more normal speed but doesn't stop. When our teacher glances at the two of us, I nudge Crispin under the table to warn him. He immediately makes a show of looking at the board and pretending to copy what Mr. Marks has written there.

It's only later that I marvel at how he knew exactly what I meant without any words.

Next time Mr. Marks looks down at his experiment, Crispin quietly slides the page back to me. I take a moment to make sure no one is watching before I read it.

Arizona? That's where you were before Minnesota? And you've lived in eight states? How long were you in each of them?

I mouth "wow" at him. *Anything else you'd like to know about my life? Hospital I was born in? Social security number?*

Just answer the questions.

I reply shortly. *Yes. New York, Alabama, Colorado, Virginia, Texas, Arizona, Minnesota, Kansas. We stayed different amounts of time in every one of them. Why?*

I was born in Arizona. I actually lived in Texas for a while, too.

That's it? That was a lot of questions to tell me where you used to live. Why did you really ask?

Crispin doesn't write a reply, and I'm about to snatch the paper back from him when I notice why. Mr. Marks is making his way back toward our table. Crispin nonchalantly slides my notebook under his own.

"Miss Weaver?" Mr. Marks begins. "Is everything alright back here?"

"Yes, it is," I tell him. I hurry to come up with an explanation as to why the pages of my open binder are blank. "I'm just a little lost. I've never taken chemistry before this, and I'm not quite as ready as I thought I was."

Crispin coughs next to me, I think covering up a laugh. I kick his stool. He glares at me. I pretend not to notice.

Mr. Marks looks confused, and I feel bad for him.

"Sorry," I say. "I'll try harder, I just came in a little unprepared today."

"Not to worry, Ms. Weaver," he says, brightening. "Chemistry is a tricky subject. Maybe a tutor?"

"Maybe," I reply, not wanting a tutor.

"Mr. Calaway here actually is quite a chemistry prodigy," Mr. Marks hints.

This time I am the one hiding my laughter. "Of course he is," I say with the straightest face I can manage.

Crispin starts to threateningly pull my notebook out from under his, so to appease him I quickly say, "I don't know if he would want to tutor me. It's alright."

"Oh, I don't mind." Crispin smirks at me. There is an odd accent to Crispin's voice, something I hadn't expected. I can't place it, and it's so faint I can't even be sure it's really there. "The more quickly you learn, the better this class will be for both of us," he says.

While Mr. Marks is thanking Crispin, I stick my tongue out at him. He gives me a that's-real-mature glance and turns to assure Mr. Marks that it's no problem at all.

"You're not tutoring me," I announce when the bell rings.

Crispin looks at me innocently. "You heard the teacher, Cara. You need to learn." He holds the door open for me. "Besides, it's not my fault I'm a chemistry prodigy." With that he walks off.

I fume for a moment, and then grumble to myself all the way to photography.

****

When I arrive at photo class, Max is sitting alone at a table with his headphones back in his ears.

"Antisocial much?" I ask, sitting across from him.

He grins and shuts his iPod off. "Little bit," he tells me. "Would you believe me if I said I just didn't like talking?"

"I would not."

"A wise decision."

"It's okay if you just don't like these people," I say, offering him an out.

"I just don't like these people," he says gratefully.

I grin. "That I understand."

"How's the first day going?" he asks me.

I think, wanting to answer truthfully. "I'm really not quite sure. It's going fine, I guess. It's pretty uneventful."

Max nods. Apparently uneventful is to be expected. "Any new friends?"

"I'm not quite sure," I say again.

"How can you not be sure if you made a friend or not? Didn't you learn how to do that in, like, preschool?"

I glower at him. "Yes." A boy with tousled black hair sits down a couple seats away from me. I unintentionally glance over at him, and then I can't help but continue to stare. The boy is paler than I'd expect someone with dark hair to be, with elegant cheekbones and a strong jaw and big eyes framed with dark lashes. He's tall and lean, and defined muscles run along his arms and shoulders and are visible under his shirt. He is without a doubt the most stunning boy I've ever seen.

Just then, his eyes flash up to my face, and it ridiculously causes my heart to skip a beat. I feel heat rush to my cheeks and I look away quickly, clearing my throat to continue talking to Max while I try to act less flustered than I am. "There was this one guy. My chemistry lab partner actually," I say to him. "And we... we argued for a lot of the period, but we still seemed to get along really well. He was immensely annoying, but it was somehow entertaining."

"Weird," Max says.

"Yeah. It was." I shrug.

"Anyone I know?" he asks.

"Do you know a Crispin Calaway?"

I see the dark-haired boy snap his head up like someone called his name, but I studiously ignore him this time.

"Crispin?" Max asks, looking at me with respect and leaning toward me over the table. "That blond senior boy?"

"I guess so?" I answer, unsure. "I don't know if he was a senior or not, but how many Crispin Calaways can there really be at this school?"

"You must be special," Max says. "I don't think that guy talks to anyone."

"Oh, I feel special. And he was quite chatty," I assure him.

Jade, looking pleased to see us, waltzes in right before the bell. She throws herself across two seats, dumps her things on the table, and knocks over the dark-haired boy's bag. She exclaims and apologizes loudly while I bend down to help him pick up the things that are now scattered around.

"So, Crispin Calaway, huh?" a lilting voice speaks next to me on the floor. I look up to find the black-haired boy watching me curiously. He is much closer than I expected. His eyes are surprisingly dark, darker than I first thought. Their color, like the sky before a storm, dances on the line between gray and deep blue. They're intense too, even in his lighthearted question, and made to look even more so because of his light skin.

I have to search for words for a moment before I can answer. "Crispin? Yeah, yeah. New lab partner." I pull away from his gaze with difficulty and reach for a few pens that I drop in his hand.

"Nice work, getting him to talk," the boy tells me quietly.

"Mm," I answer ambiguously. "I hear it's hard to do."

The boy smiles to himself. "Not if you know what to say." He holds out his hand and I shake it, hoping he can't feel my untimely rapid pulse jumping in my fingertips. "James Sable," he introduces himself.

"Cara Weaver," I reply.

"I know," James says.

"So Crispin's talked to you too?" I ask, somewhat relieved. I've just been trying to get through the first day, not draw attention to myself. "Well, I'm sure you were smart enough not to share that with the world. I didn't realize it was something you keep quiet about."

"Oh, people know he and I talk," James tells me as he sits back on his heels and watches me curiously. "But there's a difference between him talking to you and him talking to me."

"What difference is there exactly?"

"Well, I'm just kind of here. In the background. I'm around, but that doesn't exactly make it worth mentioning. But the new girl getting him to talk on the first day they meet? People are going to want to know what's special about you. I'm wondering myself."

I refuse to be distracted by the way his eyes rake over me, as though he'll be able to see the reason for my peculiarity if he looks hard enough. "And what, they don't care what's special about you?" I ask him.

James waits for a long time before he answers, and I wonder if I've somehow offended him. I'm about to apologize when he speaks again, quietly, jaw set. "No. If they remembered me I'm sure they'd be curious. But next to Crispin I'm rather forgettable." He doesn't say it bitterly, as I'd expect a statement like that to be; he says it like it's a fact.

James Sable is by far the best looking boy I've seen, bar none, so without thinking I answer just as quietly, "Forgettable is not how I would describe you." I regret the words as soon as I say them, and I blush furiously, wishing I could take them back. When I finally meet James' dark eyes again there's a small smile tugging at the corners of his mouth.

"Thanks for your help, Cara," he says to me. His mouth softens the C and makes the A's taller. An irrational thrill of pleasure shoots through me when he says my name.

It's only when James stands and dusts off his jeans that I realize that we've been down on the floor longer than necessary. I stumble to my feet. He doesn't look over at me as class starts.

"What was that?" Jade demands when I take my seat again.

"What?" I say.

She crosses her arms on the table and angles herself toward me. "He dropped about five pencils. It doesn't take two people that long to pick them up. What'd he say to you? He's cute." Jade says everything in one rushed whisper.

I blush again, because James is still in earshot, and he's undeniably cute. "Take a breath," I tell her, and in need of a quick distraction I say, "And never mind that. I think I've got something to tell you. Max found it interesting at least. You know Crispin Calaway?"

"Umm, *yes*. The gorgeous blond senior?" Jade gasps.

Distraction successful. "Why is the only thing people know about him is that he's blond?" I wonder aloud. Then, "Sure, him. He was pretty cute, I guess. Not the point. He's my chemistry lab partner." Jade lets out a squeak of disbelief. "Yep. And he *talked* to me."

"Oh. My. Gosh." Jade stares at me in wonder, her hand flying to cover her mouth. "No way! No way, he never talks!"

"Shh!" The majority of class has turned to look at us as I start to laugh, including the teacher who was beginning his lecture.

"Sorry, Mr. Lincoln!" Jade calls out a bit too loudly.

Mr. Lincoln strolls over to our table. I manage to glare at Jade before he reaches us. "What seems to be the problem?" He sounds more annoyed about the fact that we were talking loudly than the fact that we were talking at all.

Jade, unable to come up with an answer, seems lost for words. And, because I thought she had an excuse prepared, I'm not ready with a good explanation either. Max looks like he's about to say something, but he can't get it out. I think I'm doomed, then I hear, "Sorry Mr. Lincoln." James Sable leans over to join the conversation. "Cara was just double-checking what we're doing in class right now. New student, you know."

I'm staring at him incredulously, but I try to compose my expression as Mr. Lincoln turns back to me. "I see," he says. "And is she caught up now?"

"Yes sir, I believe so," James continues smoothly. "Turns out she actually took photography at her last school, so she's quite adept. It's rather impressive really."

I squeeze my eyes shut, willing him to stop there. I'm not even kind of impressive when it comes to photography.

"Well then, Cara," Mr. Lincoln says to me, "I'll be waiting to see your work." And then he strides away, back to the front of the class.

Torn between thanking him and scolding him, I fix James with a hard look.

"What?" he asks, eyes glittering. "You're welcome, for getting you out of that tight spot."

"He'll be waiting to see my work?" I hiss at him. "James, I can barely wind the film into the camera properly!"

"You might need to work on that then, huh?" he tells me with a crooked smirk.

I spin around to face the front of the room again and mutter about how "the dang people at this school keep getting me in trouble with the teachers on my first day". I catch a grin on James' face that reminds me instantly of Crispin, and it seems to me he knows exactly which other person I'm talking about.

I spend the rest of the hour alternating between trying to remember exactly what Crispin and I talked about so I can relay the information to Jade (who is hanging onto my every word), watching the people in the class work so that I know what to do, and staring at James Sable.

I find it impossible not to compare James to Crispin, especially now that I know they are friends, or at least something like it. Though very little about them seems similar, James' lack of concern for anyone else in the class, as well as the brooding expression on his face, reminds me of how Crispin was when I first sat down in chemistry. Something about them sets them apart from others around them, but no matter how hard I try, I can't put a finger on it.

James seems to be working on a project more advanced than what Jade and Max are doing. They're in the process of comparing their negatives and choosing the best ones. James has four different prints spread on the table. One is cut into strips and woven back together, one is tinged a sort of sepia color, and he's working on painting a third, adding bright splashes of color to the black and white picture. He either doesn't notice me watching or doesn't care that I am.

Mr. Lincoln comes up to me near the end of class and hands me an outline of the project I need to start. He then gets me a camera out of a back room and asks me to shoot the pictures in the next couple days before I fall too far behind.

"Texture Project," I read off, sitting back down with Jade and Max. "Doesn't sound too hard."

"Well, it is," Jade tells me, frowning at her negatives.

"Thanks for that," I reply. "Good to know I have something to look forward to."

At the end of class I check my schedule quickly to make sure I know where I'm going, then I stuff it back into my bag.

"Third lunch, right?" I ask Jade and Max as we walk out the door.

"Third lunch," Max affirms. "We'll meet you by the staircase."

I smile appreciatively. "See you in an hour!" I can't help but chance one look back at James Sable before I walk away, and I find, to my surprise, that he's looking at me too.

****

There's a sub in math, meaning no one actually has to pay attention (so I don't), but I rush out the door when the bell rings in order to find Jade and Max before the herd of students swallows them. Luckily, Max found a chair sitting in the hall and is standing on it so that he can see me. When he does, he shouts my name loudly over everyone's heads, and I pretend to look around with everyone else to see who it is he's calling to.

"Smooth," he tells me when I finally reach them.

I shrug modestly. "I do what I can."

I find that the lunch period goes by much too quickly; before I know it, there are only ten minutes left until we have to go back to class.

"The rest of the day will go fast, you'll see," Max says when he sees me glancing repeatedly at the clock with a frown. "After third lunch the last two classes fly by."

"You don't know that will happen," I say, without knowing if this is true or not.

Jade starts to say something, but before she even gets a word out, she leans back against her chair and frantically whispers: "Oh my gosh, oh my gosh, oh my gosh," Her wide eyes are locked on something behind me.

"Are you okay?" I ask her, slightly concerned.

Before she has time to reply, someone pulls out the chair next to me and sits down.

"Hey Cara," Crispin Calaway says to me. "Just wanted to drop these off for you. You need to get cracking on your chemistry studying if you want to understand the class." He sets a notebook down in front of me.

I pull it toward me with one finger, as if it's diseased. "Who says I want to understand the class?" I mutter.

"That's the spirit," he tells me pleasantly. Then he stands back and pushes the chair in. "See you tomorrow!" With that, he makes his way back through the maze of tables and meets James Sable at the door. They both glance over at me, Crispin still smiling and James looking curious, and then they walk out.

I look back up at Jade and Max, who are staring at me with ill-concealed awe. When I glance at the nearby tables, the students seated there are doing the same.

"What was that?" Jade asks.

I hold the notebook up for her to see. "Chemistry notes. Apparently I will fail the class without immediate help."

"Your teacher actually said that?" Max asks me.

"Well, he may not have used those exact words..." I confess.

"Wow. I know you said he's your lab partner and that you guys talked, but I didn't think that you guys..." Jade trails off.

I smile at how flustered they both are. "That we what? Were at the notebook-sharing stage in our relationship? I'll admit it, things are moving awfully fast between us." I look down at the notes. "Maybe I shouldn't have accepted this. After all, I don't want to give him the wrong idea."

"Wrong idea about what? Is note sharing now a form of dating?" Max asks.

"No," I reply. "Don't be silly. It just that, he probably thinks I'm actually going to look over these soon."

Jade shakes her head at my foolishness. "Cara, if a hot guy gives you his notebook, you accept it happily, and you read every damn word."

"I'm sorry," I tell her, "maybe you didn't hear me. These are *chemistry* notes."

The bell rings then, saving me from further conversation about Crispin and his special notebook. I flip to the first page as we walk out, and written there in Crispin's tight cursive I see written: *That actually is exactly why I asked. I guess I'm just a curious person. See you in class!*

I shake my head when I read it, but I can't help the small chuckle that escapes me. At least he answered my question.

James Sable is waiting with Crispin outside the lunchroom. He is leaning lazily against the wall with his arms crossed and is unseen by Cara Weaver as she exits with her friends. He sees her smile down at the notebook before snapping it shut and following Jade Thatcher down the hall.

Her short, dark brown hair seems to annoy her, he notes. She's continually pushing it out of her face. James is trying to figure out what Crispin, who is standing next to him, is thinking about her. Finally he just asks. "So, who is she Cris?"

Crispin, unexpectedly, shrugs. "No idea," he replies honestly.

They both watch her until she turns a corner and disappears from their line of sight.

Crispin's usually bright face is serious when he turns to look at James. "There was just something about her when she took her seat in class today. There was this pull, this odd connection. I don't know how to explain it."

"You don't think she...?" James doesn't have to finish his thought. Crispin will know exactly what he means.

"Oh no, I don't see how she can be," Crispin replies, but James can tell his heart isn't in it, because his green eyes darken slightly. "I hope she's not. For her sake," he says.

James silently agrees. He waits patiently while Crispin collects his thoughts.

Crispin finally gestures toward the door. "Come on. I've got to get a message to Verne." James nods in assent, glancing one last time at the hall where Cara was moments before.

She's too good for this, he thinks. *She's still innocent. She has a life here.* And, even though he isn't sure whether anyone will hear it, he sends up a prayer. *Don't let it be someone like her. Please don't let her life become like ours.*

Crispin has been standing off to the side, but now he claps James on the shoulder. His expression is one of complete understanding. "We've got to go."

Unnoticed, the two slip quietly out the door into the parking lot and dash away.

2

My last two classes of the day are both art classes; I have sculpting with Jade and then drawing and then, finally, the day will be done.

I soon discover that sculpting involves the teacher, Mrs. Prominian, handing you a lump of clay, telling you to be "one with it", and then waltzing off, humming to herself.

"So she's crazy," I whisper to Jade.

She stifles a giggle and quickly wipes the back of her hand across her cheek to hide it as our teacher flounces past. She ends up with a smear of red clay down the side of her face. Having no idea what I'm making, I dig into my clay. I don't think it matters though, because the class is between projects right now, so today is just "getting to know the clay".

Jade slides her chair closer to mine. "Do you want to talk about those guys you appear to be such good friends with?" she asks, grinning slightly.

I snort. "You do, huh?"

"Oh, so badly! I mean, my gosh! They're both so..."

"Gorgeous?" I finish with a smile, remembering the word she used to describe Crispin earlier.

She remembers, too. "Well yes. They are. You're going to have to accept that."

I hold up my hands. "I'm not denying it." I pound my clay into the table before continuing. "But, don't you think there's something...I don't know, just a little different about the two of them? Like they're in on some big secret?"

"They're high school boys," Jade says. "How big could their secret be?"

"I don't know," I answer. "I'm just saying. They seem different. They talk different. They act different. Not much, but still. You don't see it?"

Jade doesn't seem to want to talk about how different they are. At least, not how they are different in a weird way. "No. I think they are perfectly good-looking boys that obviously like you, so you should accept that. What I want to know is, do all boys from Arizona look like Crispin?"

I shake my head. "I lived in Arizona, remember? If all the guys there were that good-looking don't you think I would have campaigned harder to stay?"

Jade nods, acknowledging the truth of the statement. Then she continues. "But I mean, did you see his green eyes? And his muscles? And how mature he looked?"

I stare at her. That's what had set them apart from the rest of the school. They both acted older than everyone else, like they had seen more. They held themselves differently. They seemed too mature to be in high school.

"What's up?" Jade asks. I'm still looking at her.

"Oh. Nothing," I say hurriedly. "You just said exactly what I was thinking."

"You think Crispin is hot too?"

I shake my head slightly, grinning again. "Kind of, yeah." James' face comes to mind, his dark hair and stunning gray-blue eyes and crooked smile.

"I suppose James is pretty hot too," Jade continues.

"I suppose he is," I tell her.

"I know *you* think he is. I was sharing my thoughts with you."

Though I had just turned away, I look back over at her. "What do you mean, you know I think so? You think I think James Sable is hot?"

"Well, yeah. I mean, you kept staring at him. But you can have him. Crispin's more my type."

"I don't stare at him," I protest.

"Oh come on, Cara. It's fine. So you have a crush on a hot guy. It's happened before." She raises her eyebrows at me when I don't immediately respond. "It has happened before, hasn't it?"

I actually have to think about that. I've seen cute guys before. At my last school there was a surplus of them. I've never really liked one before, not right off the bat like this. No boy has made me blush with just a look. I've never been truly intrigued by anyone the way I am with James, and Crispin too, I suppose.

When I don't answer, Jade's eyes widen. "It's never happened before?" Her voice raises and a few people turn to look at us. Muttered conversations were going on throughout the room, and ours had been low key until that point. Jade sees their heads turn, and she quiets back down. "Well then, this is a big day for you."

When the bell rings, we all dump our clay into a huge bin at the front of the room. Jade and I run to wash our hands in the bathroom before our last classes. We part ways by agreeing to meet each other at the same entrance we came in this morning.

"Hang in there," Jade says as she walks away. "There's only one class left, and then we're home free!"

Since I'm not much of an artist, drawing proves to be a little painful for me. But my teacher is great, walking by occasionally and giving me pointers, not seeming to care one way or the other if I take them.

"Drawing *is* about capturing reality," she says, "but it's how that reality looks from your point of view, not mine or anyone else's."

Personally I don't think the bowl of fruit I've been assigned to draw is supposed to look like a bunch of blobs from anyone's point of view, mine included, but I just smile and thank her. She seems to know what I'm thinking, because she says with a wink, "I've always thought pears were a blobby-looking fruit anyhow." And I decide this class will be all right.

****

Max follows Jade and me to my house when school gets out.

"It's a mess," I warn him, unlocking the front door.

"Oh, like he cares," Jade says. "Max lives in a state of perpetual messiness."

"Hey, I take offense to that," Max, acting insulted, tells her.

"That was the general idea," Jade replies, smiling.

I usher them into the kitchen and assign Jade to be on cookie duty with me. I start pulling the dough out of the fridge and once again hunting through the maze of cardboard boxes to find our spoons and a cookie sheet.

Max and I clear off the counters and table, then he begins handing me anything he can find. I either find a place for it in the kitchen or toss it in an empty box to be put in another room.

Once the cookies are in the oven, Jade helps us too. As we work, we talk. After all, we have entire lives to share with each other. They tell me about Shawnee Mission East: the students and the teachers and the classes, which rules to watch for and which ones no one cares if you break.

I tell them about the states I've lived in and the people I've met. We share the names of our first crushes and our oldest friends. Jade hesitantly explains how afraid she is for her father, who's fighting overseas, and how her mom, the lawyer, is having a hard time handling it. Max tells me about his single mom who spends too many hours at the hospital, where she works as a nurse, but how she never wants to ask for more time off because they need the money. He talks about his douche of a stepfather, how his mom doesn't have the time or money to divorce him, and how he, luckily, isn't around very often.

For the first time in a long time, I find myself venting about my parents to someone. About how they constantly move us from one place to another with no regard for Sophie and me and the lives we're trying to build. How my artist mother thinks the movement is good for her creativity, and my father, the renowned professor, thinks that he can get all kind of new angles on his research if he doesn't stay in one place for too long. About how worried I am for Sophie because we don't stay still long enough for her to make real friends, and she doesn't have a way to stay in contact with the friends she does make.

"I just don't get it. They don't know what to do with children or how to be parents, so why did they have us? And why won't they try harder?" By now I've given up on the kitchen and am sitting at the big wooden table with my head in my hands.

Jade finishes emptying her box before she comes to sit with me. She offers me a cookie.

"That sucks," she sums up.

I nod without looking up.

"But you seem to be doing a pretty good job, despite the roller coaster that is your life."

"I wish my life didn't have to *be* a roller coaster."

"Well, roller coasters come to an end." Jade says, continuing the metaphor. "Eventually you get to hop off and let somebody else take your seat. And you get to walk away and never ride again, if you choose. But you *could* grab a friend and jump right back on. You could enjoy it."

I look at her for a long moment. "Do you just ever feel like you don't belong? Like maybe you were made for something else and no one has bothered to tell you yet?"

"I think," Jade tells me, "that people belong wherever they are. You belong here because you're here now. And you belonged in Minnesota before that. And, what was it, Texas before that?"

"Arizona," I correct her quietly.

"Oh right. That one. Well, the point's the same no matter where you were. It's where you belonged then, and this is where you belong now."

"So what? The universe is conspiring to eventually lead me exactly where I'm supposed to be? No matter what?" I ask.

Though I haven't even eaten the first cookie, Jade pushes the whole plate of them at me and smiles softly. "Yep," she says simply.

Overwhelmed, I take a moment to stare at her. I then stuff a cookie in my mouth and spring up to help Max, who is trying to put my mom's fine china in the cabinet with the rest of our plates.

We move onto lighter subjects. The topics of bands and books leads to movies, which leads to us talking about hot actors and beautiful actresses, which leads us back to crushes in general, which leads us to Max's senior crush, Abigail.

"And why do we like her?" I ask the two of them.

Max is taking his embarrassment out on the empty boxes by tearing the packing tape off the bottoms and folding them up before he throws them into the hallway.

"I don't know," he says.

"Oh please," Jade tells him. She yanks her hair up into a ponytail and turns to me. Her eyes are glinting mischievously. "I know why. If he won't tell you I will."

Max, apparently, is not going to tell me.

"Fine." Jade sits on the counter and begins her story. "We used to be friends with this guy. In high school, he turned into this huge jock so we had to give up on him eventually, but freshman year he became really popular and he got invited to all these parties. Therefore, we did too. And Abigail Bell was at practically every single one.

"People's favorite game to play was Spin the Bottle. Don't ask me why. I didn't participate. But one time Max did. And every time he or Abs would spin, they would get each other. Abigail started going on and on about how it had to be fate. But she was pretty smashed at that point, so by the next day she didn't really remember any of it.

"But Max did! And, being the superstitious oddball that he is, he too is now convinced that it was fate's way of showing them they are meant to be together." Jade finishes her story and looks at me like she's waiting for applause. I don't give her any. She hops down from the counter and continues, "Of course, by now I'm pretty sure it's just a normal old crush. He just won't admit it."

"I do admit it. All the time." Max scowls at the two of us. "I only believed that fate thing for a couple weeks," he explains. "Jade was just never able to let it go."

I'm about to tell him that it's no big deal when I hear someone trying to open the front door. There are some loud voices, and Sophie bursts into the house crying. She sees me and immediately stumbles over and buries her face in my shirt. Bewildered, I hold her tight.

"Cara, I'm so sorry." Mrs. Finch has followed Sophie into the house. "I tried to calm her down before we got here, but she just kept asking for you."

"What happened?" I ask. "Sophie, are you hurt?" I turn to Mrs. Finch. "Is she okay?"

Mrs. Finch looks flustered. "It seems as though she got in a fight at school. I couldn't get much more out of her." She looks at the front door like she's planning an escape. "I'm so sorry," she repeats, "but I have to go. Rodney is waiting in the car." And with that she rushes out.

I stare after her for a moment in disbelief, and then I turn my attention to Sophie. "Soph. Sophie, please look at me. Are you okay? Can you tell me what happened?"

Jade taps me on the shoulder and hands me a tissue. I nod at her gratefully before she retreats, backing up to continue emptying boxes with Max and giving Sophie and I some semblance of privacy.

I sit cross-legged on the floor and pull Sophie into my lap, passing her the tissue. I rock her back and forth until her sobs subside and she can speak.

"I d-don't want to go to school with Rodney anymore, Cara. P-please don't make me go."

"Honey," I say softly, "can you please tell me what happened?"

"H-he told all of the kids that my parents don't l-l-love me enough to drive me to school so his mommy h-has to do it."

I feel a surge of fury that a fourth grader would be so cruel. Sophie continues, "So I hit him. Only he hit me back and ripped my shirt. So I hit him again, and the teacher got mad at *me*. Cara, he d-didn't even get in trouble." Sophie starts to cry again. "She didn't believe me. She t-thought I was lying."

I draw her close, shushing her. She rests her head on my shoulder. I feel her tears staining my shirt. It seems ridiculous that a fourth grade playground fight could get me so worked up, but I guess when it's your darling little sister taking the brunt of the blow it's hard not to.

I notice the torn shoulder of her favorite shirt.

"Jade?" I ask quietly. She rushes over and sits next to me. "Can you sew?"

"Yeah, pretty well," she responds, looking sadly at Sophie nestled in my arms.

"Hey, Soph? Do you want to go upstairs with me and change shirts? Then we'll find the sewing kit and Jade can fix that one?"

"No!" Sophie cries. "I don't want to wear this shirt anymore! He'll just rip it again. He said it needed to be torn up because no one likes Pokémon anyway."

I was going to have to have a serious talk with Mrs. Finch about her son.

I give Sophie a long, tight hug before I stand her up and walk her up the stairs. "Well, I do want it fixed," I tell her. "It's my favorite shirt that you have. And I'm sure there were plenty of kids that loved it and just didn't say so. Now come on, Soph, please."

Sophie changes quickly into the plain t-shirt I hand her. Then we go back downstairs, and I sit her at the table with the cookies. Unhappily, she eats one. Normally she would eat three in a heartbeat.

Max stays in the kitchen with her while Jade and I search the dining room for the sewing kit.

"She *knew*," I say furiously, talking about Mrs. Finch. "She knew her son was the reason Sophie was bawling, and she just ran out. What kind of parent is she? She couldn't just own up or explain it to me before she waltzed out the door?"

I notice Jade, who looks like she's struggling for words. I look at her questioningly.

"I'm sorry!" she bursts out. "Cara, I swear I had no idea. I only met Rodney once, when he was five. I didn't know he was such a little…"

"Jade!" I cut in. "Jade, it's all right. I know it isn't your fault. I'm not blaming you."

"It feels like my fault," she sighs. "If they hadn't ridden together, then he'd of had no idea that her own parents didn't drive her."

I'm suddenly and unreasonably angry with my parents for not sticking around to take Sophie to her first day of school themselves, but I don't say so. "Jade, it sounds like this kid would've found something to tease her about no matter what."

"I guess so." She digs around in the box by her feet. "Here it is," she tells me, pulling the kit out and showing it to me.

"Great, thanks."

Jade runs upstairs to get the shirt that I left on Sophie's bed, while I head back to the kitchen. Max is trying to get Sophie to speak, but she's only giving him one-word answers.

"Soph, I'm sorry honey. We didn't know Rodney would be so mean," I tell her.

"I know," she says in a small voice.

"We'll figure something else out for you, okay? You don't have to ride to school with the Finch's again."

"Okay."

Max and I leave her be and finish the kitchen. We find my dad's tools and hammer nails into the wall for pictures, then we hang artwork and old family photos on the fridge. Everything soon has a place. Jade sits with Sophie and works on fixing the sleeve of her shirt. Neither Max nor Jade show any signs of leaving me yet, even though dinnertime is rolling around.

"Sophie, what do you want to eat tonight?" I ask her.

"Do we have spaghetti?" She's still using the same small voice.

"We do indeed. Coming right up."

Max finds a little radio in one of the remaining boxes and sets it on the counter, tuning it to some alt-pop station. We all begin to sing along with the songs and invent our own dance moves. We use kitchen utensils to act out the verses while we cook. We get Sophie to smile and even sing a few times, which is the whole point.

When the doorbell rings, I hand the spaghetti off to Max. I ignore the nervous look on his face when he glances at the boiling water, then go to answer the door.

There's a handsome, dark-skinned boy who's probably about seventeen standing on the front step, along with a striking little girl, who looks about Sophie's age, with caramel-colored skin and big, dark brown eyes.

"Hello. Can I help you with something?" I ask. I can hear Jade howling along with a song behind me (I assume it's another attempt to make Sophie laugh because Jade actually has quite a good voice).

"Does Sophie Weaver live here?" the little girl pipes up, looking at me hopefully.

"Yes ma'am, she does," I answer. "Do you know her?"

"Uh-huh. She's in Mrs. Philips' class at school with me."

I wince when she mentions Mrs. Philips. The young man notices. "Pardon us. Is this a bad time?"

"No," I answer hastily. "I'm just not sure anytime is going to be a good time right now. Sophie is a little..."

"Upset?" he finishes for me.

"Yes. She is. So you know what happened?"

I was asking the older boy, but the girl answers instead. "Yeah. Rodney was being mean to her, so she hit him!" She sounds proud. I find myself liking her.

"I'm Sophie's older sister, Cara," I introduce myself.

"Hi, Cara. I'm David Anthony. This is my little sister, Isa," the older boy says.

"It's nice to meet you," I say politely. "Do you want to come in?" I stand back and hold the door open for them.

"Sure, only for a moment then," David says. "Sorry to barge in on you like this."

"It's no problem at all," I tell him. "We're just making dinner."

"Are your parents here?" he asks, looking around at all the boxes scattered through the hall.

"No, I'm sorry they aren't. They aren't here very often at all, really." This last part I add quietly, almost to myself.

Sophie pokes her head around the kitchen doorway then. "Cara?" she asks. She freezes when she sees I'm talking to people. "Sorry," she says.

"It's okay," I say, "come on in here. Do you remember meeting Isa Anthony today at school?"

Sophie looks closely at Isa and then nods slowly.

"You have on a different shirt," Isa tells her. "Where's your other one? I was going to ask you where you got it. I want one."

She couldn't have known it, but Isa just said the one thing that Sophie most needed to hear. A slow smile makes its way across Sophie's face. "Really?" she asks.

"Yeah! I have all kinds of Pokémon cards at my house. Your shirt was so cool!"

"Do you want a cookie?" Sophie asks her. "We have some in the kitchen."

Isa looks at David for approval before she follows Sophie back into the kitchen. I hear Sophie introducing her to Max and Jade as "her friend from school today". My wonderful friends don't question her; they just welcome Isa into the kitchen warmly.

"Would you like a cookie?" I smile and ask David.

He smiles back. Before he answers Max calls my name. "Hurry," he adds.

I gesture for David to follow me. Max is watching, horrified, as the water on the stove boils over the pot. I grab a potholder from the drawer we just put it in and rush over to pull the pot from the stovetop. It instantly stops bubbling.

"I probably should have thought of that," Max says, watching me.

"Yeah, probably," I agree.

"Ah, well. Spaghetti saved!"

I laugh, emptying some of the water into the sink and drying the burner as best I can before I put the pot back on.

"Wow, it's like the Iron Chef in here," I hear David say from the doorway.

I chuckle, but Max and Jade whip around to look at him when he speaks.

"David?" Jade says in a strangled sounding voice.

"Hey there guys," David says, suddenly looking nervous.

"Oh, good," I say, "we're all friends. Hey Sophie, do you want to take Isa upstairs and show her all *your* Pokémon cards? Maybe you all can trade sometime." I give her our look, the one that means "please listen to me, just for now".

So Sophie and Isa dash upstairs.

"So, what's happening in here?" I ask the three remaining in the kitchen with me. Max and Jade still look shocked, and David looks uncomfortable.

No one answers me for a long moment. I wait.

Finally Max speaks up. "You remember Jade's why-Max-is-in-love-with-Abigail speech?"

"I do," I answer.

"This is the jock—no offense, David—that got us invited to all those parties."

"Oh!" I say, looking over at David with a smile. "You're the jock! That...actually isn't too surprising. You look like one. What do you play, football?"

David nods. He looks a little unsure about where this is going.

"That's what I thought," I continue. "You have that whole tall, dark, and built thing going on."

"You forgot handsome," David tells me.

"It was implied," I say.

David relaxes a little and takes the seat Sophie vacated moments before. "How are you guys?" he asks Max and Jade. Trying to let them talk, I turn around to finish making dinner. I can't help listening.

"How are we?" Jade manages to answer. "How are we? You mean since you dumped us for your football buddies? Since you got *popular* and started ignoring us? Since you...."

"Yes." David cuts her off. "Since then."

"We're great. Thanks," she says sullenly, picking her sewing back up.

"How's life going for you, Dave?" Max asks him. "I mean, I realize that being popular and well-known by the whole school has to be difficult, but apart from that."

I almost whack Max over the head with my spoon, but I remember that I'm pretending not to listen so I refrain.

"Guys—" David starts, but Max stops him.

"No dude. You sold out on us."

I thought David would get angry, would try to defend himself, but he is quiet for a while. When he does speak again, he sounds tired. "I know," he says. "I know what I did, and I've regretted it ever since. I just got so caught up in being *known*, for the first time in my life. In being popular. But I'm tired of it, I really am. I love playing football, but I hate myself for letting you both fall by the wayside. I've wanted to make things right with you for a long time, I just didn't know how."

"Apologizing might be a good start," I say without looking at any of them.

"Right," David says. "I am sorry, guys. I really am. By the time I realized how much I needed you two in my life, it was too late to go back to the way things were. I know that doesn't excuse it or make up for it, but I do hope it helps."

I turn around to see how Max and Jade react. They both look a little stunned, and neither says anything immediately. Then Jade drops Sophie's half-completed shirt. I'm surprised to see that her eyes are wet. "Damn it,

David," she whispers. "Do you know how much we missed you?"

David stands up and draws Jade to him. Jade wraps her arms around him, too.

I grin.

Max still looks a little wary, but I think Jade is softening him up.

"You all are ridiculous," I mutter. Secretly, I'm thrilled. Over the last week, Jade has made more than one vague reference to the good friend she and Max used to have. Apparently, they all used to be inseparable. They told each other everything. It had been obvious to me that she missed him, even when she tried to deny it. I'm glad he's back in her and Max's lives. He's in mine too now, I suppose.

"Not to break up your little reunion," I say, "but David. Why are you here?"

"Yeah, Dave. Why *are* you here?" Jade echoes. "You clearly didn't come to see me and Max."

"No, that's become an added bonus," David says, smiling down at her. "I'm actually here because I wanted to talk to Mr. and Mrs. Weaver."

"Oh," I say. "Well... Look, David, they're not here. And aren't very often. So, I can give them a message or something, if you want."

"Oh, sure, that'll work," David says. "My parents saw what happened with Sophie this morning. Or, more accurately, they saw Sophie crying when she left, and Isa explained what happened. And they figured that Sophie probably wouldn't want to ride with Rodney Finch anymore, and that your parents probably wouldn't want her to have to."

"Your parents were right," I tell him.

"I figured. Rodney's a brat. Always has been." I laugh at his matter-of-fact-ness. "So," he continues, "if your parents were okay with it, and Sophie and Isa got along, my mom was thinking she could start driving Sophie in the mornings."

I'm immediately relieved; I had no idea how much the Mrs. Finch situation had been weighing on me until a solution presented itself. "David," I say, "you have no clue how great that would be. Thank you. Thank you, thank you. And I think she and Isa are going to be fine."

"And you're sure your parents will be okay with it?" David asks.

I breathe out a laugh. "When I say my parents aren't here much, I really mean they're not here. Practically ever. They leave before I get up in the morning and don't come back until about midnight at the earliest. So it doesn't matter if they're okay with it, really. I am, and I'm the one who's been making these decisions for Sophie for a while now, so if your mom really is willing to drive her, that would be fantastic."

David looks relieved.

"If Jade doesn't mind, we'll just bring Sophie by your house before we head to school in the mornings," I continue.

"Jade, you got a car?" David asks her.

"Sure did!" Jade replies. "It's the cute little Land Rover out front."

"Little?" David says with a smile. "It's nice." He looks like he's about to say more, but he doesn't.

"Did you ever get that F-150 you wanted?" Jade asks.

"No. No, I didn't. We used the money for...something else."

Jade doesn't push him for information. You can tell in the way that Max and Jade handle conversations with him that they know David inside and out. He strikes me as a private person, and they know exactly when they can ask for more and when to let him fall silent.

"Well, since we'll be bringing Sophie over now, if you ever need a ride just let me know," Jade says to him.

"Jade, that would be wonderful," David tells her.

Jade smiles.

"Dinner's ready!" I call out. I hear Sophie and Isa shuffling around upstairs, and then hurrying down.

"Isa, you and I have got to head out now, all right? But Sophie is coming over tomorrow to go to school with you." David looks over at Sophie. "That is," he says, "if you want to ride to school with Isa and my parents."

"Yes!" Sophie exclaims. She appears to be back to her old self.

"Bye, Sophie," Isa says happily.

I walk her and David to the door. "You know you can stay for spaghetti if you want, right?" I ask David quietly.

"Thanks, but we've got a family dinner tonight. Dad is cooking." David grimaces. "Should be interesting."

I laugh. "Well thanks then. For everything."

"It was nice to meet you, Cara. See you soon." I watch as he helps Isa put her helmet on, then they hop on their bikes. I wave, and soon they've disappeared down the street.

****

After dinner, Jade and Max help me clean up. Then they have to leave, too.

"What a crazy day," Jade says as they're leaving. "First the hot senior boys and lunch, then Sophie's little tiff with Rodney, now we're reconciled with David?" She gazes at me gleefully. "I knew being your friend would be fun." With that she skips off the porch and down to her car.

Max is shaking his head after her. "What a weird one." He turns to me, smiling. "Thanks, Cara. I can't wait to see what tomorrow is going to be like," he says with false cheer. I elbow him and he chuckles.

"I can't re-introduce you to an old friend every day. I'm good, but not that good," I say.

I stand in the doorway until they both drive off. By now, it's time to get homework done, because if I don't do mine, Sophie won't do hers. The two of us settle down together in the newly straightened kitchen.

"It looks good in here," I muse, taking it in now that it isn't full of people.

Sophie looks a little troubled. "Sorry," she eventually says. "About my meltdown earlier, I mean."

I glance at her fondly. "Honey, it wasn't your fault. I'd have been just as angry as you. No one minded. Though saying you didn't want your shirt anymore was a tad dramatic."

She manages a giggle.

After a while, when it's time to go to bed, I, like I always have, get Sophie ready and tuck her in. I see her listen hopefully for the front door, and I feel a surge of frustration at my parents when I see her face fall at the silence of the house.

"Good night, little lady," I say softly. "Love you."

"I love you too, Cara," she answers.

"Someday they'll be here more," I tell her. "I promise."

When I shut the door to her room and enter my own, I wonder how I'm going to keep that promise.

3

The next day starts in a very similar way, except it's pouring rain outside. Sophie and I get ready for school and rush out the door with Jade because we're a little late, again; but this time we drive over to the Anthony's and see David and Isa waiting for us on their front porch.

Isa smiles hugely when she sees Jade's car coming up the street and hops around waving at us. David has to hold her back by her shirt to keep her from running into the deluge to meet us, but he looks pleased when we pull up.

He rushes to our car with an umbrella to help Sophie out. I turn to look at her. "You going to be all right?" I ask before she shuts the door.

Sophie looks a little nervous, but then she glances at Isa and the serious look on her face vanishes. "Yeah. I'll be okay. I'll see you later, Cara."

David walks her to the house and then comes back and slides into the backseat. I watch Sophie and Isa dash into the house with one last wave at us.

"She looked happy," David notes as we drive off.

"Which one of them?" I ask.

"Both, I guess," David answers.

"Yeah." I sit back comfortably. "Yeah, they did."

Today Shawnee Mission East already seems familiar to me. I don't flinch away from the building as we enter (at least, no more than a normal person does from school), and I even introduce myself to some of the people Jade and David seem to know. A group of kids that are clearly the popular clique call David over to them. He hesitates, but Jade waves him off.

"I'll see you guys after school, right?" he checks before he walks away.

"We'll be right here," Jade confirms. The group of people he's walking toward are giving Jade and me some looks, like we should know better than to talk to David Anthony. Jade winks, infuriating them further, and calls out "See you later, Dave!"

He shakes his head without turning around, but I can see the smile on his face. He clearly knows exactly what she's doing. Jade grins more widely as the group closes in on him, bombards him with questions, and shoots us more glares.

Max is in the classroom when we arrive for first period.

He smiles up at us. "Sophie doing all right?" he asks me.

"She's doing great," I tell him, touched that he remembered to check to see how she is. "She seems really excited for today to happen, actually. I think she and Isa can handle Rodney. I hope so."

"Isa looked like a tough little girl," Max agrees. "I wonder when the Anthonys adopted her?"

Jade shrugs, clearly wondering the same thing.

"Adopted?" I ask, perhaps a touch too loudly. "How do you know Isa was…?" I trail off. "David was adopted." It's not a question. "Is that why he keeps to himself?"

Max looks a little pained. "I forgot you didn't know."

Jade's expression matches his. "Oh, we should have let David tell you himself. But…yeah. When he was eight or nine or something, the Anthonys adopted him. And they must have adopted Isa in just the last couple years. She's adorable. David obviously loves her. I think it's good for him. To have a sibling, I mean."

Max nods, his expression thoughtful. I let the conversation drop. If David wants me to know more, he'll tell me himself.

"Cara," Max says, turning to me. "Would you mind if I hang at your place again after school today? Mom's at work all day, and I never know when the stepfather from hell is going to make an appearance at home. I don't want to be there if he does."

I grimace in sympathy. "Sure you can," I tell him. "I can't guarantee it'll be as exciting as yesterday was though."

"We'll ask David if he wants to come too," Jade says, inviting herself over without a second thought.

I smile at her. "Sounds good."

****

I beat Crispin to chemistry this time, and I'm sitting anxiously at our lab table when he enters. Yesterday could've been some fluke, and he could have retreated back into his "I don't talk to anyone" shell. But he seems genuinely happy to see me here.

"So be honest," he says as he gets his books out. He's wearing an emerald sweater that makes his eyes look even greener than they did yesterday. "How much of my notes did you actually read?"

I pull a face. "I read your note to me," I tell him. "But after that I seem to recall tossing the entire spiral into my bag and forgetting about it for the rest of the night."

He looks exasperated. "How do you expect to learn if you don't even try?"

"Well, clearly, the plan here is not to learn..." I say.

Crispin smirks. "Fine then. I guess I'll just have to talk to Mr. Marks and tell him we should start tutoring right away. I'm sure he'll agree when he hears just how far behind you really are."

My glare doesn't seem to faze him in the slightest.

"Your choice," he says with a shrug and an I-just-won-the-argument expression.

"Why do you care how *I* do in this class? Shouldn't you be more concerned with your own grade than you are with mine?" I ask him.

"I don't have to be worried about my grade. But I don't want to be responsible for you failing the class."

"First of all," I notify him, "who says I'm going to fail? I was picturing a solid D. Possibly even a C, depending on how well I cram. And second, what makes you responsible if *I* fail?"

"Because I would have had the ability to help you not fail but done nothing. So it would reflect just as heavily on me as it would on you. And then there's the personal regret I would feel..."

I appreciate his point, but I will not be swayed. "Still sounds like it would be my fault," I say. "Tell you what, I will accept all responsibility for my poor grades, thereby liberating you from the 'personal regret' and agony you would otherwise feel."

Crispin grins, but there is something behind it that gives his next words more weight than they might have otherwise had. "It doesn't work like that, Cara."

We end the conversation there. Class is starting anyway.

Crispin passes me a note halfway through class. *So, I hear you met James yesterday*, it reads.

Before replying I write, *Is this going to be a thing with you now? How can I learn if you continually distract me with note passing?*

Crispin just smiles and passes it back. I respond, *Yes, we met. He's in my Photo class. You guys seem rather chummy. Which is odd, given your reputation for talking to no one.*

I suppose James is just an exception, Crispin writes. *Our parents moved here together; they work for the same company. So we're neighbors and whatnot. Funny, people don't usually count James in the list of people I talk to.*

I noticed that. James actually said something like that too. He said that next to you, most people found him forgettable.

Crispin seems slightly surprised when he reads that. *He said that?*

I simply nod, so Crispin takes the page and writes, *Well, it would appear that not everyone thinks so anymore.*

I blush and try not to let Crispin see. *But I think he does anyway. You should ask him to help you out in Photo, if you need it.* Crispin continues. *He's quite good at art.*

Do you think I need help in ALL my classes just because I'm having chemistry trouble?

I don't know. Are you exceptionally good at photography?

I don't write a response, and Crispin laughs quietly, recognizing that the answer must be no. Just as I start to reply, an enormous clap of thunder rumbles across the sky. The rain drums loudly against the windows.

The lights flicker to accompany the thunder, so students start talking excitedly, clamoring for the power to go out so that school will be canceled. It takes Mr. Marks some time to calm us down, and by the time we get back on topic, the bell is about to ring.

"Seriously though," Crispin says when Mr. Marks gives up and lets us start packing up our things early. "Ask James for help."

I pretend to be touched. "Crispin, are you...trying to help me make friends?" I wipe away a fake tear.

He rolls his eyes. "I'm helping you and James both. You need to meet some people, on top of needing art help, and he isn't exactly talkative. Someone has to break him out of his comfort zone."

"And that person should be me because...?" I ask.

Crispin grins. "You got me to talk, didn't you?"

****

The overcast sky has turned an alarming shade of purple-gray since last time I checked. When the lights flicker again as I walk down the hall, I find myself hoping for a power outage despite the principal's announcement that a power outage is not expected. He said we should continue on with our day. When I get to photography, most of the students, Max and Jade included, are staring at the light bulbs hopefully. James is already here too, looking immensely bored and just as gorgeous as yesterday, but even he glances up at the lights briefly. I grin. He catches the look, meeting my eyes and smiling slightly.

"What do you think?" Jade asks me with a meaningful glance at the ceiling.

"I say... Twenty to eighty percent chance. Not in our favor," I answer.

She pulls a face and uses her backpack as a pillow to lay her head down on the table. Max pats her shoulder comfortingly. "That's what I was afraid of," I hear her mumble through her bag.

"Only twenty-eighty?" I hear James murmur to me.

Max and Jade don't seem to hear him, so I mutter back, "Why? You have a better guess?"

James smiles crookedly. "I say fifty-fifty. Maybe even sixty-forty, us."

"Pretty confident over there, aren't you?" I whisper.

He chuckles as Mr. Lincoln starts class.

Jade only raises her head when the lights flicker once again. "This cannot be safe," she declares. "When, yes *when*, the lights go out, wouldn't it be better if we've all left the building already? If not, there will be a thousand high school students rushing through dark hallways. Someone may die."

I roll my eyes, and I see Max do the same. "You should take that up with the principal, Jade," I tell her seriously.

"Mr. Sable!" Jade, Max, and I all whip out heads around, though it's James that Mr. Lincoln just called for. "How's the project coming?" he asks, approaching our table.

"It's coming," James replies vaguely.

"Good, good. Then, since it would seem Jade and Mr. Fedderman are not quite as far along with their own work, would you like to show Miss Weaver here the darkroom, how we process film and prints, how to work our enlargers, and all that?"

James looks at me studiously, and I can feel heat start to rise in my cheeks.

"T-that's okay," I stammer, the suggestion completely unexpected. "Jade said she'd—"

"That's quite all right," James says, cutting me off. "I don't mind."

Mr. Lincoln strolls off with a nod of gratitude.

"You don't have to do this," I mutter to James.

"I see no reason not to," he tells me evenly.

I follow him obediently through the odd revolving door that leads into the darkroom, knowing Jade's eyes are glued to me the whole way. I stand still in the middle of the room to give my eyes some time to adjust. James moves off, seeming to have no trouble navigating in the dark. The red light bulbs in here don't give off much light. All I can make out is a waist-high shelf running along the three walls of the room, and a shorter one jutting out from the other wall. There's a sink running in here somewhere, but no other students are around as far as I can tell.

He disappeared from my side for a moment, but now James is back shinning a bright red light directly into my face. I flinch away.

"Sorry," he says, no real apology in his tone, and averts the light.

"Is that...a headlamp?" I ask. The red light appears to be coming from his forehead. When he turns his head away, I can see the band wrapping around his head. "I thought your outfit was missing something... Hold onto that thing, we may need it when the power inevitably fails in this building."

As if in answer, the lights flicker again. This time I can barely hear the accompanying thunder. Even the chatter of the classroom has faded away. There's no sound besides the running water of the sink and James and me.

"Come over here." Breaking the silence, James shuts his headlamp off, takes me lightly by the arm, and leads me through the dark to the back corner of the room. The shelf we're walking beside is lined with enlargers, each with their own drawer full of supplies. The eerie red glow is brightest in this corner, so James uses it to show me where everything is located.

The red lights, while uncanny, illuminate the bones of his face sharply and cast the rest into shadow, making him look ethereal. His hair and eyes look darker than ever, tinged crimson. He doesn't even start when the lights flicker once more, twice more, and then go out, plunging us into complete blackness.

I, however, leap about a foot in the air at the whip-like crack of thunder and immediately grab for the shelf, trying to get my bearings. As far as I can tell, James doesn't move a muscle. Now I can hear the overly dramatic shrieks and laughter and excited shouts of the class outside.

"Sixty-forty it is," I mutter, mostly to myself. "James, how do we get out? Where's the door?"

James laughs as if it's the easiest thing in the world to navigate a never-before-seen room in absolute blackness.

"James?" I say again.

"Cara, relax," he says easily. "It's no big deal. I'm just waiting to see if the lights come back on before you go blundering through the darkroom. The last thing we need is a chemical spill or something."

"Just because I can't see doesn't mean I'm an accident waiting to happen! How would I even find the chemicals to spill? They're on the opposite end of the room."

James places a hand on my arm just as another equally loud crack of thunder splits the sky. I jump again, and this time my foot slips on something I can't see that's lying on the ground. I fall backwards into James. My shoulder knocks against his chest, but he catches me easily. For a moment I'm leaning back against him, and his surprisingly strong arms are around me. Then he steps away. I'm grateful for the dark; it means he can't see the blush spreading across my face.

I hear James move off into the darkness. Before I can ask where he's going, the lights flicker back on. I breathe a sigh of relief. James sets down the headlamp he had evidently just picked up; without a word, the two of us step back out into the classroom.

It's a madhouse, but Mr. Lincoln is doing his best to hush everyone up because the principal has come back over the intercom. School's canceled.

Whoops of delight ensue, not only from our classroom but from the ones next door as well, and students flood the hallway. I rush over to grab my bag. Max and Jade are already packing up their things. Jade grins at me.

James has gotten caught on the wrong side of the line of people hurrying for the door, so I snatch up his backpack as well and take it over to him.

"I guess I'll see you tomorrow?" I say hopefully.

He almost smiles, some emotion hidden in his stormy eyes. "See you tomorrow." While I wait for Max and Jade to catch up with me, he disappears from the room.

****

The three of us wait by the door where we told David to meet us. It's an effort not be trampled by the hoard of students rushing the exit, so there's a lot of shifting around being done as we try to stay out of the way. David finally comes into view and grins broadly when he sees us.

"Did you think we'd left without you?" I ask when I see his happily surprised expression.

David shrugs. "Maybe. This is just so weird to see you all waiting and know that it's me you're waiting for. It's been a long time since that's happened."

Jade pats his arm, and we make our way out the door. I didn't think it could be raining any harder than it was this morning, but now it's like a sheet of water is falling from the sky. I can barely see out the door. Students are mere blurs as they step with a shriek out into the downpour. I have to shout to be heard as we stand just inside the door.

"Who's car are we going for?" I ask the other three.

Jade and Max look at each other briefly. "Hers," Max yells back.

I nod, link arms with David on one side and Jade on the other, who grabs Max's hand, and with a deep breath I sprint, laughing, into the rain. We join the masses that are trying to find their cars. Jade has to lead the way because I don't even know where to begin to go. I can hardly keep my eyes open as we run, and I'm immediately soaked to the skin.

Ridiculous as it seems, running around in the rain makes me actually feel my age. I spend so much time being an adult and trying to be mature enough to raise

Sophie, that it feels good to race through the water arm in arm with my friends.

Jade keeps turning us around; she clearly doesn't have a good idea of where we're headed either. We find her red Land Rover in the middle of one of the rows of cars, and we all pile quickly in.

Jade doesn't start the car yet, just sits in the driver's seat and catches her breath. Her eyes are shining, and her hair is a mess. But her smile is huge as she turns to me giggling. "That might be the first time since we were in elementary school that the power has gone out during a school day. Isn't it wonderful?"

I have to agree that yes, it is. Then a thought hits me. "If the power is out here, then is it out other places? Other schools, I mean? David, will Sophie and Isa need to be picked up?"

"Oh," David says, "I didn't think of that. Jade, can we drive by? I'll call dad."

Jade pulls out of her spot and joins the line of cars slowly making their way out of the parking lot. I can't make out what David is saying into his phone. I listen as he laughs, clicks off, and leans forward to say, "Yeah. Power's out at Belinder too."

"No problem," Jade says, inching along with the other cars. Then she slams on her brakes suddenly enough that I have to brace myself on the dashboard to keep from being thrown forward. Some boy has run in front of the car and thrown himself to the side when it started moving. Now he comes to my window and pounds on the glass.

When he presses his face closer, I recognize Crispin.

"Holy mother of pearl!" Jade swears and looks at me incredulously. "See what he wants!" she urges when I don't move. Reluctantly, I crack the door open. Water comes rushing in. Crispin pokes his head in, his curls dripping water onto me. He looks around the car.

"Hey guys," he says without a trace of embarrassment. "How's it hanging?"

"What do you need?" I ask him. Two or three different cars honk at Jade for not moving as the line does. She ignores them.

Crispin looks at Jade. "A ride?" he asks with a small grin.

Jade stares at him until I punch her in the arm. "Yeah!" she says. "Sorry, hop in!"

Crispin shuts my door for me and jumps in the backseat with Max and David.

Jade continues to let the car crawl forward as I make introductions. "Everyone, this is Crispin Calaway. Crispin, this is Jade Thatcher, Max Fedderman, and David Anthony." They all wave at each other. "Crispin and I are chemistry lab partners, which apparently means he can bum rides off my friends in the middle of a storm…"

Crispin nods. "That's exactly what it means."

I smile. "Where to?" I ask him.

"Could you all just drop me off at the Village?" Crispin asks. The Village is a small shopping center just down the street from my new house. It's kind of on the way to Belinder Elementary. "I'm meeting James there soon," Crispin continues.

"How's James getting there?" I say curiously. Jade shoots me a look, which I studiously ignore. I know what she's thinking. And she might be right, but I'm not going to tell her that.

"Oh, I think he's already there," Crispin says dismissively.

I start to ask how he got there, and why Crispin didn't go with him. Then Jade flips on the radio and we finally get out of the parking lot, so my question is lost in the noise.

Max and David and Crispin thankfully start talking to each other as Jade drives, so I look out the window at the pouring rain.

Jade quietly interrupts my thoughts as she pulls onto a side street. "So... Who you thinking 'bout?"

"What makes you think I'm thinking about someone? And who's to say it's not Sophie? Or my parents?" I reply with a laugh.

"Are you thinking about Sophie?"

"...No," I admit.

Jade pumps her fist in triumph. "Ah-ha! I knew it! Are you bummed 'cuz we aren't giving James Sable a ride too?"

I frown at her. "Please, be more obvious about it. The rest of the car might not have heard you just now."

Jade grins evilly. "Hey guys!" she calls to the back seat.

I practically climb over the seat to clamp a hand over her mouth as she chuckles. "You are a horrible person," I tell her.

The boys have stopped talking and are now staring at the two of us. Jade sees them in her rearview mirror and starts laughing harder. I give her a friendly shove and sit back down.

"You have something to share with the class up there?" I hear Max ask us.

I turn to face them. Max is concealing a grin. David looks confused, and Crispin is looking at me in a way that suggests he knows exactly what's happened. I glare at them all. "As far as you are concerned, that conversation never happened. Kapish?"

They chuckle. "Understood," Max says crisply, complete with salute.

I point at him. "Don't push it."

He holds his hands up in mock surrender, and Jade cruises to a halt in front of Macy's in the Village. "Anywhere in particular you wanted me to drop you off?" she asks Crispin.

He glances at the window at the still pouring rain, and then shrugs. "Nah. Here is good. Thanks guys! Max, David, don't forget about next weekend!"

The two chorus that they won't, we all wave goodbye, and Crispin steps out of the car and disappears.

"What are you doing next weekend?" I ask Max and David curiously.

"He and James have got tickets to some concert downtown!" Max answers excitedly.

"Ooh, what concert?" Jade asks.

"I don't know," Max says. "Does it matter?"

"A little," I laugh. "What if it's someone who sucks?"

David shakes his head. "I'm sure it'll be great. Do I detect a hint of...jealousy?"

"...No," I reply, with the same pause I gave Jade a few minutes ago.

Everyone in the car smiles at me. Apparently I am not very subtle. I'll have to remember that...

Soon we've arrived at Belinder Elementary, so Jade stops the car in front to allow David and me to jump out. There isn't anywhere to park. Jade motions that she'll search for a spot while we get the girls. We both nod and sprint to the entrance. There's some process we have to go through with the secretary to prove that we're actually related to Isa and Sophie, but we eventually get visitor's stickers and get waved down the hall to Mrs. Philip's room.

There are only a few lights still on in the hallway, but it's bright enough that I can take in the school that my little sister has to go to everyday.

"This place is *nice*," I tell David as I look around.

"Isn't it?" David says. We sidestep a young mother ushering her son down the hallway. "They just had all kinds of construction done. Now it's pretty much nicer than East."

"Yeah, it is," I agree.

I gasp and duck into a doorway as we near the classroom. David turns to me quizzically, hiding laughter behind his hand. "How you doing?" he asks me.

I point down the hall. "Mrs. Finch is there," I hiss, pulling him into the doorway too. Before I fell asleep last night, I had rehearsed all kinds of speeches to give her about the behavior of her son. I had been determined to use those speeches the next time I saw her. Now that's she's here they all fly from my mind, and I just want her to go away. What does a sixteen-year-old have to tell a grown woman about raising children, anyhow?

"Ah, I see the problem." David peeks around me to see. "What are you going to do about her?" he says.

"Something very adult and mature," I inform him.

David takes my arm and steers me toward the door, ignoring all my protestations. "You're going to ignore her?"

"That is the plan," I say grimly.

And I do. Sophie throws herself happily into my arms, and she and Isa start chatting about the day as David and I say goodbye to Mrs. Philips. I don't spare Mrs. Finch a glance. At one point, I swear she moves to talk to me, but I'm not in the mood so I allow Sophie to pull me over to show me her desk.

"Good work," David murmurs as we try to find Jade's car by looking out the front windows.

"Why thank you. It was a rather successful venture, wasn't it?" I smile.

Sophie spots the car first, so I hold her hand, David holds Isa's, and we brace ourselves to rush into the rain that has yet to let up.

"This is ridiculous weather!" I yell to David the moment we step out the door.

He laughs out loud and holds out his hands apologetically. "Welcome to Kansas."

"So, we've decided something," Jade announces when the four of us climb back in the car. Max has taken the front while we were gone, so David and I put Sophie and Isa in the middle of the backseat and I double-buckle them in.

Max turns in his seat and gives Sophie and I a lopsided grin. "We're taking you on a tour of the town!"

I look dubiously out the window at the rain then back at Max.

"The indoor parts of the town," Max revises. "Come on! There are some great places that you'll never know about if you don't let us show you." He turns to David. "Dave, you got anywhere you need to be soon?"

David shakes his head and looks at Isa. "Isa, do you want to go on a tour?"

"Yes!" Isa cries, pumping her fist in the air. "Soph, come on, let's go!"

So Sophie turns to me. "Cara, please?"

I catch Jade's eye in the rearview mirror. She's grinning at me. "Cara, please?" she says.

I sigh. "Fine." I try not to smile, but I can't help it. "Let's go on a tour!"

They all cheer.

We drive around the Plaza, past the Nelson-Atkins Art Museum to see the giant badminton birdies on the lawn, and to a large park that looks beautiful from what I can see through the sheet of raindrops. David points out the way to the baseball stadium and the amusement park. They show Sophie and me the house down the street from our high school that is so decked out with lights and decorations during Christmas that the neighbors have complained about it multiple times.

"So maybe not the best day for a tour," Jade says eventually, watching me as I squint out the window, trying to spot Hi Hat, "the littlest coffee shop in the world", according to Max.

"No, guys. It's great," I say, trying to appease them all. "We can do it again sometime, no big deal. It was a really good idea."

"Just one more place," Jade tells me. "And then we'll head for home."

I agree cheerfully, truly enjoying myself despite the barely visible tour destinations, and Jade takes us down some more narrow streets to stop in front of a crooked brick building.

"And we're actually going into this one," Max says, unbuckling, "so everybody out!"

We pile out of the car and into the rain, which has lessened at this point, to push through the door of the small shop. I stand for a moment, taking it in. Then: "This place is ah-ma-zing," I announce. "I think I am going to live here. Sophie, let's away! I must pack up my things at once!"

Sophie wisely ignores me and walks with Isa to the back and the children's books. Max sniggers in the background, and I can practically hear Jade shaking her head at me. David just smiles.

"But really," I say, more quietly. The place is perfect. Or, my version of perfect: a quiet little independent bookstore. I can see a spiraling staircase leading down to another floor, but up on this one there are tall, old bookshelves winding their way seemingly haphazardly about. A rolling ladder is attached to the shelves that line the walls. Behind the counter there are precarious stacks of books waiting to be shelved. And, besides us, there is not a soul that I can see.

I breathe in deeply the smell of old books and ink and walk off to peruse the shelves. The murmurs of my friends fade into the background. I don't recognize many of the titles, but I do recognize the authors. I become so engrossed in flipping through the books that I don't hear it when a man comes up behind me.

"You must be a reader," he says in a quiet voice, making me start so violently that I nearly drop the book in my hands. When I turn, I'm facing a small, gray-haired, Hispanic man with dark brown eyes that glitter knowledgeably from behind wire-rimmed spectacles. "I recognize a fellow spirit when I see one."

I return his kind smile. "This place is wonderful," I tell him. "Do you work here?"

"Work here? I've owned this store since 1987."

"Lucky," I mumble.

"I have to say," he continues, "I don't usually get so many young people in here. Not unless the school year is about to begin. Then everyone is looking for books priced as low as they can find them."

I put the novel I'm holding back on the shelf. "My friends are showing me around the town," I say. "My sister and I just moved here, and they thought I would like this place, so they included it in the tour." I shrug. "I don't know how they knew, but they were right."

The man nods. "Funny, isn't it, how people you've just met can know things about you that you didn't even realize they noticed?"

I look at him curiously. "Yeah. It is funny. But it's a good feeling."

"Of course it is," he says, walking toward the counter. "It means they really care about you."

I glance around the store. David is helping Sophie and Isa reach the books on the top shelves. Jade is laughing and clutching at the rolling ladder as Max pushes her along the shelves.

"How can you tell?" I ask the man after a moment, following him to the counter.

"Oh, my dear, anyone would be able to tell," he smiles. "In fact, close as you all seem, I never would have guessed that you were new to their lives."

A rush of true warmth floods through me; I knew they liked me, sure, but I didn't realize how much. I didn't know it was so obvious to outsiders too. "Thank you," I tell him sincerely, "Mr...?" he isn't wearing a nametag.

"Pelegro," the man says, holding out a hand to shake.

I take it. "Hi, Mr. Pelegro. I'm Cara Weaver."

"Very nice to meet you," Mr. Pelegro says to me.

"Hey Cara!" Max calls. "You're the one who said you love *Jane Eyre*, right?"

I hurry over to him. Max is holding a worn black hardcover with gold lettering on the front. He holds it up for me to see. "You said you don't have a copy?" he continues.

"Max!" I cry, throwing my arms around him and slipping the book from his hands. "This is amazing! But...how did you remember I told you that?"

He shrugs. "Jade remembers too."

Jade is still up on the ladder, but she grins down at me. "Which copy do you like better? That one, or this one?" She pulls a red volume off the shelf and drops it to me. I hand it back to her.

"I like the black one."

"Told you, Max," Jade says as she places it back on the shelf.

Sophie skips over to us. She's holding a stack of books in her arms. I stop her. "I will buy you two. Pick," I tell her.

She frowns at me, and I raise my eyebrows at her. "Okay," she eventually concedes. Sophie sets them all on the floor and sorts through them. Eventually she holds up four.

"Two," I say again firmly.

Sophie sits and thinks seriously, but before she decides Mr. Pelegro comes and kneels down next to her. "Big decisions?" he asks. He doesn't seem to mind that she's strewn books about his clean floor. I nod at him. He winks.

David, with Isa balanced atop his shoulders, comes out of children's books to join us. "We're ready to go when you guys are," David says.

"Hold on," Sophie tells him sternly. "I haven't picked my books yet!"

"Young lady," Mr. Pelegro says to Isa. "If you had to pick one of these for your friend to read, which would it be?"

David walks over so Isa can see the titles Mr. Pelegro is pointing to. Isa contemplates her choices carefully. "*The BFG*," she finally says.

Mr. Pelegro then looks questioningly at Sophie. "Do you trust this girl?"

Sophie meets his eyes earnestly and nods. "And you want this one the most?" he asks pointing to another. Sophie nods again, so Mr. Pelegro stacks up all the others and hands Sophie's books to her. She smiles up at him. "Thank you, sir."

He waves her off. "It's my job, ma'am."

I take the books from Sophie and pile them on the counter with my own. "Thank you," I say as Mr. Pelegro rings me up.

"It was a pleasure, my dear," he replies. When he pushes the books back to me, he beckons me to lean closer. "I have been searching for someone to help me look after this shop. But it has been more difficult than I anticipated. I know you've only just arrived, but I don't suppose that you would be interested in the job?'

I gape at him. He doesn't know anything about me, and he wants me to work here? "Be interested?" I finally manage. "I would love to!" Then I pause. "Only...I don't have any way to get here. No car."

"Ah," he says. "Well, if you ever figure out a means, give me a call." He passes a card with the name and number of the store to me, and I gratefully tuck it into my pocket.

"I will," I promise him.

As I grab my purchases, everyone else calls out thanks to Mr. Pelegro. Already wondering how I can convince my parents to help me find a way to take the job, I follow them out the door. I've never actually had a job before; we've never stayed in a city long enough that it's been worth the trouble. But working in a bookstore—especially an obscure, independent one—is a dream job for me. Not typical of many high school students, I would imagine, but there it is.

"Thank you guys," I tell them sincerely as we begin the drive home. "That was exactly what we needed."

"Hey." Jade meets my eyes in the mirror and smiles. "What are friends for?"

They're for this, I think, leaning my head against the window and closing my eyes. *They're for this*.

4

When James enters The Scarlet Letter Saturday afternoon, it isn't Mr. Pelegro sitting behind the sales counter. In his place is a girl, her fashionable boots propped on the countertop and her head buried in a book. She doesn't seem to have heard him come in. James, without making a sound, slides a book from where he hid it last time he was in the shop and pads to the wingback chairs to settle down in one.

He has plenty of time to read while he waits for Crispin to arrive.

James and the girl, whose face he has yet to see, sit in what he considers to pass for companionable silence. Neither one looks up from their books until an older woman pushes open the door. Even then, James is the only one to glance over. The only sign that the girl at the counter has heard anyone enter is when she unconsciously shifts her position to sit more comfortably.

James has never seen anyone so engrossed in what they're reading. He tries to catch a glimpse of the title, but the cover is so old and worn that it is illegible. He watches as the girl begins to bounce her foot to the rhythm of some music only she can hear. He can feel the ghost of a grin on his face. Watching her, so lost in her world, is oddly relaxing for him.

So he is almost upset himself when the woman, who had been browsing the shelves, leans over the counter to interrupt the girl's reading. The bouncing foot stops, and the girl simply closes the book around her finger so as not to lose her place and smiles up at the waiting customer.

James feels his heart skip a beat in rare surprise. Her warm brown eyes and bright smile are immediately familiar to him. Cara Weaver speaks happily to the older woman and gestures to a section of bookshelves before leading the woman there herself. They disappear behind some shelves, but he can still hear their murmurs.

He considers pretending to be intent on his book and acting like he hasn't noticed Cara is here; but before he can, the two have reappeared. Cara has just finished saying something to make the older woman laugh when she sees him.

She stumbles forward a step but catches herself just before falling. She waves away concerned exclamations from the woman and averts her eyes from James' own. Cara, shakily brushing her short hair away from her face, rings up the woman's purchase quickly. The woman casts a confused glance at James. Then she thanks Cara, who smiles easily back at her, and she exits the shop.

Cara takes a moment to unnecessarily straighten things on the countertop before she turns slowly to face him. Her face is carefully blank. Is she happy to see him? Upset that he's here?

"How long have you been sitting there?" she asks him finally.

James takes the time to carefully note his page number and then closes the book and places it on his lap. He wonders momentarily what to say in answer. "Just a short while. I didn't know you worked here."

"It's only been a few days since I started," she says with a small frown. "I didn't know you were normally kept informed of the employees. Or is it me you're keeping track of?"

He can hear the joke in her tone but also the serious question behind it. "There has only been one employee, Mr. Pelegro himself, for me to keep tabs on. So it's not that I stay informed, it's that I didn't know he was hiring. Why would I be keeping track of you?" James answers her reasonably.

He watches as her face flushes pink, and she drops his gaze. "No reason," she mumbles. She twists the ring on her finger around nervously.

James stares at her while she's looking away. Crispin had tried to explain to him the odd pull he felt toward Cara when she first sat next to him in chemistry. He had been puzzled to learn that James hadn't felt it too. What James hadn't mentioned to his friend was that he *had* felt a pull, but he didn't know if it was for the same reasons that Crispin had. It could have been the same connection Cris felt, or something else entirely. He still wasn't sure. But here, in the empty shop, was as good a time as any to find out.

James knows that he has to concentrate much harder than Crispin ever would, so he bows his head, closes his eyes, and braces his hands on his legs. He is aware of Cara's eyes back on him, but he pushes past it, allowing no distraction.

Just before the door to the store swings open again, James feels it. A pulsing energy thrums between them. It's like an invisible thread connects them briefly. Or in this case something bigger and stronger, like a rope. Shock forces him to his feet before he knows he's even standing. The only other person he'd ever felt such a tie to is—

Crispin's powerful presence sweeps through the room, and James loses the connection to Cara. But he felt it long enough to know, to be sure, and remorse courses through him, because this is the last thing on Earth that he wanted.

The last couple of days have run together in a blur of classes, homework, and studying as I try to catch up with my classmates. Max and Jade have been lending me assignments from earlier in the semester to use as guides for current projects. Crispin has continued to give me pointers everyday in chemistry. When I finally shot my first photography project, James spent a class period showing me how to develop film and hang it up so that the negatives dry properly.

On top of everything I had to do for school, I also had to help Sophie with her work, set aside time to run to the store for groceries and school supplies, and work on putting the house in order.

The only notable exception to the routine had been when my parents let me accept the job at The Scarlet Letter. I had stayed up late one night to catch them when they got home, which was past one in the morning, and I had explained Mr. Pelegro's offer to them. They hadn't understood why I didn't accept the job on the spot, until I told them that I would have to drive there, and I didn't have a car to use. My dad had laughed and said if I gave them my schedule in advance, either he or my mother could easily leave one of their cars for me to drive on the days I had to work.

I had thanked them profusely, and the first thing I did the next day after school was call Mr. Pelegro and take the job. He'd seemed genuinely delighted to hear from me. He told me that my first day would be Saturday and hung up with a promise to see me soon.

Now it's finally the weekend. Sophie is spending this morning at Isa's dance recital with the Anthonys. They promised her that they would introduce her to Isa's instructor after the show to talk about Sophie joining the class. She'd chattered excitedly about it all day yesterday.

Mom and Dad work again today, and my shift began at lunch. I was worried about Sophie's plans overlapping with my work schedule, but I talked to Jade. She'd agreed to bring Sophie over to the shop as soon as the recital was over. I'd apologized to Jade for asking for the favor, for taking up her time because of my busy schedule, but Jade had said she was more than happy to do it. So she's borrowed my key and is waiting in my house for Sophie to arrive.

When I got to The Scarlet Letter, Mr. Pelegro was waiting to show me around. He told me how to organize and shelve the books, how to ring up customers, where the money goes at the end of the day, and then with a theatrical bow, he had handed me a key to the shop. A few shoppers came and went, and so when he was confident that I would do fine on my own, Mr. Pelegro left and said he'd be back in a bit.

Everything was going well, really well. I'd made my first sale of the day, and then I saw James.

It wasn't that seeing James ruined the day. For a moment, it had actually made it more interesting. I was oddly excited that he was here. But he seemed to be lost in thoughts of his own. Just when I decided to leave him be, Crispin strode into the shop and James, looking like someone had struck him, leapt out of his chair.

Before I could process the unexpected action, James dropped his book on a table and hurried out of the store. Crispin just gave me a funny look, waved, and then followed him.

I don't know what to make of it.

What in the name of all things holy was that about? I wonder, watching them go.

James' expression is burned in my memory: horror, guilt, and terrible sadness, all directed at me, played their way across his face in quick succession.

I stand still, trying to work it out in my mind, until another customer enters and I make myself look busy. I sweep the book James was reading off the table and carry it behind the counter with me. *Maybe he just got to a weird part in the novel? Maybe that's what surprised him,* I try to tell myself. But with one glance at the title, I know that's not the case. Roman mythology. Nothing too horrifying in there.

I'm still mulling it over when Jade and Sophie come in half an hour later.

"How's the first day going?" Jade asks, handing me a cup of hot chocolate and grinning.

"Umm..." I say. I hold up a finger to halt the questions she's already bursting with at this simple noise. We wait. Soon we can hear Sophie entertaining herself, pattering around the maze of shelves and talking as she plays some games I'm sure she's made up on the spot.

Now I beckon Jade to come around the counter and sit with me. "James was in here," I say before she can ask me anything.

"James, the hot boy from photography class?" she clarifies.

"Yes," I say.

"Best job ever!" Jade cries out. "So what happened? Something happened, right? Otherwise, why are you acting all secretive?"

"I don't know," I say, holding up my hands. "He was in here, I saw him after I helped a customer, and then he got all weird, and then Crispin came in really fast, and then they both ran out!"

"Wait, what?" Jade asks. "Define 'weird'."

"Weird!" I exclaim quietly. "As in, he got all serious for a second, and then he gave me this look like I was the ghost of Jacob Marley and rushed out. And Crispin, even though he *just* came in the store at that point, rushed right out after him."

"Why though?" Jade says. "What happened?"

"Jade, that's what I'm saying. Nothing! Nothing happened, except that one second everything was completely normal and the next they were both gone."

Jade takes a good amount of time to think it over, just like I had. She comes to the same conclusion: "That doesn't make sense."

"I know. I keep thinking something had to have changed. But I swear nothing did. I saw James, rang up a customer, asked him how long he had been in the store because I hadn't noticed him. He said 'not too long', looked away, then stared at me as though he was suddenly afraid of me. Crispin ran in, James ran out, Crispin followed. That's it."

Jade scrutinizes me. "I think you look fine."

"What?" I ask.

"He couldn't have been afraid of you. You're short and cute, and you work in a bookstore. James Sable could not have been afraid of you."

I tell her quietly, "You didn't see the look he gave me."

"No," she concedes, "I guess I didn't."

We sit in silence, lost in thought, until Sophie wanders out from the shelves and settles into a chair to color on some printer paper from the back room. Jade walks off to explore the lower level of the shop, and I pick up a book to continue my reading. But it isn't *Jane Eyre* that I absentmindedly begin to flip through. It's James' book of Roman myths. I can tell by looking at it which page he stopped on because the book has practically never been opened, so the read pages don't lay as flat as the pages James has yet to get to.

Curiously, I read the story James just finished. It's about someone named Proserpine, but as I read it I recognize the story as one I know well. It's about

Persephone, except with her Roman name rather than her Greek one. So I stop and stow the book on a hidden shelf under the counter. I read enough myths in middle school to hold me over for a while. Besides, James might want the book back sometime, and I don't want to be the reason it isn't here if he comes looking for it.

****

Mr. Pelegro doesn't come back to the shop until around seven-thirty in the evening, and only then so he can show me how to close the shop for the night.

"Why do you close so early?" I ask him.

"Ah, I only close early by comparison to others. Eight o'clock is a perfectly reasonable time to shut the shop down. How many people do you know that go looking for a good book to buy after eight o'clock? Apart from myself, and now you, I don't know a single one. And if there is someone else like that out there, they can go find another store! My customers know that this is when I close, so there's no good reason to stay open."

I can't argue with his logic, so I follow him around to shut off lights and turn on the alarm. Then Sophie and I (Jade left a couple hours ago) grab all of our things, and Mr. Pelegro locks the door after us. He didn't seem the least bit surprised to see Sophie in the shop, nor did he mind when I told him that she'd often be spending her days with me as I work.

"Books are good for children," he had told me. "And children are good for books! All books need to feel young again, to be tossed about and handled with a little less care than usual every once and a while. As long as there is an adult around to dust them off again. These books could do with some life."

I help Sophie pile her things in the back of my dad's Corolla. "I'll see you Wednesday, Mr. Pelegro," I call to him.

"I know you will, my dear. Thank you for your good work."

I don't think he has any idea whether my work is good or not, seeing as he was out most of the day, but I accept the compliment as I start the car and head home.

Sophie and I watch a movie before we go to sleep, though I let her stay up much later than usual to do so. James and Crispin's appearance at the store continues to nag at me. Despite many attempts to think about something else, long after I crawl into bed my mind circles back to their inexplicable reactions to whatever it is I missed.

Maybe it's nothing. Maybe my memory is making the encounter more vivid than it actually was. Maybe James really was surprised that Persephone had to stay in Hades for half her life.

Even as I fall asleep, I cannot convince myself that that's the truth.

5

After only a few days here, the too familiar routine of school is already beginning to feel crushing. So on Monday morning, I join all the other students walking like zombies through the halls and spend the first half of the day waiting impatiently for lunchtime.

I am dismayed to see my math teacher is back today. She's in a foul mood due to being home sick with the flu for the past week, and it would appear that she thinks we all are to blame for her illness. This leads to a wonderful class period.

"Why haven't you turned in any assignments besides the ones for last week?" she snaps at me halfway through class.

I haven't been paying much attention, so it takes me a moment to realize she is talking to me. But I finally reply: "Oh! I wasn't here. Sorry, I just arrived the other day. I didn't know you needed them from me."

"Well that's no excuse!" she barks.

It seems like a completely reasonable excuse to me, actually, maybe the best reason anyone has ever had for not getting homework done. I'm biting back frustration when I answer: "I'm sorry? I can—"

"No, no!" she cries. "Too late! Don't bother."

"I... Okay," I say.

She fixes me with a glare that I decide to return. Not my best decision.

She now finishes out the period by making sarcastic remarks about me under her breath (which I can hear perfectly), threatening to call my parents (I have to bite my tongue to stop from daring her to try), or arguing at me. I can't get a word in edgewise.

Finally the lunch bell rings and, barely holding back a sharp retort, I storm out the room and collide with someone in the hall. When I look up to apologize, I see it's none other than Crispin Calaway.

He peers past me into my classroom, then back at me, apparently amused at my furious expression. "Rough day?" he asks.

"Oh, not you," I moan, too frustrated to be civil. "I don't have time for this." I start to walk away.

Crispin falls in step with me. "Time for what?"

I gesture between us. "This. Whatever it is. Yes, it's a rough day. I can handle it. Good talk." I speed up, dying to see Max and Jade.

"What's eating her?" someone asks Crispin. Someone with a familiar lilt in his voice.

I stop and whirl around to face them. James Sable and Crispin both stop too.

"Yes, ma'am?" Crispin asks.

James, who stands a couple inches taller than Crispin and almost a head taller than me, has no trace of the expression he wore at the bookstore as he regards me. In fact, neither of them suggest that anything out of the ordinary has passed between us at all. Which is frustrating for me, because I spent the better part of my weekend worrying about it. "Don't you all have somewhere to be?" I ask at last, not sure why I want them gone. We are getting some weird looks from the passing students though.

"We do, in fact," Crispin tells me. He and James both step around me and continue down the hall in the direction I need to go. "Lunch."

I stare after them for a moment, and then I run to catch up. "Oh. I forgot you have the same lunch as me."

"Don't you feel lucky?" James says without looking back at me.

"No, as a matter of fact, I don't," I mutter.

Waiting right where they always are, I see Jade and Max scanning the hall for me. With a hurried goodbye, I scoot around Crispin and James to get to them. "Guys!" I call out.

They turn and wave me over, but I've barely taken three steps before I notice them looking behind me. I glance back over my shoulder and see James and Crispin didn't go into the lunchroom like I'd expected. Instead they are standing a few feet away and clearly waiting for me but chatting at one another like they have nothing better to do.

I glare at them, but they both give me their best innocent looks. Then, leaving me to follow yet again, they walk over to meet Max and Jade.

"Hi guys," Crispin says to them cordially. "Good to see you again. This is James Sable. We asked Cara if we could sit with you all today. I have some chemistry notes I need to talk to her about, and I think some freshmen stole our table yesterday anyway. She said it was all right, but we thought we'd check with you too."

From my spot in the background, I roll my eyes at no one in particular. I know the unspoken rules of the lunchroom. Freshmen do not just take tables, especially not in the middle of the semester, and not when that table belongs to hot senior boys.

I seem to be the only one who thinks this is a poor excuse though. Jade is about to hyperventilate, and never having been formally introduced, Max is shaking hands with James. I intervene before anyone says anything more.

"All right!" I clap my hands together. "This'll just be *super*. Crispin, you mind grabbing me some cookies on your way through the lunch line? Thanks so much. We'll meet you over there." I steer Jade and her sack lunch through the doors without pausing before Crispin can protest. Max, who has also brought a lunch, follows us. We make for the table toward the back of the room.

"So..." Jade prompts when we take our chairs at the round table. She and Max are both seated to my right.

"So what?" I try to ask nonchalantly.

"Being his lab partner is just lucky. But inviting him to sit with you at lunch? That's straight up courageous. And after Saturday..."

"I didn't invite either of them! They invited themselves. Trust me when I say I think this is as unexpected as you do."

"What happened Saturday?" Max asks, looking back and forth at the two of us.

I relay the story to him as quickly and clearly as I can. "I guess I just don't understand what they're doing," I tell him. "Why would they sit with us now? Didn't you guys say that they never talk to anyone? What changed?"

"We said that *Crispin* never talks to anyone. Honestly, I'd never really noticed James before you talked to him in photo," Jade says.

I stare at her for a moment. She's the queen of noticing cute guys. She pointed out four in first period the other day. "You're kidding, right?" I ask. "He's in your photo class. He's been sitting two feet away from you! How could you not notice?"

Jade shrugs. "I don't know. I just never noticed."

I shake my head but don't push it. "Okay then. Why are they sitting here today?" I ask again.

"You know what? I'm not sure it matters why. They're super cute. I think we can deal." Jade takes a bite out of her sandwich. "Hey, maybe Cara can find a sexy senior girl to sit with us tomorrow for you, Max."

Max has unfortunately just taken a sip of water, and he all but spits it back out on us both. He swallows it with a painful expression. "I think I'll pass, thanks though."

"Really? Not even if it's Abigail? We already know you like her." Jade says this last part in a singsong voice, gesturing to a pretty brunette a couple of tables away.

Max turns red, either embarrassed or choking on his drink, I can't tell which. I step in for him.

"Sorry Max. I think my magic powers only work with annoying boys."

"Who has magic powers?" Crispin and James have already made their way through the line. They take seats on my left, the side opposite Jade and Max, leaving me in the middle of the group. Crispin is waiting for an answer.

"Oh I didn't tell you earlier?" I say, "It's true, I'm magic. Cool, huh?"

Crispin makes a noncommittal face.

"Fine. Act unimpressed."

"I will, thank you. I'm sure it will be an incredibly difficult act to pull off, but somehow I believe I'll find a way to convince you that I am truly not impressed by your 'magic'."

I snort. "You can try to convince me all you want. But I think we all know that you're not *that* good of an actor. And may I ask where my cookies are?"

"You mean these ones?" Crispin holds up an empty bag. "Yeah, the line was longer than expected, so I had to eat something."

"That's it," I say. "First you doubt my magic powers, now you eat my cookies? Those were your ticket to the table, my friend. I'm afraid you'll have to leave."

James looks amused by mine and Crispin's back-and-forth, but Jade and Max are watching us in amazement. I bump the table so they snap out of it before Crispin looks back at them.

"Max, how was woodshop?" Jade asks quickly. Max has told us more than once that woodshop is the class he dreads because East's new teacher hates him.

Max launches into a passionate rant, and he includes hand gestures that occasionally send bits of his sandwich flying. He has Jade and me giggling at his impersonation of his teacher, and I can't help but glance over at James and Crispin to see if they're laughing too. When I do, I find James' dark eyes trained on me. We both look away quickly. I blush. Jade notices and kicks me under the table harder than I think is necessary.

"What was your last class again?" I ask her, giving her something to do besides gape openly at Crispin. By this point Max has settled into a content silence, having said all that he needed to say. Jade grins.

"Oh, yes, science. Well, considering chemistry is in fact awful and that it has yet to get better, it went wonderfully. The lecture was quite boring, but I did draw an excellent picture of a moose on a snowboard."

I don't look at Crispin when she mentions chemistry but instead congratulate her on her moose drawing. She pretends to bow. "Oh the joys of chemistry," I sigh.

"That's right. You and Cris are lab partners now. I hear that's going well," James says, sounding like he knows "well" is the wrong word. I'm about to say something in reply when I realize that this is the first thing James has said since we met up with Max and Jade. So I raise my eyebrows at him. He raises his back and grins slightly, as though he can tell what I'm thinking. I search for the guilt I saw in his expression the day before, but there is no trace of it.

Crispin turns to me. "Speaking of chemistry, Cara, here are those notes for you to look over tonight. I think if you start learning this stuff now"—he slides the same notebook I gave him back yesterday across the table to me—"it'll be easy to just jump into tutoring when we start."

I can practically hear Jade's jaw hit the floor when Crispin mentions tutoring, and I know she's wondering if she can get him to help her in chemistry too. "Did you have to say that?" I ask him, making a face and pulling the notebook over.

"I've marked the pages you'll need," Crispin continues as though I haven't spoken. "And, if it works for you, I'll drop by your house tonight or tomorrow. The sooner you get it all, the better."

"Whoa," I say. "You know you could just do my work with me, and I could watch while you do the labs. Then you wouldn't have to worry about tutoring me, and you could save a ton of time! Think about it."

"Not a chance. Don't worry, we'll have you chemistry ready in no time."

"Crispin, I just got here. Do you really think I'm going to invite you to my house to teach me chemistry the first week I'm at school? Or the first month, even?"

"I know you weren't going to invite me. That's why I invited myself. Tonight actually works best for me, if that's all right. We won't go over much, just the basics so you're ready for class this week."

"Oh, please, please, please, say you're kidding."

"He doesn't kid about chemistry, Cara. He is a very serious student," James tells me.

"Uh-huh. It's obvious that you aren't in our class. Serious is not even close."

That stops James' next retort. He and Crispin exchange glances; James looks warningly at Crispin, who shrugs slightly. I wonder about it for only a minute.

James turns to say something to Max about woodshop; I gather he knows and dislikes the teacher too. Jade leans in to add to their conversation, so I take the time to talk unnoticed to Crispin.

"What are you doing?" I ask him quietly.

"What do you mean?" Crispin says, not quite meeting my eye.

I feel a little bad for asking, but I continue anyway. There's something tugging at the back of my mind that I can't escape, something more than what happened in the bookstore—something that I know only Crispin can tell me.

"Oh, come on. Everyone at this table thinks this is weird, Crispin. We met a few days ago. So far, you've broken out the shell I've been told you spent your first week here building up, you've done a one-eighty with your lunch routine to include us, and now you've invited yourself to my house. Not to mention you've asked for rides from my friends and invited them to a concert with you." I sigh, realizing how controlling I'm starting to sound. "It's not that you *can't* do those things," I continue more calmly, "it's that I don't know why you are."

Crispin nods and thinks for minute before he speaks again. "Okay," he finally says. "First of all, just because this is odd does not mean that there's some hidden agenda to it. How long have you known Max and Jade here? And how much time have you spent together since you met?"

He waits while I eye him uncomfortably. Crispin doesn't look triumphant, just resigned. "That's what I thought. See, Cara, you told me how much you've moved. But I didn't tell you how much *I* have. James too. We have parents whose jobs require us to move a lot, and we never know when we'll have to leave again. So no, we haven't taken the time yet to branch out and meet a ton of new people. But we saw that you did. Have you ever thought that that's what gave us the courage to try?"

That can't be true, I think. To him I say, "You got your courage...from me?"

"Is that really so hard to believe?" he asks me curiously. "I think you're braver than you've given yourself credit for."

"I haven't done anything," I feel compelled to point out to him.

"You put yourself out there. You didn't allow fear to hold you back. You showed me that I could do the same."

This is getting a little too serious for a lunchroom chat, and I tell Crispin that. He grins. "Yeah. But there it is. Be honest here, Cara. Do you really mind spending time with us?"

He's right. I don't. And I have nothing left to say. Just like that our quiet conversation is over.

We rejoin the group and enter in on the discussion about whether we should be allowed to take naps in study hall (Jade and James are fervently saying yes, while Max is wondering where else he'd get his homework done). We spend the rest of the lunch period like that, so intent on one another that, for the first time, none of us notice the stares or whispers or general confusion of the rest of the people around us who refuse to believe Crispin Calaway and James Sable are joking and laughing like normal students.

****

When Sophie gets home from school, we spend the afternoon cleaning up her room. Between the two of us, we manage to drag a toy chest and a small bookcase up the stairs. We realize the lack of cardboard boxes makes her room look sadly bare. I laugh when she reverently places the two books she got the other day on the top shelf.

All the empty boxes get shoved into the hall. Sophie starts to clear the floor while I stand on her desk chair to press glow-in-the-dark stars around the light on her ceiling. When I look down, she's curled up on her bed watching me.

"What'cha doin'?" I ask her.

Considering me carefully with her light, coffee-colored eyes, she sits up and cocks her head to the side. "Just thinking."

I climb down off the chair to sit next to her. "About what?"

"We move a lot," she replies.

I nod slowly, unable to see the direction the conversation is headed. "Yes, we do."

"So, do you think people remember us? You know, when we leave? Do you think they ever wonder about us after we're gone?"

"I'm sure some of them do. Why are you asking?" I ask her, somewhat worried.

"Do you think Isa will forget about me when we move again?"

A tight, aching sort of pain makes my heart throb because this, more than anything else in the world, is what my little sister has to worry about. I lay back on her bed and she lays down next to me, using my arm as a pillow. Studying the ceiling I answer: "No, honey. I don't think she will."

"But everyone else has," she whispers.

I pull her nearer to me. "No one else has cared about you as much, or as quickly, as Isa has. No one has loved you the same way David and Max and Jade do. You can't compare your friendship with Isa to any of the other friends you've had, because none of your other friends have been quite like her, have they?"

I wait as Sophie thinks about that for a while. A few minutes later she asks me, "So you don't think she's just being nice to me for now?"

"Did you know that Isa is the one who told her parents about the fight you had with Rodney your first day at school?" It feels like ages ago. "She's the reason the Anthonys came over to offer you rides to school. I don't think that's something she would do if she only felt sorry for you. It sounds like something someone does because they've found a person they truly want to be friends with."

"I think she's my best friend," Sophie tells me quietly, the way she does when she's voicing a thought she's worried I'll laugh at.

I never do. "I think you just might be hers too," I reply.

Sophie soon hops off the bed and happily begins telling me about the stuffed bear named Hunter in her classroom at Belinder. Apparently everyone gets to take a turn taking him home to care for. "I get to bring him here next week!" she declares. "And we have to take pictures and everything to show what we did with him."

The doorbell interrupts her mid-speech. I'm now in the middle of shifting misplaced boxes of sheets and towels out of her room, so Sophie skips down the stairs to answer it. I set down what I'm carrying and slowly follow suit.

The door is already open by the time I get there, and Sophie is peering curiously at the boy standing just outside.

His tousled black hair is immediately familiar to me, though I can't quite see his face because he has knelt down to talk to Sophie. When he hears me, he straightens up and fixes his striking gray-blue eyes on me. The corner of his mouth curls up when he sees my surprised expression.

"James," I say finally. "What are you doing at my house?"

He leans against the doorframe and stuffs his hands in his pockets. "Wow. You don't exactly roll out the welcome wagon for your guests now, do you?" He has an unbuttoned black shirt on over a plain gray tee, and the sleeves are pushed up to his elbows, despite the chill. He doesn't give me time to respond before he continues. "And

I'm actually here with Crispin. You didn't forget about your tutoring date with him, did you?"

I wrinkle my nose. "I thought I told him no?"

Just then, Crispin comes into view on his way up the walk.

"I thought I told you no," I call out to him.

"Ah," he replies, joining James in the doorway. "You did. But I've been told that when a woman says no, she really means yes. So I read between the lines."

"Well, whoever told you that was wrong," I say, trying to regain my composure. "Unless you're asking that woman if Brad Pitt is sexier than you. In that case, no always means yes."

Crispin looks faintly amused, but James arches an eyebrow. "Always?" he asks.

Personally I'm not overly fond of Brad Pitt, but I unconvincingly reply, "I'm just telling it like it is."

James shrugs carelessly. "Well, there's no accounting for some people's taste."

"Amen," I murmur. James smiles slightly as though he can hear me, but I know I spoke quietly enough that he couldn't have.

"Look, Cara, can we come in?" Crispin asks.

I pretend to think about it, but Sophie pipes up before I do. "Sure! We're going to make cookies!"

Crispin smiles kindly down at her. "Cookies? My word, now we have no choice but to come in." Then he acts serious. "Although...what kind, exactly, were you planning on making for us, little lady?"

Sophie giggles. "Snickerdoodles!"

"Stupendous! Lead me to them!" Crispin announces grandly. He links his arms through hers, and they waltz to the kitchen together.

"Damn," I mutter.

James looks at me questioningly, a crooked smile still on his lips.

"Now Crispin will have to come over everyday, just to hang out with Sophie." I explain grudgingly.

James laughs soundlessly as I shut the front door and lead him to the kitchen, where Sophie and Crispin are already chatting like old friends. I lift Sophie up and set her on the counter. The boys roam around the room and examine the drawings hung on the fridge and the pictures nailed to the wall.

"I don't remember telling you we were going to make snickerdoodles," I say to Sophie as I watch them. James seems particularly engrossed by the Dala horse my father brought us back from a trip to Sweden a few years ago, and he takes it over to Crispin to show him.

"Yeah, you did," Sophie tells me. "Remember? When you and Jade were making chocolate chip cookies and I asked for snickerdoodles, you said we could make them 'next week'. And then I didn't even ask yesterday, which was actually the real beginning of this week, so we can make snickerdoodles now!"

"I think she's got you there," Crispin calls from across the room.

"Well I suppose you're right. I promised you snickerdoodles." With a sigh I begin getting the baking supplies out of the kitchen cabinets. Sophie slides off the counter to join Crispin and James where they've settled down at the kitchen table, and she begins to explain Hunter the Bear to them. I let her for a while, and then I say, "Hey Soph, why don't you go call Isa about spending the night this weekend? Before we forget."

Sophie happily obliges. Crispin helps her look up the Anthony's number in the phonebook I bought the other day at her school, and then she scampers into the hallway to talk.

"Thanks for listening to her," I tell the boys. "I know she can kind of talk your ear off."

Crispin stands up and waves the comment away. "She has interesting things to say," he insists. "I have an adopt— a, err...cousin, about her age. good to know not all younger kids are as stoic as he tends to be." Apparently eager to cover up his fumbled explanation, Crispin comes over to me and asks: "What can I do to help?"

I'm measuring sugar, but I tell him to get butter from the fridge and melt it into a bowl. James comes over to help too, so soon I'm doing more directing than actual work. I'm trying to watch them both at once.

"So you've never baked before?" I ask them, even though I already anticipate the answer.

Somehow James has managed to get streaks of flour down the front of his black shirt and in his hair, though I'm pretty sure it's Crispin that I told to measure the flour out. "Is it obvious?" he asks, whisking the eggs so violently that some of it slops over the side of the bowl.

He throws me an impish grin when I sigh. His dark eyes are glittering mischievously. "Not at all," I say. "Anyone would think you were professionals. I would be tempted to leave you both to it and run a few errands, but I'm afraid if I exit the room the result may be inedible. And after all this work, that would just be sad."

Sophie comes running back into the kitchen then. "Cara! David wants to talk to you!"

I take the phone from her. "Watch these two," I instruct her. I nestle the phone between my ear and my shoulder so I can pull a chair over for Sophie to stand on, that way she can see over the countertop. "Hey, Dave. What's up?" I ask him.

"Hey there, Cara," David's deep voice says from the other end of the line. "I hear Sophie gets to bring Hunter home next week."

I groan and turn away from Sophie so she doesn't hear my next comment. "I'm so sorry. She told you too?"

David laughs. "I don't mind. Isa was just as excited when it was her turn."

"This bear must be something," I mutter. When I turn around to check on my baking crew, I practically dive across the counter to stop James from pouring baking powder into the mix instead of baking soda.

"That felt a little dramatic," James tells me when I snatch the container from his hands.

"Hang on a second, David," I say into the phone. I ask Sophie to hand me the baking soda, and then I show James his mistake.

"Oh," he says ruefully.

"Yeah," I reply. Then I put the phone to my ear again. "Okay, I'm back."

"What are you doing?" David asks me.

"I think I'm teaching a cooking class," I tell him. "It's hard to tell at this point. If I am, then both my students are failing. I'll probably have to retire after this due to the stress." I show Crispin which measuring spoon size to use as I continue. "What did you need to talk to me about?"

"The sleepover," David says.

"Oh. Why? Does Friday not work for you guys?" I ask.

"No," he says, "Friday is fine. Isa was just hoping Sophie would want to come over here to spend the night instead. My parents are kind of hoping the same thing. Isa doesn't have people over very often, and they love Sophie. Entertaining guests is one of my dad's favorite things. And I thought it might be easier on you too, not having to worry about Sophie *and* Isa."

"I'd love to have Isa over here any time," I'm quick to reassure him. "It would never be any trouble at all! But it would be fantastic for Sophie to go to your house. I'm sure she'd be ecstatic."

Sophie nods excitedly to show me that she would.

"Perfect," David says, sounding just as pleased as I feel. "My parents will iron out the details and call you back. And Isa wants to talk to Sophie again, if that's okay."

"Of course. I'll put her on. Thanks, David."

"No problem. I'll talk to you later."

I hand the phone back to Sophie, who starts talking to Isa about all the toys she can take over when she goes.

"David Anthony has a younger sister too?" Crispin asks me when we start dropping the finally completed snickerdoodle dough onto a cookie sheet.

I smile. "Yes, thank goodness. She and Sophie are already thick as thieves. It's been a lifesaver." I explain to them, quickly and quietly, how Sophie got in a fight her first day at Belinder. "If it weren't for the Anthonys, I think every morning would start with her arguing with me to get out of going to school."

We put the cookie sheet in the oven and all traipse into the living room. I push some boxes off the couch for them to sit down, and I pull an armchair over opposite them. I fall into it wearily. "Who knew baking could be so exhausting?" I say, to no one in particular.

"I have new respect for the cooks," Crispin says, propping his feet up on one of the boxes like it's an ottoman.

"What cooks?" I ask.

"Oh... All of them. I have respect for cooks in general now."

I eye him closely. He meets my gaze evenly.

"Where's my big suitcase?" Sophie calls down the stairs.

"Why do you need it?" I call back.

"For the sleepover," she says.

"You're not taking your big suitcase to the Anthony's."

"But I can't fit everything in the little one!"

"Soph, honey, make it fit, or else take some things out. That's the suitcase you're taking this weekend, small or not."

"Can I take your suitcase?"

I don't answer, which is an answer in itself.

"Fine," Sophie says. "I'll take the small one."

"Don't forget that you have to fit clothes in there too!" I call, shaking my head. "You'd think she was going on vacation for a month the way she packs," I tell the boys, who have been listening with some amusement. "I take it neither of you have younger siblings?"

James says no, he doesn't. After a barely perceptible pause, Crispin does too.

Minutes later the timer on the oven goes off, and, though I told them they could stay in the living room, James and Crispin follow me back to the kitchen. Crispin takes his chemistry book from his backpack as I retrieve the cookies. I grimace at it.

"You've got to learn sometime," Crispin tells me.

"Not true," I say. "I believe I can live quite happily for the rest of my life without ever learning anything about chemistry."

"Would you quit fighting me on this? It might actually come in handy someday."

I gesture at all the dishes piled in the sink from our baking exploits. "I would love to, really, but some things have to be done first."

"Fine," Crispin says. He leans against the counter and opens the book. "I'll quiz you while you work."

I groan as I turn on the water in the sink and dig dish soap out of the cupboard.

He pretends not to hear me. James steals a cookie.

At some point I get lost and stop trying to answer correctly. I know Crispin can tell, but he continues on doggedly. After saying something about acids and bases, he asks me another question that I don't know the answer to.

"Umm... pH?" I guess.

"Titration," he corrects me. "What about the relationship between—?"

"Crispin, what about this do you find interesting?" I cut him off.

He considers the question seriously. "I suppose I just enjoy knowing how things work. Why things happen the way they do. And chemistry tells you a little bit about everything you could ever want to know." He gives me a good-natured shrug.

I hand James a dishtowel and pass him the now clean and dripping dishes. He looks reluctantly at them. I wave the whisk under his nose threateningly. "I washed them all, you help dry. You baked, too."

James takes another cookie, his fourth, and points to Crispin. "He baked too." He offers Crispin the dishtowel.

I press the measuring cup into his hand for him to dry. "*He* is furthering my education, albeit slowly. Dry."

He mumbles something unintelligible. I raise my eyebrows warningly. James ducks his head when he sees my expression, but not quickly enough to hide his boyish grin at my severity.

"Just do it!" I can't help but laugh.

When the kitchen is in order, Sophie has had some cookies, and I've failed at least two more of Crispin's quizzes, I call it quits and collapse on the living room sofa just in time to be roused by the doorbell.

"Goodness we're popular today," I say to Sophie where she's perched on the back of the couch. "Should we ignore it?"

In answer, she scurries off to see who it is. "As long as it's not another boy trying to make me learn something," I mutter.

Crispin smiles at me.

6

It hadn't been. Someone was trying to sell us something we didn't need, so I politely declined, said my parents weren't home, and then shut the door firmly.

Jade called me later in the evening. She had decided we should go ice-skating. She'd talked Max into it, and then David. Now she wanted to know if Sophie and I would be game. Sophie was an immediate yes, partially because Isa was going. I offered for Crispin and James to come along, as long as they promised to leave the chemistry book behind, but they had other plans.

So an hour later, I'm lacing up my borrowed ice skates and updating Jade on my interactions with the senior boys as we sit on the bench outside some ice rink. Jade never fails to be amazed by the ordinary happenings of my stories.

"They were at your house?"

"You baked together?"

"He's actually tutoring you?"

"Why didn't they come skating?"

"You offered, didn't you? You better have offered. I'd love to see Crispin Calaway on ice skates."

She continues to question me as we make our way over to the others. Max is doing some faux skating stretch, while David tries to convince Isa to leave her winter jacket on.

"And none of you said anything about what happened at the bookstore?"

"They're acting like it never even happened. And maybe it didn't. Maybe I really did imagine it," I answer her millionth question gamely.

Jade shakes her head. "No. You looked way too spooked to have imagined it. But hey, if they're going to forget about it then you can too, right?"

I applaud as Max steps on to the ice tentatively and nearly falls over. He bows. "I guess so," I reply.

Jade looks unconvinced by my unenthusiastic response. "Just don't let a possible friendship with them be ruined over one weird thing, okay?" She smiles conspiratorially. "Besides, if you become friends with them, then I can too."

She winks and steps onto to the rink next. She skates around once and skids to a wobbly halt in front of us again.

"That was a warm up," she informs us as Max chuckles. "Let's see you do better." They take off.

I help Sophie finish tying her skates, and we slide together onto the ice. Sophie's gloved hand is holding tight to mine as she tries to find her balance. Her cheeks are rosy from the chill, and her eyes are shining. Her tasseled hat is pushed low over her forehead.

When Isa and David skate past, Sophie becomes more confident. Soon I let go of her hand and watch as she glides forward, laughing happily. She turns to wave at me.

Then she catches up to Isa, and the two link arms to skate next to each other.

Jade is wearing fluffy green earmuffs, and David skates past her like a professional to snatch them off her head. She shrieks as he takes off again and gives chase. Max, who apparently can ice skate backwards, comes up next to me. With an expert move he twists to face forward and slows to match my pace.

"Nice," I tell him.

"What can I say? Ice skating is my sport," he replies.

I grin. "It takes a very secure man to admit that."

We watch David let Jade within a few inches of him. She makes a wild grab for the earmuffs, misses, and David shoots off again. Jade pushes off the wall to give herself more momentum as she follows.

"Jade told me Crispin and James were at your house earlier," Max says as we skate along.

"Do you think that's weird?" I ask, not surprised that Jade confided in him. "After the whole bookstore thing?"

"Well... Was it awkward to have them there?"

"No," I tell him. "It was surprisingly unawkward, truth be told."

I grab Sophie as she slides by and tell her and Isa to go help Jade retrieve her earmuffs. They do so happily.

"They were perfectly normal at lunch too," Max muses. "So maybe...try to forget about it? Acknowledge that it was weird, and try to move past it?"

"I know I should, I just can't stop wondering about it."

"Cara, you've only known them for a couple of days. It could have been any number of things that made James act the way he did. And Crispin is his friend, so of course he followed James out. Jade and David and I would rush after you if you ran out of a store for no apparent reason."

"Which would be a real comfort, I'm sure, if something frightened me enough to make me sprint out of a store."

Max has deep, serious brown eyes, and he gazes at me steadily with them as he awaits a better answer. "You're right," I tell him. "And you know you are, so stop looking at me like that." I shove him away from me, smiling. "Go skate. Show me that backwards thing again."

He does. I slow down and skate next to the wall—it makes for the longest loop around.

Eventually David glides over and links his arm through mine, just as Sophie and Isa had been skating earlier. He's now wearing the earmuffs.

I smile and shake my head. "Those clash horribly with your leather jacket," I inform him.

"I heard this jacket goes with everything," he says with mock seriousness. "In fact, I was told by the very woman who sold it to me that there is nothing I cannot wear with this leather jacket."

"And that sounds nothing like something a saleswoman would say," I agree.

David smiles and takes the earmuffs off. He throws them so that they hit Jade in the back of the head. She shakes her fist at us, but she's grinning, skating around the rink holding hands with Sophie on one side and Isa on the other.

"How you doing?" David asks me. "Honestly?"

I shake my head. "That's a somewhat complicated question right now. Ask me later?"

He switches questions. "Okay. Then what were you thinking about just now?"

I answer truthfully. "You guys. Do you remember the other day, when you said how odd it was for you to see Max and Jade waiting after school, and knowing that they were waiting for you?" David nods so I continue. "I was thinking about that. Because that's how I feel when I'm spending time with you guys, only I feel it everyday."

He watches me as I explain further.

"Moving is so...hard. It's just hard. And I'm not outgoing enough to make friends as easily as I need to. So this? This is the first time in a long time I've had people to call up, to spend time with, who are truly my friends. Who I can tell my secrets to without being judged, and who give me advice without being asked to give it. It's wonderful, don't get me wrong, but it feels a little bit unreal. Too easy, too good to be true for very long."

"You're paranoid," David tells me.

"Yes," I agree. "I definitely am." I switch topics so fast that I barely know how I get from one to the other. "Do you know that Isa is Sophie's best friend?"

We watch the girls. They're playing tag around the rink, and they've recruited Max and Jade. It looks like Max is it.

"You know that even if you do have to move again someday we won't stop being your friends, don't you?" David says to me after a long moment, getting straight to the heart of the matter.

I sigh. "Dave, you say that now, but you don't know that."

"Please. Cara, you're the best girlfriend Jade has had in her entire life. Did you know *that*? And you accomplished that in two weeks. Max is too content to branch out at all, but you made him by introducing yourself and Sophie into his life. Now he has another safe place to land when his stepfather is making his life hell. And I'm pretty sure that Isa will no longer be able to live without you and Sophie around."

Isa, as if called, rushes up to us now, Sophie hot on her heels. Isa's dark eyes are glimmering with excitement. "Sophie says you have a tire swing in your backyard. And that I can come over and use it sometimes! Can I really?"

I laugh at her eagerness. "Honey, you can come over whenever you want. The tire swing is yours to use any time you feel like it."

David looks at me triumphantly as Isa and Sophie manage to drive his point home for him.

The younger girls cheer just as Jade announces across the rink, "I figured out how to do that spinning move that professional skaters do!"

She hasn't, but it's fun to watch her try nonetheless. She laughs at herself, taking up half the rink as she attempts to gain enough momentum to make it work. Sophie and Isa both try to imitate her, and they all end up falling more than they spin.

David is still standing next to me, watching not Jade and Isa, but my face. "And, for the record, my life wouldn't be complete without you two either. You mean as much to us as any friend we've ever had." He smiles. "I wish you would stop worrying about something that hasn't even happened yet, that may never happen. I know its rough, but stop living in the future. This is your life; this is real, *right now*. Nothing else matters."

****

I stay up for a long time after I get Sophie ready for bed that night. I busy myself by working on cleaning out my new room, but my mind isn't focused on the task. I'm running through the conversations I've had with my friends and with people like Mr. Pelegro and Crispin.

It seems to me that they can see my life more clearly than I do. Or, more correctly, they see it differently than I do.

I want to be as brave as Crispin thinks, as caring as Mr. Pelegro sees, as friendly and out-going as Jade hopes, and as carefree as Max and David expect. Their advice is good, their points are valid, but I don't know how to be all those things.

Sophie, probably awoken by the sound of me accidentally toppling a stack of yet more cardboard boxes in the hallway, comes stumbling into my room around midnight. She blinks up at me sleepily, and then without invitation curls herself up on my freshly made bed. I've also finished clearing off my desk, and I'm working on finding room in my closet and dresser for my clothes after I hunt them all down.

"Why are you still awake?" Sophie asks with her eyes closed.

"Oh, I'm just thinking," I reply, tossing a blue blouse onto a hanger.

I should have known to give her a straight answer. She'll keep asking until I do. "I know *that*," she says. "What are you thinking about?"

I sigh. "I'm thinking that it's too late in my life for me to change who I am."

Now Sophie does slit her eyes open. "Who wants you to change?" she asks.

"It's not that people want *me* to change, exactly. They want me to change the way I think. The problem is, I've been thinking one way for so long that I don't know how to do it any differently. I don't know how to be brave and happy-go-lucky all the time. I think I'm stuck the way I am." *Cautious and stressed.*

"Well, I don't want you to change," Sophie tells me.

I look at her. "Not even if it made me fun and cheerful all the time?"

"Why would I want you to be cheerful all the time? No one can be cheerful all the time."

"You wouldn't rather I spent less time worrying about things like unpacking and cooking?" I ask her, moving to the bed to sit next to her.

Sophie's eyes are closed again, and she yawns as she answers. "Well if you don't unpack and cook, than who's going to? I think you have to be serious and sad sometimes. But you're happy when I need you to be. Like today, ice skating with me... And making cookies with your friends." She's dozing off now, her voice growing quieter with every word. "I liked those friends. When are they coming...over...again?" She falls asleep with the question still on her lips.

I watch her for a time before I stand up to work again. While I would love to be carefree all the time, I can't be. I've got Sophie depending on me. I've got a nine-year-old girl to raise. While I know there are people out there who could do a better job of it than me, I think she's turning out wonderfully.

And then I think, *Maybe that does make me brave. And friendly, and outgoing, and caring. Maybe they're all right. So maybe my friends are seeing the real me after all.*

I've been so caught up in the idea that I've been showing them I'm someone that I'm not, I never stopped to think that maybe they're seeing exactly who I am, and much more easily than I ever have.

I toss a blanket over Sophie and keep cleaning. Clothes in the closet, pictures on the dresser, books on the bookcase, the drawings Sophie's made for me over the years taped to the sky blue walls.

When I finally shut off the light and crawl into my bed next to my sister, David's words play over in my head until I fall asleep. His advice, above everyone else's, has the words that I need to listen to. "Stop worrying about something that hasn't even happened yet...Stop living in the future. This is your life; this is real... Nothing else matters."

****

I doze through most of my classes the next day. Jade and Max keep me awake during the periods that we have together, but there isn't anything they can do about classes like history and math where I get called out more than once by my teachers. My math teacher actually makes me sit in the hall for being disrespectful, which is no real punishment, if I'm honest. It gets me out of class. I lean my head back against the wall as I sit and try to close my eyes against the fluorescent lighting.

While I wait for my teacher to allow me back into her classroom, James and David walk by. They both stop to grin at my predicament.

"Why hello!" I exclaim fondly. "What are you doing out here?"

James cocks his head to the side and studies me. "We could ask you the same question."

I wave toward the door of the math room. "Apparently in Kansas, sleeping during class is frowned upon," I say with a shrug. "Who knew? Not to mention my teacher hates me, which clearly only helps."

"We do have some odd rules in this state," David admits. "But you know what they say: When life gives you lemons..."

"Chuck them at people, yeah, I know."

The corner of James' mouth turns up, and David laughs.

"What class are you guys in?" I ask them. "Or do you often have mysterious rendezvous in the hallways?"

"Well, yes to the rendezvous," James says, "but at this moment David and I are actually in the same class. We have physics together."

I pull a face. "Physics. The only class that's worse than chemistry."

"No class is worse than chemistry," David says.

When the door to my classroom begins to open, David and James give me hurried goodbyes before racing a few steps down the hall so I don't get in more trouble. My teacher, Mrs. Horn, eyes their backs suspiciously.

"The class period is almost up," she tells me briskly. "Come in and collect your things for lunch. And I still expect you to hand in tonight's homework to me tomorrow, just like everyone who was actually in class."

She obviously has no idea that spending the period in the hall made this the best math class I've had to date.

Crispin and James sit with Max and Jade and me at lunch again. It feels almost natural to have them around. I try to catch either of them looking at me with any amount of fear or guilt, but neither do.

I admit to Jade in sculpting that I really must have imagined the whole ordeal in the bookstore.

She sighs. "That makes for a much less interesting story. But it'll be much easier to be friends with them now!"

"Which is really the goal here," I say with a smile.

Jade gives me a look with a glimmer in her eyes. "I'm serious here, Cara. I like these guys. Yes, partly because they're hot and mysterious, but they're smart too, and funny, and we are the only people since they've arrived at

East who have gotten them to talk. I mean *really* talk! Isn't that a pretty clear sign that we're meant to be friends with them?"

"How do you know they don't talk to anyone else? Okay, sure, people seem fairly taken aback that they're chatting with us, and that they've shifted lunch tables to join us rather than sitting at their own exclusive table, but really? Do you know someone in every single one of their classes? Is someone confirming the fact that they don't speak to any other students in this school?" I ask. I can't get my head around the fact that these boys *only* talk to us. "Don't get me wrong, I like them both too. But you're telling me we're the first people they've talked to? Ever?"

"Well maybe not *ever*," Jade rolls her eyes. "I'm sure they didn't go their wholes lives without speaking before they met you."

"You know what I mean."

"I do," Jade admits. She sighs, the way she does when she remembers I just moved here and am not quite as up-to-date as she'd prefer. "Okay. So at East, there are always some guys that every girl in the school, by mutual agreement, thinks is hot. It's a big school, but word gets around. Word about Crispin and James went around fast, lightning fast. And where a hot boy is, gossip is sure to follow. So no, I don't know someone in every class they have, or who watches them constantly for me. But there is an entire student body's worth of information going around about them that I hear a lot of. So I can tell you with some certainty that they do not go out of their way to make friends. Sure, they're polite if someone talks to them or asks them a question. But we're the first people they've shown any amount of real interest in."

Jade pats the top of my head, wincing for me as she realizes her hands are covered in clay. "And it's all thanks to you," she concludes hurriedly.

I rub some of my clay on her cheek with a smirk. "How'd you figure that?"

"Please. Crispin passed you notes in class. He talked to you first. He asked you if he and James could join us at lunch. They went to your house. This was not hard to work through."

She lets me pretend to work on my sculpture project for a while as I mull things over. I guess what she's saying is true. I seem to be the one who has spent the most time with these guys.

"But like Crispin told me yesterday," I say, "it's just because I'm new too. He said something like, 'You were brave enough to make new friends, so now James and I are inspired to do the same.'" I try and fail to imitate Crispin's faint accent.

Jade is looking at me dubiously.

"So it's not like I'm special," I try to convince her. "I'm *inspirational*. And those two are ruining the lay-low-and-don't-attract-attention-to-yourself plan I put in place for myself the fifth time we moved. Instead, I've managed to become the focus of half the school."

"You say that like it's a bad thing," Jade says.

"I still think they're different," I tell her. I continue before I hear her next comment, knowing what she'll say. "And again, no, not different because they're sexy. Different because they're *different*. I don't know how, or why, but they are."

Jade shrugs. "I think you should let that go."

"I will when I figure it out."

Each lost in our own thoughts, we fall silent for the remaining few minutes of the period. *Why am I the only one who thinks they don't quite fit in? They set themselves apart from everyone on purpose, clearly, but why? And what changed when they met me?* Because although I'll never tell Jade, I do think something about me interests them. I don't think they're in love with me—Jade's current theory—or that I met them in another state and they're waiting for me to remember—Max's—but I do think there is something they aren't telling me. And I want to find out what it is.

****

When Jade drops me off after school, the first thing I do is dump my things by our front door, stagger into the family room, and fall onto the couch. I have to kick some boxes to the floor in order to do so, but I finally pull a blanket over myself and curl up to nap. I feel like I've earned it.

David's family was going to see a movie this afternoon, and they'd invited Sophie and me. Sophie had been thrilled at the offer, but I needed a day where I didn't have to do anything. I told David that, and he'd understood immediately.

"You've been going nonstop since you arrived," he'd said. "Take a day to yourself. We'll pick Sophie up from school and bring her home afterward."

So I don't have to go to work, don't have to worry about Sophie for most of the afternoon, and have almost no homework left to do. No plans. Gratefully, I snuggle down into our old sofa and shut my eyes.

About half an hour later, I haven't moved but I haven't fallen asleep. The silence of the house is unnerving. Normally I love peace and quiet because it's so rare, but it seems odd to be in this new house and have no noise. I've become so used to having Sophie pattering around, or Jade singing in the kitchen, or Max telling some story, that the house feels empty without them.

I stand up and wrap the blanket around my shoulders. Then I dance around some boxes to grab the kitchen radio and plug it into the living room wall. I flip it on, decide to leave it on the country station it's tuned to. I'm about to collapse back on the couch when I hear a solitary, hesitant knock on the front door.

I groan. I consider ignoring it, but I finally pull the blanket more tightly around myself and go to the door.

When I swing it open, I find James Sable looking down at me. He appears to have walked here because there's no car in the driveway, and as it often does, an expression of mild amusement crosses his features when he sees my bare feet and blanket.

My gaze challenges him to make a comment. He refrains, and we both end up standing in the open doorway, neither of us saying a word.

James starts to look slightly uncomfortable, like he didn't put much thought into what he would do when he arrived at my house. He drops my gaze and studies the doormat. I continue to look at him until he meets my eyes again. His hair is rumpled, and there is no way that the jeans and navy sweater he's wearing are enough to keep him warm in this chilly weather.

"You know this is my day off?" I ask him eventually.

He mouth quirks. He seems grateful for the conversation. "Day off from what?" he asks.

"Everything," I reply. "Work, homework, parenting... You name it, I don't have to do it."

"Cleaning?" he says in a way that suggests he knows the answer.

My expression darkens slightly, making him grin more widely. He runs a hand through his black hair. "Can I come in?" he asks. "I promise not to get in the way of your day off. Or your cleaning. Whichever it is."

"No Crispin today?" I ask innocently, shutting the door behind him.

James looks at me carefully. "No. He's checking some things out for his parents. They've got him busy all the time." He smiles at some joke that I've evidently missed. "Why? Were you hoping he'd come?"

I shake my head, too quickly, but I try to pass it off nonchalantly. "No, it's fine. I just don't usually see you two apart when you can help it."

"Well we couldn't help it," James says. "And I am sorry for coming over uninvited. I was just out wandering, bored, and thought maybe you might be home. But I can leave if you were enjoying your time alone."

James is leaning against the wall now, arms crossed, watching me with his dark eyes. The last thing I want is for him to leave. I reply, "If you can help me clean and promise not to be too demanding, than you can stay as long as you like."

He promises. I drop the blanket back onto the couch and shiver in the cold air we let in before we'd shut the front door. I gesture around the room.

"This is the project. Make the living room presentable, so when company comes over without being invited we aren't caught off guard."

"Good plan," James says.

"So... Just start unpacking boxes and finding a place for things," I instruct him.

It only takes about thirty seconds of silence for him to ask, "What are you listening to?"

The country music is still playing in the background. I walk over to turn it up. Way up. "Garth Brooks. Don't tell me you've never heard it?"

James raises his eyebrows. "Do I seem like the kind of guy who listens to country music?"

I frown good-naturedly. "You do now." I turn it up even louder until we'd have to shout to be heard. Then I start singing along, quietly at first, but as the song reaches the refrain I can't stop myself from belting it out and occasionally jumping around to the beat.

Part of me is consciously aware that James is in the room. I should be at least kind of embarrassed at my behavior, but I ignore it.

Then James starts singing too, and he knows every word. I laugh out loud as I watch him. He shrugs, smiles crookedly at me, and pretends to drum on the still-full boxes. His baritone voice is full and rich. When the first song ends, James sings the next one, and the one after that. At one point we cross paths, headed to different parts of the room, and he offers me his hand. Heart in my throat, I take it.

He spins me around to the music, grinning softly, then bows when the song ends and walks off to put a potted plant on a small table by the door.

I watch him go. How he's acting now doesn't quite fit with the picture of James Sable I have been putting together in my head. He's seemed so aloof, so self-assured and reserved, that I never thought of him as simply quiet or kind or at all willing to make a fool of himself. But I see that he is those things too. My heart pounds a little faster when he turns back around and finds me looking at him.

Eventually we turn the music down, and he begins to hand me items from the last few boxes we have left to unpack so that I can find a place for them. We don't speak much, only a bit about school and friends. We mostly keep to ourselves and hum along to the songs still playing.

Silence is awkward with some people. Usually it's because you have nothing to talk about, nothing in common, or nothing you want to say to the person you're with. But when James and I lapse into silence, it's nothing like that. It's a feeling of being respectfully left alone to think about whatever is on our minds and allowing the other person to do the same.

As he leaves me to think though, my thoughts circle back to the only time he and I have actually been alone: Saturday in The Scarlet Letter. I pause momentarily in our work. James waits for me to speak, somehow knowing that I have something I need to say. So I take a deep breath and, without looking at him, I ask: "James? What happened the other day at the bookstore? Why did you leave like that?"

I don't turn to see his reaction to my question. I can tell that he becomes still; he stops trying to put things away for me. I stand to continue organizing books and pictures and decorative knick-knacks on the dark-wooded bookshelves that surround our fireplace. James takes so long to answer that I'm getting ready to tell him to forget it, that it's really no big deal.

Then, dancing around the straight answer, he speaks carefully. "I...realized something. Something that Cris had been trying to tell me about for a few days, but that I didn't really understand until that day in the store. And it was such a shock, so unexpected, that I had to get away. I had to think about it myself."

I arrange a few family photos on one of the lower shelves. "Did I have anything to do with what you were thinking about?"

"You mean was I thinking about you?" James drawls.

My face flames as I realize how he's taking my question. I'm quick to backtrack. "No, that's not what I mean. Well, kind of it is, but not really. I meant, that realization that you had? Was I part of it?"

This time James really doesn't answer. When I glance over at him, he's seated on the couch and turning a candle over in his hands. I take a seat on the arm of the chair next to him. "I think I must have," I answer for him, "because you looked scared of me."

Now James looks up, intensity in his gaze, his eyes willing me to understand what he's going to say. "Not scared *of* you," he murmurs. "Scared *for* you."

I hear a car pull into our driveway just as James reaches up a hesitant hand to brush a loose lock of hair back from my face. I freeze as his light fingers find my cheek, and then the moment is gone as Sophie rushes in the door.

His hand falls as Sophie calls out, "Cara!" and runs to me. I sweep her up in a hug. She turns in my lap to wave at James, who has wiped his expression clean of whatever emotion was running through him a moment ago. I'm thinking about his response, his hand on my face, so I miss the first part of whatever Sophie is telling me.

"—can dogs really do that?"

"I'm sorry sweetie. What movie did you see?"

David, smiling when he spots us, pokes his head around the door. "Hey. Just making sure you're home before we leave her here." He accepts without question the fact that James is sitting in my living room with us.

"Well, I'm here!" I tell David. "Thanks again for taking her with you."

"She was great," he replies. "See you 'round."

"Bye, Dave." Sophie echoes me, James nods at him, and then David shuts the door and I hear a car door shutting and the Anthonys driving off.

Soon James stands and says he needs to head out. I walk him to the door. Before he leaves, he turns to gaze at me searchingly. His gray-blue eyes are even darker in the dying light of the evening, and he doesn't say anything for a long moment. "Cara, please be careful," he finally requests.

I don't even have time to ask what I'm supposed to be being careful of before he walks briskly off.

Sophie and I pass the rest of the evening reading, doing homework, and talking. I'm proud to have most of the house put together. Now there are only a few rooms left before it'll officially feel like ours. Because Jade will be upset if she hears it from David first, I text her to tell her James stopped by.

R U kidding me??!! she replies instantly. *What for?*

Just to hang out. He said he was bored so he came here. I'll tell you about it tomorrow.

I already know I'm not going to tell her everything. I won't tell her about the country music, or the dancing, or his cryptic responses to my questions. And I don't think I'm going to tell her about my growing feelings for the strange, gorgeous boy that I know next to nothing about.

7

Unfortunately, Tuesday is the last day I'll have off for a while. Now it's back to school, work, and parenting.

I tell Jade about James coming by my house on our way to school. David listens patiently to our chatter from the backseat.

"I told you he and Crispin like you," she says when I finish and we enter the school building. We take our usual seats in first period.

"Well yeah. They like you too. That's not the point I was making. Actually, I wasn't making a point at all. I was telling a story," I reply.

Max cuts off her response when he walks in the room with a swollen, dark bruise on his jaw. Jade and I look at him with wide eyes as he sits down. He hardly glances our way.

"Hey," he mumbles in greeting. There's no iPod on him today, a first for Max Fedderman. That's how he usually gets ready for his morning.

"Max." Jade speaks slowly, gently, the way you would if you were talking to a scared or injured animal. "What happened?"

"I think you can probably guess," he says, hatred in his voice and his brown eyes. He's wearing tennis shoes and a plain gray sweatshirt, completely different from his normal attire. It looks like it was an effort for him to drag himself to school this morning.

Jade puts it together faster than I do. "Max," she breathes, "your stepfather did this?"

He bites his lip and turns his face away from us. Jade and I exchange glances. Class is starting. Though we usually all sit in a row, I switch seats quickly so that I'm right in front of Max and we can continue talking. The girl whose normal seat I've taken gives me a haughty look when she enters class, flouncing past me to sit next to Jade.

I repeat Jade's question. "Max, what happened? Please tell us. He hit you?"

"Not exactly," Max says in a low voice. "He went after my mom. So I hit him. *Then*, yes, he punched me."

Jade passes him her water bottle with a shaking hand. He takes it gratefully and calms slightly as he takes a few swigs.

"I had to sleep in my car. Mom went back to work for the night shift, and I told her to stay there all day and spend the night in the on-call room. He's furious, guys. Worse than I've ever seen him."

I reach under his desk, find his hand, and hold on to it. I don't know what to say, so I hope this is enough. Max squeezes my fingers in thanks. I don't let go for the rest of the period, even as my arm starts to fall asleep, and by the time the hour is up, none of us have listened to a word our teacher has said.

Before they have time to disappear down the hall, I pull Max and Jade aside by some lockers. I press my house key into Max's hand. "First of all," I tell him in a hushed voice, "I have another one of those at home. I'll get it after school today. You keep that one. Now, you come over whenever you need to, do you hear me? *Whenever* you need to. Your mom too. Don't tell your stepdad about it "Obviously," Max says quietly. But he looks grateful.

"I won't tell my parents either." Max's awful home life is the biggest secret he's got. "Secondly, I'm going to call the school office and pretend to be your mother, and I'm going to pull you out of school for an appointment. Go over to my house. Stay as long as you need to. We've got a ton of food in the fridge and my dad has some extra clothes you can borrow for tomorrow, if you can't go home."

Max starts to protest, but I simply nod goodbye to him and Jade before they can argue and walk off. I rush to my next class, and ask the teacher if I can use the restroom. When he hands me the pass, I rush right back out. I check to make sure the bathroom is clear and then dial the office. I have the number saved to my phone after all the calls I had to make to transfer here.

Luckily, there are enough students at Shawnee Mission East to guarantee the receptionist will have no clue what Mrs. Fedderman actually sounds like. It's easier than I had guessed to convince them to let Max out early, but I still breathe a sigh of relief when I hang up. I'm always uncomfortable with breaking the rules, but sometimes it has to be done.

****

Jade sits down next to me in photography class and takes James' usual seat. We both look at each other, waiting with baited breath until the bell rings. No Max. We manage to exchange small smiles at our little victory.

"I can't believe it," Jade says when Mr. Lincoln's lecture is over and we're given work time. "Poor Max. He never... Why didn't he tell me things were this bad?"

Shocking as Max's present situation is for me, it's harder on Jade. She and Max have been best friends forever. She should be the first one Max goes to when he's in trouble, and he didn't even tell her. Jade feels pain for Max, but she's hurt too.

I wrap an arm around her shoulders comfortingly, and she leans into me. "I think he was afraid," I answer. "If his stepfather found out Max was coming to you for help, you'd be in trouble too. He cares about you too much to drag you into his problems."

"Does he really think that I would mind?" she murmurs.

"No," I reply. "But *he* would."

Since his was occupied when he'd gotten to class, James is now sitting in Max's seat across from the two of us. When I look up at him, I know that he's heard every word we've said. His dark eyes are unfathomable. He nods at me when I catch his eye, then he drops his head and continues his work. I feel an overwhelming rush of gratitude for his silence. Jade doesn't notice the quiet exchange.

"I know he's protecting me, in his own way, but I wish he didn't feel like he had to. I'd feel so much better if I knew he would come to me when things got hard."

"So, maybe you need to go to him?" I suggest. "Come over after school. I still have to go to the bookstore, but you can stay at my house with him. Talk to him. He needs you, Jade."

"I'll still have to bring Sophie over," she says.

I nod. "Yeah, I still need you to do that. Sorry. But after she's with me, you can spend the whole evening at my house. You can spend the night there, if you want to."

"But your parents..." she begins.

I scoff. "Right. Because Mom and Dad are so in tune with my life, they'll be horrified to learn I'm having a sleepover on a school night." I roll my eyes. "Please."

She flashes me a grin. "Okay. Sleepover. Your house. I'll convince Max."

I massage my temples, feeling a headache coming on. I'm more than happy to have them over and help Max through his crazy life, but I can't help wishing I had a few less things to deal with.

Jade notices my expression. "Hey, Cara? Thanks. I'm glad you're here." She laughs without any mirth. "We couldn't do this without you."

I understand her laughter, though most people might not. Had this happened only a week ago, Max would be sleeping in his car again tonight.

"Well, it's like you said," I tell Jade. "The universe put me where I needed to be."

Despite how little time is left in the period, Jade begins to work on her project. I can't help the way my eyes seek out James' face as soon as I have the chance. And I find James is looking at me curiously too.

When Jade stands up a few moments later to get a drink (Max still has her water bottle), James leans over to ask, "What was that about the universe?"

I explain. "Oh, last week Jade and Max and I were talking, and she said that . .despite how hectic my life is, it's been taking me where I need to go. The universe has been plotting my entire life to get me where I'm meant to be. And right now I need to be here. I don't usually buy into that kind of thing, but in this case at least, it looks like she was right. And I thought it would help her if she knew that."

James watches me as I explain. And when I finish, he smiles. "I like that," he muses. "The universe is taking you where you're supposed to go... I hope that's true."

I stare at him. "Are you naturally this enigmatic, or do you have to put in some effort?"

James smirks, and we stop the conversation there as Jade reenters the room.

We pass the rest of the day quietly. I had expected James to ask Jade and me what happened to Max, or for Crispin to ask where he is but neither do. I thank them, once Jade is out of earshot, but they shrug it off easily.

When I get to work that afternoon, after making sure Max let Jade into the house, Mr. Pelegro doesn't press me for details about my silence. He and I work side by side for a while, shelving books and sweeping the floor, and then he heads out as he does every time I come in, with the same promise to be back soon.

Jade's Land Rover soon pulls up across the street from The Scarlet Letter. She peers through her window to make sure I'm in the shop. I wave to her. She waves back grimly, points at Sophie as she steps out of the car, gives me a questioning thumbs-up, and then points back the way she came.

I nod. I know what her weird sign language means. She's making sure she can leave without walking Sophie into the shop. Things with Max must be tense back at home. So Jade pulls away with another wave. I watch carefully as Sophie looks left and right and then skips across the street and through the shop door.

"Max is really upset. He's at our house," she declares as soon as she walks in.

"I know, honey," I say.

She settles down into one of the chairs and cocks her head to look at me. "Well, how come?" she asks curiously.

I sigh. "Sophie, I love you, but I think Max would rather I didn't talk about it. We might tell you sometime, but right now the less people that know, the better."

Sophie thinks about this response for a moment. "Oh. He has a bruise on his face."

"Yes. He does."

"Can you not tell me about that either?" she asks.

"No Soph, I can't. I can tell you that he has a bruise because someone punched him, and now he's mad about it, and he's probably going to be spending the night at our house."

I see Sophie working through it all in her head. She doesn't put everything together, but God bless her, she doesn't press me. Over the years we've come to the understanding that there are very few things I won't at least try to explain to her, however there are some secrets that I'm allowed to keep until I believe she's ready for them.

She asks a final question: "Is he going to be okay?"

I beckon her over, lift her onto the counter, and look her in the eye. "Yes, Sophie. He's upset, but he's tough. Max is going to be just fine."

I then busy her by teaching her how to read the copyright dates of the books stacked nearby, and I ask her to help me put all books from before 1950 in one pile and the ones after 1950 in another.

This keeps us occupied as a couple customers enter the store. I glance up at them for a moment to see if they'll need my help. One is a nervous-looking, tall, red-haired man in dark jeans, and the other is a blond man in a suit. They eye me briefly before disappearing behind some shelves. I turn my attention back to Sophie.

For a while, I can hear the men muttering to each other, but eventually they fall silent. I can't see them next time I look up from my work, but I do see Crispin and James walking down the street toward the store. I smile at them.

Just then the blond man steps out from a nearby aisle and faces me. He looks awfully serious. "May I help you?" I ask him politely.

There's a shift in his expression when I speak. It's nothing I can put a name to, but something in me clenches instinctively. "Sophie," I say, in a low voice that causes her to look up. The man reaches behind him and beneath his suit jacket in one hard, swift motion. A kick of pure fear shoots through me for no reason as I say, "Get down." I pull Sophie from the counter myself just as the man points a handgun in my face. Sophie is safe and mostly hidden now, but she still sees what's happening. With a small sob she wraps her arms around me and hides her face in my side. I place a hand protectively over her shoulders and hold her to me as I flinch away from the weapon.

"We want the money out of the register," the man barks. I assume "we" includes him and the red-headed man, who has come to stand just behind him.

My heart is flying in my chest. Sophie stifles another sob into my shirt, so I tighten my hold on her. "I-I'm sorry?" I stammer out.

"The money," he growls. He gestures to the register with his gun before moving it closer to my head. I wince.

I can't think straight. I can barely breathe.

"I...I don't..." I still haven't formed an answer when I notice Crispin and James peering in the window of the store. They don't seem as terrified by the situation as I am, which gives me the confidence I need to somewhat steady my voice. Though I'm still full of fear, I say to the men, "We r-really haven't had much business. There can't be more than...seventy dollars in the register."

The blond man has a stony expression and angry eyes. "Get. It. Out." His voice is demanding.

Through the window I see Crispin make a motion at me to keep talking. So I try. "Okay, okay, I'll open it. But please...could you move the gun? You're scaring her." I squeeze Sophie's shoulder.

Both men chuckle at the suggestion. The red-haired man makes as if to move behind the counter with us. I jerk back a step and take Sophie with me. He smirks.

Terrified as I am, I feel a glare in my eyes. "Stay back," I say warningly. Crispin and James have disappeared. I feel a weight of fear settle on my chest. I can't call the police without the men seeing. I can't trigger the alarm because it isn't turned on during the day. I can't do anything except comply.

I take the few steps back to the register without taking my eyes off the men. *I don't know what to do. Oh, God, I'm so scared. Sophie has to stay safe.* I click open the register and hand whatever bills there are over to the man without the gun.

When I risk a glance around to see if anyone is nearby who'll notice what's happening, out of the corner of my eye I see James. Somehow he has made his way into the store and is hiding behind a row of bookshelves. He holds a finger to his lips and disappears again without a sound.

But now I know he's here; he and Crispin didn't leave me. Courage rushes through me, even as the blond man walks up to the counter and reaches over to press the handgun against my head. The cold barrel is solid next to my temple. I shut my eyes briefly at the feeling. "What else do you have in this godforsaken shop?" the blond man asks.

I know I have to keep their attention on me to give James and Crispin time to do whatever they have in mind to help me.

"Umm... Books? We have a few books that are kind of valuable," I tell him. He taps the barrel on the top of my head. "Then, ma'am"—his partner gives me a mocking bow as he grabs my arm—"show them to us."

"They're back here," I say, yanking my arm away. I push Sophie completely behind me. The men are getting more confident by the second as they realize I have no idea what to do.

The blond man leans lazily against the counter. "Show them to us," he requests with a jerk of his head. There's a small smile playing around his face as he eyes me, and I feel suddenly uncomfortable under his cold, blue-eyed gaze.

It's then that James and Crispin make their appearance. Crispin moves without hesitation to yank the red-haired man away from the counter by the collar. Before the man has time to cry out in surprise, Crispin has bent him backwards and kneed him in the spine. Crispin twists him around and throws him to the ground with enough force that his head hits the wooden floor and he lays still, groaning.

At the same time, James leaps onto the counter and in a seamless motion sweeps the gun from the blond man's hand. It clips my head on its way to the floor, but I can't bring myself to care.

James' expression is one of white-hot fury. "Don't you touch her," he growls in a voice so dangerously low I know he's used it before. Even though I'm not the one his anger is directed at, a nervous chill runs down my spine. This is the boy from photography class, the boy who baked cookies and sang along to country music with me. Now he seems to be someone entirely different.

Crispin leaves the red-haired man where he fell and goes to retrieve the handgun. James is still crouched on the counter and looking down on the now confused man.

"I hate guns," Crispin says airily, as if he's discussing the weather. He waves it around before planting his feet and using both hands to point the gun back at the man. "But, I suppose I should use what I've got. Back off," Crispin demands, waving the man back a few steps with the point of the gun. As the man obliges, James slides off the counter to stand next to me. His livid glare is still fixed on the man.

"Cara," he says, "call the police."

I hurry to do so, pulling Sophie with me. We return from the back room just in time to see James smash his foot into the face of the blond man, who's now kneeling on the floor at the boys' feet. The man lets out a muffled roar of pain and presses a hand to his nose.

"James!" I cry. "What the hell?"

Sophie, already frightened, shrieks at the sight of the blood gushing from between the man's fingers.

James hardly blinks an eye at what he's just done, or the fact that a nine-year-old girl saw.

"Don't act like he didn't deserve it," he shoots back.

Crispin is duct taping the men's hands behind their backs. "This was in a drawer," he says, waving the roll at me and ignoring James' outburst. "I hope you don't mind."

My lips parted in surprise, I stare at them both. They're so unshaken by the fact that they just took out a gunman, and they, especially Crispin, have stayed so calm.

"Soph, will you go wait in the back room, please?" I say softly.

Sophie turns and flees without a word.

"What in the name of all things holy is going on?" I enunciate every word in a strangely collected voice when I question the boys.

James takes a deep breath in through his nose before finally locking his intense eyes on me. Every muscle in his body is tense, and rage is still radiating from him. I'm shaking slightly. I try not to let him see. His unscathed face is a sharp reminder that he and Crispin just fought off two grown men who didn't get in a single hit. I realize with a jolt that I'm afraid of them, that James' dark eyes and lean body seem dangerous to me now, and Crispin, squatting on the floor tying up the crooks seems more lethal—his defined muscles and sharp gaze speak of something more than just staying in shape and doing well in school. There's a purpose to them, one I feel I've just seen.

James and I stare at each other for a time, and then I turn away. I'm not sure I want to know the answer to my question. I'm not as afraid as I should be, but there is still a good amount of fear clawing its way through me.

I move to sit on an armchair. James comes over to stand next to me. This time I'm the one refusing to meet his eyes. Sirens start to wail in the distance.

James speaks in a low voice. "Cara, we can't explain right now. I know you have no idea what that was or where it came from. But we couldn't just stand by and let you get robbed, could we?" He's trying to convince himself as well as me. "I'm so sorry. But Crispin and I need you to focus now.

"All you have to say to the police is that the men came in and demanded the money, and that Cris and I were around to help you stop it. Say we were in the store the whole time, but the men were so focused on you they hardly noticed. Say we were able to knock the men out when they had their backs turned. He dropped his own gun when we hit him from behind, and we used it to subdue them."

The sirens are closer now, police cars and ambulances rushing to the scene.

I'm shaking my head, mostly for lack of a better reaction than actual disagreement. James uses the crook of his finger to turn my face toward him. Despite my fear there is still the all too familiar rush of heat to my face that I get when James is close to me. My eyes slowly travel from the floor to his face. He bends down so we're at eye level. His gaze is anxious and angry. "Can you tell them that?"

I manage to ask: "You want me to lie?"

"I want you to fudge the truth, and get these men put away."

I twist away from his hand but continue to look at him. And I know that what he's telling me to do really will help. He and Crispin just saved me, the store's money, and got my sister out of harm's way. The least I can do is keep their secret. I nod once.

Police cruisers pull up in front of the store and uniformed men rush out. Some have guns drawn, but Crispin is now standing up and looking out the windows, and he waves to let them know we're okay.

"Sophie?" I call into the store. I watch as she emerges from the back room. Tears stain her face. I hold out my arms to her. After hesitating for only a second, she runs to them. I pull her onto my lap, stroke her back, and bury my face in her strawberry-scented hair.

James is standing in front of me protectively. The men are still unconscious on the floor, but he seems just as uneasy about the police. Without thinking, I reach for his hand hanging at his side. I may be scared of him, but I'm much more afraid of the situation, and I feel stronger with him next to me. James seems to know what I need. He squeezes my hand tightly.

"I'm sorry, sir, ma'am, but we need to talk to you both separately, if you would." A police officer comes up to James and Sophie and me, and I see another go to Crispin. Our officer speaks in clipped, down-to-business tones. He's short and has dark hair cropped close to his head.

James looks at him for a time; the policeman clears his throat warningly, and James holds on to my hand a moment longer before releasing me. I feel a sharp stab of loss when his warm strong grip leaves mine, but I have no choice except to let him go.

He is shown over to yet another police officer. The one who spoke to us stays with me.

Sophie's head is pressed into my shoulder. She doesn't look up, even as more and more people enter the room. I watch Crispin explain the duct-taped men to some officers, and James answers another's question with an expression of cool indifference on his face.

My officer looks carefully at me. I see him taking in my clean and unscratched face and clothes, and the lanyard around my neck that proves I work here.

"What is your name, ma'am?" he asks.

"I'm Cara. Weaver. And this is my sister, Sophie."

"Hello, Cara, I'm Officer Turner. Can you tell me what happened here a few minutes ago?"

I have to wait a moment and work out everything that's happened in my head before I can form a response. "Those two men, the ones that your officers are trying to revive right now, they came into the shop, pretended to look around, and then they came and held a gun to my face. They told me to give them the money out of the cash register. Sophie was with me behind the counter." I'm reliving it as I speak, unintentionally drawing Sophie closer to me when it hits me, again, just how much harm could have come to her.

"But Crispin and James were in the shop, too. I don't know how the men didn't see them. They caught the men off guard. They knocked them to the ground, and the gun fell out of that man's hand." I gesture to the blond man who is coming-to on the floor. "It knocked the men out when they fell." I decide not to go into more detail than that when I remember James' hurried explanation of what I should say.

"So Crispin found some duct tape in one of the drawers around here and he tied them up. And then you guys showed up."

I silently hope that will be enough. I *need* to talk to James and Crispin, but I know it isn't going to be that easy.

"Okay..." Officer Turner mumbles, writing something down on a notepad. "And you took no part in the fight?" he clarifies.

"No, sir. I'm not even sure it qualifies as a fight. They took the men by surprise," I repeat.

Officer Turner nods and writes.

When the blond man actually regains consciousness, it takes two officers to restrain him as he spots Crispin. I'm distracted from Turner's next question as I watch.

Though obviously still groggy, the man makes a desperate lunge for Crispin. The officers hold him back. The man lets loose a stream of profanities, causing me to unwittingly pull Sophie against me. I consider covering her ears, but it's not really worth it at this point. The man starts to go on and on about how "this goddamn blond boy and his friend" jumped them out of nowhere, and how the two boys "fought like madmen" so he and his friend didn't stand a chance.

I tried to ignore how his ranting is contradicting my story. Crispin is looking at the man distastefully. But when the blond looks over to Sophie and me with a sneer, I shoot him a look of pure loathing—a look that I've never given anyone before, but that I find I can wear easily.

I see Crispin's head turn my way when the man's does. When I finally drag my glare away from the man's face, I meet Crispin's eyes. His hardened expression is set, but he nods at me; a nod that wills me to stay strong, that encourages me to keep going, and that somehow gives me the impression that he's proud of me.

Officer Turner is waiting for my answer, so I turn back to him. "I'm sorry, what did you say?" I ask.

"Money is all the men wanted?"

I call on all of my acting skills, which I'll be the first to admit are limited. I allow the tightness that has been building in my throat to emerge, causing my voice to break and tears to streak down my face. "I don't know. They never got the chance to ask for more. For all I know, they could've—" I let my voice crack and I stop talking, allowing Officer Turner use his imagination to fill in the blanks.

I feel somewhat guilty as I see that's what he's doing. His expression hardens as his eyes flit to the man on the floor, and then back to Sophie and me. Sophie is trembling; the voice of the blond man is scaring her. With a nod at me, Turner calls to another officer and walks over to meet him.

Ignoring his own officer, James rushes over to me when Turner leaves. I try to smile at him to lessen his concern, but the effect is ruined by my red eyes and wet face. He rakes a hand though his black hair and stares down at me.

I recall what he said yesterday, about being scared for me, and I wonder what he's feeling now.

The officer that was questioning James is now comparing notes with Turner and a third policeman in murmured voices across the store. James, without a word, takes a seat on the table in front of the chair Sophie and I are in. He drops his face into his hands. I let him sit there for a long time, and then I unwrap one of my arms from around Sophie and reach out to lay a hesitant hand on James' shoulder.

His muscles tense under my touch at first. Slowly they unlock, relax, and he raises one of his hands to trap my own underneath it. I can feel the corded muscles of his arm beneath my fingers. We sit like that until Crispin shakes hands with the man who had been questioning him and comes over to join us. He sits on the arm of my chair, rubs the top of Sophie's head soothingly, and nods to James.

"Are you okay?" he asks in a voice so low no one more than two feet away would be able to hear. I don't know who he's asking, so I don't answer.

"This is no good, Cris," says James in the same voice.

"I know," Crispin breathes. He fixes me with a look. "Did you tell them anything?"

"You mean did I tell them the truth?" I ask, matching their tones. I look at James. "No. I didn't. I told them the men were knocked out when you both jumped them from behind." Nerves cause my voice to shake.

"Don't worry about them," Crispin says, misreading my anxiety. "The police are going to take our word over the stories of some thieves. They're going to prison, Cara."

"I'm not worried about them," I tell him. "Not anymore, at least. I'm worried because we're lying to the freaking police. Or withholding information, or whatever the technical term for it is!"

Crispin sighs. "Yes. We are. But they can't know the truth."

A news van pulls up outside The Scarlet Letter.

"Son of a gun," James swears.

Crispin follows his gaze, grumbles something unintelligible, and then stands and strides over to the officers and has a hushed conversation with them.

All I hear of it is, "None of you?" And then Officer Turner hurries outside to talk to the other uniforms. Crispin comes back over to us.

"What was that?" I ask.

"I told them we didn't want to be on camera," Crispin explains. "We don't want interviews or pictures, and we'd prefer to have our names kept out of the press for our own anonymity."

"Good thinking," I admit.

Crispin takes the compliment. "It pays to be prepared."

"Have you guys been in a situation like this before?" I ask them quietly. "Because you're very well prepared."

They hesitate. "We've been in...similar situations," James answers.

The three of us watch the would-be thieves get handcuffed and pushed into police cruisers, while the press snaps photos the entire time.

"Could we close the blinds, please?" I ask the officers still in the shop with us. Keeping our pictures out of the paper seems like a good idea to me.

The men oblige. We all sit in silence for a few minutes, and then Officer Turner comes back in. "We just have a few more questions."

****

I'm exhausted when the last police car finally pulls away. I've closed up shop, but I have to wait for Mr. Pelegro to come back before Sophie and I can leave. Crispin and James stay with us. I'm still wary of them, but they refused to leave us alone and truthfully, having them in the store makes me feel safer.

Sophie is done in—still afraid, hardly speaking, and now finally asleep; she is curled up in an armchair with a jacket thrown over her. I'm too keyed up to sit still, though I tried. Instead I'm ignoring the boys and shelving one of the many stacks of books behind the sales counter. The events keep turning over in my mind, and I feel like crying every time I realize that today I could have lost Sophie. *She could have easily been taken from me, and there's nothing I would have been able to do about it.* I have no idea if the thieves would have done anything like that, but now that the idea has been planted in my head, I can't seem to shake it.

So, although I'm furious with them for not telling me the truth and for making me keep things from the police, if either of the boys asked me to, I would get down on my knees and thank them for keeping my little sister safe when I wasn't able to.

Crispin is having a muted discussion with James in one of the corners of the bookstore. Their conversation has been going in circles.

"So what do we tell her?" he asks his friend for the tenth time.

"Nothing," James argues emphatically. "Cris, the first thing she'll want to know is where we learned how to do all that, and that's the one thing we can't tell her."

Crispin throws his hands in the air, exasperated. "We have to sometime, James! Why shouldn't it be now?"

"We're not telling her like this," James says ardently. James rarely contradicts Crispin outright. So, though their opinions differ, Crispin knows that this is important to James, which makes him willing to give in, but not without arguing his side first.

James continues: "She won't believe us anyway. Not without some kind of proof, and besides what happened today, we've got nothing. And we aren't even sure—"

"Yes," Crispin cuts him off, "we are. You know it. You felt it too."

Crispin watches as James wars with himself. He rubs a hand on the back of his neck. "Look," Crispin relents. "We won't tell her the truth. Not the entire truth. But we can't lie to her anymore."

His eyes follow Cara around the store as she paces back and forth between the counter and the bookshelves. He sees a myriad of emotions play across her face; she's probably reliving the day in her head. Her brown eyes dart around the shop: to Sophie, to her work, back to Sophie, to them, to the door.

"I wish we were wrong as much as you do," he tells James.

James' dark eyes meet his own. "Not quite as much, I don't think."

Crispin doesn't deny it. He knows what James is thinking, how James is feeling. His friend is only this passionate when it's something that truly matters to him.

"This is so much harder than they told us it would be," James says.

With a nod, Crispin replies: "At least no one pretended it would be easy."

8

When Crispin and James start following me around the store, I do my best to pay them no attention. But it becomes impossible.

"What do you want?" I finally hiss at them. I whirl to face them so fast that they almost run into me.

"We want to know if we're...okay," Crispin answers, studying me closely.

Mad and scared about everything, I've been working my self into a rage while I work. But it all goes out of me at their concerned faces. I drop my hands to my side in sudden defeat. "I don't know," I tell them both. "I don't know if we're okay. I don't know what's going on. I'm confused and I'm tired and, honestly, I am scared out of my mind! Do you realize what happened? I had a gun held to my face! Inches away from Sophie. And you two came out of nowhere, and you took those guys out like it was nothing, and then we all lied about it! So I have no clue whether we're okay or not. How about you tell me?"

I stare them both down. They both had remained calm through my little rant. Now James says, "We came from the back room. We realized there was no way to come in the front door without making things worse, so, after weighing the options, we broke through the lock on the back door."

"...You weighed the options? There were options?" I seethe.

James looks at me oddly. "Of course there were options," he says, eyebrows coming together in a frown. "We thought about breaking a window and running, just to set off the alarm, but then we figured the alarm wasn't active during the day. We thought about just calling the cops on the spot, but neither of us has a phone, and we didn't know how long it would take them to get here. And we also considered coming through the front door or jumping in through a window to take them by surprise."

"And why didn't you do that?" I ask coolly.

"Because that option put you and Sophie in more danger. Actually all of those options put you and Sophie in tricky positions, which is why we decided on the back door."

James is being much too reasonable about everything, and irrational anger stirs in me. "I had an idiot holding an effing gun *in my face*, and you two stood outside to weigh your options?"

Crispin shrugs. "In our defense, it only took a few seconds to go through them all."

"What does that even mean?"

"It means we both thought the same things at about the same time, and came to the same conclusion. We didn't take a seat on the sidewalk and map through the plan or something while you stood in here and tried to avoid a bullet to the head."

"That might actually be worse, Crispin!" I say. "You both just knew what to do? Without even talking about it? How many fights have you two been in?"

He thinks seriously about the question, which makes me roll my eyes. But his answer is sincere. "With gunmen? This is the second. Although, the first was really just a big misunderstanding. Fights in general, though?" He looks to James for help. James doesn't give him any. "A lot."

I stare at him.

"It's really not that uncommon, where we're from."

"And where is that?" I ask.

James winces. Crispin just meets my eyes evenly. "A few places, as a matter of fact."

"And you're not going to tell me which one you were referring to just now?" I guess.

"No, I don't think I am," he answers.

I throw my hands in the air. "Fine! Then why bring it up in the first place?"

"I was just trying to reassure you that we knew what we were doing," Crispin says calmly, not batting an eye at my reaction.

I don't feel reassured. I tell him so. He smiles.

"Can you at least tell me how you learned all of that...stuff?" I ask them.

James looks pointedly at Crispin who says, without looking over, "Congrats, you were right. I'll get you a medal." James scoffs. I don't even pretend to understand.

"We were taught," James answers me finally.

I shake my head, defeated. "Don't tell me then," I say. They both know I was looking for a better answer than that. "Can I please just work now?" I stomp off without letting them reply.

****

Mr. Pelegro comes back just before closing. He takes everything in with a single glance: Sophie tear-stained and asleep, Crispin and James sitting on the floor with their backs to the counter, quiet but alert, and me pacing the floors getting very little actually accomplished.

"What happened in here?" he asks.

"We almost got robbed," I say without inflection.

"Tell me," he says immediately.

So I do. I tell him the same story I told the police, still keeping James and Crispin's secret for them. "And I didn't have a way to let you know, or I would have called immediately," I finish. "I didn't know where you were, so I couldn't reach you." One of the first things Mr. Pelegro ever told me is that he despises cell phones and will never own one himself. I hope he's seriously reconsidering that opinion.

Mr. Pelegro comes up to me when I fall silent and takes my hands in his. We're the same height, and he meets my eyes with something akin to fatherly concern. "My dear," he says. "I am so sorry you had to go through that. I should have been here with you."

"Where were you?" James asks from his seat on the floor.

I shoot him a glare, but Mr. Pelegro doesn't seem insulted by his hostile tone. "I make deals with large bookstores and booksellers to get extra copies of certain novels for the shop," he replies. "Since Cara started I have been able to spend more time doing so. That's how we acquired that collection of Dickens' works the other day," he says, turning to me.

Some of my fear and anger shifts to excitement when I hear about where he's off to everyday. "Could I come with you sometime?"

There's a twinkle of amusement in his eyes. "You need a good poker face and a stiff upper lip to work deals with these people, but you just might have it in you."

I glow with the compliment.

"Now, I want you all to head home. It's been a very long day, no doubt the little one is ready to be in her own bed, and I know how to close up my own store," Mr. Pelegro says, shooing us out the door. Crispin scoops Sophie into his arms so I don't have to, and she nestles into his strong chest.

"I'll see you tomorrow, Mr. Pelegro," I say on my way out the door.

"I don't want you back here until you're good and ready. You can take some time off," he tells me severely.

I smile at him. "I know. I'll see you tomorrow."

****

James takes my car keys from me, helps me into the front seat, and drives us home. I don't protest much, because his expression is still hardened and wary, and there's no way he'll listen to me. Crispin sits in the back and holds onto Sophie.

James drives carefully, alert the whole way. I comment on it as he stops at yet another yellow light. "You know you're allowed to drive through those," I say. "It's not encouraged, but if you can make it, then go."

He barely looks over at me, eyes on the road ahead. "Better safe than sorry."

"You expect me to believe that this is how you always drive?" I ask.

"I don't usually drive," he replies.

When we arrive at my house, I invite them in. When they say no, I offer to at least drive them to their houses. They refuse that too. "Just get yourself inside," Crispin says. "We can walk."

They watch me the whole way to the door. I wave as they stride away.

"Welcome home, Cara! And Sophie!" I hear Jade call from upstairs. I find her and Max lying in opposite directions on my bed. Her head is on my pillows, and his is hanging upside down off the foot of the bed. Max seems slightly more cheerful.

"I'll be back in a minute," I say to them. I carry Sophie into her own room and tuck her in, fully clothed, for the night. I bundle her in blankets and stuffed animals, slide her shoes off her feet, and turn her fan on. Then I kiss her goodnight and shut her door.

Jade has made room for me on the bed, so I take the seat gratefully.

"Sophie looked beat," she says. "She okay?"

I take a deep breath and relay the story of the thieves for the third time. They're both shocked. Jade pulls me into a tight hug as I speak, and I sink into her embrace. Real tears, not the forced ones I used on the police, spill from my eyes. Max slides to my other side and wraps an arm around my shoulders as best he can. Jade's dark hair forms a curtain around my face as I cry.

I tell them about how utterly helpless I'd felt, how part of me couldn't believe they would really hurt me and part of me was afraid they would. If James and Crispin hadn't been there, I honestly can't imagine what could've happened.

Max's expression is an exact copy of Crispin's earlier concern. "Cara, did they try something? Other than the robbery?"

Jade pulls away from me just enough to look at me in alarm.

"No," I say, "they didn't. But... Oh God, you should have seen them. They were getting so cocky, and the way they were starting to look at me...I thought—"

Max looks disgusted. "But they didn't...touch you?"

I shake my head. "No, Max. They never got the chance."

He lets out a breath I didn't know he was holding. I lay a hand on his arm. "Thank you."

I curl back into Jade's arms and hold Max's hand. They murmur to me and comfort me as best they can until I've calmed down. Then I hug them, hop off the bed, and go to the bathroom to splash cold water on my face. I glance at myself in the mirror.

My eyes are red-rimmed and anxious, my hair is tangled about my face, and there are fever spots high on my cheeks. I rip a brush through the knots of my hair and dab my face dry.

Jade and Max are waiting patiently for me to return. I stand in the doorway for a moment, looking at them, surprised that my feet are still holding me upright. "Thank you guys. And I'm sorry for that. Max, this night was supposed to be about you."

"You had a good reason," Max tells me. "I don't mind."

Jade glances back and forth between the two of us. "You both look so exhausted," she whispers, just loudly enough for us to hear.

"You all need fuel. And a second alone. What if I ran out to the grocery store and grabbed some ice cream? So you can get some sugar in your systems before we all crash for the night."

I know she's offering mostly to give Max and me a moment to talk, but a carton of chocolate ice cream sounds amazing right about now. Everyone needs comfort food after a trauma. "Do you need money?" I ask by way of reply, managing a small, genuine smile.

She grins and grabs her black purse from the floor. "No," she says as she pats it and stands up. "I'm set. I'll be back soon." With another quick, one-armed hug for me and a smile for Max, Jade disappears out my bedroom door.

I can hear her rush down the stairs and the front door slam shut behind her. Only then do I fully turn to look at Max. "I might have had a good reason, Max. But my reason is over now. I came out of it shaken up but unhurt. You didn't. So are you okay?"

I'm sure that, just like me, Max is already tired of recounting his own story. But, as I move to sit next to him on the bed, he hugs me again anyway. I lean my head against his chest and breathe in his guy smell, cologne and detergent, and close my eyes.

He exhales into my hair. "No. I'm not okay. But I'm better." His voice becomes muffled as he rests his mouth against the top of my head and says, "Thanks, Cara. I needed this. More than you probably realized. Thank you for getting me away from East, for letting me come here. I would have gone crazy if I had been cooped up in school all day."

"Do you want to talk about it, what really happened, or did you and Jade already get it out of your system?" I ask him seriously. This is his day. And if he wants to sit here in silence until Jade returns with ice cream, I'll let him.

"Do you want to hear about it?" Max asks in reply.

"Not unless you want to tell me."

Max thinks for a moment, and I let him. "Would it be enough if I said my stepfather came home furious—not very drunk, which was unusual, but mad as hell—and the first thing he did when he walked in the door was go after my mother? He swung at her. She's smart, she ducked, he missed, but it was too much for me and I leapt at him. Got a couple good hits in too, before he threw me to the floor. You haven't seen him, Cara, but he's a big man. I yelled at my mom to get in my car, S.F.H. picked me up and knocked me in the jaw, hence the bruise, and then I got away to the car too. He chased after us, but the Charger is fast. And you know the rest: mom staying in the hospital, and me in my car. I called her a while ago, by the way, and she thanks you too, for everything."

My heart heavy, I nod into his chest. "S.F.H?" I ask.

"Stepfather From Hell," he explains.

After everything, this makes me grin. "I like it."

"How can you not?" he asks, his tone suggesting that he's matching my small smile.

I pull away from him slightly and take the time to really look at him. The bruise is even darker now than it was earlier, and there are tired circles under his eyes. He's paler than usual; his hair is mussed up. But his eyes are steady. And I feel close to him, more so now than I ever have. He's the only friend I've had that has a home life comparable to mine. We both know what it's like to have to be an adult when we're not ready and to take on more responsibility than we want because we have to. To have someone under our protection and see them in danger.

His face the picture of understanding, Max falls back on the bed and gestures for me to do the same. I do, happily, and we lie there together chatting aimlessly and otherwise just steadying one another until Jade eventually slips back into the room. A plastic grocery sack is in one of her hands, and three spoons are in the other.

She crawls on the bed next to us and we all sit in a circle and open the ice cream. I don't know how long we spend together before we fall asleep, but it must be hours before our conversation ceases and the half-empty ice cream cartons are set on the floor to melt as we rest.

****

When I wake up in the morning, the first thing I notice is that it's brighter outside than usual. The second thing I notice is the smell of breakfast wafting into my room. The third thing is how uncomfortable I am. The fourth is why.

I've fallen asleep with my head on Max's chest, my feet hanging off the far corner of the bed, Jade using my legs as a pillow, and Sophie—who joined us sometime early in the morning after waking up in the middle of the night and being unable to go back to sleep—using the crook of my arm to rest her head. I groan and try to shift my position. This causes everyone else to wake up.

After some giggling and accidentally knocking each other over the head a couple times, we all managed to untangle ourselves and stand up.

Jade stretches languidly. "What time is it?" she yawns.

I chance a look at the clock. "Late."

Jade follow my gaze. "Shit."

We're two hours late for school.

She dives across the bed to dig in her backpack for her phone, whips it out of one of the pockets, and dials. "Mom?" she says to the voice on the other end. Jade pulls a worried face at me.

"Tell her you're helping me through a trauma," I whisper quickly.

Jade does. She quickly explains the bookstore hold-up to her mother, and says my parents weren't home and I was scared (she shrugs in apology for making me sound like a wuss). "...and we overslept because we were up so late," she concludes. "Mom, I'm so sorry. But Cara is still really shaken up..." Her mother starts to speak again, and a slow smile steals across Jade's face. "Are you sure?" And then, "Okay! Thank you!" She hangs up, beaming.

"I'm out of school for the rest of the day!" she announces. Then she swears and grabs her phone again. "What about David?" she asks, in answer to the confused looks from Max and me.

Sophie, who had left the room a few minutes ago, now races back in. "Mom and Dad are home!" she cries. She rushes out again.

"Mmm..." I say. "I should probably go explain to them why we're here..."

Max nods. "You probably should."

"Do you think your mom will let you out of classes again today?" I ask him.

"She already has," Max tells me. "I asked her last night."

I brace myself for the explanation ahead of me. Max notices. "You were held at gunpoint, Cara. I'm thinking the odds are your parents won't make you go to school today either."

By the time I get downstairs, I find Sophie is already concluding her story of the incident at the bookstore. My mother is stroking Sophie's hair, and my father is cooking eggs. When she sees me, my mom comes running over and pulls me into a hug.

"Sophie's been telling us what happened! Oh, Cara dear, are you doing all right? Do you need anything?" she gushes.

I find myself consoling her. "No mom, everything is okay now. It all worked out. I'm fine. But..."

"What, darling?" she asks.

"Well, we're seriously late for school, and I know neither of us really feel like going today," I say. "Is there any way you could call our schools and tell them? And give us the day off?" I meet Sophie's eyes across the kitchen and will her to help me out.

She knows exactly what to do. "Please, Mommy?" she chirps. "I don't think I could get much work done today. I'd be too afraid."

Mom, who has let go of me and is already considering my request, smiles kindly at Sophie. "Of course," she tells us. "Just let me go find the phone numbers." I give Sophie a swift thumbs-up as Mom glides away. I watch her go. My mom is beautiful, tall and willowy, with big blue eyes and thick hair. Luckily for me, I inherited most of my genes from her. Everything but her height and coloring. I got my father's dark hair, brown eyes and tan skin, yet somehow my mother's slenderness and build despite my 5'6" stature.

When I see she's found the school directories and telephone, I pull up a seat next to Sophie to talk to my father, who's been quiet throughout the exchange. "Dad?" I say cautiously, "Are you okay?"

My father is a broad, usually boisterous man, and to see him cooking so quietly is a bit unnerving. "I don't like to hear about you girls being in danger," he says without looking at us.

I walk over to wrap my arms around his waist and lay my head on his shoulder. "Everything turned out all right, Dad. We're both absolutely fine. See?" I hold out my hands. "Not even a scratch." This isn't strictly true. When James knocked the gun away from the blonde man it had nicked me, but the cut is hidden under my hair and I choose not to mention it.

Dad looks less than convinced. "Besides," I continue, "some of my friends were with us the whole time. Two even spent the night. We were never alone, the police handled everything, and the thieves left empty handed and in cuffs. It couldn't have gone more smoothly." *Except for the fact that you and mom could have picked up your phones yesterday. I really needed to talk to you after all that. I needed you home before I fell asleep last night.*

Of course, I can't say any of that.

So I plaster a smile on my face. "Did you make enough breakfast for a couple guests?" I ask him.

"I made enough food for an army!" my dad cries. He appears to be back to himself. It's easy to appease him.

"Sophie, will you get Max and Jade and tell them breakfast is almost ready?" I ask.

Mom comes into the kitchen while I'm setting the table to tell us everything is all sorted out with our schools.

During breakfast, it's almost like having a normal family. I can almost pretend that this is what every meal in our house is like: mornings and evenings spent together, laughing as my parents regale my friends with tales of Sophie and I when we were little kids.

But my heart sinks a little when I see my mom checking the clock more and more often. I keep the disappointment off my face when she stands and reminds my father that they both have to be at work before noon.

I kiss them goodbye, my friends thank them, and then they're gone.

I sit in my chair, allowing myself ten seconds of self-pity. And then I stand, start stacking dishes to take to the sink, and smile at Sophie. "Well, that was a fun surprise, wasn't it?" I ask her. She nods, some of the sadness lifting from her face.

Jade ushers her upstairs to brush her teeth and do her hair. I shoot Jade a grateful glance before they disappear.

Max stays to help me clean. "So...that doesn't happen often?" he guesses. His bruise isn't swollen this morning, but it's a dark purply-brown that makes the rest of his face look pale by comparison.

"No. But at least you guys met them on a good day."

"What's a bad day?"

I sigh. "When they ignore almost everything Sophie and I say because they're caught up in getting ready to go somewhere, or because they're so caught up in some new project, or when I don't see them for a week because they're only home for a few hours in the middle of the night."

His brown eyes are sympathetic. "You don't have to feel bad for me, Max," I say. "I'm not the one with a bruised face because my stepfather's a jackass. The worst my parents do is forget that they're parents."

Max's expression doesn't change. "Yeah. But I've got my mom to help me when S.F.H. is on a warpath. Who do you turn to?"

I can't answer.

"Me," Jade answers from the doorway.

"You're not her mom, Jade. You've only known her for three weeks. It's not the same thing," Max says.

"Well you don't have to make her feel worse about it," Jade replies hotly, rushing to my defense.

"I don't feel worse about anything," I break in. "I'm fine. I'm used to it."

Sophie bounds down the stairs, so we turn to a new topic of conversation. After some discussion, Max and Jade offer to take Sophie and me to the mall for a few hours.

"It's out in Olathe, but it's huge!" Jade explains. "We can eat lunch while we're there; they have this one stand that sells the best pretzels you've ever eaten."

Because I notice Sophie is more serious than usual and assume her mind keeps making its way back to yesterday, I agree to go on the condition that I'm back in time for work. Jade rolls her eyes but accepts the terms.

It actually turns out to be a great idea. We spend the rest of the morning and early afternoon exploring all the shops at Oak Park Mall. Jade and I try on ridiculous outfits that we have no intention of buying, Max takes way too long studying watches in the Fossil store, and I have to drag Sophie away from the Build-A-Bear Workshop. The pretzels are, in fact, delicious. The only thing wrong with the day is my unshakable feeling that we're being watched. I catch myself constantly looking over my shoulder. I never see the same person twice, and the other three don't seem to feel anything. So I convince myself it's nothing.

Eventually, worn out, we collapse at a table in a small coffee shop and drop our shopping bags at our feet. We're tired, the combination of a rough previous day and little sleep the night before. But Sophie is grinning from ear to ear as she holds tightly to bags of See's candy and Claire's merchandise that I couldn't deny her. Max didn't purchase anything other than food. Jade, however, bought two new outfits and even talked me into getting a soft, dark brown leather jacket that I promise her I'll wear to school tomorrow.

Max and Jade start to update me on some school scandal: supposedly there's a cheerleader whose parents caught her sleeping with this guy who is on the basketball team and already has a girlfriend.

"How could you possibly know about that?" I ask them.

Jade shakes her head at me. "You've clearly forgotten all about the intricate web of gossip I told you existed at East. I heard it from Angelica Wilson, who is friends with a girl who's best friends with the now-ex-girlfriend of the disgraced basketball player."

"Anyway," Max says. "To make himself look better, the basketball player is now saying that this cheerleader slept with half of the team, so he isn't the only one at fault."

"As if everyone didn't already know how much that girl gets around," Jade tells me.

Max gives her a warning look.

"What?" Jade asks him. "I'm not saying she's a slut. I'm just saying I don't think she sleeps in her own bed very often.

I choke on the hot chocolate I've just taken a sip of as I try to force back a laugh. Max groans. Jade looks to Sophie and realizes what she just said.

Sophie raises her eyebrows dismissively. "It's okay. I know what a slut is."

Jade only looks slightly abashed, and I laugh harder.

In Minnesota, the first girl I'd befriended cussed heatedly every other time she spoke. It was almost amusing because the girl was so little but acted so fierce. Anyway, that's how Sophie got educated in a new aspect of the French language.

Jade's phone rings, interrupting any attempt to get a new conversation started. After a moment, she passes it to me. "For you," she says unnecessarily.

"Cara?" David's voice asks. "Where are you guys?" He sounds a bit out of breath, and whatever he's doing involves moving around.

"We're at the mall. Why? Is everything okay?"

David sighs audibly and something gets knocked over. "I'm fine," he tells me. "But Crispin and James think—"

His voice disappears. There's a scuffle, and then James Sable's anxious voice is in my ear. "Cara! Why weren't you at school today?"

"What? Why do you care? What happened?"

"'What happened'? Yesterday you were held at gunpoint, and today you don't show up for classes? We thought something happened to you!" James sounds strained, angry.

I lower my voice. "The whole world isn't out to get me, James. I'm capable of surviving from one day to the next. Chill, would you?"

Crispin's voice calls from the background. "Tell her we're waiting at her house!"

"You're where?" I ask, standing up from the table in surprise. "Why are you at my house?"

"Great work, Cris," James grumbles. "You made her mad."

"I appreciate the concern," I tell him in a voice that suggests otherwise, "but you don't have to babysit me!"

David, apparently, has snatched his phone back because it's his voice that speaks next. "Are you really okay? This morning, Jade told me what happened to you and Sophie."

"Yeah, David, I'm doing better now. It was just a shock. It was kind of terrifying, but we're okay."

He sounds relieved: "Good. Now...you might want to get here soon. You know, before these two break into your house. They're really worried about you, Cara. It'd be sweet, you know, if I didn't think they were going to attack the first person who looks at them the wrong way."

I cover my face with my free hand. "We'll be right there. Try to calm them down."

"I'll try," he says dubiously.

I hang up and give the phone back to Jade. "We've got to go," I tell them. "Crispin and James are at my house."

Sophie leaps up, excited at the news. They're her heroes. Max and Jade look confused.

"I know. When I wasn't at school they assumed some new terrible thing had happened to me. Apparently they're freaking out," I say.

"Okay," Jade says. "Then yeah, we should probably go."

The car ride is made in silence, except for the radio. When we pull up in my driveway, James pauses in his pacing of our front step, David hurries to the car to meet us, and Crispin simply raises his head to watch us.

"You should go talk to them," David murmurs to me.

I nod. "Will you guys take Sophie inside?"

They all file through the front door when Max opens it. James and Crispin, somehow knowing that I'm hanging back to talk to them, don't follow the rest.

"You guys care to tell me what this is all about?" I ask, stopping a few feet in front of them. "Because you went from being the heroic boys that saved me from thieves to being creepily over-protective in less than a day."

"We got worried," Crispin says.

"And it didn't occur to you that when normal people go through something like that they need some time to get over it? Or that I was probably with Jade and Max seeing as they weren't at school today either?"

"We didn't know Jade and Max were gone too," James tells me. "When you weren't in chemistry, Crispin told me, and we came to look for you."

"You skipped school to look for me?" I ask baffled. "Why?"

"Because we got worried," Crispin repeats, leaning toward me from his seat on the steps. His anxiety is clear in his green eyes. "We're sorry. Yes, we probably overreacted, we just jumped to the worst conclusion."

"But why are you so worried about me?" I ask more calmly.

Crispin smiles. "We seem to have gotten it into our heads that it's our job to protect you when you can't protect yourself." He stretches and stands. "You should be flattered."

"How often do you think I'll need to be protected?" I ask, not sure if I should be offended that they think I'm so helpless or pleased that they care so much about me.

"We'll find out, won't we?" James asks quietly.

Sophie starts to come back outside just as I'm about to go in. "Aren't you going to work today?" she asks me.

"What time is it?" I ask, dashing inside.

"Time to go to work," Sophie answers in an isn't-that-obviously-why-I-asked voice.

"Max! Jade! David!" I call into the house because I'm not entirely sure where they all are. "I've got to go! You can stay here, if you want. See you later!"

"Wait, wait, wait!" I hear Jade cry. Max and David follow her down the stairs, pulling on jackets. "We're coming."

"To The Scarlet Letter? Why?"

"We don't want to let you out of our sight," David tells me.

I glare at Crispin and James where they stand in the doorway. "I blame you two for putting this idea in their heads," I say.

They seem unaffected by my expression. "It's probably our fault," Crispin agrees. "So we might as well come too!"

Everyone starts deciding who should ride in what car. James catches my eye and shrugs. I grab Sophie's hand. "We'll meet you there," I say to them all as I stride out to my father's car.

"Why are you mad?" Sophie asks as we pull out of the driveway and leave the rest of them to follow.

I realize that I'm frowning at the road, so I soften my expression. "I'm not mad, sweetie. Not really. I think they're all being a tad over-the-top, that's all."

"But they're keeping you safe," she reminds me. "Shouldn't you be happy about that?"

You should be flattered, I hear Crispin's voice in my head. I sigh. "Yes, I should."

"I know you're used to being the one taking care of people," Sophie continues. "But now it's your turn to be taken care of. It makes them happy, keeping you safe. You should let them do it."

I stare at her with a small smile. "When did you get so smart?" I ask.

She giggles. "You taught me."

Leaving one hand on the wheel, I pull her into an awkward hug. "I love you."

"Love you too," she replies.

9

When Sophie and I troop into the shop, I barely have time to warn Mr. Pelegro before all of my friends file in after us. Mr. Pelegro raises an eyebrow.

"My, someone's awfully popular." He winks at me. "Keeping you out of trouble, are they?"

"They seem to think so," I reply.

At the same time, from the chair he's already thrown himself into, James says, "We are."

Mr. Pelegro seems to be hiding a smile.

"I see. Well, carry on. I'm off! Don't burn the place down while I'm away!"

And he leaves.

David looks at Sophie. "Do you want to come pick up Isa with me? You can tell her all about your day off."

"Yes!" Sophie says excitedly. Then she looks to me guiltily. "Can I go?"

"Of course you can go," I laugh.

She pumps her fist in the air. "I'll drive you," Max says. "I need to talk to you, Dave."

David, already guessing what they're going to be talking about, eyes the bruise on his face. He nods appreciatively, and I feel a little bad for not telling him to come over the night before to hear the same explanation Jade and I did. But he doesn't seem to mind. With a wave back at the rest of us, they all follow Mr. Pelegro out.

Heavy silence hangs in the air when the door swings shut behind them. Jade breaks it with a loud sigh. "Well if no one else is going to talk. Did I ever tell you guys about the time I cut myself with a steak knife trying to open a popsicle...?"

****

Hours later I find myself surprised all over again at how well Crispin and James get along with my other friends. Besides James' general moodiness and Crispin's careful eye on any customers who enter the store, they joke and swap stories like pros.

The only actual work I do all day is when I help an old man find our poetry section. I spend most of my time thinking quietly and pretending to listen to Crispin's stories.

How can they act like yesterday was nothing? I wonder, watching him and James laugh. *They took out a man with a gun like it was the easiest thing in the world, they won't tell anyone, they won't explain it, and the only sign that a single thing out of the ordinary happened is the fact that they left school to make sure I was still okay.*

When Max and David return with the girls, they get caught up in trying to teach Crispin the finer points of football (a sport I thought all guys were born with the ability to understand). James vacates his armchair and comes to stand across the counter from me while they talk.

"You left this here the other day," I say before he speaks, getting out the Roman myths and passing it to him.

He turns it over indifferently in his hands and sets it down.

"Why are you reading them?" I ask.

James studies me for a moment and then answers: "I haven't read them before. I was curious."

"I thought they were required reading? The Greek versions, at least, for school. And they're basically the same stories. How haven't you read them before?"

He doesn't answer immediately. He's thinking much too hard about his reply, and I know he's about to lie to me.

"Forget it," I tell him irritably.

"Why are you so mad?" he asks in a low voice.

"How can you act so normal?" I say. "After everything that happened, your and Crispin's weird behavior, how can you keep putting up this front of being some average teenage boy?"

James frowns. "What makes you think I'm not?"

I stare into his gray-blue eyes with a frown of my own. "I don't know. But I know there's something different. Besides the fighting, besides the strange comments, I can tell there's... something."

James smirks. "But you don't know what it is?"

"No. I don't. But I can tell. And I'm going to figure it out, eventually. You might as well just tell me."

"Now where would be the fun in that?" he asks.

Book in hand, he pushes himself away from the counter and joins the boys back by the chairs before I can form a reply.

"Whoa, that looked intense," Jade says, hopping onto the counter and spinning to face me. "What was that about?"

"His inability to believe I can take care of myself," I grumble. "Or that it's possible I could be right and he could be wrong."

She shakes her head and flashes an impish grin. "You two were made for each other."

I look across the store to James, whose dark eyes meet mine with an unreadable expression. I glance away quickly and heat floods my cheeks.

Jade chuckles. "I love having a girl friend! Why haven't I done this before?" Then she looks at me. "Oh yeah. Because she was traveling the country without me."

I shove her affably off the countertop. My ring catches on her sweater, unraveling one of the threads. "I'm so sorry!" I say. "Stupid thing."

Jade takes my hand and turns the ring right side up. "Cara! Oh my gosh, this is stunning! Why don't you turn it around?" she gushes. "Show it off!"

"Because," I tell her. "It's really ostentatious, and I don't want to have to explain it to people."

"But it's so pretty!" I flip it back around. Jade sighs. "You and your weird fashion sense."

I hand her a pile of old novels. "If you're going to insult me you might as well help me out while you do it," I smile.

Mr. Pelegro comes back even earlier than usual, and he shoos me out of the shop like he did yesterday, proclaiming he can close up himself. My friends, each making sure that we'll be okay alone, walk Sophie and me all the way to the door of our house.

"I'll see you in the morning!" I finally call out, shutting the door in their faces. I hear them all stand outside for a moment longer before making their way to their cars.

I roll my eyes at Sophie. "Good heavens," I sigh. "We may never be left alone again."

"We're alone now," she points out.

"Yes. Just in time to do homework and go to bed. Now, hop to it!" I steer her upstairs. "We have two days worth of work to get done."

****

The first thing I notice when I step outside in the morning is how unseasonably nice the weather is. March is beginning; the worst of winter has already started to fade away. The day only gets warmer as it goes on, so, ignoring all of my friends' protests, I decide to walk home from school by myself.

"Why?" Jade asks. "Is it something we did? Are you okay?"

"I'm fine," I say, laughing at all their anxious expressions. "It's just been stressful around here, and I need some time to myself, that's all. I need to clear my head. I'm all right, I promise."

They halfheartedly try to talk me out of it, but I assure them that I need this.

"But will at least one of you make sure you're around when Sophie gets home? Just in case she makes it back before I do?"

Max and Jade agree. So I zip up my new jacket and with a wave, I head off.

I wander along slowly, not thinking about anything in particular. My thoughts bounce between the new city, the new school, work, plans for the upcoming weekend, everything clamoring to be considered first. I take the time to work it all through, leaving nothing out.

I sigh contentedly. It feels good just to be able to think.

I'm crossing through the middle of the Village Shopping Center when my phone rings. *If it's Jade or Max or David, I'm hanging up.* But it isn't.

I answer it. "Lily?"

"Cara!" she cries. "Ohmigosh hi! How are you? How's the new house? How's school? What's life like in Kansas? Any tornadoes? I just watched the *Wizard of Oz* and realized that's the state you're living in now..."

I fall silent as she prattles on, waiting for her to run out of breath. Lily is my cousin. She still lives in New York like we used to, and we don't see her often, but she's the only one of our relatives that I really keep in touch with. A year younger than I am, she's a whirlwind of energy who loves to hear about our travels. I feel guilty for not having called her sooner.

As I listen, I absentmindedly rub the palm of my hand over the statue of the lucky bronze boar that I've ended up standing next to. People around here think that if you stroke his nose he'll bring you good luck, so I trace his smooth snout where it is more brass than bronze-colored, worn away by the touches of hundreds of hands.

"But how are you, really?" Lily finally pauses to ask.

Lily is the only one, until now, who has ever let me speak whatever's on my mind without judging me for it. I used to call her in the middle of the night and vent. She helps me think, and I start talking without even realizing what I'm saying, at first. I walk over to sit on one of the wooden benches nearby.

"I'm okay, Lil. Mostly things are great, actually. It's just...when I really stop to think about it I feel...weird. I mean, here's what I know: I have a place, finally, where I belong, where I *know* I belong, and people that I love who love me too. I have a city that I'm really happy in. So I should be ridiculously happy, all the time. Sophie has a best friend and she's thrilled, which is all I truly want, but now I have a few close friends also, and a job, and my parents are being supportive. All should be well. But it's just... It's just not yet. There's still something that I'm missing. And I know how selfish of me it is to want more when this much has been given to me, but I can't help it, no matter how hard I try.

"I've met this girl, Jade, who said that she thinks people are put where they need to be when they need to be there. And I thought I had finally found out why I was here: to help this boy Max, to be someone he can run to when his life is rough. And I am that, but I still can't escape this weird tugging inside me.

"I know it makes no sense. I *know* it doesn't. But the more I ignore it the more it's there. And you know what?"

I stop suddenly, realizing something that I haven't been able to put words to before. *Those boys. The ones I complain about and worry about and think about. Crispin and James bring that yearning to the front of my mind. When I'm with them the pull is stronger than ever.* But that makes no sense, so I don't say it out loud.

"Figured something out, have you?" Lily inquires.

"I just might have," I say. "But I'm not sure it makes much sense."

"Oh, who needs sense?"

I frown at the phone. "I think I do, as a matter of fact...."

"Uh-oh. Mom's on a rampage. Crap. I'm in so much trouble. Gotta go Cara, love you, call you tomorrow, bye!"

And before I even have a chance to speak again, Lily hangs up.

I shake my head, glad she called but wishing she could have talked longer. It's always easier to work things out with her than it is alone. I drop my phone onto my lap and curl my legs up under me, turning my face to the sky to catch the sun's last rays of warmth for the day.

As clouds begin to roll across the sky and the wind starts to pick up, I wonder what it is about the mere possibility of poor weather that sends everyone packing. For, despite how early in the evening it is, hardly anyone is still out. I close my eyes and lean back.

Without warning, a horribly deep and unfamiliar voice speaks behind me. "So, you're the one the little prince and his pet have been spending time with."

I sit up quickly, startled, having not heard anyone approaching. I had assumed I was alone.

Whoever it is doesn't give me time to answer his question, which is a good thing, for I realize I have no idea what he is talking about.

"I wonder what it is that makes you so special. You don't look like much."

Stung, I start to stand, wanting to leave, but a heavy hand clamps onto my shoulder, forcing me to stay seated.

The man quietly lets out a coarse chuckle. "Now," he says, "don't be like that." He is speaking soothingly, but there is an angry undertone to his voice that makes my heart fly to my throat.

He releases my shoulder, but now I am frozen to the spot, fear belatedly and inconveniently stealing over me. Slowly, he walks around the bench, stopping next to me. His fingers curl around the armrest that I had been using moments before. His nails are like claws, longer than mine and coming to thin points. What I can see of his arms are broad and muscular. His skin is a deep honey color. I shut my eyes briefly, then fix them straight ahead, willing someone to walk out of a shop or around a corner.

"Unfortunately, no one stays out for weather like this," the man hisses to me, as if he knows what I'm thinking. "No one but you." I can hear him smiling as he speaks, but I still refuse to look. "Didn't they teach you anything?"

They who? "You mean things like don't talk to strangers?" I find that my voice works fine, despite my fear. I try to match his quiet, angry tone, but my voice wavers. I quickly clamp my mouth shut again, but he has already heard. He chuckles again.

Out of nowhere, I hear a voice call out, roughly and angrily. Unexpectedly, the voice is familiar. I have been waiting for anyone at all to help me, and it is Crispin who strides into view, his face dark and his expression one of barely contained fury.

"Panus!" he calls warningly, lengthening his steps to reach us. It takes me a moment to figure out that "Panus" must be this man's name.

As soon as Crispin had appeared, the man's hands vanished from the arm of the bench. Now I hear knuckles crack above my head. I wince, then, slowly, I look up at the face of the man that Crispin appears to know. His looks aren't striking, but they're intense. His stringy black hair is long and it's pulled back from his broad face. He's tall; every inch of him is muscle. But it's his eyes that at last cause me to jump off the bench and back away. The irises are a cold, shocking black, and, although Crispin is still calling his name, they are directed at me with a hatred that I had never encountered.

He reaches for me as I stumble back, but suddenly Crispin is there, knocking his arm away. Almost before I know it, the two are fighting. Or I guess battling would be a more accurate term. And both are experts. I scramble to get out of the way, finding it impossible to keep my eyes off of them.

I thought I had seen a bit of what Crispin was made of back at The Scarlet Letter, but it's nothing compared to this. This is terrifying, mesmerizing. They are flying into each other, just as quickly diving out of range, and then spinning around to leap back into the attack, faster than I'd thought was possible.

Panus snarls as Crispin lands an uppercut to his jaw, but the man hardly seems fazed. He sends Crispin spinning into the boar statue. Crispin simply takes the hit and uses the few seconds before Panus reaches him again to clamber up to the boar's head and leaps off, smashing both feet into Panus' chest. As Panus falls with a roar, he grabs Crispin and pulls him down too. They crash into a flowerpot, toppling it. Crispin rolls away to bounce back to his feet before Panus can move.

Crispin seems the faster of the two, but Panus is stronger. And I don't know which will win.

An arm circles my waist and pulls me back just as Crispin is knocked to the ground where I had been standing. I twist to get free as I am hauled to my feet, thinking another man has joined the first. I continue struggling until a voice hisses in my ear. "Stop it, would you? It's me!" And I am spun around to face James Sable.

"James?" I breathe, heart pounding, stunned for the third time in as many minutes. James has time to flash me a crooked smirk before he yanks me back. Panus is lunging toward us. But Crispin is there again, fighting him back. Crispin takes a crushing blow to his ribs and falls heavily. He doesn't make any sound of pain as he heaves himself back to his feet; instead he looks at James and me and yells, "Run!"

So, without a moment's hesitation, James grabs my wrist and takes off. I am nearly pulled off my feet, but right myself in time to keep up. James doesn't slow down for me. Had his hand not encircled my wrist, he would have left me in the dust. However, the speed keeps me from looking back, from seeing the battle that rages behind me. James never breaks stride.

What happened, what is happening now, finally hits me, flooring me. I don't understand what is going on, and it seems that I am the only one who feels that way. I can't catch my breath. I stumble. But James catches me, holds me up, and slows just enough that I can run next to him. We cross the bridge into Mission Hills, still sprinting at a breakneck pace.

"What's going on?" I whisper. The wind tears the words from my mouth, but it seems James hears me anyway.

He looks over at me, his gray-blue eyes dark in their intensity. "I'm sorry," he says as rain begins to fall. He slows down, finally stops, and turns to face me. A raindrop falls onto his cheek like a tear as the clouds open up, and the misty rain catches in his windblown hair. He looks pale and otherworldly in the dark. "Don't be afraid," he tells me quietly. "Trust me." He reaches for my hand, smiles sadly, and, before I've even had time to catch my breath, Mission Hills fades into blackness.

Haley Fisher

Book Two

"The two most important days in your life are the day you are born and the day you find out why."

- Mark Twain

Haley Fisher

10

It feels like I have gone blind. In these seconds there is nothing but darkness pressing in on me. I think for a moment that I might be fainting. Then I am slammed back into my senses, and a world of green erupts before me.

Dizzily I fall to my knees and press the heels of my hands to my eyes. It is quiet but for the wind in the trees, and sunlight now blinds me—all traces of a rainy day gone. The ground I'm kneeling on is covered in dirt and grass, rather than the concrete I had been standing on seconds before. Breathing heavily as if I'm still running, I gasp for air. All I want to do is sit here and stop my head from spinning.

But wherever I am James is still with me, his arms pulling me up, his voice in my ear. "It's okay, Cara. Trust me, it's going to be okay. You need to stand up. We need to keep going."

I open my eyes and struggle to my feet. Now that we are no longer running, my adrenaline has quickly shifted to overwhelming weariness.

"We're in a forest," I murmur, disoriented. James releases me and doesn't answer. There is little to say because I'm right. Towering trees replace the winding roads of Mission Hills. When I move, dry leaves crunch softly beneath my feet.

"James, how did we..." I start, but my questions die on my lips when I see him. He clearly does not share the surprise I feel at our surroundings, which, in light of recent events, does not shock me. He is completely still, intent on something between the closely packed trees and out of my line of sight. Every muscle in his body looks tense.

I take half a step forward, reaching out a hand to touch him and ask what's wrong. Hardly have I moved before James snaps his attention to me. Quickly he is at my side again. He protectively circles an arm around the front of my waist and pushes me slightly behind him, so I stand on my toes to see over his shoulder.

At any other time, my heart would race at his proximity, so close I can smell his odd scent of pine, rain, and musky earth. But the way his eyes dart back and forth at the unrecognizable sounds of these new woods makes my heart pound with something much different.

"James?" I repeat, all awe gone from my voice.

He hushes me gently. "Cara, listen." He's still scanning the trees and turns his head so his mouth is close to my ear, then he lowers his voice. "You're going to have to run again. Run dead ahead, just until you can't hear me anymore, then go west, right, and keep going until you see the biggest tree in this forest. Wait there. Hide."

"Wh-whoa...wait. What?" I manage. *This isn't happening,* I think.

James fixes me with a hard look, his dark eyes wary. "Did you get that?" he demands.

"No! ...Well, yes, but—"

"No. There isn't time. If you understood, repeat it back to me."

I stare at him for a moment. Then, "Run until I'm out of hearing. Right. Big tree. Hide," I whisper.

He nods curtly.

"First the bookstore, and now... James, what do you know that you're not telling me?" I ask quietly, wanting answers before I rush off into the woods.

Slowly James steps away from me. The look he gives me is slightly superior, the same smirk he used only minutes ago when he dragged me away from the Village, but when he answers his tone is almost mournful. "So many things, Cara. Things it appears you'll have to learn soon enough." Then he pushes me forward, and, just like Crispin had, he says only, "Run."

So not knowing where I am, where I am going, or what on earth is happening to me, I run.

Within seconds, an explosion of sound breaks out behind me spurring me on. Clanks, yells, and the howl of an animal, clearly audible in the stillness of the forest, echo around me.

Dogs, I think frantically, dodging between trees and under branches. *That howling has to be dogs.* And aren't dogs used to track people? *What do I do if they catch me before James does?*

I don't even know who or what "they" are, and I am worrying about them.

I feel like crying, like curling up on the ground and waiting for someone to find me, but I can't. So I keep moving.

At some point I wonder if this is some kind of trick Crispin and James are playing, though I can't imagine what purpose that would serve them or how they would have managed it.

At another point I wonder if I really did faint and this is a dream I'm having before I wake back up in Mission Hills. But that doesn't make sense either. I'd be done running by now if this were my dream.

I love fiction as much as the next person, but I never imagined I'd have to live it.

After what feels like eternity, I notice that only my own pounding footsteps and panting breath penetrate the silence, so I swing right, praying I've been going straight the whole time. It's hard to tell when the only landmarks are hills and trees. I am losing speed; my fear of pursuers isn't enough to keep me running quickly anymore.

"Where's...that...dang...tree?" I wonder aloud, taking a deep breath between each word. I look quickly around me. Every tree I see is both wider and taller than any tree I have ever seen. They all look like the biggest to me. I curse James' poor directions.

Then, minutes later, as I stumble into an opening in the trees, I see how wrong I was. Only this monster, so big that in this dense tree-packed forest it forms a clearing beneath its own branches, can be what James had been talking about. I don't think it can even be lumped in the same category as the rest of the trees around here. The rough brown trunk is easily large enough to drive a few semis through, with room to spare. I strain my neck, looking for the top, but the branches seem to extend forever and conceal the highest point from me.

Only the fatigue that threatens to engulf me stops me from spending all day gaping at it. I stagger forward into the giant root system that's so twisted together it could offer an array of hiding spots to even a fully-grown man. I wriggle into one near the trunk. And there, nestled between tree roots and an unfamiliar forest floor, I wait.

****

When I wake up, I have no idea where I am. My face is pressed against dirt and leaves, my legs are stiff, and, though it takes me a moment to realize it, there is absolutely no sound except for leaves rustling around me. No traffic, no people, nothing.

Too soon, everything that happened comes rushing back to me and I gasp, scrambling to sit up. My head collides with something coarse and hard, and for a moment I feel trapped. Then the rest of the memories fall into place, and I remember the tree and the massive roots and hiding, and I realize I must have fallen asleep.

Angry with myself for letting my guard down against whatever it is that's out to get me, I find an opening to poke my head out of. The light seems to have changed drastically since I last looked. I start to feel frantic. *What if James has come and gone? What if he couldn't find me? What if... What if he didn't make it out of the forest after me at all?*

Right in the middle of freaking myself out, I hear murmuring and someone stepping across the roots nearby. I can't make out the individual voices, so I try to burrow back into my hiding spot. Before I can move, a head of blond curls pops into my line of sight. I yell and lash out, and then my brain registers what I'm seeing. I try to draw my hand back, but it's a little too late. My loose fist strikes the side of Crispin's face.

I feel overwhelming relief and at the same time horrible guilt. "Oh my goodness!" I cry out while trying not to grin like an idiot. "Crispin, I'm so sorry! I didn't—I didn't know it was you!" I climb quickly out of my little hole and rush over to him.

"You know we've just spent the last couple hours trying to save your life? And you thank me by punching me? You're kidding right?" he asks angrily.

My guilt evaporates and now I'm annoyed. I think he's overreacting because he doesn't even touch his cheek where I just "punched" him. Then I actually look at him, and I see what bad shape he's in. His jeans are torn at the knees, and long, bloody scrapes accompany the tears. One arm has rows of gashes that I'm sure would match Panus' fingernails perfectly. A large bruise is forming on his temple, and more are at his throat.

"Oh Crispin," I breathe. "Are you okay?"

"He's fine," another voice says, sounding both weary and amused.

James limps out from behind one of the roots. I thought Crispin looked bad, but James looks about ten times worse. His hair is matted down on one side of his head with what I assume is blood, and I see some of it drip down his cheek. He has the beginnings of a black eye. His shirt is gone, so I can see bruises and slashes across his chest. Both of his shoes are missing too, and his feet are cut up from the forest floor. Even the palms of his hands are scored with little scrapes.

I exhale quickly and sit down, trying not to stare at the wounds they received protecting me from some unknown assailant. "What happened?" I ask.

They both sit down gingerly nearby. "Well, I think you saw most of what happened with Panus. It didn't last long after you two left. The noise eventually drew some people out of their shops and at that point I was losing, so they pulled Panus off me, and I had to get out of there," Crispin explains. He sounds frustrated, as though he is blaming himself for doing something wrong. "I got here in time to help James finish off his own battle, then we came to find you."

I want to ask what happened to Panus after that, if the people that were holding him back are safe, but I decide it's not a good time. I make a mental note to find out later. I look to James expectantly, thinking he'll elaborate on his bit of the story now, but he avoids my eyes.

"And?" I demand impatiently. "After all this, that's really all you're going to tell me? Not who Panus is, not who James was fighting, or what happened to them, not where the hell we are, not how you showed up out of nowhere and saved me just in time to drag me off to a forest—?"

I break off. They both look nervous, which is an expression I have never seen on them. I hadn't realized how scared I was until I started talking. There is so much I don't understand, and it would appear that they know I'm in some sort of trouble and just risked their lives to keep me out of it.

"Who are you, really?" I ask in a small voice.

"That, I'm afraid, is going to have to wait," Crispin answers after a slight pause and stands suddenly. "We're losing daylight. We've got to get home."

"Home?" I say cautiously. Why would they drag me all the way here just to turn around and take me home?

Crispin is the one looking guilty this time. "Err... Sorry Cara. Not *home* home just yet."

"What?" I ask. "Where else are you talking about?"

He rubs his nose ruefully. "We...can't take you home. Yet. We can't take you home *yet*. But we will. Soon, I mean. Just not yet."

I stare at him for a moment in bewilderment. "That was probably the least articulate anyone in history has ever been," I finally say.

James snorts.

Crispin pulls a face, and I can't tell which of us it is directed at. Right then something clicks for me. It has taken me a minute, but I finally clue in. "You live here?"

Now they both looked pained, as if this, after everything else, was the biggest secret they had, so I know I'm right.

"Come on, Cara, we really have to go," Crispin tells me tiredly, not offering any explanation.

I hesitate. Do I really want to go running through the forest, again, with these two, still without the explanation I think I deserve? I suddenly wonder if there is someone following us, so I begin to look around, and then something else occurs to me.

"James," I say slowly, "what happened to all those people? The ones you fought when we got here?"

James has already started to make his way across the tree roots, but he stops. He half-turns back to me. "I did what I had to. They would have followed me and gotten to you if I hadn't." He started to say something more, but stops to begin walking again.

I sit there in shock as his words sink in, amazed that I remain surprised by their answers. "All of them?" I ask. "You killed...even their dogs?"

He stops again, this time swinging around to look at me intently. "What dogs?"

Crispin, who had begun following James, halts too and watches him warily.

"The dogs," I say blankly. "I heard dogs when I..." I trail off because James is looking at me apprehensively, as though afraid of what I'll say next.

I must look as shocked by his reaction as I feel, because James shakes his head, ridding himself of some thought before he continues walking.

"No," he says over his shoulder. "The dog lived." His voice sounds oddly tight, but I let it drop. It doesn't matter that much.

It's then that I notice something else. "Where did you get those pants?"

They're the only article of clothing he has on, crudely made of dark cloth, ragged at the hems, and definitely not the jeans he was wearing earlier.

He sounds exasperated when he answers, "Off of one of the soldiers in the woods."

I have to process that information before it hits home. "You took them off a dead man?"

"Well I needed them, and it seemed he didn't anymore," James replies, walking away.

I'm aghast at his flippancy, but there is nothing to be done about it. I realize with a start that he must have been in battles like that before if he can brush it off so easily. He must have had to kill before.

Trying not to dwell on this new revelation, I push myself up off my seat on the tree roots to follow the boys. But when I do, something slices my finger and I inhale quickly. It takes a moment to realize that I'm not actually hurt. It's just unexpected. I look down and see that my ring has turned around and cut into the side of my finger.

I laugh softly at myself and start my climb over the roots. But I haven't taken more than a step before I notice Crispin making his way quickly back toward me.

"What happened?" he asks.

It didn't occur to me that either of the boys had heard me gasp. They must still be on alert, though I'd felt assured that the danger had passed for now.

"Nothing at all," I say, somewhat touched by his concern, but feeling foolish after seeing the boys' injuries. "Just a scratch." I hold up my hand for him to see.

Crispin takes my hand, inspects it carefully, and slides my ring off in the process.

"Oh please, it's nothing. I'm perfectly fine!" I say, snatching my hand back. "I thought we had to leave."

"We do," Crispin tells me. He seems just as annoyed as I am at the hold up. He makes a move as if to toss my ring back to me, but he stops at the last second and looks at it closely. And then, for the first time since we've met, I see an expression of true astonishment cross his face. And my breath catches, because if something around here is enough to startle Crispin, then it's big.

In a strained voice, Crispin calls out to James who comes bounding over. Crispin doesn't even glance at him, just hands over my ring and sits down heavily. The same look of total astonishment steals over James' face.

"That's not possible," James eventually whispers.

Crispin is still sitting, shaking his head back and forth slowly. "Crap," he breathes.

Then, simultaneously, the two raise their heads to look at me.

What now? I wonder, feeling my stomach lurch. *I don't think I can take anything else.* I feel drained, empty, and I have the same heroic urge to curl up and weep that I had when I first arrived.

I hear my name. I do my best to focus again and realize James is speaking to me and asking where I got the ring.

"I don't know," I mumble. "It's just a ring. I don't know."

Crispin's voice was persuasive: "Yes, you do. Think about it."

So I do. "My uncle." I remember, the memory coming to me out of nowhere. It was my seventh birthday, back when my aunts and uncles and grandparents still celebrated holidays with us, when we still lived near them all. We'd already had cake and opened presents, and most of our guests had started trickling out the door. My Uncle Amos brought a friend, and they were some of the last to leave. His friend had pulled me aside while my parents were thanking my grandparents for coming, and he had pressed the ring into my hand. "I thought it was a toy at first," I explain, "because I'd never seen a real ring with so many jewels." He told me it had real diamonds in it, and that the green stone in the middle was an actual emerald. He'd said: "Your mommy and daddy probably wouldn't like it if they knew I was giving this to you. Let's keep it a secret, okay?" Since I trusted my Uncle Amos and therefore his friends too, I readily agreed. I had tried to slip it onto my finger, but it was a few sizes too big. He had laughed and told me I would grow into it, and that I must always keep it safe. I didn't see him again after that.

I quietly relay the whole story to James and Crispin. Neither says a word until I'm done.

"Crap," Crispin says again.

James sighs and nods in agreement.

Then Crispin looks me square in the eye. "Cara," he says seriously. "Think. Do you remember this guy's name? Did this friend of your uncle's, or your uncle himself, ever, *ever*, mention the name Demesne? Or Lyria?"

I try to think back and hope I can tell him yes, but I have no idea what he's talking about. I shake my head.

I can't tell if Crispin is relieved or disappointed with my answer.

"Why?" I ask.

"This ring," he tells me slowly, "is the ring of the royal family of Demesne." Crispin removes one of his countless rings, the one on the ring finger of his right hand, takes my ring back from James, and walks over to drop them both in my hand.

I have to stare at them for a minute before my brain registers what I'm seeing. "We have the same ring," I say. I mean for it to be a question, but it comes out a statement.

"Almost," Crispin answers, finally offering me information I don't have to beg for. "See here," he points, "the number of diamonds, there, are different than the number on mine."

Sure enough, as I look more closely at the rings, I see Crispin's is encrusted with diamonds, almost ridiculously so, and mine has only eight in comparison.

"But," I begin, then stop. I don't know how to ask what I want to know, and I'm afraid all my questions are going to come out at once. I pick the most important. "What does that mean? For me?" I look Crispin right in the eye. He's always treated me like he already knew everything about me and didn't care much if he ever learned more. But now he looks like he doesn't know what to make of me.

"It means we have to get moving," James answers for Crispin, who nods in agreement.

This time I don't hesitate for an instant to follow them. I'm scared to death and immensely curious, but somehow I know, despite everything, these two are going to keep me safe. So I follow them back into the woods.

11

"Okay. So here's the thing. I get the whole secrecy bit. I really do. What I don't understand is why you all zapped us in here nowhere near where we actually needed to be. And why you don't just zap us there now. I really do think my feet may fall off soon." I am talking to the back of the boys' heads. They are a little ways ahead of me.

"Would you stop calling it 'zapping'?" Crispin calls back to me without turning around.

"Well, it may help us all if you'd just freaking explain it to me," I mutter loudly. We have been walking about an hour and a half (my Chucks weren't made for treks through forests), most of it in silence. So I've had plenty of time to get over my initial fear and stop cringing behind trees in terror every time a twig snaps. Now I'm tired and frustrated and, quite frankly, bored. Apparently, they can fight full-grown men, but walking and talking at the same time is a bit over their heads.

Both Crispin and James stop and wait for me to catch up for the first time since we started. "Oh how kind," I say when I reach them. "You remembered me."

Crispin scowls at me, but James looks faintly amused. "I've never seen you this cranky," he tells me.

I cross my arms over my chest and rearrange my expression to match Crispin's. I don't think I succeed because James just raises an eyebrow. I give it up a moment later and sit on the ground. "I'm not cranky. Now, why did you stop?" I ask, shoving my hair back from my face.

"Wait...are you saying we *imagined* all that talking you were doing back there?" James asks in mock confusion.

This time my scowl feels successful. James and Crispin join me in the grass. "We know we haven't been very helpful," Crispin begins, settling himself down comfortably, "but, even if you don't believe it, this is just as weird for us as it is for you."

"Uh-huh," I say, unconvinced.

"I know. You don't have any reason to believe it. You've trusted us so far though, right? So just...keep trusting us. It's important."

I'm still skeptical, but he's right. Why stop trusting them now? I've already followed them through an unfamiliar forest after letting them "zap" me to Lord knows where. Which reminds me of my question.

"All right. Then if it's not zapping...?" I prompt them.

"Right," Crispin says with a sigh. "Well, we call it 'jumping the tear'."

I'm startled. I didn't actually believe they were going to answer me. "Okay," I say, trying to take it in stride. "Jumping the tear. So far, so good. What tear?"

"Well," Crispin says again, choosing his words carefully. "The tear that's..." he looks over at James who shrugs, so Crispin turns back to me, "between your world and ours."

I sit still for a long time. Crispin is gazing at me nervously, and James is tense off to the side. I wait for someone to jump out from behind a tree and yell "Gotcha!" But the boys' expressions are dead serious, and, while I'm sitting there hoping that they're kidding, I know, with the same certainty I knew I could trust them, that they aren't lying to me.

So, I take a deep breath to prepare myself, and, with the steadiest voice I can muster I say, "Oh."

"Yeah," Crispin tells me quietly.

No one says anything for a few moments more. Then I speak again, "Okay. So when you 'jump the tear', it takes you from one world to another? From...my world to *yours*. Which means there's more than one world? And that makes you *not* from my *world*?"

"Yes, to all of the above," Crispin answers.

I close my eyes and breathe deeply.

"Cara, we know how this sounds. How this seems. And you must think we're crazy. But please, be brave. Trust us. We wouldn't have brought you here, not like this, if we'd had another choice." Crispin is trying to be calm; I know he's only being this composed for me. The anxious edge to his voice betrays the fact that this really is new to him too.

I open my eyes to look at him, but I still can't find the words I want to say. He continues, "We have never shown or told anyone else what you're seeing now. Never once in the eight years James and I have spent in your world. So we don't really know what to do right now either. All we know is, clearly, it's not safe out here. And I know I can't imagine what you're feeling, but you have to believe in us."

I want to believe him, I do, but it's too much, too good to be true. "When I was little," I find myself saying, "there was nothing I wanted more than for this kind of thing to be true. Other worlds, and all that. There are some days where I still find myself wanting it. So, how can it be that, all this time, it was real? How could I want something impossible so badly, and have it be attainable the entire time?"

"Because you're one of the lucky ones," James answers. "You get to have your dreams, or this one, at least, come true."

I snort derisively. "James, I've learned from experience that dreams like this don't really just come true. Especially for people like me."

"And which people are those?"

"The ordinary ones who dream of something impossible. Impossible things don't happen."

"Not always. Maybe less in your world." James smiles crookedly, his storm-colored eyes warm and sincere. "So it's a good thing we're not there anymore."

In my head, I hear David telling me that day at the ice-rink to quit worrying about what might happen someday and focus on what's real right now. And, now, this is real—very real. So I look at Crispin and James, and I try to believe them. And it is such a relief to let it go that I can't help the grin that steals across my face. It eases the tension from me as my fear and apprehension slowly disappear.

"So," I say, smiling at the pure ridiculousness of it all. "Jumping the tear. Check. What about the other stuff? Like the rings?" I pull mine off to study it again, seeing it in a whole new light now that I know what it is.

Crispin looks up, I think at the sun, then back down at me. "Can we explain on the way?"

I smile more widely and stand up, brushing off my jeans. "So far you have proven that you cannot, but I'm willing to give you another shot."

James snickers at Crispin's disgruntled expression, and they both get to their feet. Crispin points in the direction we need to go. This time I fall in step next to them.

"All right. You want to know about the rings first?" Crispin asks me after a few minutes of more walking. He and James nod at each other, and then James breaks into a jog and is soon lost among the trees. Curiously, I watch him go. "Scouting ahead," Crispin explains in response to my unspoken question. "Just in case."

"I just don't understand why this ring matters so much. I mean, okay, ring of the royal family, sure, but why did you guys care so much that I have one?"

"Well," Crispin says, rubbing the back of his neck uncomfortably, "like you just said, it's the ring of the royal family. I guess you wouldn't know, but those rings are kind of a big deal. In Demesnian history, each and every royal has had one, and when they die, their rings are kept well-guarded in the treasury of the Demesnian castle. No ring is used twice. And because *only* the royal family has them, anyone with one has claim to the title of Demesnian royalty. But they're so heavily protected that it has never happened. In history." He gestured to my ring. "Until now."

"Oh." I process that quietly for a moment. "How did one of them end up with my uncle's friend, then? With me?"

"I'm curious about that myself," Crispin admits. "I didn't know that one had even gone missing. I think it would be quite a big deal."

"Hmm. And they really don't go out to anyone else besides your royalty? Ever?"

Crispin shakes his head.

"So...you're royalty then?"

He doesn't answer me for a long time, which only confirms what I've said. Eventually he looks over to gauge my reaction, but I look straight ahead, not meeting his eyes.

"A...what was the word? Demesnian? A Demesnian prince. Are princes allowed to go journeying across worlds and wandering through forests?" I ask him.

"This prince is," he says evenly. And it sounds like a line he has used before.

"Oh my gosh," I say, feeling a bit like I've had the wind knocked out of me. "You're a prince. I mean, of course you are. Why not? Any other bombs you want to drop on me? Please, please do it now, while I can still handle it, because I think this is all going to catch up with me, and I'm probably going to go into shock any time now."

James comes bounding back to us just then. "James!" I call out. My eyes wide, I point a thumb at Crispin. "He's a prince!"

James skids to a halt in a spray of leaves and stares at Crispin in false disbelief. "A what?" he asks.

"Oh stop," Crispin says in annoyance. James is grinning, clearly not amazed at this bit of news.

"You already knew, didn't you?" I ask.

"Not at all," James replies. "I am incredibly shocked by this remarkable turn of events."

"Ha, ha," I say, making a face. Then I'm serious again. "Oh no. You're not a prince too, are you?"

James barks out a laugh, waggles his ringless fingers at me, and effectively ends that line of thought. I'm relieved. Crispin being a prince seems almost obvious now that I know about it. He has that kind of air about him that I can now see could come from being respected and in charge and used to being listened to. But it's still a slightly uncomfortable thought, like I've unwittingly been spending time with Prince William. Exactly like that, actually. And it's not that James doesn't carry himself with confidence. His is just more hardened, like he came by it himself.

"There's about ten minutes of forest left," James reports to Crispin.

"How do you know that?" I ask him.

"Well, I carefully timed myself and ran until the trees stopped. Then I came back here," James explains slowly, speaking to me like I'm five.

I glare at him. "Obviously," I say, insulted. "I meant, since it takes ten minutes to get there and that's about how long you were gone, how did you get there and back so fast?"

He doesn't answer.

"James," Crispin says, "do you think—"

"I'm fast," James tells me shortly.

"Fine," I reply curtly, knowing full well he's keeping something from me. I'm annoyed all over again. "Sorry, I thought we had decided to share everything with Cara since, you know, she's been dragged to your world because someone is *after her*. But I guess I'm still on a need to know basis. My bad." I storm ahead of them, but still catch the look that Crispin shoots James, and the frown James gives him in reply.

Crispin jogs a few paces to catch up with me, and this time James is the one lagging behind. "We decided to share *almost* everything with Cara," Crispin tells me in a somewhat apologetic tone. "But James has some of his own...stuff, and I can't make him tell you unless he chooses to. Some of it you may just have to figure out on your own."

"Just how many secrets are you going to keep from me?" I ask. "Only going to share with me when my life is in immediate danger?"

He gives me a withering look. "Stop acting like a child, Cara."

I pull up short, so he stops too.

"Look," he tells me irritably, "you're the one who has to make the impression here, not us. So quit moping. You need us right now, and frankly, I don't care if you like it or not. But when we get home, people are going to have to choose whether they want to help you. And you're making the decision pretty easy right now."

I'm stung. "Whatever you say, your majesty." I say bitingly, curtsying at him.

Crispin winces like he's been struck, and I'm suddenly aware of how ungrateful I'm being. He's shared the biggest secrets he has in the world with me, and because I can't handle it, I'm punishing him for it. No wonder he didn't tell me earlier.

I take a deep breath. "I'm sorry, Crispin. I'm...feeling a little lost here. A lot lost, actually. I'm walking blind, and I don't like it."

"Understatement of the century," I hear James mutter behind us.

"That we can relate to," Crispin tells me. Thankfully, he ignores James' comment as we continue walking. "Walking blind? James and I have been in your world for a long time because we're the ones who are supposed to find...an answer to our problems. And we didn't even know what we were looking for. Instead of searching for something, we were searching for anything. Do you know how hard that is?"

It feels like a rhetorical question, but I shake my head just in case. Although I know he's still mad, Crispin grins at me.

I look at him curiously. "Did you find it? The answer you were looking for?"

"I'm not entirely sure yet," Crispin responds, choosing his words carefully. "But I think we have. Though it's not quite what we were expecting."

I know he isn't going to elaborate any more than that, so I ask, "Will you tell me what it's like here? Will you tell me about home?"

A slow, genuine smile steals across Crispin's face. "What do you want to know?"

"Everything," I reply.

So Crispin talks, more freely and enthusiastically than I've ever heard him. He tells me that Demesne is one of five kingdoms east of the Aurian Ocean, and his and James' home. One kingdom, Krela, is empty, abandoned a long time ago. There was a war once, and the Sheiks (Panus' people) and the Krelans had allied and tried to overthrow the other kingdoms. They succeeded with Nava, the first kingdom in their path, but the remaining Navites rushed to the Demesnians and the Cairnes (the final two kingdoms), joined forces, and fought back. They won. But there was a battle (all details left out by Crispin) that ended in the annihilation of the Krelans. None have been seen since, and the land is unoccupied.

Demesne is the kingdom nearest the coast. It's green and fertile, and it's been peaceful for a couple hundred years now. King Rennar and Queen Andromeda are Demesne's rulers. "There are different territories within the kingdoms, just like there are cities within your countries," Crispin explains. "My mother was the eldest child of her parents, the previous king and queen. She's the one with royal blood. My father was the Duke of Kenstral, one of said territories, after his father died. He and my mother were betrothed, so when she came of age they were married."

"So the oldest kid becomes the next ruler, regardless of gender?" I ask, impressed by this system. I know too much about times in history where women couldn't become rulers.

"Not always." James comes up from behind me to answer.

Before I can ask him what the exception is, the trees thin and suddenly we can see rolling hills speckled with yellow and green, and a wide, shining blue river. Strong breezes blow cool, salt-laced air to us. James and Crispin let out whoops of delight, abandon the conversation, sprint to the river, and splash across a shallow section that they've clearly crossed before. They race up to the top of the nearest hill, and Crispin throws himself rolling down the other side.

Hearing Crispin talk about this place made it sound like his home, but seeing the two of them here, the immediate shift in their attitude…it's evident that this is where they belong, and that they've been waiting to come back. I can still hear them yelling to one another, though they're both out of sight, all pain they may have felt at their injuries forgotten for the moment.

Their joy is infectious, and I find myself giggling at their childishness. I walk much more slowly than them to the bank of the river, take this in, and stroll along until I come to the place where they crossed. I can't tell if it's manmade or not, but there is a path of rocks a few feet wide that spans the river's width inches below the surface. On either side of the path the river drops straight down from the banks and looks to be about ten feet deep in the middle. There's hardly a current. I can hear the boys coming back, so I sit carefully on the low, steep bank and, removing my shoes and socks, dabble my sore feet in the cold clear water.

"Good thinking." Crispin and James finally come back over the hills and cross the river to sit next to me on the bank. I lay back and close my eyes. After the stress and shadow of the forest, the warmth of bright sunlight feels amazing on my face. So does the fact that we actually get to rest. The boys aren't on guard for once, and that makes it easier to relax. And when they start chatting about something or other, I take some time to think over everything I've learned, as well as the things I still need to find out. And I start to doze off.

The boys don't let me sleep for long. They must have cannonballed into the water because just as I feel warm again, I find myself drenched. I sit up, sputtering. Crispin's shoes and shirt are thrown haphazardly by the water, and he's pushing James under the surface of the river. I laugh and pull my feet out. "What on earth?"

"In Lyria, I think you mean," Crispin corrects me, grinning. "We aren't on earth anymore."

"Lyria." I try out the world. It sounds musical, fitting. Then I pounce on the offered information. "I didn't know that this world wasn't on earth," I tell them. "I mean I figured it wasn't on *earth* necessarily, but still. If it isn't on earth, what is it on?" I'm aware the question makes little sense, but I don't know how to word it any better.

James seems to understand what I'm asking, and he spits a fountain of water at Crispin before he answers. "We don't know. Technically it could be on earth, or something like earth. But really Lyria *is* our earth, assuming it's a planet. It might be called different names other places. We don't have a way of knowing how our world compares to yours in the physical sense. It's different in so many ways. It could be flat where yours is round, and the stars could revolve around Lyria just like Earth revolves around the sun. Who knows?"

"Why don't you know?" I ask.

"Well, we don't have your technology," Crispin tells me matter-of-factly. "No maps of the entire world, no cruise ships taking us from one end of the world to the other, definitely no spaceships or anything like that. What we know we've found out from the cartographers of our five kingdoms."

"Really? That seems strange. You have the ability go back and forth between our worlds, so did you never bring any of our stuff back here? Or introduce your things to our world for that matter?"

Crispin gestures back toward the trees without answering. "Hey, Cara, will you run right over there"—he points—"and grab the bag that's hidden in those bushes?"

I stare at him for a moment. "We aren't going to run off or something while you're gone; it'll take like thirty seconds," Crispin laughs. "Please?"

I brush myself off and jog over to where Crispin pointed. There's bunches of bushes gathered around the trees nearer the river, and the handle of a brown bag is visible between some of the leaves. I tug the bag out of its hiding place. Curious, I dig through it quickly before I take it back to the boys. There is a bundle of cloth bandages, some bottles of liquids that have different colors and consistencies, some weird shapeless mass made of what I think is animal skin, a few sets of clothes, and something hard wrapped in cloth. I don't have time to look at it more closely, because Crispin calls out to ask if I found it.

"Yes," I yell back as I quickly repack the bag and swing it over my shoulder.

"You know," Crispin says as I approach, "if you wanted to know what it was, I would have told you."

I flush. I didn't know he could see me. He hoists himself out of the water, joins me as I sit back down on the bank, and takes the bag from my hands. "It's nothing magical and secret, if that's what you were thinking."

One at a time, Crispin pulls everything out and lines it up neatly in the grass. "I'm sure you figured out the bandages. And the clothes, hopefully." I nod. "All right. Canteen and medicine," he says, pointing to the animal skin thing and the bottles in turn. And, with a sigh, he unwraps the last item. Or items. A big, thick, emerald-studded gold band falls out, along with two daggers, a small bag of coins, and a ring that matches yet another of Crispin's—this new ring is a duplicate of one on his left hand. "And then there's this."

He pushes the band firmly onto his head. I can't help but gape at him. "How's it look?" Crispin asks, smirking and turning his head to the side.

James swims over, shakes his head, and tells him, "Quit showing off. "Crowns look good on everyone." Dripping water, he lifts himself out of the river and grabs the ring from the grass to slide it on the little finger of his left hand.

As I look at the two of them, the last traces of my world seem to fade, and suddenly I can't imagine them being anywhere besides this place. Then I realize that I am sitting next to two incredibly good looking, otherworldly boys that are both soaked to the skin, and blushing furiously, I avert my eyes to the river.

Crispin is busily studying the bottles of medicine, but I think James notices my discomfort. Thankfully he doesn't say anything as I sit there splashing my feet.

"Here," Crispin says to James as he tosses two of the bottles at him. James snatches them out of the air easily, sits down behind me, and opens the larger of the two. It is half-filled with a pale green liquid. I swing my feet out of the water and turn to face them both with my back to the river. James pours some of the liquid on a wad of excess bandages, then he dabs at the deepest of his cuts with it, wincing slightly. The river had washed away the blood that had dried on their wounds, so, as best I can figure, this stuff is some kind of disinfectant. Crispin is efficiently treating his own injuries with something similar to what James is using, but his liquid is more blue than green.

"Cara," James says. I snap my eyes up to his and realize that I'm blatantly staring. I feel my face burn, but I try to hold his gaze That same crooked smirk he's been flashing all day steals across his face again. "I need your help. I have some kind of scrape on my back, near my shoulder blades, and I can't get to it." He holds his antiseptic out to me.

I hesitate for only an instant before I grab it from his hand. "What exactly does this do?" I ask, standing to walk around behind him.

"Kills bacteria that's in the wounds. Starts the process of sealing them up," James explains. He's already unstopped the second bottle, full of an orange paste, and has begun rubbing it into the recently disinfected cuts.

"Some kind of scrape?" I exclaim when I see James' back. He has a long deep gash running from the top of his left shoulder down to his right side. "James! How did you walk so far with this?" *How did I miss this earlier?*

"We couldn't exactly have done anything about it before, could we?" Crispin joins me behind James to look himself, so I suppose he is the more medically advanced of the two. "Wow. That *does* look bad." Then Crispin walks back to where he was sitting to start bandaging his remaining scratches.

I roll my eyes. "Thanks for your help." I douse the damp bandage James used with more green liquid, then press it gently against his wound. James yelps softly and jerks away.

He hisses out a breath. "Sorry."

"It's fine. Are you okay?" I ask, worried I've done something wrong.

"Yeah." James slides back over to me carefully.

"Was it something I did?"

"No. No it wasn't you. I just wasn't ready. It must be worse than I thought."

"You think?" This time I brace one hand on his uninjured shoulder. His skin is smooth and still cool from the river, and water droplets cling to the ends of his dark hair. I see an odd scar at the base of his neck. It looks like something large bit him once upon a time, and I can't stop myself from tracing it softly with my thumb. James doesn't move and doesn't say anything, but I recognize what I'm doing and snap myself out of it. "Are you ready?" I ask him quickly.

James nods once, so I again press the bandages to his back. He inhales sharply, but I dig my fingers into his shoulder and hold him down as best I can so he doesn't move. I feel his shoulders shake under me, and after a moment I realize he's laughing.

"What?" I ask, not stopping my work.

"It's like you think you could hold me in place," he chuckles deep in his throat.

I pause long enough that he looks over his shoulder at me with his eyebrows raised. His gray-blue eyes don't have a trace of mockery in them when he says, "Thank you, Cara."

So I finish up and then go over the cut with the orange paste like I saw him do on his other wounds.

"Heads up!" Crispin calls, then tosses a bunch of bandages at my head. I barely manage to catch them before they hit James in the face. He takes them for me and begins winding some lightly around his feet and chest. So I stand and make my way over to Crispin.

"Anything I can do?" I ask him.

He looks up. "Yes, there is actually. Can you bandage my arm up?" He raises his left arm slightly. "I'm left-handed, so it's slow going when I do it."

"Of course," I answer. I kneel next to him and wrap the cloth carefully and tightly around his bicep.

"Perfect." Crispin leans back on his other hand and closes his eyes. His crown is still perched on his head, and it glints in the sunlight. "I missed this place," he tells me.

"I can tell," I answer. "So, what comes next?"

"I think we'll camp here tonight. It's safer in the tree line than it is out in the open. We've got about another half a day of walking before we reach the nearest town, so we'll get up early tomorrow and head out. We'll go there, commandeer some horses, and head home. The ride to Geler is a few hours or so from there."

"Commandeer? Geler?"

"The capital city. Home."

"So we're almost there?"

Crispin smiles widely as I tie off the bandage. "We're almost there."

I head back over to James and slide the remaining bandages out of his hand to take care of his back for him. By the time I'm done with them, have stopped the bottles once again, and have put the extra bandages back in the bag, I feel like I'm quite an accomplished nurse.

"Cara, could you do us a favor?" Crispin asks me.

"Depends," I answer.

"Just...look that way, for a minute," he tells me. "We have to change."

He and James walk toward the trees. "Wait!" I call out.

"Unless," James says with a smirk, "you'd prefer we didn't." He gestures to their bare chests. His is pale and sharply contrasts with his black hair. Crispin's chest is tan and perfect for his blond curls. Both have lean muscles along their arms and stomachs. I try to make a face at James, but I can't quite. *Damn, why do they both have to be so attractive?*

"No, you feel free to put a shirt on," I tell him halfheartedly to keep his ego in check. "I was actually wondering if I needed to change too?" I'm wearing jeans and a long-sleeved shirt, exactly what Crispin is about to go change out of.

"Well, we don't really have clothes for you with us. So no, you're good for now. We'll borrow something for you when we get into town." Crispin says.

"Who's going to just give me clothes?" I ask dubiously.

"No one," Crispin answers with a grin. "They're going to just give *me* clothes."

"Oh... You're going to pull the royalty card."

"Works every time," Crispin tells me. Then they walk off and I turn to stare across the river.

12

When the boys come out of the woods in their new clothes, I can't help but laugh. It's either that or ogle them.

They are dressed in outfits that I've only ever seen in movies. Crispin has the full ensemble: beige, fitted pants that end at his shins, a white shirt with a high square collar and baggy sleeves that tighten only around his wrists, a fitted, light green, gold-embroidered vest, and tall brown boots. His rings shine around his fingers, and his crown is set neatly on his head.

He looks good. It's what he belongs in.

James wears something very similar, but while Crispin's clothes are buttoned up and straight, James looks like he's just slung his on. And his clothes are darker in color. His pants and boots are black. His white shirt is actually tucked in, but the dark blue vest over it is completely unbuttoned. Even his hair is disheveled.

All their injuries are hidden by their new clothing. From the way they move, you'd never been able to tell they were in pain just a few hours ago.

I marvel yet again at how different they both are in looks and personality, but they don't give me the time to marvel for very long.

"Let's get camp set up!" Crispin says, clapping his hands together. James glances at me and rolls his eyes but motions at me to stand up. "James, I need you to hunt. It doesn't look like our aides thought to leave food with the rest of these supplies. Cara and I will get firewood and see if we can find the pack that's supposed to have food and blankets in it. We'll meet you in the clearing."

James nods silently, picks up one of the daggers, tosses the other to Crispin who catches it deftly by the hilt, and then disappears into the woods.

I watch him go apprehensively. Night is approaching fast. The last of the sun's rays are fading from the sky and leave a darkness unlike any I've ever encountered. Normally I love nighttime. I love the shadows and the feeling of being able to walk about unnoticed. But the dark here is unfamiliar, new, and nerve-racking.

Crispin puts a hand lightly on my arm. "Don't worry," he says gently. "There's nothing to be nervous about. We're the only ones around. I'm here to help you out."

"How do you always know what I'm thinking?" I ask him.

He looks genuinely pleased with himself, but he answers seriously. "All I have to do is wonder what I'd be most anxious about if I were in your shoes," he tells me. "Right now, I'd be wondering how James will be able to find his way alone, part of me would be wondering *if* he'll make it back, and most of me would be trying to convince myself that there's nothing to be afraid of in these woods because we just walked through them and came out all right."

I look him in the eye. "And what would you tell yourself to make you less afraid?"

The last beams of sunlight catch in the crown on his head and the rings on his fingers. It gives an odd weight to his words. "I would tell myself, 'You made it this far. No matter how you feel now, you can make it farther still.' Trust yourself."

Though the line is somewhat cheesy, I take it seriously. "And that would be enough to make you keep going?" I ask.

Crispin takes my hand and leads me slowly forward. "If I had an expertly trained man with a knife at my side? Absolutely."

I shoot him a look. "Expertly trained?"

Darkness has fallen now, and everything is bathed in dim moonlight. Crispin gives a must-we-go-through-this sigh, drops my hand, and without a moment's hesitation throws the knife, end over end, toward a small tree. It sticks perfectly in the middle of a small knot, handle swaying with the impact.

Crispin's hand finds mine again as we walk to retrieve it, and he gives it a quick squeeze before letting go, comforting me without words. He lets me examine the dagger where it's still stuck in the tree trunk before he pulls it out.

"Is that actually where you were aiming?" I ask him with a smile. I'm both alarmed and impressed by his ability.

He shakes his head. "You know it was," he says.

I consent, and we re-enter the trees.

I wouldn't have thought so, but even under the thick cover of the trees, the moon and stars outline the forest with a soft silver glow and provide enough light to see by. I manage to keep up with Crispin even though he constantly picks up the pace, veers off course without warning, and generally leaves me blundering along behind him.

After a few minutes of walking, Crispin holds out a hand and motions for me to stop. "That pack should be around here somewhere," he explains.

He crouches down and presses one hand, fingers splayed, against the ground. He closes his eyes, his face the picture of concentration, so I don't ask him what he's doing. It only takes a minute for him to straighten back up and grin at me. "Thanks for being patient," he says. "We're going that way." He points and starts off again.

I trail behind him. "So..." I begin. "Do I get an explanation about that? Or is this some of that 'we'll tell you when you're ready' stuff?"

Crispin, uncomfortable again like one of us seems to have been all day, rubs the back of his neck. "Well, I *can* tell you, but I'm not sure you'll like the answer much."

"I think I'd like to take my chances," I reply.

"Of course you would," he sighs. "Okay then. The easy answer? That right there, was me doing magic."

He clearly anticipates my reaction and turns to face me as I halt.

"I know, I know," he says. "But remember? Walk and talk. If James and I can do it, so can you." I force my feet to slide forward. "A little faster," Crispin urges. "James is going to meet us in the clearing, and if we're not there soon, then he's going to come looking for us. And we may not pass by each other in this forest in any reasonable amount of time. Do you want to spend the night wandering about looking for James?"

I manage to raise my eyebrows at him. "You couldn't just use *magic* to signal him?" I ask weakly.

"Well yeah, I could," Crispin tells me as though it's obvious. "But any type of signaling magic, especially at night, is going to be bright and attract unwanted attention. Have you forgotten that there may be people after us?"

I follow Crispin mutely as he jogs a ways forward. He stops at a tree with branches that hang only a few feet above our heads. "Really?" he mutters under his breath. He bounces on the balls of his feet, bends his knees, and then in one swift motion he leaps up to grab a branch with both hands. He dangles there for only a second, arms straight, before pulling himself up and swinging his feet onto the limb, standing, and then bracing himself to do the same thing again.

Eventually he jumps back down next to me with a large pack on his shoulders and a grin on his face. "It's been a long time since I got to do something like that."

"That was impressive," I admit, my mind still whirling.

Crispin hands me the pack. "Carry this. I'll get firewood on the way to the campsite. And you can ask those questions you've been so patiently carrying around for the last minute and a half."

I dutifully take the pack, and I'm surprised at its light weight in comparison to its size. I shuffle through the questions in my head. "Magic?" is all I'm finally able to ask.

"You already jumped the tear, and that's about as big as magic can get, traveling between worlds like that. I'm surprised you're this shocked," Crispin says to me. He stops to pick up sticks and branches as we walk along. "I feel like it should have been kind of obvious after that."

"I didn't really think about it," I say. "Once I got over the whole 'other world' thing, it just fit that there would also be a way to get from one world to the other. I didn't know that meant magic was real or that it was common or anything."

Crispin nods understandingly. "We told you that we don't have Earth's technology here, and that's the reason. Magic and science don't exactly mix. They interfere with one another. And we have no need for all the technology in Lyria because most of the things it does we can do with magic. And vice versa for you guys on earth. I could list a few other reasons, but the main point is…yeah, magic."

I think quietly for a moment. "Can everyone do magic?" I ask.

"Everyone in Lyria? About half the population is born with any amount of potential for it. Some don't have the opportunity or the drive to ever pursue it; some learn important casts and stop there. And then others take the time to learn and master every cast they can. So there are a lot of people that *can* do magic. But the aptitude for it varies."

"Are there different kinds?"

"What do you mean?" Crispin asks.

"Are some people better at one type of…cast than others?"

"Not anymore, no. There are some casts that people focus more specifically on than others, but not really any types of magic."

"Not anymore?" I ask him.

Crispin cocks his head to look at me and shifts the pile of wood in his arms. He leads me around a line of trees. I know the look he's giving me. It's the same one I give Sophie when I'm trying to decide how much to explain to her.

And then my stomach lurches as I suddenly think: *Sophie.*

"Damn it!" I cry suddenly. "Crispin! You have to take me home. We have to go back!" I grab his arm.

Crispin looks startled, my question forgotten as he glances around to see what's frightened me. "Cara, what? What's wrong?"

"Sophie! Crispin, what's Sophie going to do when she realizes I'm gone? Who's going to take care of her? She needs me! We have to go back!"

Crispin looks sympathetic but not alarmed, as though he'd guessed this outcry would occur eventually. "We can't. I'm so sorry, Cara. But there's more going on here than you realize, and we can't leave yet. Sophie will be okay."

"What exactly do we have to stay here for?" I ask, my voice lowering dangerously. I'm immediately fiercer and less willing to be led around now that I remember the importance of returning home. I'm angry that I forgot at all. "Sophie is more important to me than some damn adventure with you and James, Crispin! I have to go back. Now." I sink to the ground, the weight of everything suddenly hitting me at once. "Oh God. What is everyone going to think when I don't come home?"

I feel Crispin sit down next to me, but I don't look at him. I'm running through dozens of scenarios in my head at once while, with my knees pulled up to my chest, I stare at the grass by my feet. In every one of them, Sophie is terrified, and my parents are furious (at least, they are when someone tells them what happened).

Out of the corner of my eye, I see something glowing. When I turn my head, I see a thin line of soft green light stretching from Crispin's fingers where they are pressed to the ground at his side. The line winds away from us, disappearing into the trees to our right.

Whatever he's doing, Crispin isn't focused on it. He's watching me.

"I have to go home," I whisper, eyes still on the shining line.

Crispin doesn't respond to that. Instead he explains, "This is for James. The other end will find him and he can follow it back to us. Forget the clearing. We can camp here."

"I thought you said signaling him was too risky," I say.

"It is risky. But we'll be fine," Crispin tells me. "I imagine he's caught something by now. You need the food. And I'll get the fire started for you."

Crispin removes the pack that I've forgotten is on my shoulders and digs into it until he pulls out a thick blanket. He wraps it around me. Then he takes his wood a few feet away and starts piling it together.

Now that he's mentioned it, I'm famished.

"What if James thinks something is wrong?" I ask Crispin as he works. "What if he thinks you're calling to him because we're in trouble?"

"A red line would mean trouble. But green is just a path. We came up with codes for things like this a long time ago." Crispin says.

I pull the blanket more tightly around myself. Crispin digs flint out of the pack and uses it to light a fire with practiced ease. He tends to it for a time before coming to sit next to me again.

"You couldn't do that with magic?" I ask quietly, nodding toward the crackling flames.

Crispin shakes his head. "No. You can't control the elements. Not with any magic that people remember, at any rate." He places an arm gently around my shoulders, and I find myself leaning into him. To my horror, tears spill from my eyes.

"Hush," he tells me softly. "You're all right. You're safe."

"Safe?" I laugh sardonically through my tears. "Crispin, as far as I can tell, there have been two attempts on my life today alone! That's about as far from safe as it gets."

"Nothing is going to happen to you. Not while we're around. We won't let it."

Crispin and I sit in silence, broken only by my sniffling as I try to get my crying under control, until James finally emerges from the trees.

James glances between the two of us questioningly.

"Shock," Crispin says by way of explanation.

"It's about time," James says, dropping whatever is slung across his shoulders to the ground. When I see feet and blood I avert my eyes. Crispin pushes himself to his feet to help James.

"What do you mean, 'it's about time'?" I ask.

"Well come on," James begins, ticking things off on his fingers. "You got attacked, you jumped into another world that you didn't know existed, you were attacked again, you journeyed through some other-worldly woods, learned that Crispin is a prince and that, technically, you're honorary royalty, apparently you were told magic is real, and you're just *now* going into shock? I mean, geez Cara. It's about time."

"It's not shock. I'm tired, and I feel out-of-place, and I just want to go home," I argue, disliking the word. I'm aware that I sound like a little kid.

Crispin sighs. "Cara, do something for me." I glance at him warily, still trying to avoid looking directly at the dead animal on the ground. "Hold out your hand, palm up."

After a moment's hesitation, I do as he asked. Crispin places his broader, more callused hand over the top of mine, so that my fingers are brushing his wrist and his are doing the same to mine. "Close your eyes," he instructs. I do. "Now," he says. "Concentrate."

Before I can ask what on earth I'm supposed to be concentrating on, a shocking pulse courses from Crispin's hand through mine. I pull my hand back sharply just as something unlocks in the middle of my chest with such a burst of intensity that I cry out. It's as though a knot that I never knew existed suddenly loosens and sends both pain and relief coursing through me.

Despite all the other shocks that I've made it through today, I faint.

****

"—and really, *that* was the best way?"

"You know it was. She never would have believed us."

"We still should have told her! She deserved to at least know what you were doing before you ripped it out of her!"

"I didn't rip anything out of her! I showed her something that was in her already."

"Something that made her pass out! Cris, it's been building up in her for sixteen years! You couldn't have found a less painful way to do it?"

"What other way would you suggest, James? You know that I..."

I wake up to the sound of Crispin and James' raised voices. When I move, even a little bit, I can feel an odd lightness in my chest and a throbbing next to my heart. I suck in a deep breath at the feeling and pull myself into a sitting position. James and Crispin's voices cut off immediately.

I blink as I look around. Everything has taken on a weird clarity that I can't explain. James' wide dark eyes are fixed on me anxiously, while Crispin looks merely curious.

"Cara?" Crispin asks. "How do you feel?"

I have a bit of a headache along with the other weirdness, so I simply reply, "Strange."

Crispin nods. "That's not surprising."

I don't say anything. *It's surprising to me.*

James comes over to offer me some kind of meat on a stick. I poke at it suspiciously. James' serious face cracks into a small smile. "It's good," he promises, sitting crossed-legged in front of me. He pulls off a piece and pops it in his mouth. "Could use some salt, but other than that..."

I grimace as I copy him, placing the piece of meat carefully on my tongue. "What is it?" I ask as I chew. It's not bad, James is right. I eat another bite.

"It's better if you don't know," James tells me.

I almost spit it back out at that statement, but it's good, and the more I eat the hungrier I realize I am.

"Crispin," I say as I eat, "what did you do to me?"

Now Crispin does look nervous. He and James exchange quick glances. "I was...showing you that you do belong here," he finally answers, "despite what you may think."

I swallow hard. "What do you mean by that?"

"You have something of Lyria in you. Cara... Somehow you...you have magic."

I drop my meal in my lap, the worry that had been playing quietly in my head coming true, and I cover my ears childishly. "No. No, no no no. I don't. I'm not. No."

No way. No, I don't. This is not happening... I can't handle any more of this.

Rough hands encase mine and remove them from my ears. "That's what he did, Cara. We knew, or at least

Crispin knew, from the first time he met you. Magic calls to magic. I felt it too, eventually. You wouldn't have fainted, you wouldn't have felt anything, if you weren't magic. That's how it works. Crispin opened it up for you." James is leaning toward me, our hands held between us. He looks calm. He truly is not surprised, and he's not lying.

Fear, excitement, and curiosity overwhelm me. "H-how, did you know?"

"You can feel it," James says. "If you try. Come on, let us prove it to you." He places my hands in my lap and lets go. "Reach out, with that part of you that Cris called out, and find me. Close your eyes."

"This is ridiculous," I mutter. But I do it. I want to know if I can.

After some internal fumbling, I figure out how to concentrate on the aching emptiness in the middle of my chest. And after I discover it I can focus on pushing it past me; I instinctively know how to search for the same thing in someone else. Then I find it.

It feels like a pulsing, rippling thread of energy stretches from James to me. At the same instantaneous moment that I feel it, I know that what James has and what I have are two completely different things. They are both magic, sure, but his is darker and slower while what I have collides with his in a wild kind of force.

Before I have any time to figure out the difference, James' presence is eclipsed by Crispin's. His power hits me like a wave and drives me to open my eyes, which breaks the connection. I have to take a couple deep breaths to steady myself. The lightness is gone, but the empty space is still in my chest.

Wide-eyed, I stare at them both.

"Well?" James asks cautiously.

"I felt it. You, I mean. And then Crispin kind of took over. But, I felt you guys. How is that possible?"

"We don't really have to explain it again, do we?" Crispin asks me.

I make a face at him. "No. I understand. Magic. You don't have to be all smug about it. But if I'm not Lyrian..." I look at them. "I'm not Lyrian, am I?"

"No," Crispin assures me. "You're not. And we're not quite sure yet what gives you the power you have. But we've been trying to find you for a long time."

James immediately stands up and walks toward the fire. His back is stiff, and he apparently has no desire to be part of the conversation anymore.

"That's...kind of creepy," I tell them as I watch James walk away. "How long is a long time?"

"Cris," James says warningly from his place by the flames, "you're pushing it."

Crispin gives no sign that he's heard his friend, but his answer is a bit more vague than it might have otherwise been. "We've known for many, many years that there was someone in your world who would be able to cast. We just didn't know it was you. We don't know exactly how whatever this is works. I promise you that, if we did, we'd be explaining it to you right now. Cara, you were made to be here. You were made for this. How can you still not believe us?"

"It's not that I don't believe you," I tell him as I pull up handfuls of grass. "I mean, I kind of have to. The proof of it all is literally right in front of me. But I don't know how to let go of everything else I've been taught. The normal, rational part of me will not allow me to accept that this is possible. But apparently every other part of me knows that it is." I rub the spot in the middle of my chest that's still aching. "Even parts of me that aren't supposed to really exist."

Crispin notes the movement. "Oh!" he exclaims. "I'm sorry! I forgot all about that." He hurries over to me and pulls me to my feet. "Usually children are learning magic as soon as they can speak. But if it lays dormant as long as yours has, then when you release it, it has all those years of not being used to make up for."

I follow his explanation without really understanding any of it. He pauses for a moment to think. "So... I've got it! Do this." Crispin makes some gesture with his fingers that's too fast for me to follow.

"I would, but..." I say.

"You went way too quickly, Cris," James tells him. He's watching us carefully.

Crispin makes the same motion again, just as rapidly.

"All right," I say. "You're not even trying now."

James chuckles. "Here." He comes to stand with us again and takes my right hand in his left. "First, you need to use your dominant hand. Eventually you can cast with both hands, two at once probably, but your right hand will be the strongest. So don't copy Crispin exactly." The look he gives Crispin suggests Crispin should have thought to tell me this. "Now." His rough hand manipulates my fingers until they're the way he wants them.

"You want me to make shadow puppets?" I ask. The way my fingers are positioned makes it look like a shadow puppet dog.

James shakes his head. "You're going to twist your wrist so that your palm is up, and as you do so rearrange your fingers so that the pinky and ring finger are pointing out, and your pointer finger and middle finger are pressed to your thumb like your middle two fingers are now. And push your hand away from you at the end."

I give him a blank stare. He demonstrates, and then Crispin demonstrates faster.

"Are you sure this is the cast you want to start her with?" James asks Crispin as they take a few steps away from me.

"We have to fill the whole void in her chest. Might as well do it all at once." Crispin says.

James gives me a weak thumbs-up. "Whenever you're ready. Just, make sure you aren't pointing that hand at us. How about that rock over there?" he suggests.

I eye my own hand before trying what they showed me. I fumble the motion the first couple times, but when I get it right heat courses between my chest and the tips of my fingers. Pressure builds at my fingertips, and when I finally shove my hand away from me, the pressure releases instantly. And the boulder I gestured toward flies from its age-old seat on the forest floor, crashes against a tree, and cracks its trunk.

I stare at the damage for a long time. "Oh, wow," I finally whisper.

When I turn to look at the boys, they seem a bit awestruck. "That is not what I expected," Crispin murmurs.

James grins at me suddenly. "We told you. You belong here."

And it's in that moment when I hear his confidence that I finally give it all up. All the fear and worry that they're playing some elaborate joke on me—that this is some kind of hoax or illusion that they've conjured up—vanishes. I laugh a bit breathlessly. "I want to do that again."

Crispin and James join in my laughter as though they can't believe it. And maybe they can't. I've been fighting them all day. But it doesn't get any more real than that.

"That was me?" I ask, just to be sure.

"That was all you," James promises. "Feel any better?"

My headache is gone, the empty feeling in my chest has disappeared, and I feel lighter and happier than I have all day. "Amazingly, yes."

"Good," he smiles.

"So part of me, at least, really does belong here. If magic is solely a Lyrian thing, that is."

"It is," Crispin assures me.

"*But*," I continue. "That doesn't mean I can stay. How do I know things will be okay at home? Can't we go back, just for a bit, so I can at the very least have a plan to keep Sophie taken care of?"

James is shaking his head. "Cara, it's too dangerous. The safest place for you, so we can figure out what's going on, why you can do that," he gestures to the fallen boulder, "is Geler. As soon as we can though, the moment we can, we'll take you home."

Because I'm finally convinced that they mean well and that I have no choice but to place whatever trust I have left fully in these boys, I accept the answer.

13

It feels like the instant I finally shut my eyes that night to get some well-earned rest, morning light is forcing them open again.

I groan. Sleeping in jeans is hardly comfortable in the best of times, but when a soft bed is traded for the cold ground of a forest floor, somehow the jeans become even less comfortable. My eyes are unbelievably heavy, and all of me aches. But I eventually push myself upright.

James and Crispin appear to have been awake for a while now. They're sitting around the cold remains of last night's fire and eating something. James tosses me a piece when he sees me stirring.

"When did we get jerky?" I ask after examining it and chew on one end hungrily.

"In the packs," James tells me. "It makes a better breakfast than it does dinner, or we would have eaten it last night."

As I glance around our makeshift campsite, I see everything that had been unpacked the night before is neatly replaced in a sack. Crispin and James are dressed, armed, and now that I'm awake they stow my blanket in the bag it came from.

The forest is less alarming than it had been yesterday, most likely because of the soft light of morning. Nothing seems as bad in the light of day as it does at night, the way horror movies are only frightening once it gets dark outside.

"I'll be back," Crispin says to James and me. He hauls the same pack we retrieved last night onto his back and strides into the trees.

I look to James questioningly, still blinking sleep from my eyes. "We don't need those anymore," James says. "We'll get supplies in Kayyar, and we already put the food we'll need for the rest of the day in the other bag. So he's returning that to its hiding spot."

"Oh," I say as I bite off another piece of jerky contemplatively.

The moment Crispin returns he says jovially: "Let's move out!"

I follow the boys silently as we cross the river from yesterday and I take my first steps up the hills on the other side. All the while I think about how far I'm getting from home.

James and Crispin leave me to my thoughts, but they seem pleased when I catch my breath at the top of the first hill.

It's not that the sight is spectacular. Away from the trees, however, away from the forest that both hid us and closed us in, the wide-open space before me is daunting. The hills, sloping gently all the way to the horizon, continue as far as I can see. The tall grass is green and yellow and it is unbroken by buildings or roads or towers. And the peace is captivating. Not a car or a plane or a person in sight.

"It's so big," I say. I feel silly for stating the obvious as soon as the words leave my mouth. But they understand.

"It's the world," James says. Then he smiles softly. "A world, at least."

After telling me about the small town we're headed for, the boys and I become quiet again, and we pass most of the journey this way. I have a million more questions, but I figure that I won't get any straight answers for most of them. As for the others, I think I might not really want to know the answers after all.

So I focus on everything that I have learned, and that's enough to keep me busy.

The first time I'm snapped out of my reverie is when, instead of grass, Crispin and James and I begin walking along a dirt path.

"Where did this come from?" I ask them.

"It's the road into town," Crispin says. "We have about an hour left."

I frown. "We're closer than I thought." I'm suddenly increasingly nervous about the village we're headed to. I don't know what to do around other people. I may be lost in this world, but I'm lost with two boys that I've come to know rather well. That isn't true of the people we're about to meet.

Crispin and James seem aware of my nerves. They start to slow down and I know they're about to try to console me, so I wipe any anxiety from my face. "Good," I say, trying to sound upbeat. "I need some new clothes."

"We'll get you some," Crispin, not at all fooled by my act, tells me. "Soon enough."

I grimace, but we all stop talking again.

James and Crispin also become more apprehensive as we approach the town. They glance around more often, stay closer to me, and Crispin flexes his fingers a lot—a nervous twitch of his that I now can associate with his getting ready to cast at a moment's notice.

Their nervous energy reminds me of the times they've fought for me. I realize that, both times I saw, neither of them used any kind of magic to win. Not that they needed it, but it seems to be Crispin's first instinct and quite an advantage. So I ask them about it.

"Why did you guys fight those thieves in The Scarlet Letter hand to hand? And Panus. When he attacked, why did you fight him? Why didn't you use magic? Is Panus magical? And if so, why didn't he cast either?"

I think Crispin and James seem to have been waiting for me to question them because they both smile as I reel off my inquiries.

"Remember how I said magic and technology don't mix? How they interfere with one another? Technology, science in general, stops working when magic is used near it. So in the bookstore? The light bulbs most likely would have burst if either James or I had cast," Crispin answers. "Your phone would have fried in your pocket, and the streetlights might have popped too. Especially since we were so angry. Magic used in anger or fear is less controlled.

"And it's not as though we needed it to win the fights," Crispin echoes my thoughts exactly. "It was a closer call with Panus. I thought he might try something. But I suppose even he would know how much unnecessary attention it would have attracted. It's hard to keep this all a secret if you walk around Earth casting and leave trails of broken technology in your wake."

He begins rummaging around in the pack he's been carrying. Shaking out his blonde curls, Crispin places the crown I'd forgotten about on his head. James gives me a quick, unexplained once over, and then Crispin says: "We're here."

I don't see the town until we come to the top of the next rise.

It's still a few minutes of walking away, but I take that time to study it as we near. The small buildings are built with white and tan stones, and they spread out across the hills. The road we're on widens as it reaches the village and cuts straight through some of the hills; shops of some kind line the street, probably for easy access for those passing through. The buildings stretch away from us for miles.

As we slowly approach, the people that are milling about the streets look up at us. Those who recognize us, or rather, Crispin, nudge those around them and they all hastily drop to the ground. I was walking next to him, but I fall behind to walk with James instead. Crispin strides ahead with his head high, and he is so naturally royal that I almost bow down myself.

My heart is flying in my chest. These people are all dressed plainly, in similar but less elegant clothes than James and Crispin. I am conspicuously out of place. With just the boys to keep me company it hadn't been a problem. But here, surrounded by others that belonged in this world...

James again seems to sense my nervousness. He reaches over and squeezes my hand. "Just stay back with me," he says. "Let Cris do his thing."

I grip his hand tightly for reassurance.

When we reach the edge of the town, a gray-haired man, still bent at the waist, comes running up to us. "Crown Prince," he gushes. "Welcome, welcome. Is there anything that you require of us today?"

"Raffin," Crispin says, kindly but still sounding lordly. "Yes, thank you. My friends and I require horses, as well as new clothes for Lady Cara here."

Lady Cara? Raffin looks up at James and me when Crispin mentions his friends. His gaze slides over James, avoiding his eyes, but rest on me long enough I can tell he's wondering who I am. Then he once-overs my clothing and, if Crispin had not been standing there, I swear he would have sneered at me.

"Is that all?" Raffin asks, clearly wanting to do something for Prince Crispin himself.

"Yes," Crispin replies firmly. "Quickly, if you will."

"Of course," Raffin tells him as he bows even lower. Then the people that had been kneeling nearby stand and back away into shops or houses, except for one woman with graying hair who stands and bows at the waist as Raffin had.

"Lady," she says to me without meeting my eye, "if you'll come with me, I can find some suitable clothing for you."

Wide-eyed, I look at the boys. I have no idea how to answer.

Crispin catches my look and hurriedly answers for me, "Tendri, thank you. James is going to accompany Cara, if you don't mind, while I fetch horses for the rest of our journey." He fishes in the bag of coins that he's tied around his waist and pulls out a few silver pieces that he presses in her hand. "Now, pardon me." And Crispin marches off in the direction Raffin went.

When he leaves, Tendri straightens and gazes at me shrewdly. She ignores James completely. In fact, everyone is ignoring James, avoiding him, going out of their way to walk around him. I can't figure out why. But he pretends not to notice. He's still holding my hand, and now I feel as though I'm the one reassuring him. I don't let go.

"Follow me," Tendri says shortly. She turns and walks a different way than Crispin had gone. I watch Crispin's retreating figure for a moment before I follow Tendri.

She takes us to a little shop down the main road. There are no signs, but the shop we walk into has a beautifully simple dress hanging in the window and rolls of fabric leaning against the walls, so I'm able to guess it's a tailor's. The store is empty when we enter.

"What is it that you are looking for today, Lady?" Tendri asks.

I look around blankly. James doesn't offer any help. "Umm..." I say. "I actually am not entirely sure."

Tendri accepts my answer as though she was expecting it. "Well, we don't want you to dress too far below your rank," she says, mostly to herself, "but Prince Crispin is not traveling grandly, and you don't want to attract unwanted attention nor outshine him..."

"No, we wouldn't want that," James muses quietly.

Tendri makes no sign that she has heard him. "But you mustn't be outshone by *him,* either." I can't tell which of the boys she is referring to.

Then she's off pulling pieces from different dresses and stacking them in my arms. I reluctantly let go of James to keep the pieces from falling to the ground.

"There," Tendri tells me. I stare at the pile of fabric I'm holding, having no idea where to start. James chuckles quietly, pulls a tight, sheer dress from the pile, and steers me toward a changing room, saying, "That goes on first."

I leave on my own undergarments, pulling on the short white dress James showed me first. Then I lay everything else out and try unsuccessfully to piece the outfit together. "Hello?" I call out eventually. "Could one of you guys help me out?" For a moment, there is silence on the other side of the changing room door, then a chair scrapes back and someone approaches.

James opens the door and looks at me lazily. "Can't get dressed?"

I feel my face flame, well aware that I have so little on. I had assumed, though I'd asked for either of them, that Tendri would be the one who came to help.

Apparently unembarrassed, James is still watching me. He closes the door behind him and shuts us together in the small room.

Without another word, he brushes past me and begins handing me one piece at a time. "Leggings, riding skirt, shirt, overdress—"

"Why are there skirts, shirts, and dresses?" I ask. No wonder I couldn't--figure it out.

"Just put it on," James says.

I pull on a long, lightweight, chocolate-brown skirt—the riding skirt, as it has slits halfway up both the front and back—over loose, blue leggings and tuck in a cream-colored shirt that looks much like the ones Crispin and James have on, only this one is cut differently to fit me. In this confined space, I'm too aware of James as I dress; I'm careful not to brush against him.

Last to go on is a green, sleeveless dress that has buttons trailing from my chest to my waist, and then V's out around my riding skirt. It is similar, again, to the vests James and Crispin are wearing.

"Good?" I ask James, holding my arms out for him to examine the finished product.

He studies me carefully before responding. He then reaches out (not far, in this little space) and straightens the collar of the shirt. He lets his fingers linger my neck longer than necessary. "You look like you belong here."

I can tell from the glow in his eyes that it's a compliment.

Too soon, he drops his hands and opens the door for me. I step out of the small room to stand in front of Tendri, and I twirl once when she motions for it so that she can see the back of the outfit.

"Perfect," she tells me, and I hear James murmur in agreement. I want to look at him; I want to see if he's still looking at me the way he was a moment ago, even though I know that he isn't. He'd never let Tendri see that look, especially with the distant way she's been acting toward him.

I see Tendri rummaging behind the counter. As I'm about to ask what she's looking for, she straightens up and is holding a light blue scarf. "We need to do something about your hair, Lady," she says by way of explanation.

"What's wrong with my hair?" I ask, reaching up protectively as if she's suggested tearing it from my head.

"You stick out like a sore thumb with it uncovered," James answers. "You didn't notice?"

"Notice what?" I reluctantly sit down on a stool so Tendri can wrap the scarf around my head.

"Cara, Demesnians are blonde," James tells me. "Almost all of them. It has to do with the history. You really didn't see that when we got here?"

I think hard, back to my first glimpse of the people in the town. I hadn't exactly been paying attention to them.

"Come here," James says, leading me to a window. I look out, studying the people that pass by. Some have strawberry blonde hair, others more honey-colored like Max, some white-blonde, but, sure enough, no one has a hair color other than yellow. I turn back to Tendri. Her hair is mostly gray, but I can see sandy streaks that haven't faded yet. And then I stare at James for a moment, causing him to run an uncomfortable hand through his black hair. *So he's not Demesnian, then?* I wonder. But I decide not to ask. Not yet.

"Why...? How?" I begin, not sure how to phrase the question I actually want to ask.

Again, Tendri takes my lack of knowledge in stride. "That may be something best explained to you by the young men you're traveling with. You have a long enough journey ahead of you. Plenty of time.

"Now," she says, handing me a pair of brown boots, "since there's nothing to be done about your eye color, put these on and be off with you. You can't keep the young prince waiting."

James makes a noise of disagreement, but I shoot him a look that silences him. It's probably best not to cause a prince to lose face in front of his subjects.

"Wait!" I say as James starts to walk me out of the shop. "What about my clothes?"

"Your Earth clothes?" James asks me.

"No," I manage to say sarcastically. "My *other* clothes."

He smiles faintly. "You don't need them anymore, Cara."

I want to explain how those clothes are *mine*; how they're the last link I have right now to home. I need them with me. But, "I want them," is all I say.

And that's enough for James. He nods to Tendri. She drags a small knapsack out from a pile of things behind the counter and hands it to James, who passes it to me. "Go get them," he says. I hurry into the small back room and stuff my jeans, shirt, and Converse sneakers into the pack.

I remember Sophie helping me pick out these clothes only yesterday (though it feels like a lifetime ago), and a sharp ache of worry and longing shoots through me. I have to push it away, close up the sack, and rejoin James in the main room.

When he's ready to be gone and gesturing pointedly to the door, I give a startled Tendri a grateful hug, sling the knapsack over my shoulders, and follow James away through the streets of Kayyar to find Crispin.

****

James leads me toward the opposite end of town. We avoid the crowds by taking the back roads. Eventually we come to a shop, set a distance apart from the others, with a large building behind it that I soon see is a stable. Crispin is out in front talking to Raffin, who looks disgruntled. There are two horses standing nearby, saddled and bridled; one is pure white and the other is a dappled grey.

"Cara!" Crispin calls, waving me over when he spots us. I hurry to him and James follows more slowly. "Lady Cara, please tell this man that you can ride a horse."

I look at Raffin. "I can ride a horse." It comes out more as a question, because I can't see where this is going.

"A lady should not have to care for her own horse," Raffin sniffs. "And I was under the impression that *he*," Raffin nods at James, "did not ride."

"But today he will," Crispin says firmly, "so we will require the brown mare I've requested."

If it had been anyone other than Prince Crispin asking, I imagine that Raffin would have stormed off and locked up his shop after being told off. As it is, he merely bows and enters the stable again.

"I don't like that guy," Crispin tells me with a shrug, "but I need him."

When Raffin leads the mare out, Crispin presses a heavy gold coin in his hand. "We'll take it from here. Thank you for your service, Raffin."

Raffin doesn't say a word, he only nods stiffly, bows, and strides into his shop. I can see him watching us from his window though.

"James," Crispin says, "if you'll saddle your horse up, Cara and I will get the other two ready." The other two horses look ready enough to me, but I follow Crispin over to them anyway. He checks the straps and readjusts the saddlebags.

Out of the corner of my eye, I see James approaching the brown mare cautiously, speaking to her softly and gently. She's skittish, and I almost expect her to shy away when he reaches out a hand to pat her neck, but she only lays her ears back and stiffens. I don't know that much about horses, but it seems like an odd reaction to me.

Slowly, James gets her ready, and he speaks to her all the while.

"You really can ride, can't you?" Crispin asks, sliding the knapsack off my shoulders.

"Trust me, I would not have said I could if I couldn't. I have enough going on without lying about knowing how to ride a horse." Horseback riding was a popular activity in some of the states I'd lived in, so my parents had broken down one year and got me lessons.

"Good," Crispin says, relief in his voice. "That would've made this quite difficult." He digs through the pack quickly and looks up at me with raised eyebrows. "Why are you keeping these?"

"Because they're mine. Can we just get going?" I ask. "I'll feel better when we're out of this town."

"And on to a bigger one?" Crispin grins. But he cups his hands together so I can step into them and mount the gray mare. He pats her neck before attaching the sack to my horse's saddle. He walks away to mount his own horse. "James, you ready over there?"

"Just about," James calls over.

Crispin swings himself up on his own mount. "That's Misty," he tells me and nods to my horse. "James has Ebony," he continues. I dubiously glance over at the brown horse. "I know," Crispin says. "Not my idea. I think she may have looked darker when she was a filly. And I have affectionately dubbed my own stallion Tumble."

I raise my eyebrows. "Tumble? The fierce white stallion?"

He chuckles. "You should've seen him as a foal. He could barely walk. He fell all over the place. Tumble is quite appropriate."

"If you say so," I say with a smile.

James finally has Ebony ready. He mounts and, with a cheeky wave to where Raffin is still watching us from his store, he wheels his horse around and starts off. Crispin and I follow.

****

For a time, the three of us ride in companionable silence. James and Crispin are riding ahead of me, and every so often one of them speeds into a gallop, only to swing around a few minutes later and rejoin the other two of us.

I have enough to think about to last me the entire journey, but I figure I also need more information than I currently have before we arrive in Geler, which is who-knows-how-far away.

So, after I decide on which of my questions is the most important, I spur Misty on to catch up with the boys. James speeds away again as I approach, so, original question already forgotten, I ask Crispin, "Why do you two keep doing that?"

"Just keeping an eye out, getting a different view. Better safe than sorry," Crispin says.

"Mm-hmm. Whatever you say," I reply. And then I remember why I sped up in the first place. "Ooh, I meant to ask you something."

"A real surprise. You, with a question?" Crispin pretends to be shocked.

I make a face at him as I reach up to adjust the scarf fixed around my head. "When I was in the tailor's shop with Tendri and James, they pointed out that not having blonde hair in Demesne makes you stand out. They also said something about my eye color, which I assume means people here don't have brown eyes. But one of them mentioned that it had something to do with the history. Of Demesne or Lyria, I'm not sure which."

When I pause, Crispin says, "I didn't hear the question you were dying to ask."

"What history were they talking about?"

"Ah," Crispin sighs. "Cara, I really do want to give you answers. But that's something best explained by someone else. It's a long story, and we'll have more time for it later."

I huff out a breath, expecting the "we can't tell you now" response but still disappointed by it. "Fine," I say. "We can talk about something else, then. Like... Crown Prince, huh?"

Crispin seems to grimace. "You caught that, did you? You're more observant than I've given you credit for."

"True fact," I say, pleased. "But *Crown* Prince? That makes you...that means you're the next king? Of the kingdom?"

"I'm the next 'king of the kingdom'?" Crispin repeats, chuckling.

"Mock all you want," I say, "but that's a big deal, Crispin. I thought you being a prince was big, but Crown Prince?"

"Yes, Cara," he nods. "Crown Prince."

James canters up just then, reigning in his horse to ride next to me. He clearly heard Crispin's comment because he adds to the conversation, "Crown Prince Crispin. That's what happens when you're the seventh son. Of a seventh son, no less. And since that's the case, no matter who is the eldest, Crispin is the next king."

I recall James mentioning the day before that there was an exception to the eldest-child-inherits-the-throne rule. "Seventh son of a seventh son," I repeat. "Sounds fancy." Then the rest of James' proclamation hits me. "You're not the oldest?" I ask Crispin. And then, finally, I realize: "You have six brothers? And you never mentioned any of them?"

"No, I'm not the oldest," Crispin replies after deliberating for a moment about which question to answer first. "I'm the second youngest of eleven children."

Before he can finish the rest of his answer, in the distance I see something gliding over the hills. I pull back on the reigns and stop Misty in her tracks. The boys circle around me.

"What's the hold-up?" James asks.

"Umm..." I say. "I saw something. Coming this way. I think. Hang on." I ride to the top of the next hill then stop there to scan the horizon. For a few seconds, all I see are empty green hills and blue skies. Finally I find it again. "There!" I call out. Crispin and James ride up next to me. "There, do you see it? It looks like another rider."

Without a word Crispin and James pull long knives from their boots.

I eye them nervously. "Do I get a weapon?" I ask, worried.

"No," Crispin says, "if this is an attack then you'll get out of here as fast as you can ride."

"I don't think so," I tell him. "If this is an attack then I'm not leaving you all again. I'm so sick of running. Besides, what's one lone horseback rider going to do against three people?"

Crispin glares at me. "That wasn't a suggestion, Cara. This could be anyone."

"Yes, it could. Which is why I'm staying right here. We have the magical Crown Prince of the kingdom standing here with his friend who fought off an army back in the forest. And I can do that hand thing." I demonstrate what they showed me last night. "I believe our chances of victory are quite high."

Crispin looks furious, but James hands me his own knife. "You win," he says, dismounting. Crispin glares at him too.

"What are you doing?" I ask James. The rider is getting closer. "How are you going to fight a man on horseback from the ground?"

"It's just a precaution," James answers.

Before I have time to ask what possible precaution getting off your horse in the face of danger is, Crispin asks James, "Hey. Don't we know that horse?"

James sets a foot in his stirrup and pulls himself up to have a look. A slow smile spreads over his face. "She is going to be in so much trouble," he says by way of reply.

Crispin waves his knife in the air, and it takes me a moment to see that he's catching the sun on the blade, which clearly signals to the rider. She changes direction slightly to meet us.

"So, no fight?" I ask, relieved, as I pass James his knife back.

Crispin laughs. "Cara, get ready to meet my younger sister, Sasha."

"How much younger?" I say, wondering how old you have to be in this place to ride out alone into the empty stretch of land where there is no town for miles.

"About three minutes," Crispin answers.

It takes a moment for that to sink in. "You're a twin?" I gasp. "And you never told me?" I repeat my previous question.

He looks at me with a shrug. "When was I supposed to tell you? On earth you would have wondered why she wasn't at school with us, and here there hasn't really been an easy way to work it into a conversation."

"That's true," I concede. Sasha is barreling toward us in a full speed gallop. She'll be here in seconds. "What do I do?" I hurriedly ask the boys. "How should I act? What do I say?"

"Cara," Crispin smiles. "Relax."

Sasha skids to a stop in front of us. She's grinning from ear to ear as she jumps expertly off her horse before it has come to a full halt. "I was wondering when you were going to show up again! It's been a long time."

Crispin and James dismount to greet her warmly. I follow suit by sliding off Misty and approaching Sasha. She's beautiful, with the same sandy-blonde hair as Crispin, only hers is twisted in to a knot on the top of her head. Her eyes are sky-blue, and she has an open face with a splash of freckles across her nose. She is the kind of girl who, back on earth, could simply roll out bed and look like a model for messy hair and pajamas.

Sasha, obviously curious, turns her attention to me. I'm not sure whether I should be nervous or not, and goodness knows Crispin and James aren't being any help at all, but Sasha smiles kindly at me and puts me at ease. She looks slightly troubled, like she was expecting someone else and got me instead.

I feel like I should curtsy, her being a princess and all, but I don't know how. Sasha solves my problem by awkwardly holding out a hand for me to shake. I take it gratefully.

"I'm Cara," I tell her.

My ring is now turned the right way, not hidden like I used to wear it, but if she notices it's a royal ring that I'm not technically supposed to have, Sasha doesn't comment on it. She just introduces herself.

"Hi, Cara. I'm Sasha. I'm Crispin's sister." She leaves off her title, which makes me like her more than if she had used it. She is also almost exactly my height. That means I don't have to look up at her, a fact that makes me oddly happy.

"Our parents are going to kill you," Crispin sings, practically skipping over to join us.

She looks at him with innocent eyes. "What makes you think they didn't give me permission? Or that there isn't a team of guards riding right behind me?"

Crispin just gazes at her steadily, a tell-the-truth look in his eyes.

Sasha sighs. "Fine. They'll be mad. In my defense, the guards shouldn't make it so easy for me to slip away. And bringing you all back should help soften the blow, don't you think?"

Her eyes dart back to me as she speaks, and I am suddenly struck with a memory. That look, it's a watered-down version of the hopeful, yet almost frightened glance of disbelief that James gave me that day in The Scarlet Letter, and that I have been waiting to see on Crispin and him ever since then. A look that seems to show they know something I don't, and they don't want to tell me, but they wonder if I know anyway.

My heart pounds just a little faster as I'm faced with the fact that maybe I don't want to know the answers to the questions I've been asking.

James is the only one who appears to notice my wide-eyed expression. He meets my eyes and holds them calmly. Then he shakes his head, almost imperceptibly, so I clear the expression from my face before Sasha and Crispin see it.

"Let's keep moving," James says loudly, interrupting the brother-sister discussion the other two have started up. Sasha looks to him with a smile that suggests she has just won the argument with Crispin, and James smiles back. An irrational surge of envy floods through me. But I snuff it out, shaking my head at my own silliness.

Forgotten for the moment as those three have their reunion, I take my place slightly behind the group as we mount up again. Now when we start off it is the boys that pester Sasha with questions: what's been happening in Geler since they left last, how people I've never heard of are doing, and the like. I want to like Sasha as they do, but with her joining us, I feel like the outsider once again.

So I spend some time admiring the scenery (grassy hills as far as the eye can see), and then I straighten Misty's mane (an impossible task, with the wind), and then quit putting it off and decide to eavesdrop because I think their conversation might give me more information than I'd get if I asked some of my questions directly.

What I actually hear them saying is much different than I expected. With a sinking certainty, I realize that they aren't talking about Geler anymore, but about me.

"—really think it's her?" Sasha is asking the boys.

Crispin answers. "Yes. We don't see how it can be, and we don't want her to have to be, but come on Sasha, you saw the ring. We felt the tie to her, even on Earth. And she cast last night. That's about as clear as it can get. And, get this, she's lived in eight states. Eight! No wonder we could never find her, she kept moving. The last two were states called Arizona and Minnesota, exactly where we were. That can't be a coincidence."

"Yes, it could be," Sasha argues. "It could be Cris. I just... It can't be her." Then she asks a serious question. Doubtful, but hopeful at the same time. "How could she save the world?"

I feel like I've just been punched in the gut; there's a hollow feeling in my stomach. I freeze. I can't breath.

Maybe they aren't talking about me. But...who else could they be talking about? Who else has a ring, has lived in eight states, just moved from Minnesota and Arizona?

I start to fall behind, way behind, and Misty does nothing to keep up now that I'm not spurring her on.

Eventually they must notice that I'm not following them closely anymore because when I look up James is heading back toward me.

"You doing okay back here?" he calls out as he approaches.

I can't answer. My lips won't form actual words. I'm numb, but I can feel terror clawing inside me, waiting for its chance to get out.

James starts to look worried as he gets closer. Sasha and Crispin have stopped up ahead.

"Cara?" he asks anxiously. "What happened? Are you okay?"

This is worse than anything else they've told me about. Harder to take than anything else they've shown me. This is impossible.

I finally look him in the eye. But all I can say is: "What were you guys talking about?"

With those words, I know that he knows what I heard.

"How much did you listen to?" he asks.

I gaze at him helplessly. "Umm...just...enough. I listened to enough."

Now James is watching me with regret plain in his eyes. "You weren't supposed..." he trails off, the end of the thought obvious to us both.

"You guys should probably look behind you more often," I manage.

James nods mutely. "Probably," he eventually agrees.

We sit there on our mounts, staring at each other, neither of us knowing what to say.

"I can't... I don't..." I stop trying to talk, and James doesn't say anything.

The awful thing is, so much more makes sense now. James and Crispin's "problem" they were looking for an answer to, the answer they found. The weird way they acted at school, not talking to anyone until I came along. Their startling reaction to my ring.

"How long have you known?" I ask James.

He shakes his head. "We still don't," he tells me firmly. It sounds like he's trying to convince himself as much as me.

"Crispin sounded pretty sure," I say.

James doesn't have an answer to that. "Please Cara," he says. "We weren't going to tell you until you were ready, until we could make it all make sense to you, but since that didn't work out... Please just let us explain. There are people back in Geler that will know what to do."

"I don't know if I can," I whisper. "James, I don't understand."

James looks sympathetic. "I know you don't. We're not sure what this means Cara, but we need to figure it out. And we need your help to do that."

I start to protest, I don't know how to help, but James stops me. "Cara, people know you're here now. And they think the same thing we do. Panus, those people in the woods, that wasn't chance. They were coming for you because they know what we found out. Only they're trying to stop you. We have to get you to safety. Please. We have to get to Geler."

My heart is pounding and I'm having trouble thinking straight, but if what he's saying is true, then I want to get to Geler soon. So I nod. "Can we hurry?" I ask James.

"Of course," James says softly. "Let's go."

He turns Ebony around and I do the same with Misty. With a nod at me, he urges Ebony forward, from a trot to a canter and then to a full-out gallop. I'm right behind him with the wind stinging my eyes and giving me an excuse for having tears sliding down my cheeks.

Crispin and Sasha see us coming, and they start off too, still ahead of us. Though the ride is still long, we don't slow down until the city we've been waiting to reach comes into sight.

14

How could she save the world? How could she save the world? Sasha's voice resounds in my head; I can't think around it, can't get past it.

Glancing anxiously in my direction every few minutes, James continues to watch me as we ride. He ignores Crispin and Sasha when they shout questions to him, so eventually they too fall silent.

More horseback riders join us as we near the city. The sprawling buildings of Geler mirror those we saw in Kayyar—though bigger and spreading as far as I can see—and they circle a tall stone wall over the top of which the towers of the castle are visible. The riders are all dressed in blue so dark it's almost black; they wear swords at their sides.

They come charging at us when they first see us approaching, but with a signal from Crispin, they shift to form ranks around us and match their horses' paces with ours. People clear the main road up to the wall for us, so we gallop on. There is an iron gate that sits in front of a giant sturdy-looking door made of metal and wood; both the door and gate swing open as we advance toward them and shut quickly behind us.

Once we pass through these, there is an extensive green lawn and garden leading up to the double doors of the palace that Crispin, Sasha, and James call home.

I get a quick glimpse of the massive building standing before me. It's beautifully constructed of tan and brown stone with towers that stretch to the sky; some stained glass windows pepper the façade, and guards studiously patrol the grounds.

Then, before the horses even come to a complete stop, people flood out of the front door and head straight for us. James leaps lightly off his still moving mount and grabs Misty's reigns from me. He brings her to a swift halt before lifting me down and putting his arms around me protectively to shield me.

"Sasha!" he calls out. "Keep them all away. Keep them busy. Cris, I need you with me!" And then, like I feel we've done too many times already, James and I take off running, him pulling me along with Crispin hot on our tail.

I don't understand why they're hiding me from everyone, but I don't really mind. The last thing I could handle right now is being bombarded with questions from strangers—questions that I won't be able to answer.

The three of us avoid the front entrance where people are still streaming out. Instead I'm led around to the side of the castle and through a small door. Neither of the boys stop. We scurry down halls and up staircases, so quickly that there is no time to take anything in. I only catch flashes of things: richly woven tapestries on the walls, thick carpets lining some of the hallways, startled passersby that dive out of our way.

We climb endless flights of stairs, turn countless corners; any sense of direction I have is soon gone. Finally, James halts us in front of a small door. Crispin gives James a fleeting look of unease, and then he seems to realize something as he takes in my frightened face.

"She knows?" he asks, trying to catch his breath.

"She knows," James affirms. And with that, he pushes open the door and we slip inside.

The room we've entered is tiny with stone walls and barely any furnishings. A small table is placed by the door with a lone, lit lantern sitting on it. There is a bed with a single sheet and a thin pillow set against the far wall that looks as though it hasn't been used for years. And there is an empty washbasin on yet another wall with a small wooden chair placed next to it. Except for the writing carved into the wall on my right, there is nothing else in the room.

Some of the engravings are pictures; still others are phrases or sentences that make no sense to me. But there are three carvings that are lengthy and structured in such a way that they resemble poems. Most of the writing on one of these three has been worn away, yet the second is still mostly intact, and the last is in pristine condition. It looks as though it was written recently.

Crispin pulls the chair over to me and I sit down gratefully, not sure my own legs will support me much longer. James moves the lantern from the rickety table and uses it to light three others placed at intervals along the written-on wall.

"How much did you listen to?" Crispin asks me the very same question James asked before.

"A lot." I pause. "I heard something about me—you describing me to Sasha—and then...Sasha asking how I could save the world," I say quietly. "But she must be mistaken or confused or something because...because she couldn't have been talking about me. And saving the world is something out of superhero movies. Not real life."

"And what part of your journey here thus far *has* been something out of your real life?" James asks, already knowing the answer.

Even as frightened as I am, I can still shoot him an irate glare.

"I'm just saying," James shrugs. He's trying to sound lighthearted, but his searching gaze gives away the seriousness of the situation I've recently landed in.

"You said you'd explain things to me when we reached Geler," I tell James. "Now we're here. So? Will you explain?"

James fixes his eyes on me for a moment without a word, and then he walks over and turns my chair so that I'm facing the written-on wall. He points at the long poem that looks new. "Read that," he says to me, "and then ask your questions."

So, after looking at both Crispin and James again once, I focus on the poem in front of me. It stretches from the ceiling all the way to the floor and is written clumsily, as though the author wasn't sure what he was doing or wasn't paying very close attention when he wrote it. And as I read it, I realize that it's more than just a poem. I think it's a prophecy.

> When the world again learns to jump the tear
>
> A time of war will be drawing near
>
> That which was lost will again be found
>
> Those who were dead rise from the ground

The wicked will be led by one

Whose strength is like the raging sun

Darkness and power run in his blood

His only weakness lies in the flood

The army to oppose him will then form

Led by the one who calls the storm

Magic seventh son of the queen and king

Partnered with the one who wears the ring

She's in the world apart from ours

Her fate is written in our stars

This One brought in by shifter's hand

Must find the strength to save the land

She must learn to fight, she must learn to cast

She must remember those of us from her past

She must release the life she's sought

the final battle must with her be fought

She has the power to choose her side

If with light she fights it will change the tide

But if this savior answers Warlord's call

Then evil will ensnare us all

I read through it multiple times, and then I sit back without a word and try to think rationally about this. "Who's the 'shifter'?" I ask the boys without looking away from the wall.

"I think it's me," James says from behind me.

"Okay," I say, not bothering to ask why he thinks that. "And the 'one whose strength is like the raging sun'? Or 'the one who calls the storm'?" I feel like I'm outside myself. I hear the odd, tight calmness in my own voice, but I'm not sure how it got there.

"We don't know yet. People have been trying to figure that one out for ages," Crispin answers my question. "The funny thing about prophecies is they don't always make sense when you read them. Usually certain events have to fall into place before the rest comes together."

"That doesn't stop people from trying to understand though, does it?" James says.

"So. You think this is about me? Why? What...What makes you think it's even true?" I ask.

Crispin takes a seat on the bed, and a cloud of dust floats around him as he settles down. "We still aren't sure that it is you. We don't want it to have to be." He said almost the same thing to Sasha earlier, so I know he's telling me the truth. "But the proof seems to be there,

Cara. You must see that too, or else you wouldn't still be sitting here."

He's right. Much more makes sense now than it did when I first got here, as though this was a puzzle piece that had been missing, obscuring the whole picture, and only now that it has fallen into place does it all fit together. If James is the shifter, whatever that means, then I was brought in by a shifter. I do have a ring, and not just any ring, one that belongs here, in this world, and effectively ties me to Lyria. Crispin is with me, the magic son of the king and queen; I'm from another world...

Even with all this clear before me, I find myself shaking my head. I reread the last stanzas.

> She must learn to fight, she must learn to cast
>
> She must remember those of us from her past
>
> She must release the life she's sought
>
> the final battle must with her be fought
>
> She has the power to choose her side
>
> If with light she fights it will change the tide
>
> But if this savior answers Warlord's call
>
> Then evil will ensnare us all

"That can't be me," I murmur, almost to myself. "I can't fight." *Even if I can cast.* "I can't...I can't 'save the land'." I finally meet the boys' eyes again, something I have been avoiding, but I need them to understand. I choke back the despair that's threatening to overwhelm me. "I can't," I repeat. "I have a life, a family, friends, a home, and I want—" I stop talking at the sorrowful look on James' face.

She must release the life she's sought. I think. "I don't think I can give up my life," I tell them. "So it can't be me. You have to find someone else." I'm vaguely aware that whatever war is being mentioned here sounds like the end-all be-all war of the world. Their land is in jeopardy, and I'm refusing to help. *But they can't ask this of me.*

And then I think: *Would I be willing to ask this of them?*

I realize that I would. If, somehow, my entire world was on the line, and I had the power to find the one person meant to save it, I *would* find him and I *would* ask him for help, even if it meant his life would be changed, possibly endangered. It would be worth it to me.

But I am still not convinced.

"Why do you guys think this is true, anyway?" I ask again. "Someone writes a prophecy on the wall of their bedroom, and suddenly it's gospel to you?"

"Normally, no," Crispin says. "Not at all. But just because we have magic here doesn't mean everyone goes around casting spells and writing prophecies.

"There was this guy," Crispin continues, "from your world, actually. Somehow he found his way through the tear hundreds of years ago. Kayyar was being built then, so people were often out looking for supplies, materials, and someone found him. We don't know who he was or where he came from, but I guess he used to freak out whenever someone suggested he should be sent home. So he was led to the palace. They gave him this room until they could decide what to do with him. And he's the one who carved all this stuff on the wall.

"Some of the pictures are spoken of in some of the random phrases up there, and many of the phrases appear in one of the three actual prophecies. It's a bit like he was working out the wording, or that the pictures came to him first and the writing was his way of working out the meaning. And the castle staff let him write because they couldn't see the harm.

"And one day, about a week after he wrote this prophecy right here, he died. For no apparent reason. So the staff buried him and eventually came to remove the writing. But what they discovered was that the first of his true writings, not the scribbles or pictures, but the actual writings, described something that had happened centuries ago. It's something he couldn't have known about: the discovery of Lyria, how people crossed over the sea, how they built their five kingdoms here, and how they chose the way they'd split the land."

Crispin gestures toward the first prophecy, the faded one on the far left, as he speaks. "But neither of the other two had anything to do with something that had happened in our past. So, some people thought that might mean they had something to do with the future.

"We shared these two with the other kingdoms; we told them the story of the strange man, but no one believed it like we did. They all brushed it off as a madman's imagination. But the Demesnians remembered it, and we kept watch for the events it spoke of. And not even two hundred years later they came to light."

Crispin points now to the middle prophecy. Most of it has worn away, but the first two and the last lines are still legible.

An unseen war is about to begin

From fire it will start, in blood it will end

And then:

And the race will be gone, to be heard from no more

"That's the war I was telling you about on the way here," Crispin says to me. "The war where the Krelans rose up with the Sheiks and tried to take the other three kingdoms. No one saw it coming, and it ended with the destruction of the Krelans. And the second prophecy came true. So, somehow this man knew what he was talking about.

"And now we're at this one, Cara, and we're all terrified. It speaks of not just another war, but the war that has the power to save or to end the world. And Lyria has been waiting quite impatiently and full of fear for years and years and years, and while we don't want it to be true, we've come to see that it is. We know that it is."

Crispin is looking at me pleadingly now, as if by sheer force of will he can make me understand. There is a battle raging in my head, and I hold my head in my hands, like it will help.

And the thought winning out is: *What if it really is me?*

Part of me is trying desperately to squash the thought out of existence, and another part is trying to raise it up, shouting that this is the kind of adventure that most people can only read about in books. The kind of adventure that I've always wished I could be a part of.

But it's different now that it's actually happening.

Crispin watches anxiously as Cara has some kind of internal battle with herself. He feels a pang of sorrow when her head falls into her hands; it's almost like he can feel her pain himself. James takes a half-step toward her, but when Crispin shakes his head slowly, James backs off, frustrated. There is a clear desire in James to protect her, something Crispin hasn't seen in his friend in a long time, and that has never manifested in James as quickly as it did with Cara. He's been worried about her since the first week they met.

Crispin knows that Cara is reasonable, and she's clever, and he can see in her eyes that part of her sees the truth to what they've been saying, but it is continually being beaten down by the part of her that's been taught not to believe it. And she doesn't want to believe it; she doesn't think she can.

Which is to be expected, Crispin reminds himself. *In these past few days we have dropped more new and unbelievable information on her than most people get in their lifetimes.*

He's known since he first met her that she's stronger than she seems, stronger than she or anyone else has given her credit for. But even he admits that this all might have been too much, too fast. Maybe they should have spent more time away from the city first and gotten her used to the idea of being here.

But he comes up with the same reason he did earlier that day. She's safer here than she would be there. She just looks so fragile and scared huddled in her chair.

When she finally looks back up, she meets Crispin's eyes first. Her own are laced with fear and pain, she's holding back tears, and remorse for what is happening shoots through him. *Oh, why her? Of all the people in any world, why in the name of all things holy does it have to be this girl?*

Crispin tries to reflect sympathy back at her, to show her that he'll do whatever he can to make things right, but he knows that it isn't working. "Please, Cara," he finally whispers. "You have no idea how badly we need you."

"But..." she says softly. She doesn't finish and he doesn't ask her to.

James, sensing his loss for words, steps in. "Cara." Crispin wonders if James knows how tenderly he says her name, or if he's doing so unconsciously. "How about this? Forget this prophecy, as best you can. I know it seems like an impossible task, but try not to think about it. Let's pretend it doesn't exist, just for a few days, and let us show you around. Let us tell you about our world, show it to you, so you can clear your head, and then we'll decide what to do about this."

Cara hesitates for a moment. "What about home? My home?" Cara asks James. "I have to go back. They'll miss me." For the first time since their race back to Geler, Crispin sees Cara's eyes grow clear as concern, not for herself but for someone else, passes over her face. "What about Sophie?"

Her sister. Crispin is repeatedly awed by Cara's unfailing devotion to her younger sister, and by Sophie's blind trust in Cara. Cara's dedication takes precedent now, as all this new fear for herself is put aside yet again by worry for her sibling.

James is already calming her. "You know Max and Jade and David will do everything in their power to take care of her. They love her too. Nothing will happen to her. They all know what to do."

Cara nods as he speaks, seeming somewhat reassured. So Crispin jumps back in the conversation. "So, for all intensive purposes there is no prophecy. Not for a few days at least. Not for us." James and Cara nod in unison.

"Good," Crispin sighs. "Now we just have to explain that to everyone else."

15

Explaining it to everyone else turns out to mean that James and I sit in the corner of a large council room while Crispin tells an immense group of people the situation that has arisen. It's a good thing too; Crispin makes it sound as though I have had no breakdown at all, but rather that I am skeptical and afraid for the consequences if they pin their hopes on me too early. Though I can't imagine how he'd be aware of the condition of things, there is a tall, broad man with white-blonde hair cropped close to his head who is backing up everything the young Crown Prince says. He applauds our wise thinking and encourages the rest of the council to do the same.

"Who is that?" I finally whisper to James as I point at the man. Despite the fact that the meeting we're at is all about the prophecy and me, I find that I'm thinking less about it already. It's hard to focus on one single thought when so much is around for me to take in.

"Verne? He's pretty much the castle's tutor. He's been teaching Crispin and Sasha and me for as long as I can remember. He's always worked for Andromeda and Rennar as some kind of record keeper and librarian, but when Crispin was born they asked him to teach their son what he knew." James has yet to refer to any of the royal family by their titles, only calling them by their first names. "The man's a genius," James continues. "And he always seems to have a sixth sense as to what's going on. He knows precisely when to turn away and let us do our own thing.

Like now. He may be at a loss, but as long as we explain it to him later, Verne trusts us."

I take more time to study the man, now that I know James has such a high opinion of him. His eyes are a steely blue and his face looks weather-beaten, not typical of a librarian I would think. But now that I know to look for it, I can see the twinkle behind his serious expression. He and Crispin are playing a game.

And they're winning. An hour later, the council has decided to give me free reign through the castle and city, on the condition that if any of the common people were to call me the warrior they've been waiting for it would be my (and Crispin and James') duty, not the council's, to set them straight. And they're requiring that I be taught the ways of the kingdom as well as it's history, and, after a time, that I start my training in magic and fighting. After a quick glance at me, Crispin concedes.

"Wow, that was boring," I mutter, standing up at the end.

James chuckles loudly, quickly turning it into a bout of coughing when two of the more serious council members walk by. They give James and me hard looks. They are mad at me for not jumping on board with the savior idea, and mad at James for who-knows-what. Probably for laughing at such a solemn time.

Crispin is having a quiet conversation with Verne, but he beckons James and me to him when we catch his eye. So we dodge through council members and curious stares to join him.

"James, good to see you, my boy!" Verne says cheerfully, clapping James on the back with a smile. "How did life treat you in the Otherworld?"

"Well, missing these meetings was difficult. Crispin and I spent hours bemoaning the fact that they were going on without us. Think of all the good times we've been so cruelly deprived of..." James tells him.

Verne roars with laughter. He seems genuinely thrilled that they're home. It is almost as though they're his own children. Then he turns to me, humor still dancing in his eyes. "You must be our own little warrior. What an unusual eye color you have, my dear."

My eyes are brown. I'm not sure how to respond.

"Not in her world," James says for me.

"I've often wanted to visit the Otherworld," Verne tells me kindly, sensing my discomfort. "Someday you will have to tell me all about it."

"Someday I will," I say. Verne's smile, if possible, widens.

"Now!" Verne rubs his hands together conspiratorially. "We must get you out of here. Preferably without drawing the attention of the rest of the council." He scans the room. We're standing in the front, but, the way the room is set up, that put us the farthest from the door. And there is an obvious build up of people in the hall who are waiting to catch a glimpse of the non-warrior.

I groan.

"Not to worry, not to worry," Verne murmurs. "First, a distraction." He mumbles something under his breath, twists the fingers of his right hand, and the carpet on the floor of the hallway squirms about. Mass confusion ensues from those standing there as everyone tries to retain their balance and their dignity.

I'm so caught up in watching the chaos that James has to catch my wrist and pull me along behind him as he, Crispin, and Verne seize the moment and pass through a narrow door hidden behind a tall tapestry. We fumble in darkness for a split second when the door clicks closed. But then I stumble after the three through a second door and into a bedroom.

This bedroom is much larger than the last one I saw. An enormous desk dominates the far wall and is covered in papers and open books. Even more papers hang on the wall around the desk. Stacks of books are scattered about the floor across the room. There is a wardrobe standing open in the corner next to the bed, but everything in it is neatly organized. The only things that don't look like they have a place are the loose sheets of paper. They are on the desk and the walls as well as in piles on the floor and strewn across the carefully made bed.

"My own bedchamber," Verne informs me as I take it in. "Conveniently located a mere secret passage away in case the necessity of emergency escapes arise. And now..."

Verne leads the way to the back of his room, next to the bed and behind a tapestry where there is a door, a real one this time. It opens to reveal a short passageway, which leads into the most beautiful library I have ever seen.

James and Crispin leave me to stare in awe around the room, knowing my love of books, and Verne follows suit. The library is a three-story room, oval in shape, with a high ceiling painted deep blue and depicting the constellations. The ground level, arranged as a normal Earth library would be, has walls lined in towering, dark-wooded bookshelves. More of these freestanding shelves stretch across the floor in rows. Breaking the line of bookcases along one of the longer walls, I can see the double doors you're supposed to enter through, and on the wall across from those doors huge windows stretch from the floor to the high, arched ceiling. These windows face the back of the castle. Or, I assume it's the back because none of it looks familiar to me.

I'm standing on the second level, which is made up of one long, wide balcony that wraps around the room. Yet more tall bookshelves cover the walls up here, but in front of the windows where there are no shelves, three large tables sit. I imagine that's where work and studying is done.

One level up, where James, Crispin, and Verne have already gone, there are two more balconies, semicircular in shape. One is affixed to either of the two shorter walls of the oval room. While there are still bookshelves up there, most of the space on the balconies is taken up by comfy looking armchairs and side tables. Tight spiral staircases lead down from each level to the next floor.

I take the time to run my fingers across the spines of the books nearest me before I follow the other three up the stairs. The titles are all unfamiliar, and some are not in English, but I have the urge to take a few off the shelf and thumb through them. I've just decided not to when a book titled *Wars of Our Ages* catches my eye. I grab it and hear Crispin calling my name, so I take it with me.

"Already found a good read?" James asks when I appear. I take a chair opposite him, with Verne and Crispin on either side of me.

"Maybe," I shrug, holding it up for them to see. Crispin and James look uncomfortable with my choice, knowing what it means for me, but Verne smiles knowingly.

"Learn what you can, when you can," he says with a wink.

I shrug again. "Yeah, I guess so. I was just curious."

"Of course you were," Verne says kindly. He slides the book from my hands. "Then the only chapters you need to concern yourself with are..." He pages through the volume quickly. "Five and eleven. Read the others if you want, but I believe you will find those the most helpful."

I thank him and take the book back, holding it tightly in my lap as though it's a lifeline.

No one speaks for a time. I continue to take in the library and the grounds outside the windows where the sun is finally starting to set on the day. Crispin and James seem to be having a silent conversation, and Verne is watching us all carefully.

I wonder how odd this is for him, I think. If it's weird for Crispin and James, two boys who at least know about me and about my world, how much more must it be for this man, who knows nothing.

"How much have these boys told you?" Verne finally breaks the silence.

"Quite a bit, but only in pieces," I say, looking over at him. I quickly sum up what I've learned. "Crispin told me about the war with Krela, and he told me, more or less, that he's the Crown Prince, and Sasha is his twin sister. He told me a little of the geography of Lyria. They told me about the man from my world that wrote the prophecies. And about magic. And about my ring."

I take it off my finger and pass it to Verne. Crispin and James and I had decided I should wear it with the jewels hidden, as I usually do, to keep any question about how it came into my possession at bay for a time. Verne's eyes widen when he sees it, and he looks at Crispin for confirmation. Crispin nods.

"She had it when we met her," he says.

"Remarkable." Verne sits forward in his chair and passes the ring back to me. I slip it on, somehow comforted by the familiarity of it on my finger in this strange situation. "Though maybe not your wisest of decisions to keep this from the council. They will be furious when they find out. But it makes one of our first orders of business paying a visit to the treasury," Verne says.

"Our first order of business is introducing Cara to the king and queen," Crispin corrects him. "They know the stress of the situation as it is, so they will be understanding of the delay, for now. But, though I'm sure the council will have long since informed them of the ruling, Cara is at the very least a guest in their home, and it is necessary that they meet. Soon."

Anxious all over again, I press myself farther back into my chair as Crispin speaks. I don't want to meet a king and queen.

James, sprawled across his seat in the same position he's often sat at The Scarlet Letter, notices my expression. "Cris, don't you think that can wait? Maybe until tomorrow? Today has been—"

"I know what today has been, James, but you know this can't wait." I've never heard Crispin talk to James with authority before. He and James have always been equals, which is why it's hard to imagine him as a prince. But there is authority in his voice now, and James bows his head stiffly in acknowledgment of it.

Crispin's expression softens. "I think it will be best if we can explain the situation as it stands, before anyone else has the opportunity. Before rumors fly," he explains.

Verne speaks now. "If that is your plan, then we shall postpone our visit to the treasury until tomorrow. And as you do not need me for your audience with your parents," Verne says, standing up, "I think I will retire for the evening. I expect you both, as well as you, Cara, my dear, to be here in the morning for our tutoring session, as usual." As he starts to walk down the stairs, Verne turns back to us. "And boys, be kind. Do not forget to feed the girl." And then he is gone.

I fold my hands in my lap and nestle back into the armchair, not sure if I'm more or less anxious that Verne won't be joining us for a meeting with the rulers of Demesne. I think having an adult present would be reassuring, but apparently that's not going to happen. Crispin gazes at me for a moment, and then pulls his chair closer to mine and places his hands over my own.

"Cara, I'm sorry. I know this is still a lot. And I'm sure the last thing you want to do is walk around and be sociable. But, around here, things are done a certain way, and it is not only necessary to be introduced to the king and queen, but it's considered insulting for you to stay in their home and not meet them. It should have been done immediately. They'll be somewhat forgiving, especially considering who you are, and they're lenient with me. And after this, and dinner, if you're hungry enough to eat, you're done. Done for the day, for the next few days, and it will be all about explaining things to you and teaching you. But first the formalities have to be taken care of. Okay?"

I nod slowly. "I know you know what's best around here," I say quietly. "But...I'm scared." It's the first time that I've admitted out loud to them just how frightened I am. I'm sure they have been able to read it in my face our whole journey, but saying it is another thing entirely.

I didn't mean to make either of them sad, but I can see that I have. Crispin pulls me out of my chair and wraps me in his arms. I lean my head against his shoulder and fight back tears. I'm tired of crying in front of these boys He holds me tighter, without speaking. He smells of cinnamon and soap and magic, and I allow myself to be calmed by his sturdiness and his strength.

Crispin doesn't let me go until I pull away myself. He looks me in the eyes as he reaches up to wipe the teardrops from my face. I laugh weakly at myself and drag my sleeve across my eyes.

"I'm going to go find Sasha," Crispin tells James and me. "You two might as well stay here for a while. This is the last place people will expect you to be."

James, who has been watching us impassively, nods in agreement, so Crispin dashes away. I collapse back into my recently vacated chair. James is quick to stand and grab my hands in order to pull me back to my feet.

"What?" I ask him. "Why can't I sit here?"

"Because," he replies, "I'm not supposed to be letting you dwell on the problems the day has brought. We're going on a tour!" James announces this last bit with a good amount of false cheer.

"Crispin just told us to stay in the library," I protest weakly.

"Do you really think that because he's my prince I do everything he says?" I start at the word "prince". Just for a moment, I had forgotten. James just shakes his head. "No," he continues, "I believe that all leaders must be challenged. Fortunately for you, this is not one of those challenges. I meant we're going on a tour of the library."

"I can see it all from here," I tell him. However, I still pick up my book and follow him as he walks away.

"You can see some of it from here," he corrects me over his shoulder. "There is much more. Feel free to address any questions you may have to your guide, me, as we walk."

I already have a question. "If you want to get to the other balcony up here, the one over there," I point, "do you have to walk down the stairs, cross the room, and then climb back up?"

"Really?" James says. "You're not even going to let me *begin* the tour before you ask?" But he is smiling as he answers. "No, you don't." The balconies are all railed in, thankfully, because it's a long way down, but James leads me confidently to this railing, to a spot near the wall, and gestures at something. I go stand next to him to see what he's pointing at.

A long, narrow beam runs from this balcony along to the other. It is set a few feet away from the wall and a hundred or so feet in the air and is made of the same tan stone as the rest of the walls.

James is watching me, waiting for a reaction. I don't disappoint.

"Holy smoke!" I finally say. "You're kidding me! That? That ledge, right there? People actually use that? Who would use that?"

James says with a crooked smirk: "Yes, people use it. I use it. Crispin does too. Normal people take the stairs, but this takes much less time."

"Yeah," I say, "unless you die on the way over there."

"Cara. Have a little faith. The key is to not look down." With a wink, James hops over the railing, lands neatly on the beams, and lithely runs across. He never shifts from his fast pace and, true to his word, he doesn't look down. When he reaches the other side he simply leaps the railing again and sticks the landing. Then he turns and, even in the dying light streaming through the windows, I can see his cocky grin across the room.

"You are such a show-off," I mumble. I didn't think he would be able to hear me, but James barks out a laugh. He places his hands on the rails once more, but I call out, "No, that's okay. I'll meet you over there."

James shrugs and starts down the stairs on his side of the room. I do the same on mine. We meet on the second floor, and James wastes no time in beginning the grand tour.

"So," he says, gesturing to our left. "On the south wall, we have history books. You, it seems, have already found that on the second level, these particular histories have to do with wars." He looks pointedly at the book in my hands before continuing. "A level down, the volumes are about Lyrian history in general. The coming of people to these lands, records throughout the years of populations and crops and trade, and cartographers' findings. The much smaller collection, on the third level, has to do with past interactions with magical creatures."

I blanch. "You...you're kidding me. What magical creatures?"

"Consider yourself lucky for not running into any during our journey here," James says to me. "Yes. Not many, not on this side of the ocean, at least, but some magical creatures do exist. Elves. Werewolves. Dwarves. The like."

I let that sink in. "Vampires? Dragons? Fairies?"

"Don't get carried away," James grumbles. Something about the topic is irritating him.

I decide I'll press Crispin for more information later. "So what about the north wall?" I ask James. "Or the..." I pause, working out the directions in my head. "East wall?"

"Come along, young grasshopper," James says over his shoulder as he strides away.

I laugh and hurry behind him. We descend the spiral staircase to the vast ground level. As soon as my feet touch the stone floor, I look up and realize the towering bookcases absolutely obscure the far side of the room. It's quieter down here, darker.

James continues talking. "The east wall. Those are novels. Some of them. Most are accounts of the lives of Lyrians, but they pass as pleasure reading around here. Very few fiction or fantasy books. Not like your world." He smiles grimly. "But then, who needs them in this one?"

As we stroll around the library, I remember The Scarlet Letter. When James pulls a volume from a shelf up ahead, I'm struck with another question.

"James?" He turns to face me. With his dark looks and lithe, easy movements, he seems as though he could disappear into the shadows at any moment. "That book of Roman Myths? Now that I know all this, can you tell me why you were reading them? Of all the books in my world, they're not usually the stories people pick out to browse through for fun."

James takes time to mull over the question. "I suppose it's because...I think they're tragic. And it always strikes me as odd when people can write tragedies without having experienced them firsthand."

"What do you mean?" I ask.

His dark eyes study my face for a moment. "Take Persephone, for example," he begins, like he knows that's the myth I read the other day. "She is swept from her home by a monstrous man simply because he covets her, and because of her innocence, she loses the life she would have known without his interference."

I surprise myself by scoffing at his word choice. "'Innocence'? James, you realize it was her fault, right? That she was stuck in Hades, I mean. She was the daughter of a goddess. Odds are she was taught well enough to know not to eat the stupid seeds in the first place. And I think there's a version where she's warned to eat no food from the Underworld, but does so because she decides no harm could come from six pomegranate seeds. So she wasn't really the brightest."

"That's how you interpret it?" James asks, sounding surprised. "She didn't have a choice, Cara. He took her life from her."

"He took *a* life from her," I reply. "Which means it probably wasn't the life she was destined to have in the first place. I suppose you can feel a little bad for her, but don't go blaming Hades for it. Not completely, at least."

"You're siding with the monster on this one?"

I make a face at him. "I'm siding with the Greek god." James' expression has slowly become closed-off as we speak, and suddenly, for an unexplainable reason, I have the urge to make him understand my point. "I just...I never liked that story. I think people read it wrong. And I'm not even sure what about their interpretations of it bother me, but something does. I just know that it isn't supposed to be all Hades' fault. Persephone got in her own way."

James watches me curiously as I finish, but he doesn't refute my opinion. He looks as though something is bothering him. I know that if I ask he won't answer, so I wait to see if he'll tell me anyway.

After a long pause, he drags his storm-colored eyes away from my face to glance up to the arched ceiling above us. When he meets my eyes again, there is a slight smile playing about his lips as if he knows I'm paying close attention to whatever he's about to do. The rest of him tenses. He closes his eyes, and I can see his lips moving, but no sound comes out.

It isn't the explanation I was hoping for, but now my curiosity is peaked.

Night has fallen. The light from the lanterns that are hung along the banisters overhead is all that illuminates the room. As James begins twisting the fingers on his right hand, I watch his movements with an even more careful eye. But my gaze leaves his face when the lanterns start to dim, until they are nothing more than soft points of light. And then the ceiling begins to glow. The midnight blue of the painted sky simply shines softly, but the constellations become bright spots of white in the now dark library. I stare around in awe, not noticing James approaching me until he's right by my side.

"What do you think?" he asks with seemingly forced lightness.

I can't pull my eyes away from the stars glowing above us. "It's...amazing. James, it's..."

"Magical?" he finishes.

"Well, yes," I admit, meeting his eyes. "That is the first word that comes to mind."

There is hesitant intensity in his expression—the same look that seems to be on his face every time we're alone. The look that makes my heart stumble over a beat. My fingers itch to reach up and sweep his tousled black hair back from where it falls over his forehead.

Then something hard and small pelts me in the back of the neck, ridding me instantly of the urge. After glancing around wildly for a second, my eyes fall on Crispin and Sasha where they're leaning against the railing a floor above us. They're grinning widely.

"What are you kids up to?" Sasha calls down.

James takes one slow, deliberate step away from me as any moment we might have had vanishes into the dim library air.

"We're keeping each other company while we wait for you two slowpokes to reappear," James calls back. "I mean really, Cris, you had to find one person."

"One person whose habits he seems to have forgotten in the last few months," Sasha says. "Honestly. The very first place he looked for me was in the stables." She shakes her head at her twin's foolishness.

"Ah," James replies with a knowing nod. "When he should have remembered that you now spend your free time hanging around the training arena. Ever since Blaine started spending less time with his brothers and more time with the soldiers..."

I know from the tone of her voice that Sasha must be blushing when she speaks again. "It's not because of *Blaine*. I'm hoping to...pick up on a few moves for next time I lose my guards and run off." Apparently riding alone, without permission, is a favorite past time of hers.

"So Cara," Crispin interrupts. "While we're being ignored, and since Sasha has evidently forgotten why I went to find her in the first place, would you like me to show you where you can get some new clothes?"

I stare up at him. "You're making me change *again*? How many outfits do you people go through every day?"

Sasha seems taken aback by the familiar way I address Crispin, and I wonder for a moment if I should have spoken with more respect. But when I glance at the boys, neither of them look concerned about it.

"Don't let him pick out your clothes for you," Sasha warns me. It's the first real time she's addressed me, apart from when she introduced herself outside the city earlier. "He has no fashion sense."

Crispin starts to defend himself and his fashion sense, so I look to James. "Why do I have to change again?" I ask him.

He gestures to my outfit. "Those are traveling clothes. You're going to meet the royal family, and those simply won't cut it." He winks at me. "You have to look your best."

Rising Calm

"How much royal family is left to meet?" I ask worriedly.

James thinks for a moment. Crispin and Sasha's voices fade slightly as they move off to come down the stairs and meet us. "Well... Odds are only the king and queen, Branshire, Elik, Saladin, and these two are around for you to meet right now. Though I suppose Divia or the twins could be visiting."

"Oh, that's all?" I say sarcastically.

"Not even close," James answers. "Assuming Divia and Arlin and Aldim aren't in the city, eventually you'll still have to be introduced to them, their spouses, and their kids. And on top of that there are the other three: Maple, Gina, Malloc and *their* children and husbands and wife." He pauses to grin at me. "And that's only the Demesnian royals. So there's a daunting prospect."

"That is a lot of people," I whisper.

James' smile softens. "It's not so bad. You've got some pretty powerful friends to help you out."

Crispin bounds to our side as if called. "He's referring to me," Crispin clarifies, like I haven't figured that out already. "By the way, James, it looks good in here. Very impressive." He's talking about the still-lit ceiling. Turning to me again, Crispin explains, "This is the first cast he ever wanted to learn. It's tough. He's become even better at it than I am."

"I would like you all to make note," Sasha proclaims, waltzing up to join the group. "Crown Prince Crispin has just admitted that he is, in fact, worse than someone at something. Let us all stand in silence, in honor of this grand moment." She bows her head just in time for Crispin to elbow her in the side. She shoots James and me a grin, blue eyes glinting.

She's happy they're back, I realize. *She's acting like it's no big deal, but I wonder what it's like for her when they're in my world.* I wonder if she's jealous that they get to have their own adventures while she's stuck here, surrounded by guards that she has to run away from if she wants any time alone.

I wonder what she thinks of my intrusion into her life.

"Sasha," Crispin says. "James and I have to get ready too. Can you help Cara and meet us in an hour or so? I'd like you to come with us for our audience, if you don't mind."

She seems to shrink a little. "I don't mind," she tells him. "They're going to demand my presence soon enough anyway. Nox is probably furious with me for ditching the patrol earlier. I'll bet the first thing he did when he came back was tell Mom and Dad."

Crispin only looks slightly sympathetic. "Those dang guards. Always worried about your safety. No wonder you can't stand them."

Sasha shoots him a glare. "You haven't had a watch on you since you were ten. You're only fine with guards because you just have one, and he happens to be your best friend."

Crispin backs down. "I know, I know," he says. "I hated them too. But I want you to be safe as much as they do. Be careful, okay?"

"I always am," Sasha tells him. When James and Crispin murmur goodbyes for now, Sasha adds under her breath, "And by 'always' I mean 'most of the time'."

This being exactly the kind of comment I would have made, I can't help grinning.

She smiles at me. "Let's go get you ready!"

****

Princess Sasha points things out to me as we walk up some staircases and down a few halls, but my anxiety about my pending audience with royalty is impairing my ability to listen. I tune in just in time to hear her say: "But for now, until your room is complete, you can use mine." There is a heavy oak door down the hall we're in that separates this wing of the castle from the rest. Sasha swings it open and leads me to one of the doors at the end of the elegant hall.

It looks like a princess' room should. Her huge bed is canopied, and the gauzy white fabric drapes down over three of the sides. Two open windows on the far wall allow the cool night breeze to float in. Lanterns are already lit. A thick embroidered rug spreads across most of the floor, intricate tapestries hang along two of the walls, and a stone fireplace with flames crackling in its grate dominates the corner by the bed. On the fourth wall, there is a long table with accessories strewn across the top. A mirror with a gilded frame hangs next to a small doorway, which Sasha leads me through.

Inside are a bathtub, a washbasin, some towels on hooks, and shelves with all kinds of soaps and bath salts and perfumes. A patch of wall next to the head of the tub is blackened. Between this patch and the tub is a tall, sturdy-looking wooden frame set over a pit in the floor. Sasha shows me everything with a wave of her hand, then studies my clothes and the rest of my person with a critical eye. "I'll call Talit in to help heat some water for you." She beckons me back out into her room. "But until then, we're calling in the tailors."

I hurry to her side as she strides across the room to ring a bell hanging by her door. "Tailors? Sasha. Princess, I mean. We don't have enough time. Can't I just, I don't know, borrow something of yours?" There is a knot in my stomach as my meeting with the king and queen nears. I can't stand around and get fitted for new clothes.

"Oh, please," Sasha says, with a toss of her head. "You will be wearing something of mine. But we'll have to at least make sure it'll fit before you go rushing off to meet my parents. And you're the one the meeting's for, so it isn't as though it will start without you."

I gape at her. "I can't make the king and queen *wait* for me. I'm supposed to be convincing them to like me."

Sasha looks me over yet again. "They'll like you fine. You're confused, and you're cute. They won't have the heart to refuse you. And I'll muzzle Saladin if he tries anything," she adds with a growl.

I don't quite know what she's talking about, but her expression and the confidence in her voice remind me so vividly of Jade that I'm startled into a grin. And I start to feel just a little more comfortable around her.

When someone knocks softly at the door, Sasha pulls it open without hesitation. Standing there is a tall, lanky boy who can't be more than a couple years older than Sasha and me. He has smiling blue eyes, but a serious expression, a mop of curly hair much like Crispin's, and hands rough from work.

Sasha smiles politely at him. "Talit, this is Cara. Cara, Talit. He does a lot of odd jobs around here for us."

I say hello quietly. Talit looks curiously at my eyes for a long time, until Sasha clears her throat and he murmurs a greeting back to me. Sasha begins explaining something to him, so I wander away, both to avoid being stared at and to look around the room.

I pause in front of one of the many tapestries that seem to decorate the entire castle. It's breathtakingly detailed. This particular tapestry is a picture of the palace from a distance with the sun setting behind it. The embroidery is perfect; each stitch has a purpose. I can see the windows of the towers and the guards on the battlements. I can see people in the town below the castle walls as well as the hills sloping away from the city. And the colors of the sunset seem to bleed together as if they were painted rather than sewn.

"It's some amazing work, isn't it?" Sasha says from behind me. I hadn't heard her approach. "And most of them don't even use magic. They just sit in their shops and houses and sew, all day." She suddenly looks pained. "You…you do know about magic already, don't you?" she asks quickly.

"The boys told me. Last night." I unintentionally flex my fingers the way Crispin often does.

Sasha notices, but makes no comment. "Well, that's good," she sighs. "I don't want to be the one to break even more astounding news to you. I hear I'm the one who told you about your prophecy?" Sasha is no longer looking me in the eye.

I try to reassure her. She seems awfully nervous about how I will react. "Better I found out now than later. I would rather not have any more secrets kept from me. Though, how many more could really be left after all this?"

She shoots me a grateful glance as Talit walks by with a tangle of leather straps. Sasha pulls the bell by her door again and walks over to collapse on her bed in a fashion I would, before now, have only associated with Otherworld teenagers.

"Crispin and James seem to be awfully fond of you," she says, her eyes closed.

Heat floods my face, and I wonder if she's implying anything. I say in a carefully neutral tone, "They've done a lot for me, but I suppose they had a pretty good reason."

"Oh, sure, they have a great reason, if you actually are who they think you are. They've just taken to you pretty quickly, that's all."

Though I've spent some time refuting the idea that I'm this girl spoken of in their prophecy, I find myself stung by the fact that Sasha doesn't believe it. "Is that unusual?" I ask.

Sasha, noticing the shift in my voice, opens her eyes. "They're fairly kept to themselves. Especially in the Otherworld. Now I hear they became friends with not only you, but your sister and your friends too. Yes, that's unusual. They must really like you."

My stomach clenches at the reminder of my friends and family. "Or they just wanted to get close to me so I wouldn't freak out quite as much when they brought me here." I sound bitter to my own ears.

"No," Sasha decides, after a slight pause. "They protected your feelings as well as they could, both here and on Earth. They wouldn't have worried about that if they didn't care about you as more than just our potential warrior."

Her claim does little to alleviate the new fear I have: that Crispin and James might only care about me because they think I'm supposed to save their world. "Do you think they're wrong about me?" I ask her, not sure what I'm hoping her answer will be.

Sasha props herself up onto her elbows and cocks her head to the side to study me. I'm leaning against the wall, arms crossed over my chest, and I resist the urge to straighten up under her scrutiny. "I don't see it," she finally answers. "But Crispin usually isn't wrong."

"How many people from my world can do magic?" I ask.

She looks surprised by the sudden shift in conversation. "Not many, I've heard. Just a couple."

"Can you?"

"A bit," she says with a wave of her hand. "That's mostly my dear twin's department."

"So, if I *could*...would that mean I was this warrior that they want me to be?"

Sasha sits up, suddenly interested. "Cris said you cast! That wasn't a lie?"

I hold my arms out. "If you're magic, you should be able to feel it in me, right? Go ahead. Tell me what you think."

She looks at me like I might be joking, but then she folds her hands in her lap and bows her head over them. Her fingers tighten as she concentrates. Eventually she snaps her head up, and stares at me with the too-familiar expression of wide-eyed surprise.

"That's a lot of power," she says to me.

I rub my chest, recalling the empty feeling there. "That's what I was afraid of."

Talit comes out of the bathroom, nodding respectfully to me before turning to Sasha. "Lady Princess," he says. "Everything is ready for her."

"Perfect," Sasha tells him. "Would you go and see what's taking the tailors so long to arrive?"

He nods again and hurries from the room. He doesn't seem comfortable being in the bedroom of the princess. I wonder briefly what other jobs he does for the palace.

Sasha has disappeared into the bathroom, so I follow her. She's in the process of pouring sharp-smelling soap into the empty tub. The once-empty wooden frame next to it now holds a large, gray caldron, which is suspended by the leather straps I saw Talit bring in earlier. It's steaming, full of water, and tendrils of smoke curl from the pit below it where a fire must have been going.

There's a handle near the top of the frame that Sasha reaches up to pull back once she's put the soaps back on the shelf. The caldron tilts, dumping the water into the tub and splashing some of it over the sides and onto the floor.

"I hope you're decent," Sasha says, reentering the small room. She grins unapologetically at my expression. "Sorry, I probably should have asked." She rummages around the shelves, pulls a bottle off, and passes it to me. "Soap. Towels are there when you're done."

I jump back as the hot water rolls over the floor toward me.

"Rats," Sasha mutters. "That wasn't supposed to happen. Ah, well."

The soap has formed bubbles on the surface of the water in the tub, and their scent fills the air invitingly. Sasha looks at me. "It's all yours," she says. "I'll wait outside for you." As she exits she pulls a folding screen in front of the doorway for me.

When I'm sure she's gone, I fumble to remove my new traveling clothes, toss the too-tight headscarf to the floor, and sink into the stingingly hot water. Few things have ever felt as good as this bath does. It's large enough for me to stretch out my legs and rest my head against the edge. I close my eyes.

I do my best not to think about anything except the warmth of the water on my aching muscles and the wonderful smell of the soaps, which is somewhere along the lines of rosemary and ginger.

I think I start to drift off.

Too soon new voices enter Sasha's room—the tailors, I can only imagine—and I begin to feel self-conscious, afraid someone is going to pull aside the screen. I sink lower into the water, thankful for the concealing bubbles.

"I hope you're decent," Sasha says, reentering the small room. She grins unapologetically at my expression. "Sorry, I probably should have asked." She rummages around the shelves, pulls a bottle off, and passes it to me. "Soap. Towels are there when you're done."

Before I can protest, Sasha has swept my clothes from the floor and taken them with her back out the door.

I'm quick to shampoo my hair, dunk it under the water—making sure to get all the thick soap out—and jump out of the tub to wrap a towel around myself. It's big and plush and covers me completely. I run my fingers through my hair to try and look as presentable as it's possible to look in a towel. And then I join Sasha in her bedroom.

Two older women are standing around her bed with her. They are studying my traveling clothes and making necessary adjustments to a pale blue dress that I assume is Sasha's.

"Oh good!" Sasha cries when she sees me. "Come here." She drags me over to the women herself when I don't walk fast enough for her. They hardly glance at me. Sasha pushes a thin, dark green skirt and some new underclothes into my arms. "Put these on," she instructs, pushing me back into the bathroom.

I do so. As soon as I come back out into the bedroom, the women begin pulling the dress over my head. I stand still and take it without complaint as they pin the fabric in place. The dress fits surprisingly well, all things considered. It isn't long before it's yanked off of me again.

One of the women picks out a needle and spool of thread to make the easy alterations. The thread is white, but after a quick glance at the dress she mutters over it, and the color changes to an identical blue. I watch closely, fascinated by the magic. Sasha strolls away to poke around her table of accessories while I wait.

The dress I'm borrowing has gold embroidery around the hem (which is long enough to brush the ground, as is the green skirt I'm wearing now). The pattern looks like ivy, twisting its way up from the bottom and fading out as it reaches the dress' waist. The neckline is low and square-cut in both the front and back, and the long sleeves are loose fitting.

The women are finished sooner than I would have thought possible, and they bow at Sasha as they exit the room. They didn't say a word to me the entire time they were here.

Sasha sighs contentedly. "Almost done," she tells me. "Now, your hair." She sits me on the edge of her bed and kneels behind me on the duvet. "Divia, that's my sister, and I used to do each other's hair all the time," she tells me as she works. Sasha spends a good amount of time simply brushing my hair, running her fingers through it, arranging it, and then letting it fall. It feels good, relaxing.

Eventually she apologizes. "I've never seen hair like yours before. The only ones with brown hair are the Cairnes, and theirs is much darker than yours is. It's so pretty. It's so unusual..."

I laugh. I'm still having a hard time believing *no one* around here has any other hair color but yellow. "It's not any different than blonde hair, besides the color," I assure her.

"Oh, I know," Sasha says. "But it seems like it should be." She begins braiding sections of my hair, pinning other sections on top of my head. "So, does everyone in the Otherworld have different hair colors? How many people have hair like yours?" she asks eagerly.

I smile at her excitement. I think their world is incredible; I didn't think they might believe the same thing about mine. "Have you never jumped the tear?" I ask her before I answer.

She sighs angrily. "No." She changes her voice to mimic who I can only assume is one of her parents. "'It wouldn't be proper for a young lady, and a princess at that, to take such a journey and be put at such risk to satisfy her own curiosity. You'll just have to hear about it from Crispin and James when they make their return.'"

It takes no time at all for me to decide that I'll tell Sasha whatever she wants to know about my world. Being treated like you're too young or delicate to handle something important is a feeling I can relate to. Even though they've made me run my own life for as long as I can remember, my parents have some weird moments where they act like I'll crack under the pressure of something absurd. Like taking care of the house when they're away for the weekend or packing up my room when we move. It's amazingly irritating.

"Well," I tell her, wincing when she tugs a little too hard on a lock of hair, "First, I honestly have no clue how many people in...the Otherworld, is that what we're calling it? I don't know how many people have brown hair. But a lot. A bunch of them have blonde hair too, and some have black hair, or red hair. And, I don't know if this is true here or not, but some people dye their hair different colors."

Sasha stops and peers over my shoulder to stare at me in disbelief. "Like, the way we dye our clothes?"

I grin. "Yep."

"Honestly? So...people with yellow hair can dye it brown, if they want?"

"People with yellow hair can dye it purple, if they want."

Sasha begins doing my hair again with a bit more vigor than before, which is a tad more painful for me. "Purple hair," she muses. "That's unbelievable."

"Or it can be blue, or pink, or orange too."

She's quiet for a long time, and I let her think it over. "What about eye color?"

"All of them," I say. "Combined with all kinds of hair colors. So, for example, I have a friend back home with golden-blonde hair but brown eyes like mine. And another friend with black hair and hazel eyes that are kind of green and gold."

"Navites and Sheiks have black hair, and the Cairnes' hair is so dark it seems like they do, but none of them have green and gold eyes too." She still sounds impressed.

I ask a question of my own. "So then, if Sheiks have black eyes, do Navites and Cairnes have a different eye color?" I ask her. The Lyrian terms still feel awkward coming out of my mouth, but I'm doing my best to use them.

"Why did they tell you Sheiks have black eyes?" Sasha asks.

I exhale quietly. "Crispin and James didn't tell me. I met Panus in my world. In the Otherworld."

"Panus? Wow. Did they fight? Did they kill him?"

She asks so easily, it surprises me. I can't get used to a world where it's natural to kill your enemies. "No," I reply quickly. "Just roughed him up enough that we could all get away."

Sasha sighs again. I think it might be in relief, but when she speaks she sounds disappointed. "He's such a pain," she mumbles, bunching all of my hair onto the top of my head and beginning to pin it there. "Panus is always in the way."

"Who is he?" I ask, the eye color question becoming less important.

She gives my hair one last twist, and then lets go so I turn to look at her. Her face is serious. "He's the right hand of the king of the Sheiks, King Orrick. Orrick never does anything for himself, but he hates us for winning the last war, and he wants to show us up as much as he wants anything. Panus is the man he always sends after us." A pause. "He came after you?"

"I guess so. I didn't really understand it then. I still don't. But I think he knows who I am, or who I'm supposed to be."

"I bet he was supposed to bring you to Orrick as soon as the boys found you. He's probably in trouble for messing up the plan," Sasha says with a satisfied smirk.

I silently hope that he is.

"Well," Sasha says, ending the conversation, "time to get you dressed. Crispin and James are probably already waiting for us." She hops off the bed and retrieves my new dress and one of her slips. I start toward the bathroom to change, but Sasha stops me. "I'll need to help you if you don't want to muss up your hair."

I'm uncomfortable with the idea, but I consent. She helps me pull the slip on over my head without another word. This one, unlike the sheer one I got in Kayyar, is a slightly thicker material that laces up in the back, almost acting like a corset (though much more comfortable, I imagine) and ends at my waist. The lightweight, dark green skirt is arranged over it, and then Sasha helps me into the pale blue dress. The wide, triangular slit in the front of the dress allows the green skirt to show through.

"Now, for the accent pieces!" she cries.

I end up with diamond pins in my hair and golden bangles on my wrist. "Turn your ring around," Sasha instructs. "My parents will want to see it." And then she sends me away to look in the mirror while she gets ready herself.

I already know what my dress looks like, but my hair is stunning. She's run three braids of varying widths through the rest of my hair, and knotted it all messily on the top of my head. A few loose pieces fall at the nape of my neck and around my ears, somehow making the whole thing look carelessly elegant. The pins sparkle in the lamplight and set it all off perfectly.

"What do you think?" Sasha asks, appearing in the mirror beside me in a light pink and gold gown. She's truly anxious for my answer. The princess wants to know if I approve of her hair styling.

I give her reflection my widest, most sincere smile. "It's beautiful, Sasha. I've never looked so good."

She squeals and hugs me, then immediately lets me go and looks embarrassed. I squeeze her hand lightly. "Thank you," I say.

Sasha finishes sliding her own rings on her hands (she has about as many as Crispin), places a golden tiara on her head, and then she leads me out of the room to my audience with the king and queen.

16

Sasha takes me down yet another convoluted path full of twists and turns and hidden staircases that cause me to get lost all over again, but that help us avoid almost all other people.

We finally make it to the second level, to the hallway I'm told is just above the front entrance to the castle. The corridor we're now in leads to a grand staircase, which will take us down to the double entrance doors. Sasha stops us just before the stairs, at the railing that overlooks the ground level. Crispin and James are nowhere in sight.

"Stay here for a moment," Sasha says to me. "Let me see who's in the throne room." She dashes away.

While I wait for her to return, I lounge on the staircase in the entrance hall. Only a few servants and soldiers come through, otherwise it's more isolated than I would have thought the main entrance to the palace would be, even at night. The thick emerald green rug that runs down the stairs continues in a curve over the tan stones to the great double doors. This staircase is set off to the side of the hall, against one wall, and large framed portraits of the royal family run up alongside it. I know it's the current royal family because I recognize Crispin and Sasha and count eleven children, plus the king and queen.

Some of Crispin's siblings look quite old—I suppose they would be, seeing as there are so many of them—and each of them, as I've come to expect, has blonde hair and blue eyes. I do notice that Crispin shares his green eyes with his father, but no one else. Since he is from a thirteen-person family, this strikes me as interesting.

I also note that there are thin banners of color beside the pictures: two on some and one on the others. A stripe of brilliant green runs along the left side of all thirteen portraits. Beside every picture except for the last three (Crispin, Sasha, and another brother) runs a stripe of a different color, on the right side. Almost all of them are cobalt blue, but next to one is a dark brown stripe, by another is a gold one, and by a third is an icy blue line.

As I'm studying the portraits, a boy who looks to be just older than Crispin and James saunters down the stairs and stops dead in his tracks when he sees me. He bears a striking resemblance to Crispin. He has the same facial structure, the same head of curls, but his hair is more yellow than Crispin's, and his eyes are a deep blue. There's a band of gold around his head.

The boy narrows his eyes at me, so I stare back. "Which one are you?" I ask when he doesn't say anything. I wave a hand vaguely at the portraits above me.

He seems amazed when I speak, notes my accent or lack thereof, and takes in my brown eyes and hair with a new look. The corners of his mouth curl into a sneer.

"So you're the girl my prodigy brother and his lackey brought in from the other world," he says without answering my question.

I frown. "I have a name," I reply angrily, unwilling to be known as "the girl" that follows Crispin and James around.

"Your name is no concern of mine. I think it's about time you run home before you get hurt. It's a more dangerous world here than you're used to," he scoffs.

He no longer resembles Crispin in the slightest. I cannot imagine Crispin looking at me with such scorn on his face or such derision in his eyes.

That disdain is what causes me to rise to my feet. I'm a head or so shorter than he is when we stand face to face, so I take a step up to make us eye level. I can feel my expression shift to match his as I whirl to face him. I'm aware that he's a prince and I should be treating him with respect, but I find myself unable to do so.

"Do you have a problem with me?" I ask the boy furiously.

"Yes. I do," he answers just as heatedly. "You have no right to waltz around here like you own the place! You know nothing about us, and I, for one, fail to see how some girl is supposed to save us, especially since she's too afraid to even take the job."

Stung, I retort, "'Waltz around like I own the place'? I'm sorry, I didn't realize how presumptuous sitting on the steps made me appear. Would you at least like to wait until I order my throne before you begin pointing out my conceited nature?"

"And I can't see what help you would be anyway," the boy continues as if I haven't spoken. "This impending war, if it even exists, is not something we need some outsider's help in winning. We're not too weak to do it on our own."

"That, Saladin, is where you are wrong. It is where you've always been wrong." Crispin and James have appeared at the bottom of the steps. There is a very unbrotherly light in Crispin's eyes when he looks at Saladin. "But how nice of you," he continues, "to graciously welcome Cara into our home."

Saladin clearly feels the same amount of contempt for his younger brother and James as he does for me; it's written all over his face. When he turns his glare back on me, James makes his way up the steps and stands protectively in front of me. Crispin joins him within seconds.

Crispin keeps talking. "You always seem to believe that the whole kingdom could run on its own. But what good would we be without allies and outsiders helping us? We're not self-sustaining, Saladin, and it's about time you realized it."

Saladin pushes between James and Crispin to reach me, and I wave them off as they try to hold him back. Saladin steps up so his face is in mine. "Whatever you think you are," he hisses at me, "whatever you think you can do, you're wrong. Having some girl underfoot is going to be more of a hindrance than a help, and everyone knows it. They're all just afraid of hurting your fragile feelings. Well, I'm not. I say we don't need you, we don't want you, and it's only a matter of time before someone else has to break the news to you."

I want to slap him, but I think better of it. Instead, I curl my hand into a fist and drill him in the nose. He staggers back, barely keeping his balance on the stairs, but it is more from surprise than pain, for when he draws back his hand from his face there is no blood.

"Damn," I mutter, truly disappointed. "I was hoping it would do more than that."

James is smirking, eyebrows raised, waiting for Saladin's reaction.

I can tell that Saladin is about to retaliate, maybe even hit me back, but Crispin grabs his arm and holds him in place.

"Leave it," Crispin says severely.

I expect Saladin to turn on his brother, but instead he actually backs off. With a final look of loathing in my direction, Saladin wrenches his arm from his brother's grasp, storms off down the stairs, and disappears out the door.

"What a pleasure to meet another one of your siblings, Crispin," I say.

Crispin looks apologetic. "I know," he sighs. "I was hoping to hold off on having you meet any more of them, especially Saladin. He's a little...touchy."

"Ah," I say with a grimace. "Exactly the word *I* was going to use."

Crispin frowns at me. "He's still royalty, Cara. You have to be more careful."

"Do you want me to just stand around and take it when people come up and insult me?" I ask him, careful to keep my voice level.

"No," Crispin says. "I expect you to think before you go off and punch a prince in the face."

James smiles slightly. "You're just upset because she hit him before you could."

Sasha is now making her way up the stairs, which leaves me wondering what took her so long.

"They're ready for us," she says to the boys and me.

Crispin takes the lead as we march down the staircase. James and Sasha fall in step on either side of me, as James filling her in on my face-off with Saladin. Sasha looks at me appraisingly when James tells her I punched her brother in the nose. "Someone had to," she says with a shrug.

Saladin doesn't seem to be too popular with his siblings.

After a couple turns that I forget to memorize (so I'm lost again, a now familiar feeling), Crispin stops us at another set of double doors. They're painted a soft gold, and engraved in the middle of each door is a small tree; boughs branch out from its trunk, bare but for a few leaves on each, and seven stars form a shallow "U" around the bottom of the symbol.

The guards posted on either side of the doors drop to their knees for Crispin and Sasha, who pay them no mind.

"When we enter, curtsy," Sasha tells me, demonstrating.

I copy her, and she nods approvingly.

"Let Crispin do most of the talking," James instructs. "When they address you directly, look to their feet unless they tell you otherwise. Always end anything you say to them with 'king', 'queen', 'ma'am', or 'sir'. Look to one of us if you don't know how to respond. Got it?"

I nod once, my mouth suddenly dry.

As Crispin turns to motion to the guards to open the doors, James whispers in my ear, "You'll be fine." I close my eyes briefly at the feeling of his warm breath on my neck. And as the door opens and Crispin begins forward, James adds, "And you look beautiful."

Then Sasha is at my other side once more, and we step through the doors into the throne room.

****

Emerald green is a popular color around here. That's the first thing I think when I enter.

There is yet another green carpet that rolls from the doors to the thrones. It's a bit like I'd think walking the red carpet in Hollywood would be; it's just wide enough for James and Sasha and me to walk side by side, and all eyes are on our party. Another rug of the same length and width runs perpendicular to the first—a line in front of the group of thrones. Otherwise the expansive floor is made of even blocks of tan stone.

Wooden benches run around the edges of the room and stop just before the green rug begins. The walls of the square room are bare, except for the one to my left. It holds row upon row of tall rectangular draperies. From this distance I can't quite tell what they are, but I can at least tell that they are different than the other tapestries around the palace. The ceiling, frescoed with scenes that I can only guess are of Demesnian history, arches over everything.

I do my best to look nowhere besides straight ahead or at my own feet, but it's hard not to take the room in. Each of the golden thrones set on the dais at the head of the room are padded with more emerald green fabric, and each is decorated with elaborate carvings. Only the front two thrones, the ones that the king and queen are seated in, have edges lined with diamonds and emeralds.

I count thirteen thrones total, one for each royal family member. One is set off the king's left side and mere feet behind it. The remaining ten are arranged in a line, five on either side of the front-most three, and all set farther back than the lone one.

Apart from the ruling couple, there are only two other occupied seats. A pale, thin man, with overlong waves of light blond hair and pastel blue eyes occupies the innermost throne on the queen's side (my left, her right). He isn't even watching us as we approach.

The second throne out from the king's side holds a younger man with broad shoulders and a serious face. His short hair is light and his eyes match Sasha's sky blue ones. His expression is curious, but he is polite enough not to stare at me for too long. He instead removes his gaze to nod at his siblings where they walk with me. They smile at him in return.

Our group of four finally reaches the thrones, and Sasha and I curtsy while Crispin and James drop to a knee. I hold my position like the others until the king, in a deep voice says to us, "Rise." We do so; I keep my eyes on the ground.

"Crispin, my boy," King Rennar says kindly, "it's good to have you back. James, welcome home." In my peripheral vision, I see Crispin and James nod in acknowledgement.

Rennar has strawberry-blond hair and a short beard. I see him scratch his cheek thoughtfully as he regards his daughter. "Sasha," he finally says. "I'm glad to see you're safe."

I feel him turn his sharp, green-eyed gaze onto me. I don't look up, but wait a long time for him to address me. "What shall we do with you?" he muses aloud. I don't move. "You may look at me, girl. I want to see your face."

Slowly, I raise my head to look into his eyes. His hair is a short mass of tangled curls with a large, six-pointed crown resting on top. He's wearing (surprise, surprise) a green robe, which is lined in fur. There are wrinkles around his eyes and a dimple in his cheek. He shares the same broad-shouldered build as the son behind him.

King Rennar regards me shrewdly. I do my best not to look away from his face.

When his expression clears, some of the tension goes out of me. "You'll do nicely," he says.

I don't know how to respond, so I bow my head as the others have done.

"What an interesting looking girl you are," the queen says to me. "Such fair skin but with such dark eyes. And what an unusual hair color."

I silently wonder if every Lyrian I meet will have something to say about my coloring.

Queen Andromeda watches me solemnly. "My dear girl, do you know what it is that you've stumbled into?"

Stumbled is the right word. "Only bits and pieces of it, your majesty." I bite my lip when I realize "your majesty" wasn't on the list of titles James told me to use. Thankfully, it seems to be an acceptable alternative.

The queen's sandy hair, braided and coiled above her head, is beginning to gray. Her gold tiara-like crown has a single emerald at the center of its base. "I see you have met our youngest," she gestures at Sasha with a heavily ringed hand, "and goodness knows you've had the time to become acquainted with our heir"—this with a nod to Crispin. "These are their brothers, Princes Elik and Branshire." I see when she waves to each of them that Elik is the elder, thinner man and Branshire the younger. "Saladin should be here for this as well, but he seems to be late." Andromeda's sky-blue eyes flash with disappointment for her son's absence. It appears family meetings such as these are a serious deal.

"In any case, what we have on our hands is a problem," King Rennar says, laying a hand on his wife's arm. "Are we to understand, as the council members have informed us, that you have refused the prophecy?"

I swallow hard, stuttering over my explanation. "I-It's not a *refusal,* sir, I simply...I don't know that I'm ready to believe it's me the prophecy talks about. Honestly, it seems that most everyone else would be better suited for the position the prophecy offers than I would." Somehow being in their presence has automatically made my speech more formal.

"Ah," Rennar sighs. "Unfortunately, it is not everyone else that the prophecy calls for. As I've heard it, prophecies are not something your world has to offer, are they?"

"Only in movies, king." When Rennar hesitates to answer, I realize he probably has never heard of movies before. I mentally slap my forehead. "Only in books. Sir," I correct.

"We're told that nothing here is quite what you're used to. So these must have been very trying days for you." I murmur that they have been. "So, the question remains: What shall we do with you?"

Crispin speaks up. "At the council meeting, it was decided that she could be allowed to remain here, so long as she was taught and trained, in case that she is indeed whom we have been waiting for. We're to be"—here he pauses, though it's hardly noticeable, as he chooses the right words—"furthering her familiarity with Lyria, as we try to figure this all out."

James is nodding along, confirming everything Crispin says.

"That is all well." Andromeda says to Crispin. "But we would like to know what you think. This girl, do you believe that she is the one?"

Crispin shoots a guilty, apologetic glance at me before addressing his mother. "Yes. That is exactly what I believe."

Andromeda nods, closing her eyes. "Then we respect the council's decision. You may stay," she says to me.

I nod, wanting to appear grateful, but I find myself frustrated with Crispin. It's not his place to tell everyone what my fate is.

Saladin enters the room, bows stiffly to his parents, and flings himself into the throne one down from Branshire.

I am satisfied to see the beginnings of a bruise under his eye.

"You're too late, Sal," Branshire says to him. "The decision's been made."

Saladin scoffs. "Safe to assume this group failed to mention that this girl attacked me?"

When the royals on their thrones all turn to look at me, I fight the desire to shout my defense at them. My face burns. I look Saladin steadily in the eyes, daring him to say more. He smirks cruelly.

"Do any of you deny this?" Rennar asks us.

No one answers for a moment, and then Crispin says, "No, Father, we do not deny it, but you should know that it was short, it was provoked, and attacked is far too strong a word."

"Are you excusing her actions?" the king asks his youngest son.

It's James who speaks next. "No, my king. We are merely explaining them."

Andromeda and Rennar exchange serious looks. My heart plummets. *Stupid temper.* I'm going to get kicked out of Geler because I punched their prince.

Rennar begins to speak. "Things are handled a certain way in our kingdom, and those ways may be new to you. They may be different than in the Otherworld. It is important that you learn these ways and that, in the time you spend here, you live by them. But because you have the support by those standing with you, this time we are inclined to believe you."

He fixes both Crispin and James with hard look. "I will leave it to you both to make sure nothing like this happens again."

Saladin is pissed, I'm trying not to let my triumph show, and Crispin and James have adopted carefully neutral expressions. Sasha is standing quietly beside us, seemingly still fearful of being reprimanded.

Rennar makes a motion with his right hand, and a sharply dressed guard who has been standing to attention in the background the entire time steps forward quickly, passes a roll of parchment to his king, and then respectfully bows and returns to his place. He is standing almost behind the line of tall thrones, which is, I imagine, why I didn't notice him before.

The king carefully reads over the parchment in his hands, glances at me occasionally, and then sets it in his lap and leans forward.

He's watching me, but he addresses Crispin. "The ring?"

Crispin takes my hand and pulls me gently up the three steps to stand in front of his father. He passes my right hand to the king. Rennar takes it and studies my ring without a word. I don't know where to look, but my eyes find the paper the king was reading. Even upside-down, I can tell that it's a copy of the prophecy.

So ignoring it isn't working as well as Crispin and James seemed to think it would.

Finally Rennar lets me go. "What did Verne have to say about this?" he asks Crispin.

"We agreed to visit the treasury tomorrow to try and find out how this came about," Crispin answers.

Rennar nods, so Crispin nudges me back down the steps to stand with James and Sasha again. King Rennar looks to James now.

"May I assume it was you who brought the girl into Lyria?"

How could he know that? I wonder immediately. And then: *Oh. Right. James is the "shifter".* And it looks like I'm the only one who doesn't know why this is.

James nods, jaw set, something about the comment digging at him. I wish I could ask what it is, but I know he wouldn't explain it.

"Her ability to cast?" Rennar asks the boys.

"You should see for yourself," Crispin tells him.

Not only the king, but also the queen, Branshire, Elik, and even Saladin close their eyes. My heart begins to pound as I realize all their focus is solely on me. My own eyes close in concentration.

I feel my magic flood through me, curling out from the space in my chest, eagerly trying to respond to them all at once. I attempt to reign it in, not sure how I should be reacting, but with a small gasp I'm forced to let it go. It snaps forward, connecting to all five points of energy at once.

I know Rennar by his calm strength; Saladin by his contempt. I'm able to identify Queen Andromeda, whose magic is soft and careful. Elik's power comes to me in a different form than the others, slightly weaker. Branshire's is easy and controlled. I know Crispin, Sasha, and James have stepped back so it will be easier for everyone to focus on me, but part of me still registers their presence: Sasha's has a curious force, Crispin's radiates like light, James' pulses quietly underneath it all with a still unnamable difference to it.

Slowly, the points of contact fade out until only the general feeling of magic is left in the room. It's then that I open my eyes.

No one speaks for a long moment. And then Branshire says: "She feels a lot like you, Cris."

Everyone nods in agreement with this statement.

When I glance at Crispin his mouth is turned down in a minute frown.

King Rennar has begun reading his copy of the prophecy once more. "Can she fight?" he asks James and Crispin.

Both shake their heads. "Part of the deal with the council is that she be taught," James explains to the royals. "She does have it in her though. She's brave. She's had to be."

I don't move my eyes from the king and queen, but it's an effort not to peek at James when he speaks. He sounds torn between pride and sorrow.

The king moves on. "And 'those of us from her past'?"

Crispin shrugs. "We know nothing about that yet."

Rennar at last rolls the prophecy back up and rests his hands lightly on the arms of his throne. "Despite the minor flaws and missing information, I have to say that the odds of finding another Otherworld girl who so closely fits the prophecy's criteria is doubtful. Only time can tell us, but it does seem as though Crispin and James have done their job well." The king never looks away from my face as he speaks; I hold his gaze, my heart constricting with every word. "What do you think about all of this, dear girl?"

I take a deep breath and try to sound calmer than I feel. "I don't think this is something I could ever be ready for," I reply. "I'm...I'm just me. I'm nothing special, and I definitely don't think it's possible that a prophecy from a world that I knew nothing about could destine me to be a warrior. But then...I didn't think any of this was possible, not before yesterday. So, sir, if I'm honest, I don't know what to think anymore."

The king and queen are both serious as they regard me. "You are not what we expected," Andromeda begins, "but I think you are what we have been waiting for."

No! I want to cry out. *I'm not. I know I can't be. Please. I like it here, I really do, but I can't stay. I can't fulfill a prophecy. It's too much.* I would love to accept it, to be a heroine, to take the challenge and prove to everyone and myself that I'm much more than I ever thought I could be. But I can't let myself. *I'm going to have to go back home. I can't spend my life here, waiting for a war, waiting for the opportunity to fight.* I can't think of anything to say out loud, so the throne room stays silent.

Elik is lost in his own thoughts, uninterested in the meeting. He's probably only here because his parents demanded it. But I notice Branshire's watchful gaze on our little group, gathered at the foot of the dais. He meets each of our eyes, first Crispin and Sasha, then James and me. He points to me, locks gazes with Crispin again, and makes some signal that Crispin seems to understand. Crispin shakes his head.

"Lady Cara," Branshire says, a little too loudly. "Have you eaten yet? You should have the boys show you to the kitchen."

"My dear," the queen says, suddenly concerned. "When was your last meal?"

"Umm..." I think. "This morning, while we traveled." Nerves have been twisting through my stomach all day, chasing off any thoughts of hunger, but now that food has been mentioned I have to will it not to growl.

"You all have missed dinner, it was served hours ago," King Rennar tells us. "But you may be dismissed to find something to eat."

James and Crispin bow once more, so I curtsy. I flash a grateful look at Branshire, well aware that he has purposely given us an excuse to leave. He returns my glance with a smile and a nod. James brushes my arm and beckons me away.

"You, we still need to talk to," I hear Queen Andromeda say, and Sasha reluctantly mumbles good-bye to the three of us as she turns back to her parents. They haven't forgotten her disobedience after all, though it seemed they had.

I sag against the wall when the throne room doors shut behind us. "You're parents are intimidating," I tell Crispin.

"They're the rulers," he reminds me. "They have to be."

James motions for us to follow him away from the room and from the guards still standing in front of it. They lead me in a different direction than the one we came from.

Neither of the boys speaks at first. So, when we pass through a couple doorways that seem to double back on each other, I break the silence first. "Really?" I ask. "You know I get more lost with every step we take, right?"

James cracks a smile. "We'll get you a map," he promises.

We descend a couple poorly lit flights of stairs that I would guess are normally used by servants rather than by royalty. As we walk the air becomes stiflingly hot, but appealing scents waft up to us.

When we reach the last landing, James leans down to whisper: "If you're going to make any friends in the castle, have them be part of the kitchen staff. Smartest move you could make."

I smile, Crispin opens the wooden door, and we step inside.

The kitchen is vast and noisy. A large woman is barking out orders while numerous staff members in white uniforms rush to and fro. It's an effort not to be in anyone's way. The three of us skirt the walls, ducking under pots and pans as people swing them about.

Multiple fires are lit in ovens and fire pits around the room, which is the cause of the heat. A fountain of water spurts from a spot in one wall and falls into a sloping trough that runs the length of the room. A shelf above this holds soaps and sponges, and a line of staff stands almost shoulder to shoulder as they scrub dishes clean and hand them off to be dried.

Wonderful scents assault me: everything from roasting turkeys and steaming vegetables to warm bread and sweet pastries.

James yanks me out of the way of a man carrying a wide tray of crystal glasses. The man begins to curse at me until he takes in my clothes, hair color, and companions. Then he apologizes profusely and backs away. I watch him go curiously and am surprised by his reaction to me, but James continues to pull me along after him so I have to tear my eyes away.

"Still encouraging me to make friends with these people?" I ask him over the noise. "Usually I prefer my friends not swear at me when I accidentally almost trip them."

"Well, as long as you don't knock them or their expensive glassware over, you'll get along just fine," James responds.

Crispin is making his way to the middle of the kitchen and the loud woman standing there. James and I follow in his wake—he clears a path more quickly than either of us could.

When the woman sees us, she stops her yelling and fixes her prince and his friends with a stony expression. "Crown Prince," she says. "What brings ya ta my kitchen at this hour?" She speaks to him like he's a poorly behaved nephew of hers; her accent is a much heavier version of what I noticed in the boys when we first met.

Both James and Crispin are grinning boyishly. James takes one of her hands in both of his and looks at her pleadingly. "My dear Frale, we were so cruelly deprived of your heavenly cooking these last few months we've spent in the Otherworld that it was a top priority upon our arrival in Geler to sample the morsels of yours that we have missed. Alas, there was much to do before we could eat, and we seem to have missed our dinner. We come to you with empty stomachs and pleas for your understanding. Is there any food you could spare such weary travelers?"

I snicker behind my hand. What a show-off.

There's a twinkle in Frale's eyes despite the sternness in her voice. "Away with 'ee, ya rascals!" she cries, pulling her hand from James' grasp and swatting them both good-naturedly. "I'll send Genia up ta the small dinin' hall with a meal fer ya. And Crispin, ma boy, yer sepal's been waiting fer ya to return. Givin' this staff a mine a migraine, she is. Ye should go an' find her before the day is out!"

She pushes between Crispin and James to clasp my hands. "And a pleasure ta meet cha, my girl," she says to me. "We have the highest a hopes fer yer future." And then she's gone, lost in a mass of kitchen staff.

James and Crispin lead me back up the same staircase. The rush of cool air that comes with the open door is a relief as it lifts the sweat from my neck and forehead.

James passes me a warm roll that was hidden in his pocket as we walk down a few more curving halls. He winks when I ask him how he got it while he munches on his own. "You've got to be sneaky about it," he tells me. "Quick fingers."

I bite into it; it's sweet and soft and eases some of the hunger tightening my stomach. "Thanks," I mumble around another mouthful.

"Wait until you try the rest of Frale's cooking," Crispin says, grinning like he knows something I don't.

The small dining hall is just that, if it can even pass for a hall. It's really just a long little room. Windows line one wall; they look out over the gardens that are hardly visible in the dark. A few armchairs, with small tables at their sides, sit in front of the windows. A longer table stretches across the majority of the floor. Places are already set with glasses and plates in front of each of the many chairs.

James walks around to light some lanterns while Crispin leads me to a seat in an armchair. I nestle down into it. "How much trouble is Sasha going to be in?" I ask them when they come over to join me.

"Oh, hardly any," Crispin replies. "She's safe, it isn't as though this is the first time she's ditched her guard, and she found us. She'll be warned not to do it again, then she'll be sent to her room for the night, which is where she would have gone anyway."

"Good." Though I hardly know her, I've developed an easy fondness for Crispin's twin sister and wouldn't want to see her in too much trouble.

Less than ten minutes later, right when I remember to ask Crispin what a "sepal" is, the girl who I soon figure must be Genia enters the dining hall with a cart of food. She's small, with quick, bird-like movements and a long braid of golden hair, and she seems humbled in the presence of the Crown Prince. Her blue eyes stay glued to either the food or the floor. She does, however, chance a swift, adoring look at James before she scurries out of the room once more.

James hardly seems to notice the glance Genia gave him. He is already piling a plate he took from the table high with victuals. But light spots of pink appear on his cheeks and betray the fact that he does know. I can't decide whether I should be amused or surprised with the serving girl's hidden infatuation with her prince's friend.

"A sepal," Crispin says through a mouth full of chicken, "is a Demesnian animal, pretty much like a large Earth cat, a puma or a leopard. For some reason they've taken to the hills and plains of Demesne instead of the forest or mountains. Anyway, they're a bit of a symbol of our kingdom. The other four have their own animals too."

"So, when Frale said your sepal was looking for you to come back, she was talking about a cat? Like your pet?"

Crispin wrinkles his nose at the word "pet", and then he looks me square in the eye and asks: "Do you want to meet her?"

I nervously bite into a pastry akin to a chocolate croissant before I answer. "I suppose so, yes."

Crispin fixes his eyes across the room for a second. "Good. She'll be here in just a moment."

"Really?" I ask.

"Yes, really. She knows where I am. She'll come find me."

We eat in silence for a minute or two. Now that I'm aware of how hungry I've been all day, I can't get enough of the food in front of me. Some kind of broth turns out to be delicious with pieces of a thin, hard kind of bread. I put chicken and some kind of gravy onto another of those rolls James sneaked from the kitchen, making an odd, but appetizing sandwich. There's whipped cream in a small bowl that Crispin and James dip pieces of fruit into. This soon becomes my favorite thing on the cart. But while the boys pour themselves glasses of dark wine from a pitcher, I settle for cold milk.

"You sure, Cara?" James asks, offering me the pitcher. "It's not as though there's a drinking age here or something. And it's quite good. Better than the stuff you call wine back on Earth, at least."

So I try a sip of his, almost spit it back out, and am glad I chose the milk.

There is eventually scratching at the dining room door. Crispin is quick to go open it and let in a silver cat the size of a jaguar. Her short fur is shiny and spotted dark gray; her eyes are mint green and intense. She's sleek and stunning and unlike any animal I've ever seen at home.

She purrs when Crispin kneels down to pet her—a sound that rumbles throughout the room. As she rubs against Crispin, he strokes her ears and neck.

"It's good to see you, too," I hear him murmur.

The cat's eyes rest on my face when she's finished greeting Crispin. There is intelligence sparkling in them.

"Cara, this is Nelma. Nelma, Cara," Crispin introduces quickly.

Nelma cocks her head to the side, still staring at me. I don't look away, curious about her and about sepals in general. Her head is held high, almost as if she is royal herself. And it's only when Crispin walks back to James and me to sit down that she finally moves. She pads over to us too, as if unwilling to be any farther away from Crispin than she has to be.

"Nelma has been with me since she was a cub," Crispin tells me. "Verne and I were out practicing what he likes to call 'survival magic', and we found her. She lost her clan, and she was injured, losing a lot of blood. Verne taught me how to patch her up so that we could bring her back to Geler. I used to think that she would leave as soon as she was better, that she would go looking for her family again. But she never left. Now the only time we ever spend apart is when James and I are on Earth."

Nelma, still watchful, has lain down at Crispin's feet. I can see two pink scars running from her stomach to her back on her left side.

"They're from another sepal," James explains when he notices my gaze.

Nelma looks up at me when James speaks, and in that moment I swear I know exactly what she would say if she could talk. *It was a long time ago, and it is better here with Crispin than it ever was out there. I'm content and healthy now. I intend to stay this way.*

She obviously says nothing, but I still find myself nodding to her, to show I understand. "I'm so sorry," I say. She blinks once, slowly, and then looks away.

And then I realize I've just had a conversation with a cat. Curious, I close my eyes and reach to Nelma with that magical part of me that has so recently become accustomed to seeking out others. Sure enough, there is a bright, pulsing force exuding from the sepal—one that I find is inexplicably tied to the power that I know to be Crispin.

I open my eyes to continue eating, and I'm aware that James' eyes are on me. I don't look at him. I decide not to ask for an explanation of anything I just felt. Easier to accept it and move on.

"So Cara," Crispin begins, "while you're staying here—"

"Which is going to be how long, exactly?" I ask. I feel as though I continually ask him the same questions, but he never gives me a real answer.

Crispin sighs. "You know we don't know that yet."

"I know. But it doesn't mean I don't need to leave. You keep mentioning all the times you and James have been on Earth, which I'm assuming means you can go back and forth whenever you want. So why I can't I leave and settle what I know is a madhouse at home, and then I'll come back and we can figure all this out here?"

Crispin's expression is set. "We've been through this. It's not safe for you."

"I realize that, but—"

"Do you realize that by going home you're putting your friends and family at risk? Panus knows who you are now, which means it's only a matter of time before everyone else does, and then everyone will be looking for you. Not all of their intentions will be bad, but the majority will. Are you willing to put Sophie and Jade and your parents in that situation?"

"No! I just think we should discuss me going back to Earth. Not eventually, not sometime, but soon. I only mean that it's been a couple of days already, and it's only going to get worse there the longer I'm gone."

Crispin opens his mouth to retort, but I stop him. "Forget it, never mind. I shouldn't have brought it up." My voice is sharp with irritation.

We both stay silent. When it's apparent that everyone is done eating, James stands and says, "Come on. Might as well get you to your room and call it a night."

This time I don't even try to pay attention to where we're going as we travel through the castle. James' hand is firm on my elbow and guiding me forward; Nelma is striding alongside me; Crispin is leading the way.

I do have enough sense to recognize the hallway that leads to Sasha's room, but the heavy door closes off the wing where her room sits. The boys and the sepal walk down the corridor in the opposite direction, stopping in front of a door at the end of the hall.

"We hope your room is comfortable enough for you," Crispin says to me. I can't tell if he's being rude about it or not. I decide he probably is, but I'm over it. As long as my room is warm and has a bed, I'll be happy.

But, of course, it has much more than that.

It's is beautiful—almost as large as Sasha's, with the same small doorway in one wall that I know leads to a bathroom and the same large fireplace in one corner. There's already a fire going; I can feel the heat of it from here. My bed is devoid of the canopy hanging over the top, but the better part of it is covered in large, full pillows. A dark wardrobe dominates another wall. Curtains waving gently in a light breeze hang open around open windows.

I note the few tapestries draped on the walls, the desk sitting by the bed, and the same tree symbol that had been on the doors to the throne room carved into the stone above the door we just entered. Now that I'm full and warm and there's an inviting bed calling to me across the room, I'm aware of the late hour. I have no idea what time it actually is, but, in Earth time, I would guess it has to be at least one or two in the morning.

Crispin is still distant. "What do you think?" he asks without inflection.

I wince internally at his closed-off expression and feel increasingly guilty for bringing up such a sore subject when the day had been ending so well. "It's great, Crispin. Thanks." I try to smile, but I falter when he only nods stiffly.

"You already know where Sasha sleeps. The rest of us are down the hall with her, if you need us," Crispin says. And then he turns on his heel and walks out.

My head is spinning. James is still next to me, and with a confused sigh I drop my head on his chest. I'm too worn out to be embarrassed by the action. I want to scream, but all I can manage is a kind of muffled, growling shriek. "First Saladin, then the king and queen, now Crispin... Why does everyone hate me?"

"Oh Cara," James says, stroking my hair. "They don't hate you. They're just as sad and confused about all this as you are, and they don't know what to do about it." He pauses momentarily. "Well, except for Saladin. He most likely does hate you."

Exhausted enough that I don't laugh, I close my eyes. "I know," I say eventually. "I know they're confused too, and I suppose they have every right to be mad at me right now. I'm not exactly the hero you've all been waiting the last couple hundred years for, am I?"

"You might be, Cara. You still might be."

I want to pull away, to tell him that I'm not and to quit expecting me to be. But the rhythmic motion of his hand in my hair and the electric feeling of his arms around me make it impossible for me to move. So I link my hands behind him and stand there until he finally clears his throat and lets me go.

James looks down at me, and the firelight flickers over his pale face. "Get some sleep," he instructs. "Crispin and I will come get you in the morning. He'll be fine by tomorrow, Cara. You'll see."

He leans down to brush his lips against my cheek and exits without another word. The door shuts quickly behind him.

I'm left alone to raise my fingers hesitantly to the spot where he kissed me and to try to interpret the emotion that was hidden in his eyes before he left.

17

When the flip did my bed get this comfortable? I huddle further into the blankets until my back presses against something large and warm. I turn over to look.

A soft-furred, green-eyed cat blinks at me lazily. I push myself quickly away before my brain catches up with my body and the events of the previous day hit me all over again.

Is it going to be like this every time I go to sleep? I wonder, falling back onto my pillows. It's exhausting, waking up and having to remember everything I've gone through.

Now that I'm awake, Nelma wants me out of bed. She sticks her nose in my face. When I roll over and resolutely shut my eyes, she grabs the blankets in her teeth, and pulls them off of me.

I open a bleary eye to glare at the sepal. "I have not gotten enough sleep yet," I tell her. "I need more if anyone in this world wants me to function at all today." My eyes are slipping shut again of their own accord, so I close them and bury my face in one of the soft pillows I surrounded myself with before I fell asleep last night.

Nelma doesn't move for a moment. Then she flops heavily back onto the bed by my legs. When I crack my eyes open again to look at her, she's curled in a ball by my feet and effectively warming them for me. I sigh happily, reach over to run my hand across her soft fur, and then draw the covers back over myself.

"What good are you?" Crispin says to Nelma, entering the room minutes later. "She's not even kind of awake. I ask you to do one job..." But I can tell he isn't at all mad at her.

"Why won't you people let me sleep?" I mumble with my eyes closed.

"It's your first day of training!" James announces grandly, coming in from the hall.

I hear a door shut down the hallway, and moments later Sasha hurries in behind the boys, and takes us all in with a glance. She fixes James and Crispin with an authoritative glare. "Get out of here!" she says to them. "The last thing a tired girl wants first thing in the morning is two annoying boys pestering her before she's even had a chance to get out of bed!"

"Are you sure that's the *last* thing a girl wants?" James asks mildly.

At the same time Crispin tells his sister "We gave her a chance to get out of bed! Cara just didn't take said chance."

"Out." Sasha points to the door.

With mock, whatever-you-say-princess expressions, Crispin and James wave to me and exit my room. Nelma looks like she considers joining them, but the comfort of my bed wins out, so she stays.

"But you do have to get up," Sasha says to me. "Verne is going to be waiting for you in the library soon. He expects you to be part of today's tutoring session with the boys and me."

"So even in Lyria I have to go to school," I say with a yawn I can't hold back. "How sad for me." I glance out the window at the dark, gray sky. "What time is it? Why are we up so early?"

Sasha follows my gaze. "Oh. It's not early. It's just stormy weather. We get a lot of that here. It'll probably be dark all day."

I draw the blankets around my shoulders, sit up, and swing my feet off the bed. "How long, exactly, does a tutoring session last?" Sasha has begun rummaging in my wardrobe. "And can I just wear my jeans?" I ask.

Someone—Crispin, is my guess—had the knapsack with my Earth clothes brought up to my room for me. It had been waiting on my bed when I'd come in last night. I pull the denim pants out to show her. Sasha takes them from me warily. "They're pants, they're not going to hurt you," I tell her.

"You wear pants, in the Otherworld?" Sasha asks.

"I'm stuck in one of those times before women were allowed to wear pants?" I ask in dismay. "Please tell me I don't have to wear dresses all day everyday."

Sasha is still studying the jeans. "No," she answers absentmindedly. "You can wear skirts too." I stare at her until she notices. "You can wear pants in battle or during training and such, but everyday clothes, especially for those of us in the palace, are dresses. Or skirts. Your choice. No, you cannot wear these." She tosses the jeans to me. With a final, woeful glance at them, I stuff them back in the bag.

"Then what am I allowed to wear?"

"Anything else." She flings wide the doors of the wardrobe so I can see what's inside. Rows of dresses (and skirts) are packed in. Sasha pulls a few out. "For lessons, I'd just wear one of these," she tells me. "This one'll suit you." She holds up a dark blue dress. It's just long enough to fall past my knees; the skirt of it is gauzy and flowing. It's got a shallow scoop neck and three-quarter sleeves.

I sigh. "Yeah. That'll do." As I pull it on (Sasha shows no sign of leaving, so I'm just going to have to get used to changing in front of her) I ask, "When were these clothes made? I've barely been here for a day."

Sasha takes my vacated seat on the bed. "Magic tailors. What part of this aren't you understanding?"

"As far as magic is concerned, so far all I know is that I can move boulders, Crispin can make light-up paths, and one of the tailors can change the color of thread. Other than that, I don't know what people can and can't do. I don't know how it works yet."

"Oh. Okay, well, the tailors are chosen because this is the kind of magic they're strongest at. Color changing, changing the kind of fabrics clothes are made from, adjusting size or length, things like that. So it wasn't too hard for them to take some of mine and my sisters' clothes and alter them for you."

Sasha reaches over to help me straighten out a few wrinkles. "Nice," she says approvingly. She walks to the wardrobe and pulls stockings and boots from the bottom, then passes them to me.

I lace up the tall, soft leather boots, slide my ring onto my finger, and borrow a brush from Sasha to run through my hair. When she deems me presentable, Sasha leads the way to the library. Nelma bounds beside us as we walk. I'm pleased to find that, though I wouldn't know the way on my own, I recognize the halls and stairs we take to get from my room to the library.

This time we enter through the correct doors, not Verne's secret magical one. Verne, James, and Crispin have apparently been waiting for us to arrive. Crispin calls down for us to join them a floor up, at the tables by the windows. At the sound of his voice Nelma races off, weaving between bookshelves, and is soon lost from view.

Sasha and I follow more slowly. Judging by the way she's dragging her feet, I'm not the only one reluctant for this tutoring to start.

James is leaning back in one of the wooden chairs, his feet propped up in the table, an open book in his lap. Crispin is standing, three books spread before him, and he is jotting something down on a scroll of parchment. Nelma has taken a seat at his feet. Verne is coaxing light from the lanterns nearby; the gloom of the day is making the library a bit too dark.

I have an almost panoramic view of the grounds from here. Before anyone can put me to work, I walk over to the windows and stare out. Rain is beginning to fall in the distance—I can see it over the hills; it looks like a sheet of gray crawling toward us. The rolling clouds are dark, the sun nowhere in sight. It's going to be one of those days where I'll never know the time, because the light outside will stay the same for hours on end.

I'm struck, all of a sudden, by the vastness of this place. *This whole world has just been sitting here, waiting, right next to us, and no one knows. How could no one know about a place like this?*

James has come to stand next to me, so I voice the question. "Why is it that you all get to know about my world, but my world doesn't know about yours? How did that happen?"

"Lyrians are the only ones who have the power to go between worlds," James reminds me. "You need magic to jump the tear. So, if you can't cross from the Otherworld, then what good would come of knowing somewhere else exists?" He falls silent for a time, and then he adds: "And your world isn't exactly ready to know."

I glance at him to find his blue-gray eyes staring at something beyond the castle grounds. "What does that mean?" I ask.

"What would your world do if they found out about us?" he asks me as he turns to lean against the window and face me. "How would they react? What would people think?"

I mull it over. "Most people would think it was crazy," I say finally. "Some people would be overjoyed, some would be terrified…"

"And everyone would want to come," James continues for me. "Everyone on Earth would want to see Lyria for themselves. They would want to explore everything, understand how it all works. They would want to improve it by bringing technology in, no matter the cost to magic. Cara, your world would want to make this one their own. They need progress, to feel like they've improved things. We've learned to leave things as they are. It's enough for us to spend time in your world, to study it, and then to come home. You can't say the same about the Otherworlders."

I frown, recognizing that he's probably right and not sure how I feel about it. "You don't feel like you're cheating us out of all this? I mean, do you ever wish people knew?"

James sighs, his expression serious. "Sometimes. Think about it. They never get to be a part of all of this." He gestures vaguely out the window, at the rolling green hills and dark sky. "We *are* cheating them. But as far as importance goes, we've put the well-being of Lyria above the thirst for knowledge of Earth. Tell me you wouldn't do the same thing."

I mirror his position, crossing my arms over my chest, no more than a foot of space is between us. "I don't know what I would do," I tell him honestly.

James' face darkens. "Well, then we have a problem."

"Another one?"

"Yes, another one. Because you aren't allowed to tell anyone about us, about Lyria."

I raise my eyebrows. "I'm not *allowed*?"

"No, you're not allowed."

"Would you care to explain that to me?" I challenge.

"It's simple, really," James says coolly. "Otherworlders can't know about us. About this. It's a secret, our secret, and we intend to keep it that way."

"I'm not saying I want to invite my world to move here! But don't some people deserve to know?"

Our voices have risen from a muted conversation to a loud argument.

"People like who?" Crispin asks me, as James and I both fall silent.

I hesitate. "People like Sophie. Like Jade and Max and David. Like my parents," I answer.

"You would tell them?" James asks incredulously. "After everything you've already been through here, your first instinct is to include them in this?" When I nod, James throws his hands in the air. "I don't think you've quite got a handle on your role here! You're in danger. Because of who you are. Now, whether or not you believe your prophecy, others do. That's what Crispin and I were trying to tell you yesterday. The more you tell everyone at home, the more danger you put them in. They can be used as leverage against you, Cara!"

This isn't James angry as he normally is; I recognize that he isn't mad at me, necessarily. He's angry because he's confused, because he is unable to see the situation the way I do and doesn't understand why I continue to hold tight to my way of thinking. And I don't quite understand it either. But it's important to me, and I can't just let it go.

"This sounds as though it's something to discuss at another time, on another day." Verne breaks the silence when I don't have a response to James' outburst. As this is the first time Verne or Sasha has heard the boys and I have this conversation, they are watching us curiously. But Crispin and James are disgruntled with me all over again.

I fall into one of the chairs around the table and stare out the window. "I'm sorry," I say, meeting first Crispin's and then James' eyes briefly. "I am. I know those are exactly the things that I shouldn't be worrying about right now. But I just can't get them out of my head."

Crispin sighs. He rubs the back of his neck and then comes over to sit next to me. "It's okay. We're trying to be more understanding, we are, but I don't think we've made it very clear how big of a deal this is."

I look to him. "The whole saving-the-world prophecy deal? No, you've made that pretty dang clear, as a matter of fact."

"Not the prophecy deal. The bringing-someone-from-Earth-into-Lyria deal."

I keep my eyes fixed on him until he explains. "The only way for someone without magic to be brought over the tear is for them to jump with someone who *is* magic. So, as everything stands, people from Earth can't jump on their own, and people from Lyria don't bring them over. Mainly for the reasons that James explained a moment ago. In fact," Crispin looks to Verne for confirmation, "I believe the only known instance of an Otherworlder coming to Lyria is in the case of the man who wrote the prophecies."

Verne nods, affirming Crispin's statement. "You have to think of Lyria as it is, as one big secret," Verne tells me, picking up where Crispin left off. "Everything: the people, the animals, the very land, is supposed to be kept under wraps. The more Otherworlders who know, the less secure the secret becomes. And it is an important secret to keep. So the solution, the most surefire way to assure everyone Lyria has remained hidden, is to refrain from telling anyone at all from Earth about it. It has been that way here for hundreds of years.

"Now," Verne continues. "That secret has been compromised. We have known for a long time that, someday, there would be one of you who would have to know. That is the way the prophecy says it shall occur. But very few are comfortable with the idea of sharing the centuries-old secret. Only because it is you, Cara, only for that reason, have the majority of Lyrians been willing to lay aside their fear and accept that this is necessary. As the one who is destined to save our land, we have put our trust in you. But do not expect Lyrians to extend the same faith to those you tell, for they play no part in our world. It does not make sense that *you* could both save Lyria and then destroy it by bringing elements from your world here. But that is not true of the rest of the Otherworlders."

"I'm not talking about all Otherworlders," I say. "I'm talking about the few I know and trust. The ones who are important enough to my life to share secrets with. I can't just shut them out!"

"Secrets have an unfortunate way of spreading, far beyond those they were intended for," Verne tells me gently. "It is, after all, our world at stake. You cannot be surprised when we are protective of it."

I'm not meeting Verne's eyes anymore. I can't decide where to look. The window, the floor, the ceiling—all seem equally inviting. But, all on their own, my eyes seek out James and hold his gaze. He's still leaning against the window with his face outlined in gray light. His hands are in his pockets. His eyes match the sky outside.

"How can we make this easier for you?" he asks me softly.

I take a long time to respond. Everything they've told me, everything they just said, rolls through my mind. "Expect less of me?" I answer.

James laughs once. "Anything else?"

"Honestly?" I say with a sigh as I cross one of my legs under the other. "I don't know." After another beat of silence I add, "I think I just need some answers, and I haven't gotten them yet."

Crispin smiles now too. "Cara, if we answered all the questions you have, we'd be here for years."

I pull a mock frown at him. "*Some* answers. Not all, *some*."

"We've been doing the best we can to tell you what you've wanted to know," James says to me.

I can think of a couple specific instances where this isn't entirely true, but I keep them to myself. "Verne," I address him. "Didn't you say we could visit the treasury today? Find out about my ring?"

"We can, my dear. That's what you want to do?"

I hesitate for only an instant before nodding. "Yes. That's what I want to do first." I wave a hand at the tables and books and scrolls. "Before we dive into all this, at least."

James grins more widely at my aversion to work.

"Then," Verne says, "you'll have to give me some time. I've asked Granite to help us determine which ring is missing, so I must go tell him we're ready," he explains to the other three. I don't know what he means, but I assume I'll find out soon enough. Verne waves to us, then starts toward the staircase. He calls over his shoulder, "I'll meet you down there in a while."

We wait only five minutes before becoming bored enough that we decide it's time to journey down to the treasury. Or, at least, Sasha, James, and I are bored enough. Crispin is so engrossed in his multiple books and scribbled notes that it takes James and me calling his name and Sasha throwing a scroll at him before he raises his head.

"Ready to go?" Sasha asks impatiently.

The three of us wait with tapping feet and crossed arms while Crispin holds up a finger and finishes his notes. When he shows no sign of moving away, James reaches over, slams Crispin's book shut, and gets in his face to say, "If you make us late, *you'll* have to explain why to Granite."

That, somehow, gets Crispin moving. While I laugh, James winks at me, Crispin matches James' mischievous smile, and the boys race each other to the railing and launch themselves over into the empty air. Sasha giggles as I gasp, my heart pounding. It's a few dozen feet down to the ground—enough for a serious injury no matter how magical you are. I rush over to grasp the banister and stare over the side.

I shouldn't have worried. They have leaped just far enough to land in perfect crouches atop the bookcases on the floor below, and now they're climbing down the shelves without disturbing a single book. Sasha is already running down the stairs to meet them.

Not to be outdone, I race after them and take the steps two at a time to reach the bottom. Nelma stays behind, curled up asleep in the shadows.

As I round a corner to meet up with them all, I have to skid to a completely ungraceful stop to avoid crashing headlong into a young girl.

It takes her a moment to notice me, even with my yelp of surprise. She's even smaller than me, thin, and her nose is buried in what looks like an incredibly heavy, large book. The kind of book most girls her age would be avoiding at all costs. She blinks up at me with big, light green eyes. Her hair is long with Cleopatra-style bangs. She seems unsurprised by my appearance—a first in Lyria.

"I'm so sorry," I say quickly, when she doesn't speak. "I didn't see you there."

"Oh, it's quite all right," the girl says. Her voice is naturally quiet.

I hesitate, expecting her to say more. She hardly blinks as she continues to gaze at me. Though her eyes hold no trace of true curiosity, I can't shake the feeling that she's studying me much more closely than anyone else has since I arrived. "Umm..." I fumble for the appropriate excuse to keep walking. I lamely decide on, "I guess I need to go...now."

"You're Lady Cara," she states.

"Yes," I reply, unintentionally making it sound like a question. "I'm sorry, I don't know who you are."

She smiles for an instant, a flicker of light crossing her face. "My name is Cassandra," she tells me.

"Well, it's awfully nice to meet you," I say. "Now, I really do have to—"

"Yes, of course," Cassandra nods, looking back down to her book. When she does I see three bands wrapped around her white-blonde hair.

Before I can stop myself I tell her: "Those are pretty. They look like something my little sister would wear."

Rising Calm

Absentmindedly, Cassandra reaches up to touch the headbands. "They're special," she says.

"Why?" I ask curiously.

"Well, let's see." She fingers each band in turn. "Black, the first, that one means heartbreak. It is the thickest band because it lasts the longest. Pink represents peace. It's small and delicate, but it always comes next." The clouds that have been obscuring her pale eyes lift slightly when she brushes the last one. "Gold. Justice."

I wait for more after she falls silent, having very little idea what she means, but she doesn't elaborate. James is suddenly by my side, nodding politely to Cassandra before taking my arm and leading me away. Just then Cassandra speaks again, "They are the steps that come after losing someone you love."

I want to turn and murmur an apology. I feel as though I have intruded on personal ground, but we are already around the corner and away.

****

"Who was that?" I ask James as we trudge down another flight of stairs. I didn't realize quite how many floors the castle had until I was told the treasury is on one of the ones underground. The library is on the second, technically, though it takes up two additional floors with its height. My room is on the fourth. The prophecy room is on the fifth. The servant's quarters are in the two floors above that, and the attic is above those. My head begins to spin while I try to picture it all.

Crispin and Sasha are ahead of us having one of their brother-sister debates. James answers: "Cassandra, and her brother Tarn, were cousins of Branshire's wife."

It takes a moment for that to register. With a sinking feeling in my chest I say: "They 'were'?"

"Arianna died giving birth to their daughter," he replies, eyes fixed straight ahead. He adds, as though obligated: "The baby didn't live through the day."

If Branshire had been anywhere in sight, in that moment I would have rushed to hug him. As it is, all I can do is press a hand to my mouth and ignore my heartache. "Did he love her?" I ask softly, after a moment of silence.

James looks at me curiously, seeming perplexed that this is the question I've chosen to ask. But he answers honestly: "Yes, he did. Very much. It took him months just to leave his room after her death. The only people who were allowed to see him were Cassandra and Tarn. Those two used to live at the manor in Kenstral, but Branshire and Arianna were more like their parents than their real mother and father, so they decided to stay in Geler with him after Arianna died."

All I know of Branshire is what I have put together from our meeting yesterday. He'd seemed smart, steady, strong, appeared to be observant and kind. He'd seemed to be happy. It's difficult to hear about his heartbreak.

"He's okay, Cara," James tells me as he studies my pale face. "He still thinks about her, still misses her, but he's okay."

"His wife and his daughter. He lost them both in one day," I whisper sadly, unable to imagine the kind of pain this would cause. "Oh, James. That's..." I can't finish my thought, and James doesn't ask me to. He simply reaches out and takes my hand, giving it one long pulse—which I return—before letting go. My heart flutters in my chest, but I don't take the time to think about it because Crispin announces we've reached the treasury door.

Swallowing my emotion, I stare at it dubiously. No guards are posted outside the door; the wood is unembellished. So I'm confused to hear *this* is the treasury, until Crispin pulls the door open. The small room inside has two guards, standing to attention in front of a wooden door similar to the first. They bow to Crispin and Sasha, nod to James and me, and then one places his palm on this second door. His fingers twitch in a rhythm I can't follow, there is a quiet click, and the presumably once-locked door swings open for us.

I am momentarily stunned by the room, but James places a hand on my back and pushes me forward so the guard can shut the door behind us. Then he, Crispin, and Sasha take a step back to watch my reaction with identical smiles.

I know how wide my eyes must be as I try to take everything in. Gold, silver, and jewels, mainly in the forms of crowns and rings, glitter from every available nook and cranny. The room is rectangular, with another door in one corner, and a long island stretched across the middle. On this is a display of crowns, dozens of them. The shelves and tables around the room hold a variety of tiaras, necklaces, and bracelets, but what finally draw me over are the royal rings.

The display that holds them looks as though it should be in an Otherworld jewelry store. A solid stone block stretches the length of the room. Its top is about three feet wide, and it gently slopes down from the wall to end at waist level. This makes the rings easier to view.

And what a lot of rings there are. Each is set in its own slot in the surface of the stone; there isn't even an inch between them. The style changes slightly from left to right, but the general design remains the same for every band. There is always an emerald set in the midst of diamonds. As they do between Crispin's and my rings, the number of diamonds varies, but they are always there.

"Goodness gracious," I finally breathe.

Crispin has moved to stand near me, and he looks as pleased as if he owns the rings himself. *Which, in a sense, I suppose he does.* I remember in a rush his status as Crown Prince. Then something hits me, and I turn to study the rows of rings once more. I frown. "Why aren't any of them missing?" I ask my companions as I twist my own ring around my finger.

"What did you think Verne was bringing Granite down for?" Crispin asks.

I raise my eyebrows at him. "I'm sorry, what?" I reply.

James snickers. Crispin sighs. "Granite," he says again.

"No matter how many times you repeat the word 'granite', I'm not going to know what you're talking about," I say. "I'm not sure this discussion is necessary *every time* you guys tell me something new. Unless my lack of knowledge is amusing to you." I think for a short moment and then add, "Actually...no. Not even then."

James takes over the explanation. "Granite is a dwarf, Cara."

I narrow my eyes at Crispin. "Now was that so hard?" I ask him. He just grins. I look at James. "A dwarf?"

"Of course," he says. "Who knows metal and precious jewels better than a dwarf?"

I hazard a guess. "No one?"

I'm rewarded with a crooked smile. "No one," James confirms. "We figured since no one's ever noticed your ring was missing, the most likely explanation was that it was replaced with a fake. People come and go in here quite often, and an empty ring slot would have been noticed. So Granite, the dwarf, is going to help us examine the rings and determine which one isn't real."

I look between the boys and then at Sasha. "Why do you all know this and I don't? Where was I when this was determined?" I ask them all, slightly irritated that I'm still so out of the loop.

"Asleep," Crispin tells me.

"You planned all this last night?"

"What else would we be doing?"

"Oh, I don't know," I say sarcastically. "Sleeping, perhaps?"

Before Crispin has a chance to retort, the treasury door swings open. Verne steps in and nods to us. "Lady Cara," he says, leaving me to wonder again when I received my title and how everyone but me knows about it. "Allow me to introduce you to Granite. He's agreed to give us a hand in finding whose ring you've been given."

It takes a great deal of effort for me not to stare at Granite when he enters, grumbling under his breath. He already looks unhappy—his rugged face seems to be set in a permanent scowl—and I don't want to make him angrier. Granite is almost a head shorter than me, which is saying something, with overlarge ears sticking out from under his thick mass of gray-black hair. He has a short, wiry beard and mustache to match his hair, broad hands, and charcoal colored eyes set above a large nose.

He doesn't look pleased to be offering his services. I try to look as grateful as possible anyway.

Granite takes the time to fix each of us with a personal glare, as though we've committed some grievous wrongdoing by requesting help. His gaze rests the longest on James, who doesn't look particularly happy either. "Wot's 'ee doin' 'ere?" Granite growls. He scowls at Verne. "You dinna say 'ee was comin'." He doesn't have the same accent as the other Demesnians. Instead he just sounds like he couldn't care less about proper grammar.

Verne's response is polite. "Why wouldn't the Crown Prince's guard be with him?"

This is clearly not the response Granite wanted. "Keep 'im," he points a stubby finger directly at James, "away from me."

James' jaw is clenched as he gives Granite a mocking nod of respect before moving to the far corner of the room.

I watch him until Granite barks out: "You! Girl. Gimme tha' ring o' yours."

Had I known him better, and had we not appeared to need his help so badly, I would have come back with a biting reply to his demand. As it is, I silently slip my ring off and hold it out to him.

He's quick to snatch it from my grasp and hold it up to his eye to examine it. He starts to mumble—I only catch snatches of what he's saying: "...after Queen Myla...not Obsidian's shoddy workmanship...no older than four-hundre' years..."

"How do you know that?" I can't help asking curiously.

Granite looks annoyed at the interruption. "Wha'?" he asks.

"How do you know it's less than four-hundred years old?" I ask again.

He opens his mouth, I'm sure to tell me off, but Crispin clears his throat. Granite closes his mouth again with a disgruntled expression. He glowers at the floor and answers, "New way a workin' the gold. Only started usin' it afer King Dar. Four-hundred years ago." He squints up at me angrily before continuing his inspection of my ring.

I slowly back away toward James and lean against the wall next to him. "So... You two have a history?" I ask under my breath.

"Don't, Cara," James warns.

I look at him. "Don't what?"

"Ask questions like that. Because I won't answer, and you'll get angry."

I cross my arms and sigh. He's right. I still know absolutely nothing about James' real past. "Fine. Do all dwarves dislike you?"

The side of James' mouth quirks slightly. He looks down at me. "Yes."

I take the reply in silence. We stand together and watch Granite make his way to the ring display. He bypasses the first third of the rings completely, and then he holds my ring up to each of those on display. I assume this is to see if there's a match. Granite works quickly—much more quickly than any of us could have.

Soon, he pulls one ring out of its slot and passes it to Verne. "Done," he states. "Ken I go?"

Verne takes a long look at the slot Granite removed the ring from. "You're sure?" he asks.

Granite looks highly offended. "Aye!" he cries gruffly. "I don' make mistakes li' that."

Verne nods, already lost in thought. Granite scurries out the door without a goodbye to anyone.

Crispin, Sasha, James, and I wait for Verne to explain whatever he's discovered, because the look on his face means he's realized something.

"This is Queen Layla's ring," Verne finally says quietly.

This, apparently, is a very serious proclamation, because Crispin, James, and Sasha all go still. I glance between them all as they turn to face me.

"Queen Layla?" I ask, for lack of anything better to say.

James and Sasha take a seat on the floor of the treasury room in anticipation of the long explanation to come. Crispin leans against the wall. Verne hands the real ring back to me so I can put it on, replaces the fake in its slot, and crosses his arms. All of them continue watching me.

As I've come to expect, Crispin finally starts to explain: "Queen Layla. She married into royalty a few centuries ago. She was the king's second wife, much younger than his first, and she was not too pleased with her marriage. Their wedding took place during the Final Krelan War, which we were losing at that point."

He pauses, collecting his thoughts it seems. "That was a time in Lyrian history where people still remembered what we now think of as old magic. Elemental magic."

Crispin locks his hands behind his head. "There's so much we haven't told you about yet," he murmurs, as much to himself as to me. He fixes me with his steady, green-eyed gaze. "Okay. When Lyrians crossed the ocean to come here, the first thing they did was establish the kingdoms. Krela was given the mountains to Demesne's northwest, Nava, the peaks farther southeast than that. The Sheiks took the land east of the river, the hills and the caves there. The Cairnes occupy the northeast desert. And Demesne took these plains, between the forest and the coast. And the kingdoms were split like this for a specific reason: obviously for the looks of the inhabitants, but, more importantly, for the reason they looked this way. For the elemental magic they could do.

"We in Demesne could manipulate the water, the Cairnes worked with wind, Navites controlled ice, Krela, fire, and Sheiks could control earth. So it only made sense for the kingdoms to separate based on their magic."

Crispin smiles ruefully. "I'm not explaining this very well, am I?" he asks me.

"It's a bit jumbled," I admit with a similar grin, "but I think I'm keeping up."

So he continues: "So, back to Layla. She was only twenty or so at the time. And, just as people now specialize in certain magics, usually, only particular people then could work with the elements. Queen Layla was one of these element workers. A powerful one.

"It's part of the king's job to lead the army in times of war. The king himself wasn't a strong enough magician to work with water, so he used Layla's power."

I could picture it: a young woman, forced into a marriage she didn't want, made to use her power whether or not she wanted to. I pull a face. Crispin notices.

"I know," he says to me. "But that's the way it was, and the Demesnian side of the war needed her. She accepted it, too. She agreed to the marriage, agreed to help, however unhappily. Layla gathered a group of elemental magicians from Demesne, Cairne, and Nava. And they formed the plan that won the war.

"The three kingdoms first took Sheik. With a small force of the army holding Krelan reinforcements back, the rest of the army captured Sheik, one territory at a time, over the course of many months until they surrendered. And when the Krelans heard about the surrender they went mad. They refused to quit; their leaders claimed they would fight to the death of their kingdom before they gave in.

"So they razed Demesnian territories, set fire to more than one Navite ice village, killed thousands of citizens from each of the kingdoms... It was carnage. And our leaders did the only thing they could think of to end the bloodshed."

With a sinking feeling in the pit of my stomach, I know I'm about to hear how Krela became uninhabited. And it wasn't by some kind of mass exodus of the kingdom or an outside force like I have been imagining. They were slaughtered. For good reason it seems, but nevertheless...

"And this is where Layla comes into play," Crispin tells me, now eying the ring on my finger. "As Demesne's most powerful water worker, she and the small army she'd gathered around her came up with the final plan. The main force of the army—the regular magicians and the foot soldiers—forced Krela back into their own territory. At this point not a single Krelan was holding back from the fight. As they retreated, the survivors were pushed back into a small valley. Everyone, from each Krelan territory, ended up there. Our armies surrounded them."

Crispin's face hardens as he speaks. His emerald eyes, generally humor-filled, are steely, his jaw set, hands curled into fists at his side. I can't tell what he's angry with: the Krelans, their final stand, the way the story is sure to end.

But he keeps talking, and I feel my heart start to pound as he does. "And Layla's brigade struck. She directed the wind workers to keep the Krelans trapped as they realized what was going on, the Demesnians to make it rain, make the valley flood, and the Navites to freeze the water as it rose.

"No Krelan surrendered. None of them survived."

I can almost understand why this was necessary. I can see myself in the battle, watching from the sidelines as this genocide—for I know no other word for it—is committed. I find my eyes are tightly closed, though I don't recall shutting them. I'm surprised by the sudden urge I have to yank the ring from my finger. It's a piece of history I don't want to be connected to.

But a hand clamps down on my wrists before I can move. My eyes fly open. James is right in front of me, and he has an iron grip on my arm. His face is as hard as Crispin's, and just as steady.

"Think about it, Cara," he breathes. It's only then I see he's afraid. For a split second, I think he's worried Crispin revealed too much. But then I realize he's afraid that I'm going to hate his world for what they did so long ago.

So I try. For him. I push past the bile twisting in my stomach and picture it. The Krelan's declaration that they won't surrender. The burned homes and the bodies, the wasted lives. I can see Layla, a small woman with a serious face and a long braid of yellow hair, her heart heavy with the weight of her decision. I can see the silent sadness of the army as they watch a piece of their world disappear and die.

There was no better way out, no better choice. Not at that point.

Verne passes me a handkerchief. I don't know why, until James reaches out to brush tears from my face. I stumble back. *Why the hell am I crying?*

Horrible remorse is welling up in me. I look, wide-eyed, between James and Verne and Crispin, and I press the handkerchief to my face. "What is this about?" I ask, waving the handkerchief in the air for emphasis.

They look as surprised as I feel. James slides my ring off my finger, and he holds it up to the light as though it's changed significantly since last he saw it. "Emotional transfer," James states, looking away from the ring and back to my tear-stained face. "There's this form of magic," he begins.

I try and fail to muffle a groan. "Again?"

James smiles fleetingly. "Yes, again. When there's an object, like a ring, for example, that is strongly attached to someone, emotions can be stored in it, unintentionally. Layla, as royalty, was wearing her ring at all times. And"—here James glances again at my face—"clearly she had some strong emotions associated with certain memories. What with you being so powerful, Layla being so powerful, the emotions being so powerful—" he breaks off with a shrug. "It's just a lot of power," he finishes lamely.

"Which you seem to have unlocked," Crispin adds.

James passes me the ring, and I turn it over in my hands a few times before slipping it back on my finger where it belongs.

I shake my head in disbelief as I finish wiping the tears off my face. "Keep it," Verne tells me when I offer the damp handkerchief back. I do.

"Now," Verne muses. "Why would someone take Queen Layla's ring and seek Cara out in the Otherworld? Why Queen Layla's, specifically?"

"I think we saw why," James says quietly, pointing to the handkerchief in my fist.

"Maybe. But how would they know about Cara's connection to it?" Crispin asks.

Sasha stands up. "Lucky guess?"

Verne holds up a hand to stop the guessing. "We aren't going to get the answers we want by making assumptions," Verne says to all of us.

He, James, and Sasha all look to Crispin, so I do too. Crispin nods once in understanding before walking to the far wall and sliding down to sit with his back against it. The other three wander off, studying the displays with sudden interest. But I can't bring myself to look away.

Crispin's palms are flat against the ground, and his fingers are splayed. He tilts his head back, closes his eyes. His lips are moving, but no sound comes out. I watch his fingers twitch—there's no real movement or twists to this cast (I know that's what it is). Instead he works in silent concentration.

James eventually puts a hand on my elbow and steers me away to look at some crowns from a few decades ago. "It could take him some time," he tells me. "He has a lot of people to work through."

"I don't know what that means," I say, my nose practically touching the tiara James is showing me as I eye the intricate design.

I swear James is holding back a sigh. "I know you don't," he says, running a hand through his ever-tousled black hair. "He's going through every person who's been in the treasury over the past twenty years."

"What?" Now I look up from the crowns at James' face.

He shrugs like it's no big deal. "People leave trails wherever they go. It takes an unbelievable amount of energy to trace those trails, but it *is* possible. And what with Cris being so strong... Well, he can do it. So, if he can find the exact trail of the person who examined your ring last, before it was taken from Lyria, we'll know who really gave it to you, and possibly why they did."

I frown. "I thought we knew why. You remember...the prophecy?"

James corrects himself. "We'll know who and *how*."

I wrinkle my nose but make no further comment.

It takes about ten minutes more for Crispin to finish his cast, and when he does all he says is, "Hey guys." He doesn't move from his place in the floor, doesn't remove his hands from their positions, doesn't open his eyes. His face is still set in concentration.

We all move to stand around him. Slowly, a steady trail of white light makes its way across the floor, from the door to the display where Layla's ring was once kept. When Crispin squeezes his eyes more tightly shut, the end of the trail twists into the air. It swirls in on itself, finally forming a translucent, life-sized man. We watch as the man bends over the display, reaches out a hand as if he's picking up one of the rings, and pockets it. From another pocket the man removes something—the fake, most likely—puts it down, and then, with a hurried glance over his shoulder, he walks away. Slowly he fades out of existence and the trail of his energy winds back to the door before disappearing.

I let out a breath I didn't know I was holding. Everyone else in the room looks confused. Pleased that the cast worked, pleased they have something to go off of now, but still confused, because what they now know still isn't much.

For the first time, I know more than the Lyrians. None of them have registered my new shock. They've started walking off, talking excitedly, wondering where to begin the search for this man.

I catch James' sleeve, who gestures quietly to Crispin. Sasha and Verne are almost at the treasury room door before they notice we've stopped. I twist my ring around my finger anxiously.

"Guys," I say after a small pause. "Guys, that was my Uncle Amos."

18

We reconvene in the library, this time on the third floor, where we have less of a chance of being disturbed or overheard.

Verne had left the treasury separate from us, saying he needed to talk to Granite once more before we all spoke, and thinking he might get more out of the dwarf if the rest of us weren't around. I couldn't help but agree with him.

So we are left waiting for him once more. Crispin has brought his books up from the second floor, while James and Sasha stare into space. Every once in a while they look at me, then away again. I'm lying upside down in one of the chairs—a much more difficult feat than I had anticipated in the dress. But I succeed, letting the blood rush to my head in a poor attempt to expel some of the more confusing thoughts from my brain.

"*That*, was your Uncle Amos?" James asks me for the third time.

"Ask me that again and I will punch you in the throat," I say calmly, tired of simply answering: "Yes."

Even upside down I can see James fight to keep the smile from his face.

Crispin is having a hard time focusing on his studying. "I don't understand," he mumbles, rubbing his eyes.

"None of us do," I tell him. I do my best to look over at him. "But what in particular?"

"Why did your uncle take the ring?" he asks.

I pull myself into a mostly upright position. "Isn't that, like, the question of the hour? None of us know."

"No," Crispin says almost before I finish. "I mean, if he's not the one who gave it to you? When you told James and me the story, you said your uncle's *friend* gave you Layla's ring. So, if your uncle was there and your uncle is the one who took the ring from the treasury, then why didn't he just give it to you? Why go through the third person?"

I frown. James does the same. "I...I don't know," I tell Crispin. I hadn't given that any thought yet. Trust Crispin to be thinking that far ahead, and doing so while studying something else.

Crispin shuts his books and drops into the armchair next to me. "It doesn't make much sense," he sighs.

"So it falls right into the same category as everything else we've learned lately," I say.

He drums his fingers against his knee and shoots me a look. It's truly bothering him that he can't figure this out.

"Your uncle would have had to be someone pretty high-ranking around here to get into the treasury," James notes.

"He couldn't have distracted the guards or something and just sneaked in?" I ask.

James shakes his head. "He wasn't in that much of a hurry. In the projection Crispin cast, Amos was taking his sweet time."

I think about that for a time, and notice Crispin is doing the same.

"Then our parents must know him," Sasha says. She's talking to Crispin, but she's looking at me. "How long ago was Amos in there?"

"About eighteen years ago," Crispin replies.

Sasha nods, as though this is to be expected. "That's right before we were born," she notes. "So mom and dad were already ruling. If Amos really did rank that high in the court, they would know him. Probably personally."

"And I believe they did." Verne apparently heard that last remark, and he appears at the head of the stairs. "Granite says there were two men, a number of years ago, who showed an interest in the royal rings—both the ones already made and the making of new ones. He doesn't remember much about them, as human features tend to slip through his mind. But he does recall only one of them was Demesnian. The other, to the best of his knowledge, appeared to be Navite."

James, Sasha, and Crispin immediately have questions for Verne, but my voice silences them all. "What do Navites look like?" I struggle to remember Uncle Amos' friend, the man who handed the ring to me so long ago.

"Pale-skinned," Verne answers. "Black hair. Blue eyes the color of ice."

I flash a glance at James. He very nearly fits this description. But James shakes his head slightly, and I look away again before our silent exchange is noticed.

"I can't remember." I sigh in frustration after wracking my brain for a long moment, trying to picture the man who handed me the ring so long ago.

Crispin crosses the first two fingers of his left hand and looks me in the eye. "Yes, you can."

I think again, harder this time, back to ten years ago. Uncle Amos' friend had stayed in the background, only approaching me twice: once to introduce himself and again to give me the ring. His raven black hair had been long enough to brush his shoulders. His face was old and weathered. I remember wondering why Amos was friends with someone so much older than himself. And I remember being awed by the man as he passed the ring to me, because his anxious, sincere eyes were lavender in color.

I blink my eyes open, unable to remember shutting them in the first place. "His eyes weren't blue," is the first thing I think of to say. "They were purple. Light purple." Then I narrow my eyes at Crispin, as understanding about what just happened dawns. "You did that to me in the woods, too, didn't you? Some kind of cast to make me remember."

"Dredge up your old memories," Crispin clarifies. He seems tired, a little too pale, but his green eyes glimmer. He's pleased with himself. "Yeah. I did that."

"And you should stop," Verne warns him, "before you exhaust yourself."

"Too late," Crispin says quietly, smiling slightly as he leans his head back and closes his eyes.

I watch him for moment, unsure if I should be concerned. But eventually I turn my attention to Verne again. "If he was Navite, why would his eyes be purple?"

"For the same reason Prince Crispin and King Rennar have green eyes rather than blue." Verne smiles at my blank expression. "We don't quite know, my dear. For years it was thought that this showed them to be stronger magicians, which seemed plausible, as both Rennar and Crispin are seventh sons. But then there are those like our own Cassandra, or Koda, who is one of our stable hands, who do not posses any magic far outside the ordinary."

"So there are some other Navites with lavender eyes rather than blue ones?" I ask, just to be sure.

Verne nods. "There are."

"So it's safe to assume Amos, being blonde-haired and blue-eyed, and this Navite were the ones questioning the dwarves about the rings?"

"It appears that way," Verne agrees.

I pause. "Okay. Then Crispin, I'm thinking your question was a pretty good one. If Amos took the ring, why did he need to use the Navite to give it to me?"

Crispin dips his head in acknowledgment of my statement, but that's the only sign he gives that he has heard. James is watching him carefully. I remember what they've said, that James is Crispin's guard. And, right now, he looks it.

"I do believe that we will have to broach this subject with the king and queen if we want fast answers," Verne tells us all.

"There's no other way?" I ask. Either Rennar and Andromeda didn't know they had an Otherworlder in their court (and if that's the case I don't necessarily want to be the one to tell them), or they knew and purposely kept it a secret from their children, James, and Verne.

Sasha seems to be thinking along the same lines. "What makes you think they'll be willing to talk about it?" she asks Verne.

He smiles kindly at her. "We simply have to hope they will." That is not quite as reassuring as I would have liked, but he continues, "It may be best for you to ask at dinner tonight. They will know of our visit to the treasury anyhow, so they will ask what we learned. It should be an appropriate time to ask them for details."

Sasha and I remain unconvinced, but Crispin, his eyes still closed, nods in agreement, so James does too.

"I think we can call it a day. For tutoring, at least," Verne says. "I think you all have done enough." He looks specifically at Crispin and me when he says this. "Unless," he addresses only me, "there is more you would like to learn."

James and Sasha widen their eyes behind Verne's back and shake their heads. I hold back a smile as I tell Verne: "I think I've learned more than enough to last me the afternoon." Sasha and James relax.

Verne heads off to who knows where, so I turn to them and ask: "Did you really think I was going to *ask* to spend the rest of my day being tutored? Give me some credit."

Sasha smiles in relief. "I didn't have to study at all!" she cries happily, making me laugh. We share an outlook on schoolwork, then.

James is still waiting for Crispin to move. When he doesn't, James stands up and walks over to him to shake his shoulder. "Cris? How you holding up?"

Crispin cracks his eyes open and glances up at James. I think he must have been putting on a brave face for Verne, because all he does now is pull his face into a grimace and mumble, "I did too much."

James nods; he expected this answer. He casts a glance at Sasha, who immediately bounds to her feet with a nod. "I'll ask Frale if we can be served lunch up here," she says (probably for my benefit) before dashing down the stairs.

Since Crispin's eyes are closed once again—as far as I can tell he's fallen fast asleep in the last few seconds—I ask James, "What happened to him?"

James is still standing next to Crispin's chair, but he draws his eyes away from Crispin's face to look at me. "You haven't cast enough to feel it yet, but the more magic you do, the more it wears you out. And Crispin did two big casts in a matter of hours. The one that showed us your Uncle Amos? That would be enough to finish anyone for the rest of the day, except for him. But that one coupled with the memory cast he just did was too much."

"He did that same cast in the woods, and he seemed fine afterward," I point out.

"Right," James nods. He takes a seat in another chair across from me. He runs both hands through his hair, making it stand up messily, before resting his elbows on his knees and leaning toward me slightly. "In the forest, all Cris did was prompt a memory. That story of how you got your ring was most likely something you didn't *really* forget, you just hadn't thought about it in a while. So it was easier to pull to the front of your mind. But remembering the features of a man you saw once, ten years ago? That's much harder. So it takes more energy."

I gesture to Crispin. "Then why did he do it?"

James frowns. "Because, in Crispin's head, the answers to our questions are more important than his own health." He sounds like he doesn't condone this way of thinking.

"So then, how much can he handle normally?" I ask.

He thinks seriously about the question. "Normally he'd be tired, but fine, even after all this. The only reason he's so beat now is because he took on two energy-sapping casts back-to-back and he's way out of practice."

"This is something you can practice for?" I ask.

"Of course," James says, causing me to roll my eyes. He grins. "It is, though. Something you *have* to practice for, actually. Practice doesn't make you a more powerful magician, but it makes you a more controlled one. And it strengthens you—it stops your energy from disappearing so quickly. The more you practice, the more that hollow in your chest stretches and toughens."

"And that's why the empty feeling went away when I did my first cast?"

James nods and adds, "It's also why that hollow felt so empty to begin with. It had never been used, so it was weak."

Now I'm on a roll, thinking of questions as fast as James can answer them. "So why didn't my cast wear me out? I had never done any magic before, so like you said, the hollow in my chest should have been really weak, right? So shouldn't my moving-the-boulder cast have made me tired like Crispin is now?"

"Ah," James says. "That. What we know about magic is from experience and from history, so keep in mind some of this ventures into guesswork. But, as well as we can figure, anyone who has magic has the ability to unconsciously store some of their body's energy in the hollow. So if you don't do magic for a time, you're still saving that energy to cast in your chest's hollow. You had been building it up for sixteen years. So the cast you did depleted some, but not all, of your energy supply. You still have plenty of energy left, you just don't have much stamina. Which is why we only had you do the one cast."

I nod, taking in everything he said. "Okay," I say after a long pause. "I think I got it."

"You haven't seen Crispin in action yet," James tells me as he settles more comfortably into his chair. "Someday soon this will all make more sense, when you actually begin to practice with magic. I know right now it must seem a little weak to you. Especially seeing Crispin, who we've been constantly telling you is the most powerful magician around, worn out before noon. But when he gets back in practice, you'll see."

I hear Sasha coming back, directing whoever is with her on how best to carry the trays of food up the stairs, so I fall silent. James stands back up next to Crispin, who is still breathing evenly in his sleep. I clear any books and papers off the surrounding tables and try to look less confused than I feel.

"Over there is fine," Sasha is saying as she appears, waving a hand vaguely in our direction. I'm quick to stand

and move out of their way. Talit and Genia are following her. Each is bearing trays loaded with food.

I smile at Talit, truly happy to see someone I recognize. He flashes me a quick smile before dropping his eyes to carefully set down his trays. Genia is a bit less sure of herself; she shakes slightly in the presence of all of us. Talit helps her steady the trays as she places them on the tables. James nods to each of them politely while Sasha thanks them.

"Genia definitely has a thing for you," Sasha whispers to James once the other two are gone in a flurry of bowing and curtsying.

James rolls his eyes at Sasha as he pours a glass of wine from one of the trays. "For no good reason. Really Sasha, she wouldn't like me if she knew me."

"Well that's simply not true." She points to Crispin and me and then herself. "We know you, and we like you just fine." She pretends to look him over carefully. "You know, most of the time."

James chuckles. He shakes Crispin's shoulder. Crispin finally blinks his eyes open and seems surprised to see all the food laid out around us. James passes him the cup.

"It wouldn't kill you to give her a chance," Sasha continues.

"It just might," James mutters with a grin. He flashes me a look. For a second, he doesn't say a word, and my face is carefully blank, as I don't have anything to add to the current conversation. But then he tosses me a roll. "You're allowed to eat you know."

We spend the rest of the afternoon up here; it's the best time I've had since arriving. Out of everyone else's sight, Sasha, Crispin, and James all become normal teenagers, catching up on Demesnian gossip, poking fun at each other, and doing their best to explain anything and everything to me. If I can think of a question (and believe me, I can), one of them is quick to answer.

"So dwarves make the royal rings?" I ask, spreading some kind of cinnamon butter on another of Frale's rolls. They're delicious.

James answers around a mouthful of apple tart. "Yep."

Sasha throws a grape at him. "Chew your food," she tells him in the motherly tone she often seems to take with the boys.

He does so, swallowing, giving her a thumbs-up, and then continuing. "Dwarves are metal-workers, the very best in Lyria. They have this way with precious stones and metals, and long ago they agreed, for a price, obviously, to make the rings for the royal families. I believe they made the same deal with the other kingdoms, too."

"That's cool, I suppose," I say.

"Not really," Crispin disagrees. "It means they have no allegiance to anyone besides themselves. Having the same deal with everyone is their way of not showing favoritism. Much like all the other magical creatures." He mutters this last part, and then immediately looks guilty.

James clears his throat loudly from his seat on the floor and leans back against the railing. "Magical creatures don't like to make permanent alliances," he explains to me. "From time to time they'll make brief treaties with the kingdoms, but it's a constant battle to win them over, and no one has ever done so permanently."

"Do the kingdoms have alliances then?" I ask.

Crispin answers again: "For the most part. Though none of those alliances are set in stone either. Demesne has a standing alliance with Cairne, one that's been beneficial to both kingdoms and has lasted for a few centuries now. Sheik had a treaty with Krela. They're still pretty upset with the way the last war went, and they blame Demesne, rightfully so, for the fact that they lost. So they refuse to make any kind of pact with us, or with Cairne as they are our allies. Nava tends to stand alone as well. They had a one-time allegiance to Demesne and Cairne during the Krelan War, but it ended when the war did. Now we are at peace with them, but we are by no means allies."

I take a long moment to work this out in my head, munching on some strawberries as I do. "Do you have a map or something I could look at?" I finally ask. "I'm still not sure I understand the layout of this world."

James stands up and starts down the stairs before Crispin has a chance to. He's still making sure Crispin doesn't exert too much unnecessary strength, which is probably a good thing. Crispin is wide awake now and his eyes are bright and curious once again, but his face is still awfully pale.

When James comes back to join us, he's carrying a large roll of parchment. Sasha and I help him spread it out on the floor. We weigh the corners down with some of the heavy books still lying about.

As we've positioned it to face Crispin, where he's still seated in his armchair, I go and kneel next to him. James takes his already-familiar position behind Crispin's chair, and Sasha sits on Crispin's other side.

I note how easily Crispin takes to being the center, and how natural it is for him to be waited on like this. It's so easy for me to forget he's the Crown Prince.

I lean forward to get a better look at the parchment. A beautiful map is laid before us: detailed, colored, encompassing the Lyria that these three have told me so much about. I brush my fingertips over Geler, trace the boys' and my journey from the forest to the capital city. The forest and the river connect to form a U—the forest curving away from the edge of the map, and the river stretching from the coast of the Aurian Ocean to join it in the center. On the forest's north side, hills, and then mountains, begin. Krela and Nava are located in this mountain range, Krela farther northwest than Nava is. The river—which the boys and I crossed on our way out of the forest—divides Demesne from Sheik. Cairne is in the northeast corner of the map.

Many cities are scattered across the map—or territories, as I remember Crispin and James calling them. One called Harena is set in the middle of Cairne, in the vast plain that spreads out from the base of the mountain range. Another, Beibrennen, is labeled right in the center of what I think is a volcano, placed directly in Krelan territory.

"So," Crispin begins when I don't speak, "Demesne, obviously, is right here." He points. "There's Geler, Kayyar, and then a couple day's journey south of the castle brings you to the Aurian Ocean. East, across the river from us, is Sheik. It's really rocky terrain over there. Hilly, close to the cliff, and the Sheiks were the only ones willing to live there."

"Sheik looks small. I mean, compared to the other kingdoms," I say.

Crispin nods. "On the surface, it is. But the Sheiks have spent centuries excavating a labyrinth of tunnels under their land, under the hills. The other kingdoms have created magical boundaries, as a matter of fact, to ensure the tunnels didn't end up under our land."

I make a noise of understanding, allowing him to continue.

"The twin peaks, right there," Crispin points to two large mountains in the center of Nava territory, "those are where most Navites live. They have cities spiraling all the way up the mountainsides. They're easy to defend and hard to get to. Plus, the weather hardly does a thing besides sleet and snow up there, especially on those two mountains.

"The desert starts in the northeast, in that valley where the mountains stop. It's also easy to defend because the Cairne cities are all grouped near the middle, and they're the only ones who have really perfected living in that environment. It's a tough place for armies to get to.

"And then Krela." He pauses for a long time. "Mount Brennen is the volcano, there. Without it Krela would be as icy as Nava, but Mount Brennen keeps it warmer. It's just mountainous over there. And, because of the eruptions that occurred a long time ago, not much grows. It's a lot of dirt and rock and ash. Beibrennen was their capital, it was *inside* the volcano." He takes a breath, like he's about to say more, but then he falls silent.

I pull my knees to my chest and rest my forehead against them. "This is so complicated," I sigh. My voice is muffled but they all still hear me.

Someone comes to sit next to me. "Not really." It's James. "It's a lot of information, sure, but you're smart, Cara. Is there really any of that you didn't understand?"

"Would you quit being logical while I'm trying to be overwhelmed?" I ask. I turn my head to look at him, my cheek still resting on my knees.

He grins crookedly. "Would you stop being overwhelmed so I can be logical?"

Sasha glances out the window briefly. "Would you both stop so we can go get ready for dinner?"

We follow her gaze. Despite the clouds that have kept the sky dark all day, the sun is clearly setting. The four of us have been snacking on the food from the kitchen the entire afternoon; I'm not hungry and I know they can't be either, but dinner with the king and queen isn't something you skip just because you aren't hungry enough.

James keeps a watchful eye on Crispin as he stands up, and then the two start down the stairs. Sasha rolls up the map and sets it on a chair before following them. I look around the balcony. It's a mess.

"We don't need to straighten up?" I ask them all.

Sasha looks at me curiously. "No. The servants will do that."

"Oh. Right."

I let her lead me to my room where we once again change clothes. I think it's ridiculous, going through so many outfits, but Sasha loves it and I know that's how things are done around here. I'm unable to talk her out of dressing me in a light pink and white gown with gold trim. She—and the boys when they reappear, dressed in their own dinner finery—assure me that the dress is perfect for the occasion. So I accept it.

The dining hall is empty but for the footmen when the four of us arrive, so I have a chance to take it in. A large, candlelit chandelier hangs from the arched white ceiling. The stone floor is almost completely covered by an immense blue and green patterned rug, but except for a few choice paintings and tapestries, the walls hang bare. The mahogany table is set for at least two dozen; I pray silently that there will not be that many joining us. The gold candlesticks set at intervals along the surface provide more light.

Crispin leads me to a seat right in the middle of one side of the table, tells me to stay there, and then he and Sasha move off, around to the other side and across from me, though down a couple chairs.

"Where are you going?" I hiss after them. They ignore me.

I continue to stand there like an idiot until James enters the room, having stopped to have a short conversation with one of the guards. He takes everyone in with a glance, eyes glittering with thinly veiled amusement at my predicament. Then he nods to everyone and comes to stand by the chair next to mine. "Need some help?" he asks under his breath.

"Don't leave me," I plead, just as quietly.

He chuckles. He and Crispin exchange glances. Crispin shrugs slightly before switching seats with Sasha. Now he is across from James, and Sasha is on his far side.

"Are you guys allowed to change seats like that?" I whisper to Crispin and Sasha. I've figured out enough about the court here to guess the answer myself.

Crispin just shrugs it off. "I'm sure our parents will make an exception."

I raise my eyebrows at him just as Branshire comes over to lean against the chair at my other side. "What is this, a seating free-for-all?" he asks his siblings.

"It is tonight," Crispin confirms.

Branshire grins at me. "Is it safe to assume this is your doing?"

I sigh. "It appears to be."

"Ah well," he says easily. "A little change around here couldn't hurt."

I smile at him gratefully. I remember James' story of Branshire's past and my heart aches for him, but he really does seem to be just fine.

I'm about to take my seat when Crispin motions at me from across the table to continue standing. I mouth, "Why?" He points to the double doors. So I wait.

After about a full minute of standing in silence—during which Elik, Saladin, and two other men I don't know enter to stand at their seats—the doors swing open and the king and queen sweep into the dining hall.

They look exactly as rulers should. Queen Andromeda is decked in the most elaborate gown I've ever seen—it makes Sasha's dress look casual and me feel like I've accidentally worn jeans to a black tie event, though I'm in a gown of my own. Layers of green and blue and brown are heavily embroidered with gold thread, studded with emeralds at the hem, and draped elegantly about her figure, managing to make her look slender and composed through the lengths of fabric.

King Rennar is wearing the same fur-lined robe from the day before. However, underneath it, he now has on what can best be described as a high-collared vest. The long-sleeved shirt beneath that is more fitted than most of the shirts I've seen men wear around here, though it seems to be made of the same material as those and it ends in the same tight cuffs. The buttons of his vest are diamonds.

I hadn't given it much thought in the throne room yesterday, but the queen and king have the same multitude of rings spanning their fingers as Crispin and Sasha do. A swift glance around proves what I've just guessed to be true: Elik, Branshire, and Saladin have the rings too, so they must have a special meaning to the royal family. I make a mental note to ask Crispin or James later.

Everyone bows when the royal couple enters, so I am quick to do the same. Only after they have settled into their positions at either head of the table do the rest of us finally sit.

We all exchange polite greetings as we take our seats. Footmen and servers pour wine and water into the goblets set before us. As Andromeda asks Elik about "his day's work"—whatever that may be—and Rennar questions Branshire about some soldier-training situation, I concentrate on what everyone is doing. There are at least a dozen different kinds of silverware set before me as well as a multitude of glasses and plates and bowls.

James nudges me under the table as the servers set small bowls of fruit in front of us. "Work from the outside in for the silverware," he murmurs. He demonstrates by picking up the farthest right fork and using it to eat the fruit.

I copy him, still glancing around constantly to see what the others do. I see that I'm the only one who doesn't drink the wine, but I'd thought it was disgusting enough last night. I don't want any more.

"Cara," Queen Andromeda says suddenly. I swallow the grape I've just put in my mouth so quickly that I'm afraid I'll choke on it. But, after a moment of difficulty, I manage it.

"Yes?" I ask weakly.

"Have you been introduced to the general of our army, Logue, or his colonel, Blaine?"

I shake my head mutely as she gestures to the man on Branshire's right and the younger man at Crispin's left.

"Well then," Andromeda says with a polite smile, "General, Colonel, this is the young woman who it seems will be fulfilling our prophecy."

My stomach drops at the ease with which she declares my future. Both men look at me curiously. Colonel Blaine—I have to fight to keep from smiling when I realize this is who James teased Sasha about—reminds me very much of Branshire. They have the same open face, same smiling eyes, similar builds. Blaine's sandy-blond hair is short. His eyes are dark blue and I can see his toned muscles under his shirt.

I can't help flashing my eyes to Sasha after I nod a greeting to him. She raises an eyebrow slightly as if to say, "He's handsome, isn't he?"

I grin and take another bite of fruit to cover it.

General Logue looks displeased with me, though I don't know why. His thin, shoulder-length, pale blond hair is tied at the base of his neck, and his equally pale blue eyes look me up and down as though I've already disappointed him. He has a slightly pointed nose and is smaller in stature than I would have thought an army general would be.

"No disrespect to your highnesses," General Logue says, without acknowledging me, "but this cannot truly be the savior we've waited for."

I nearly choke on my food. James, noticing, pats me on the back. Luckily no one but Blaine is looking our way. All eyes are on Logue or on the king and queen.

Crispin speaks first, breaking the heavy silence that has fallen: "And why not?"

Logue practically sneers as he responds: "She is hardly more than a child! I mean—" I'm sure he was about to say: "look at her", but he stops himself. "How much does she know of our world? Of battle? Of magic?" he asks instead.

"She has to be taught, of course," Queen Andromeda says patiently. "As would anyone brought here from the Otherworld."

"She's catching on remarkably fast," Crispin adds.

"And she has plenty of time to learn more," Branshire tells him.

Despite my doubts about my fate, it's gratifying to hear the royal family stepping up to defend me. It takes a good deal of effort not to smirk at the general, but I continue to eat quietly as they talk.

"And how do you expect her to learn everything in time?" Logue asks.

I shoot a look at Crispin. *In time?*

He sees and answers Logue, though I know the explanation is for my benefit. "We may still have decades to teach her. You, as our general, should need no reminder that there is no sign of war, in Demesne or anywhere else. Nothing to suggest the prophecy is ready to be fulfilled in the near future."

Logue recites the beginning lines of the prophecy, "'When the world again learns to jump the tear/ a time of war will be drawing near'." He glances around at each of us. "The tear opened nearly twenty-five years ago, Crown Prince. How long do you think 'the time of war' will wait?"

Crispin has no answer to that.

So I speak up for the first time. I feel my face flush slightly as everyone turns to look at me. I address Logue, "How soon, General, are you expecting this war to come? Shouldn't it take years for something of this magnitude to escalate? Won't we have some kind of warning before the battle begins? And wouldn't that, then, give me sufficient time to be ready?"

James coughs, quite possibly covering a laugh, but I don't look away from Logue. He looks disgruntled. "Should I take this to mean you have accepted the prophecy for yourself?"

I pause. That *is* what it sounded like. Then King Rennar speaks before I have a chance to respond: "General Logue, we have no control of the prophecies. They do not speak of things as we prefer them, but rather of things as they are. It is not up to us to change them, nor to interpret them to fit in our lives the way we believe is best. We instead need to do our best to understand them, and to use them so that we are prepared for what lies ahead. So it matters not if people look to Lady Cara and see a warrior. The prophecy says that this is what she is. Who are we to deny that?"

He has spoken with quiet authority. It effectively ends the conversation.

I know Crispin and James' eyes are on me. I can feel them waiting for my reaction. But I avert my gaze to stare into my fruit bowl. It's slightly less appetizing now, with my stomach knotted from the king's words, than it was moments ago.

When I finally do look up again—after other conversations have begun—Crispin meets my eyes first. He sees that I've finished my fruit, so making sure I watch, he sets his fork next to the bowl to be taken by the servers. I do the same. In moments my fruit is replaced by a bowl of stew.

I stir my stew in silence for a little while and listen to the conversations floating around me. After a while of watching Blaine and Logue talk to the king and Branshire, I'm struck with a question that I can't help but ask. "What exactly do an army general and his colonel do?"

Blaine smiles at my bluntness, but Logue seems insulted. "Is it not obvious, Lady?" he asks, hiding contempt in my title.

I ignore it. James and Crispin look bemused by my question as well. "I know what they *do*," I correct. "Lead the army and whatnot. I got that. I meant when you all aren't at war. I'm sure there are soldiers to be trained and drills to be run, but is that all you do, every day, when Demesne is at peace with the kingdoms around it?"

Logue is irritated again. "Of course that's not all we do," he practically growls. But he offers no more explanation.

So I turn to Blaine, who is hiding a grin behind his spoonful of stew. "Well, Lady Cara, we do a little of everything. We, the soldiers, are the eyes and ears of the kingdom." He glances somewhat apologetically at King Rennar. "To an extent," he adds.

The king nods, unoffended.

Crispin takes over the explanation. "In your world, Cara, your police and your army are separate entities. You have officers and sheriffs in every city, in every state, who take care of crime. And then you all have your army, for wartime. That's not quite how it works around here."

"Of course it's not," I mutter. Only James hears me. He chokes on his bite of stew. I pat his back lightly so he can play it off as an accident. "How does it work around here, then?" I ask.

"The soldiers are in charge of it all," Crispin says with a smile. "They are the police and the FBI and the army, all at once. So, if they aren't training, they're working, or being assigned to work, or teaching others, or on guard duty somewhere. They, apart from the council and the royal family, are the justice system."

I think about that, taking a contemplative bite of my stew before I can remember that I'm not hungry.

Sasha and Andromeda have been engaged in a rather animated conversation for a while now. They ignore the rest of us for the most part, and Sasha is looking more excited by the second. She flashes a wide smile at me. My stomach twists at that look—there's no way I'm going to be as thrilled as she is.

My suspicions are confirmed when she whispers excitedly in Crispin's ear, and he nearly spits out his stew. He manages to keep his face composed for a minute, but then he gives me a brief, highly entertained grin.

Even James lets out a quiet exhale of amusement.

"How do you know what's going on and I don't? I'm right next you," I say quietly.

He just shakes his head and keeps eating.

I frown and pretend I don't know I'm being talked about.

It's when Saladin rolls his eyes and shoots me a dirty look that I know I'm really in trouble. But before I have time to dwell, or change the subject, Queen Andromeda announces, "Sasha and I have just had the most wonderful idea!"

I drop my spoon into my mostly full soup bowl and fold my hands in my lap as I await the news.

"We're going to have a feast, to celebrate the arrival of our warrior," she says grandly.

Sasha begins to explain the details excitedly to an intrigued Branshire and Rennar. Saladin and Logue look sullen, Elik looks only slightly interested, and James and Crispin are both trying not to laugh while I do my best to adopt a pleased expression.

"A feast?" I manage to ask politely.

Sasha nods. "Oh, it will be wonderful! If we hold it just a few nights from now it will be a full moon, and we can have it in one of the courtyards under the starlight! We'll invite all of Geler, the soldiers and townsfolk and our family, of course. Frale will cook food like you've never imagined, and there will be music and dancing, and—oh!" She breaks off, finally taking a breath, a dreamy look in her eyes.

"You want to arrange all that in just a few days? Isn't that a little ambitious, Sash?" Branshire asks.

Sasha scoffs. "If the announcement is made tomorrow, and the cleaning, cooking, and decorating crews are set to work immediately, it should be easy enough to pull off."

This sounds like a statement only someone who wasn't in charge of actually *doing* the work would say.

Andromeda speaks next. "Of course, we'll have to plan another evening in the near future for the Cairne, Navite, and Sheik royals to meet you, Cara dear, as well as the rest of the Demesnian nobles, but it's far too late to invite them to this. No, this will merely be a celebration for us, that our warrior has finally come."

I blanch, hopefully not visibly. Inside I'm a turmoil of emotions. Yes, a feast would be grand, it would be exciting, and it would be fun, and it would give me a good chance to see the kind of life people around here live. But I don't want the feast thrown for my benefit. I don't want to be the center of attention for something this big. And I can't dance. And I need to go home, eventually.

Really, the feast is seeming like a worse and worse idea by the second, but I put on my bravest face, match the glowing smiles of the queen and Sasha, and say, "That sounds amazing."

They positively beam at me, soon ducking their heads back together to discuss the details.

James waits for the servers to remove the soup bowls and replace them with small plates of mini pastries before leaning over and murmuring in my ear, "That was very kind of you."

He stays angled toward me so I can whisper in his own ear, "That's the hardest thing I've ever done."

He chuckles under his breath.

I'm about to inform him that I'm not joking, when someone pounds on the entrance doors. Before anyone can make a move to let them in, whoever it is shoves the doors open and practically falls through them. She's gasping for breath. All the men are immediately on their feet; Andromeda and Sasha follow suit more slowly, as do I.

The woman is wearing brown leather armor over her lithe frame, and a short sword at her side. It's clear she's been running. The guards who I know must've been posted outside are flanking her, but they make no move to stop her. So they must know who she is.

I hardly have time to be pleased by all I've noticed before Rennar is speaking. "Fern. What's happened?"

In one rushed breath, Fern replies, "The marauders are back."

19

Logue and Blaine immediately sweep out of the room, closely followed by Branshire and Saladin. Crispin steps up to his father's side. After placing a hand on my arm and murmuring close to my ear, "Stay here," James joins him. Elik exits out the other doors.

Andromeda and Sasha remain standing at their seats. Though I'm bursting with questions and desperate to know what's going on, I stay quiet and do the same.

"They've attacked the northwest outpost," Fern is telling Rennar. "Fifty or so men. A dozen of our own escaped, but the rest were captured. That's roughly twenty captives, sir."

"Rorck!" Rennar calls to one of the guards still at the door. "Go to the barracks. Tell the men to arm themselves. Fifty men cannot stand against half an army."

Rorck bows and is about to do as he's told when Fern stops him. "Your majesty, the marauders have proposed a deal. If you bring no more than two dozen men to a meeting, the group will release the captives and give up the outpost in exchange for safe passage off Demesnian land."

Crispin and James exchange glances. Rennar looks thoughtful. "They've never agreed to a meeting before. Not once," he muses.

"What's changed?" Crispin asks quietly, as though he doesn't really expect an answer.

I'm clueless; truly, I have no idea what's happening. I understand what they're saying, but the significance of the event escapes me. However, I do know of one thing that has changed in Lyria, in Demesne, recently. Something this world might consider worth fighting over.

"It's me." I speak so softly that I think only Sasha hears me. She looks up at me sharply. The king, James, Crispin, and Fern continue talking. So, heart-pounding in my throat, I say more loudly: "It's me. I'm what's changed."

Now the discussion ceases. Fern, taking in my appearance with wide eyes, seems to notice me for the first time. King Rennar is gazing at me steadily, considering my statement, but Crispin and James look stricken. Which is how I know I'm probably right.

James slowly shakes his head, looking very much like he wishes I would stop talking.

I shrug at him. "What else could have changed around here?" Though for my life I can't think what a band of "marauders" would be interested in me for.

Apparently nothing else could have changed, because Rennar says, "Boys, find Logue and Blaine. Gather the proper amount of soldiers; make sure at least half are good shots and bring bows with them. Mount up and meet me at the front gate.

"Fern, come with me to the stables. Rorck, if you would fetch my sword and armor, and meet us there."

King Rennar walks over to his wife and takes one of her hands, raises it to his lips, and kisses it lightly. "My dear, I'm sorry for the abrupt end to our meal. It would seem that duty calls."

Andromeda pats his hand reassuringly. She is smiling tightly in worry rather than annoyance. "I understand," she tells him. And I can see that she does.

"Boys," Rennar says firmly as he exited with Fern in tow. "Quickly."

I glance over at Crispin and James to find them both looking at me. Reluctantly, as though they'd prefer to stay and talk to me, they both back out the door and dash away.

"You girls are excused as well," Queen Andromeda says to Sasha and me. "To your rooms, I think would be best."

The servers are standing off to the sides as they have been the entire meal. They are waiting for us to leave so they can clear the table. With a curtsy to her mother that I'm quick to mimic, Sasha hurries around to my side of the table, grabs my wrist, and pulls me out of the dining hall behind her.

She's running and I'm forced to keep pace. We race up the main staircase, and I now easily recognize the well-worn path to our bedrooms.

"Sasha?" I start to ask when we skid to a halt in front of my room.

She stops me. "There's no time," she says quickly, opening my door for me. "Change into your riding clothes. Quickly, Cara, quickly," she adds when I just stand there.

Before I can protest, she's disappeared down the hall to go to her own room. Though I can guess what she's planning and have no real wish to be caught up in it, I rush into my bedroom and close my door. It takes me only a moment to yank open my wardrobe and pull out the first riding skirt and shirt I see. It takes a little longer for me to slip out of my gown, but I manage it.

I've slid on leggings and am in the process of putting on my boots when Sasha bursts back in. Her hair is braided down her back, but otherwise she's dressed in the same thing as I am.

But she's shaking her head. "You need a darker-colored shirt. White is too obvious during the night. We're being stealthy." Sasha walks to my wardrobe and tosses me a shirt that's deep blue.

I don it without argument.

"Come on, then," she says as soon as I've laced my boots up. She is already on her way back out the door.

I almost laugh at her unusual brusqueness, but I'm becoming anxious about what we're doing. "Sasha," I say again.

She seems to know exactly what I'm about to tell her, because she stamps her foot as she looks at me. "No. You will not talk me out of this. I deserve to know what's going on. Just because I'm the *youngest* and a *girl*, I'm never included on these missions. I'm going, Cara, with or without you. I just thought, since this meeting might be about you, you'd want to come."

I frown. She's completely determined. Her expression is set, and her eyes dare me to challenge her. This is the most princess-y she's ever looked.

When I sigh, Sasha comes back over to hand me a dagger, which she instructs me to hide in my boot. Shaking my head, apprehension curling in my chest, I dutifully follow her out of the room.

Now we're being sneakier, no longer running. Sasha leads the way along the walls of the corridor, both of us listening intently for sounds of someone coming. It would be pretty obvious to anyone who saw what it is we're doing. I feel I can safely assume that ladies of the court don't often sneak through the palace after dinner in their riding clothes without an escort.

"What's your plan?" I whisper as we move.

Without looking back at me she answers quietly, "When my father leaves the stables, the stable hands will head out too, to the gate with him, and they'll check each of the horses before the soldiers leave. We'll use that time to grab our own horses and sneak out the side gate. Then we'll go around the castle wall, stay in the back alleys of town, and follow the soldiers to the meeting."

There is no hesitation in her voice. "Is this something you've done before?" I ask.

Sasha sets her shoulders, but doesn't say anything.

"So yes, it is," I conclude from her silence. We're on our way down one of the servants' staircases. She then leads me down a small, dimly lit hall. Then she opens another door, ushers me down one more flight of stairs, and produces a key from somewhere to unlock the wooden door at the bottom.

A cool gust of night air whips around us as we step outside; we're in one of the castle's courtyards, as best I can tell.

Sasha doesn't give me the time to look around that I would have liked. She beckons me to follow her once more when she has shut and locked the door, so I do. We hurry along a pathway to the courtyard gate, pause to make sure we haven't been spotted, and then—with no warning from Princess Sasha as to what we're about to do—we sprint across the wide expanse of the castle lawn. This leaves us completely exposed for ten, twenty, thirty seconds. We stop and pant for breath in the shadows of the towering castle wall a few dozen yards away,

My heart is pounding loudly, so loudly Sasha can probably hear it. I don't know what the punishment for sneaking out of the palace is, but based on the secrecy Sasha is using, I can guess. It would be bad to get caught.

But it might be worse for us not to be.

"Sasha, it doesn't really seem like the best idea to follow a group of trained soldiers to a meeting with a band of marauders."

"I didn't say it was the best idea," she grumbles. "I said I was doing it."

I try not to smile at her response. "Okay. Can I ask what the deal with these marauders is? Why is the king so keen to meet with them?"

Sasha is inching forward again, staying low and keeping to the shadows. I understand why she had me change shirts now. She is wearing one of a similar color, and they are dark enough to blend in nicely with the shadows.

"We've been dealing with this group for almost ten years now," she explains in hushed tones. "They raid the cities and villages and outposts on the outskirts of

Demesne usually, but they've been getting bolder as time goes on. They've been attacking closer to Geler without explanation. They haven't killed many men, but they destroy what they touch and supplies are important around here, especially in the more distant towns. There isn't any order or reason to their attacks, so we can't track them, and we don't have enough soldiers to spare to guard *each* of the towns. We've never caught any of them. One was killed once though. We never did find out who he was.

"Point is, this meeting is the first time they've done anything like this. If we can find out anything about these guys, it'll be much more than we know now. Safe passage out is a small price to pay for information. Besides, safe passage doesn't mean the soldiers can't follow them. We'll be able to see where they go, maybe even where they've been hiding out."

I process this all and come to the conclusion that if these marauders have been operating for ten years without being caught, they have some plan to get away without being followed. But I don't say anything out loud. Sasha probably knows better than I do anyway. And we're coming within sight of the stables.

She and I fall silent and sneak around the side, between the stable and the castle wall. At her signal, we sit and lean against the stable's side next to one another. We keep quiet so we can hear when the king, Fern, and Rorck leave with the stable hands.

Their voices are muffled through the wall. Though I would like to know what they're saying, I can't make out any individual words. Sasha, patiently waiting, is staring up at the sky. I try to do the same. Patience has never been my strongest suit.

Out here it's quiet—so quiet I can imagine I hear the soldiers that James and Crispin were sent to gather; the clink of their armor and their murmured conversations are practically audible.

It's not my imagination. Sasha yanks me to my feet and dashes farther into the shadows. The stables are set in a corner of the lawn and nestled right where one castle wall meets another. There is only a few feet of space where we've been sitting between the stable and the wall. Sasha pulls me around the corner and crouches down in the thick, tall weeds surrounding us.

Rather than staying behind her, I kneel next to her so I can peer around and see what exactly we're hiding from now. The soldiers I heard are still moving away from us at this point, but three people are standing together just outside the stable door.

I have to strain my eyes and ears to make out their faces and what they're saying. But I find I soon recognize Crispin, James, and Colonel Blaine.

James is speaking rapidly and quietly: "What if they *do* ask for Cara? We all know we can't give her up, but what will happen to the captives inside the outpost if we refuse? What if the gang asks to trade them for her? What will we do then?"

I understand immediately why they're talking in the shadows. No matter what their personal feelings, when it comes down to it, this isn't really their decision. When they get to the meeting, King Rennar will be in charge. So they need to clear the air now, and maybe talk to the king when a decision has been made.

I'm gratified, despite the serious situation I know we're all in, that Logue is not being included in this secret conversation.

"Is her one life worth the many?" Blaine asks the other boys softly.

I know why he's asking; I know it's nothing against me personally, but rather a question asked in concern for his own men being held hostage. Even so, my stomach drops. Sasha shoots me a look, but I don't meet her eyes.

Without hesitation, Crispin and James answer in unison, "Yes." My rush of fear is instantly alleviated.

"She's not a bargaining chip," James says so softly that Sasha and I can barely hear him.

Crispin continues, "Generally, Colonel, no, one life is not comparable to twenty. And I would prefer not to lose any of our men. Twenty captives is nothing to turn up our noses at. But her life is infinitely important."

They all fall silent, lost in their own thoughts. Crispin finally speaks. "Cara isn't coming with us. And we'll have to hear these men out no matter what. If it is Cara they ask for, at the very least we'll be able to say we have to come back to the castle to fetch her. We'll have time to think of something then. In the meantime, our men are still stuck in the outpost, and any time we waste here puts them in danger there. Let's move."

Blaine and James, unsurprisingly, don't disagree with their Crown Prince, and soon the three have disappeared to join the soldiers at the gate. I let out a breath of relief, both at the fact that we weren't seen and because of their decision to protect me.

"Well now we just *have* to go," Sasha whispers with a grin. Curiosity officially peaked, I don't argue.

I am pleasantly surprised to find that Sasha's plan goes off without a hitch, though I can't tell if this is due to luck or practice on her part. Once the king, Fern, and Rorck are followed out by the stable hands, we sneak in and tack up a horse. As getting two separate horses ready without help would take too long, we've decided to ride together.

Then we're off. We exit out the currently unguarded side gate and into town.

We're walking our horse for now; it's only slightly less conspicuous than riding. "It's late, and few townspeople have the need to be out at this time," Sasha explains when I ask where everyone is.

Any other time, I would love to stop and look around. This is the capital city, and I have yet to see it. Everything—the roads, the houses, the shops—are made of the same tan stone as the castle and its walls. The city sits around the castle in a circle of winding roads and one-story buildings. It's actually quite pretty, with patches of flower gardens and small trees scattered about.

But Sasha is moving quickly and quietly, and I have to do the same. As the shops end, and we come to the start of the hills and smaller homes, there is less need for secrecy and it becomes easier to see the king's men and to follow them. Now we can mount up.

Sasha is more adept at tracking than I ever would have guessed, so we let the soldiers get far enough into the distance that there is no way they can look back and see us. It is astounding just how bright it is out here on the Demesnian hills with only the moon and stars providing light.

"They're not taking the traditional route to the outpost," Sasha notes as we ride.

I wonder if that means anything important, but, as she doesn't elaborate, I figure it is simply something she's pointing out.

Eventually, Sasha pulls our horse to a stop. "They've slowed down," she explains. "We're getting too close to them, and to the outpost."

I shrug. "And?"

"And we need to walk from here so we aren't seen," she tells me.

I'm sitting behind her, so I dismount first. Once Sasha's feet touch the ground, she twists her fingers in a cast and murmurs in the horse's ear. It snorts and dips its head before turning in the direction we came and galloping off.

I follow Sasha toward the outpost. "What did that cast do?" I whisper curiously.

"The horse will have no trouble finding its way back to the castle now," she tells me quietly. "Shh, now, we're getting close."

We stay low, keeping the hills between the soldiers and ourselves. Few of them are looking around; most of the soldier's eyes are fixed on the outpost in front of them.

All I can see of it is a wall made of stone and wood. There must be a building of some kind inside, but it isn't visible. There are platforms on each of the four corners of the wall, and I assume a sort of walkway connects them all as there are men walking between them. Most of these men vanish with the appearance of King Rennar and his soldiers. And, even in this lighting, I can see that the men are blond. *So the marauders are Demesnian, then.*

With luck, Sasha and I manage to stay hidden. She leads me to the bottom of a low hill, and we crawl up to lie on our stomachs and peer over the top. It's the perfect position to hear and see all that's going on while remaining nearly invisible.

There is one man left on the outpost walls. He holds out his arms in greeting. "King Rennar," he says grandly. "It is about time we met, face to face."

Even from here, I can see easily Rennar's expression. It could be carved from stone. "What brought on this sudden change in tactic?" he calls. "What inspired you to call this meeting, when you have never reached out to us before?"

This man must be the leader of the gang. He wastes no time in getting to the point. I would have expected more formalities to be exchanged, false promises and accusations to be made. *Maybe I've watched too many movies.* "This time, we have information that may be of interest to you. Valuable information." I watch as the man scans the group of Demesnian soldiers. "Where is this warrior we've heard so much about?" he finally asks.

Though I have to say I've been expecting the question, it still shakes me to know the man was expecting me. My mouth close to Sasha's ear, I murmur: "How could they have heard about me? Who would have told them?"

Sasha shrugs once, without ever tearing her eyes away from her brothers and father. "Word gets around the kingdom. We don't know who's part of this marauding band, but it isn't as surprising as you may think that they've heard of your arrival. You're a big deal, Cara."

We fall silent as Rennar answers the man. "She is safe, back at the castle."

I feel a pang of guilt at his words, as he truly believes them; I'm the farthest thing from safe right now.

"Pity," the man on the wall says conversationally, "as what we have to say will affect her most of all."

"Then we'll make sure she receives the message," Crispin practically growls. He's sitting stiffly on his mount, eyes fixed on the enemy ahead. When it glints in the moonlight, I see he's drawn a dagger and is clutching it in one hand along with Tumble's reigns. I pray he doesn't have to use it.

The man must realize he has struck a chord with the Crown Prince, for his tone takes on a bit more confidence. "We're proposing a trade. The guarantee of our safe passage away from here, in exchange for the information we have."

King Rennar shakes his head. "We will make no such promise. We have no way of knowing whether we care for the information you possess, and you have made no mention of the safety of my men who you hold captive."

"For every one of my men who walk away without being pursued, we shall release one of your men to you," the marauder says.

"You have more men than captives," Rennar is quick to counter. "What will you do when you have no men left to release?"

The man on the wall appears to have been waiting for this question. "The rest of my men will leave, again without pursuit of any kind. Once they are out of sight, only then, will I give up to you the information I have."

"And how do you expect to get away once we have our men *and* our information?"

To Rennar's latest question, the man merely smiles.

Chills run through me at that look. I want the king to demand an answer, to make the man talk, but I know he won't.

"One man at a time?" King Rennar says instead.

The man's grins more widely. "One man at a time," he agrees.

Sasha and I watch for what feels like a lifetime as the exchange of men begins. The gates of the outpost swing open and closed as pairs of men, one marauder and one Demesnian soldier, exit together. Each marauder takes off in a different direction than the man who left before him. True to their word, not a single soldier follows them, though I see more than one of Rennar's men shift on their horses and watch the members of the marauding gang until they can no longer see them. One by one, the once-captive Demesnian soldiers stumble to their king's side, bow to him, and then enter the circle of riders where they are safe.

Finally, it is announced that the last captive is being released. I watch with bated breath as he walks to Rennar without contest. Sasha exhales quietly, but I'm still tense, watching the marauder that the soldier exited with jog off into the distance. *Surely it can't be that easy.*

Now a group of the remaining couple dozen marauders in the outpost slowly step through the gate as their leader watches it all from the wall above. It seems to take a lot of restraint on their part for Rennar's soldiers to remain where they are as this group splits into three, and all three set off in separate directions. It's clearly rehearsed. These men knew what they were doing.

It's pure luck, along with our proximity to the Demesnian soldiers, that keeps any of the departing men from passing too close to where we're hidden.

I belatedly realize that Sasha and I could follow any one of these men, and they would most likely lead us to where the marauders have been hiding all these years. But a combination of fear, instinct, and desire to hear this news their leader says he has for me holds me in place, even as the last of the men disappears into the shadows of the night.

I expect Rennar to demand the information now that part one of the exchange is over. Instead though, he turns his horse and speaks to his men. It's impossible to make out much of what he's saying, but I can see the men obeying him. His soldiers are dismounting. It takes me a curious moment to understand what they're doing.

Each of the dismounted men helps one of the once-captive soldiers onto their horses. The hostages are clearly weak, possibly injured, and I feel a rush of warmth for the Demesnian king, whose first order of business is to care for his wounded men. Crispin, James, Rennar, Blaine, Logue, and a handful of soldiers are the only men still mounted.

Then the horses holding captives are lead back to the castle by the recently dismounted men. Five men remain with the king, general, and prince. Even Branshire and Saladin, who rode out with the group, have given up their mounts and left with the other soldiers.

The king doesn't speak until his men are out of sight; the man still on the wall does not ask him to. "What is this information that you claim to have?" Rennar finally calls.

My breath catches. I hadn't realized just how anxious I really am until now. "What information could they have about me, Sasha? What could he know?"

Sasha finds my hand and grips it tightly without answering. Either she doesn't know, or she doesn't want to tell me. Soon it doesn't matter though, for the man has begun speaking. I squeeze Sasha's fingers.

"We," the man says. "Our band of... What are you calling us? Marauders? Fitting, I suppose, isn't it? Our band has heard quite a lot about your Otherworld warrior. We hear even King Orrick's right-hand man had no success in bringing her to him. So we were hired to find a way."

"A way to what?" Crispin asks, when the man pauses.

Answer, please answer, please answer.

He doesn't. The man spreads his arms wide, seemingly an attempt to include everyone in front of him in what he is about to announce. "Your warrior has a sister, does she not?"

Sasha's hold is the only thing keeping me grounded as everything stops around me—her hand in mine, her fingers gripping my arm. *Sophie. No, please no. Not Sophie.*

I didn't know I was speaking aloud. "Hush, Cara. Hear him out. He still has more to say," Sasha reassures me.

"They know about Sophie," I can't help but whisper. Sasha hushes me, and we both focus again on the man on the wall.

The king and his men have not graced the marauder's question with a response. None is needed. The man smiles.

"With help, we found where your warrior lives. We found her family. We found her sister." Normally, in a situation such as this, my heart would be doing its best to beat its way out of my chest. This time is different. This time, I feel as though it has stopped. It has frozen in place.

"And now, we have her."

Time is standing still, so much so that James' voice barely carries over to me. "Where? Where do you have her?" I have enough sense to recognize that he's probably out of line; I don't think he's supposed to be speaking at a meeting like this. He's only a guard after all. I have to close my eyes for a moment against my appreciation for him. He sounds just as desperate to know as I feel.

"Well, that, my friends, is the real genius of our plan. You see, in order to get her sister back, your warrior will have to come get her alone."

"Like hell we're letting her go alone," James snaps.

Now Crispin silences him with a look.

"I was under the impression that it wouldn't be so easy for you Demesnians to cross into Sheik territory. Not without reason. And, somehow, I doubt the Sheik guards will see this as enough of a reason to let you through." The man is smiling, I can tell. *How can he be enjoying this? How can he be happy about the idea of Sophie being stuck with the Sheiks?*

I thought I knew what terror was. I was scared the first time my parents told me we were going to move. I was scared once when Sophie and I were at the mall, and I had turned around to find she wasn't by my side like I'd thought. I was scared when Crispin and James brought me to Lyria, when they showed me their prophecy, when they told me it was my fate.

But none of that compares to the rush of pure fear that courses through me when the man speaks. All that is nothing in comparison to hearing that Sophie is here, alone, in the Sheik's hands.

"You're telling us that the Sheiks are in on this plan of yours?" King Rennar asks, voice carefully neutral.

"I'm saying the girl is being held across the border," the man answers.

I tap Sasha's arm rapidly. "What does that mean? Sasha, what does he mean you can't cross the border? How else can we get her?"

Sasha shakes her head once, an attempt to silence me. I bite my tongue hard enough that I taste blood.

"Is the girl injured? Have you hurt her?" James asks sharply.

"Now, what purpose would it serve to hurt the girl?" the man on the wall asks.

"That doesn't answer the question," Crispin says as Tumble takes a step forward.

The man continues as if he hasn't heard them. "For three days, we will have your warrior's sister. She must come to the border, alone, if you want her back. Anything else we have to say is for her ears only."

Had Sasha not had a hold on my arm, I might have jumped up then and there and agreed to go with the man.

As it is, her grip tightens as though she's guessed what I'm thinking.

"What is your plan if we don't agree to let our warrior come to you alone?" King Rennar asks the man.

I can hear the smirk in the man's voice as he answers simply, "I think you can guess."

If there was a single thing this man could've said to make my already aching heart hurt even more, that was it. I may not have been in Lyria for long, but I know what he's suggesting. If I don't go... Sophie may not be hurt yet, but she will be.

"Enough of this." Logue speaks now for the first time. He and all his men move forward toward the gates of the outpost. "There is no need to continue the conversation like this. You have used everything you have to offer us. You have no men left, nothing left to bargain. So, would you like to come out to us, or should we come in and get you?"

No, Logue. I need more information. That's not enough! Keep him talking. Again, Sasha's hand in mine is almost all that keeps me down, keeps me hidden. To my utter surprise, the man does not seem at all nervous about his predicament. Instead, he chuckles down at Logue and his men.

"General, you are mistaken. I do, in fact, have a third option available to me."

Logue draws to a halt in evident surprise.

The man looks again to the king. To *his* king. "Do not forget to give your warrior the message." Almost, but not quite, before I know what he's doing, the man has drawn a long knife from the sheath at his side. He stands up straight, turns the blade in toward himself, and plunges the knife into his stomach. He doesn't cry out as he topples from the wall.

I turn away before he hits the ground. My eyes are tightly shut, and I'm drawing in shuddering breaths. I'm shattered, broken into a million desperate, sickened, terrified pieces. My face is hidden in Sasha's shoulder, and I feel her face buried in mine.

Rennar's barked orders to Logue and his men don't register with me. I was already stunned, shocked, hurt. I couldn't think, could barely breath for fear. The added disbelief of seeing a man take his own life rather than being captured is almost more than I can take.

When Sasha draws away from me, I come back to myself. Barely. Enough to recognize the sound of hoof beats coming toward us. We don't have time to move. So when Crispin and James draw up next to us we're kneeling in the grass together, stricken by what we've seen.

Both Crispin and James leap off their horses to join us on the ground. I expect to be reprimanded. After all, we're not supposed to be here. But instead, James drops to his knees beside me and pulls me into his arms. I fall into him and feel hot tears tumble from my eyes. I don't want to cry right now, but no matter how fast I am to wipe the tears away, they continue to fall.

I'm shaking. "Never once, the whole time I spent worrying about not being home, about being here, about what was going on, did I even think there was a possibility this could happen," I whisper into James' shirt.

None of them answer, and when I can finally open my eyes, their grim expressions tell me they *did* think if this.

My emotions are out of control, because I go from overwhelming fear to wild fury in half a second. "Why didn't you let me go back to her? If I had been there, if I had gone home, this wouldn't have happened! I could have protected her! She'd. Be. Safe!" I punctuate each of the last three words by pounding James in the chest with my fists.

It doesn't faze him in the slightest; he's still sitting disarmingly close to me, and he takes the beating without comment.

"Or, Cara, you both would have been captured and no one would know where you were. And you'd be stuck with the Sheiks too," Crispin says.

I scowl up at him. "You're saying if it was your younger sister, if it was Sasha, and the Sheiks had *her* and wanted you in exchange, you'd be thinking: 'Well, at least I wasn't with her when she was captured'? You'd rather she was there alone, so people knew where *you* were, than be there with her? Because I can't think like that, Crispin! She's a nine-year-old girl who knows even less than I do about Lyria. And now she's—" I stop and take a deep breath.

Crispin has been standing above us, but now he kneels down too. "Of course that's not what I'd think," he tells me softly. "But you and me, Sasha and Sophie? You can't compare those situations."

I don't say anything. Crispin sighs. "You're more help here than you would be if you were with her, okay? Try to remember that."

Rennar and his men have long since moved off, disappearing into the distance. And they've taken the marauder's body with them. The four of us are sitting in silence, complete and utter silence. I soak it up, needing the quiet, the dark, the odd comfort it gives me to know we're alone.

"How long have you known we were here?" I ask quietly.

"The whole time," James answers, his voice tight.

I pause for a heartbeat. I don't ask him how he knew. He probably won't tell me. "Thank you," I say instead.

"For what?" Crispin asks me.

I answer softly: "For letting me stay and listen."

"We're rethinking that decision right now," Crispin says.

I nod. I would be too.

Now James moves away and gets to his feet. It's colder somehow, without his nearness. He holds out a hand to pull me to my feet, so I take it. "We need to get moving," he says.

"Okay." The boys start to mount their horses again, but I stop them. "Can we walk? Just for a minute? I need to move around."

I think I must look slightly ill—just like I feel—because they agree.

I feel weak, as though in the past few minutes something vital, something that keeps me going, has been stripped from me. I'm empty.

"You still with us?" James asks me after a few minutes of walking in silence.

I have one hand gripping Ebony's mane, holding me steady, and James is in front of me leading Ebony forward.

"I'm here," I tell him. He looks unconvinced. "I'm not doing *well*, but I'm still with you."

That he understands. "We're going to figure something out. I promise, Cara. We're going to figure this out. The Sheiks wouldn't risk hurting Sophie." I don't think he realizes I can hear the implied "not yet, anyway" at the end of his assurance.

I grimace in a silent response.

"If she's here, we will get her back," he promises.

I look at him. "What do you mean 'if she's here'? They said she was here, James. So we will be getting her back."

He sets his jaw. "We were talking to the leader of a band of thieves, Cara. There *is* a chance he was lying."

"I'm not risking Sophie's life on a chance."

"Well, we're not letting you go to the Sheiks alone based solely on potentially faulty information," he retorts.

"Then I won't tell you when I go," I say flatly.

He glares at me. "You're not going, Cara."

I pull up short. "You can't stop me from going after my little sister."

James keeps walking, and I think I hear him mutter, "Watch me," but I can't be sure.

Eventually, Crispin stops and helps Sasha mount Tumble before following suit and settling in front of her. James and I have stopped talking. He pulls himself onto his own mount before reaching down a hand to me. I catch hold of it, and he swings me up behind him with ease. It isn't long before we've broken into a canter.

My arms are looped around James' chest, my face pressed between his shoulder blades.

We're finally coming in sight of the castle when James speaks again. "Is Sophie the only thing bothering you?" he asks.

Without moving my face and feeling guilty about my answer, as Sophie should be the only thing on my mind, I shake my head. James doesn't press me to explain, but let's me do so myself. I keep my explanation short. "I watched a man die. And I don't even know his name."

I know many responses James could give me: "I've seen many people die", or, "At least you didn't have to watch someone kill him", or, "That man was a thief, don't mourn him". But James doesn't say any of those things. In fact, it takes him a long time to say anything at all.

"I wish I could tell you things will get better, will get easier for you from here." We ride through the castle gates, and he falls silent again as we pass groups of guards. He finishes the thought as we ride across the lawn. "But I don't think they will, Cara. I'm sorry."

Somehow, Sasha and I aren't in enough trouble to warrant a meeting with the king and queen tonight. After Crispin and James wave off the stable hands and put up their own horses, the four of us make our way to our rooms.

Crispin, James, and Sasha look like they want to stay and talk to me, but I don't have the energy. And I would have thought that, with everything going on in my head, sleep would be hard to come by. But as I fall onto my bed, fully clothed, I only have time for one thought: *James is right. Everything about my being in Lyria just got so much more complicated.* And I'm not quite sure I can handle it.

Haley Fisher

Book Three

"Anyone can give up, it's the easiest thing in the world to do. But to hold it together when everyone else would understand if you fell apart, that's true strength."

- Dr. Seuss

20

Two days. Two days I have to wander angrily about the castle while the council, king, princes, and Logue decide what to do about Sophie. Decisions that I have yet to be included in, no matter how much I pester everyone. Both the guards and the servants are avoiding me as best they can; I'd be avoiding me too.

Verne and Crispin and James spend whatever time they can spare talking to me, though they adamantly refuse to tell me what's going on in these closed-door discussions.

"She's my sister! And I'm *your* warrior! Shouldn't I be kept informed about this kind of thing?" I burst out once. It's early evening, and we've been spending the time after dinner holed up in my room. I'm sitting cross-legged on my bed. James is sprawled out beside me, and Crispin is sitting in an armchair nearby. Nelma is curled up by the fire. I'm no longer surprised by the fact that Crispin has an old, heavy book in his hands. That boy does nothing but study.

"You're on board the prophecy train now?" he asks, looking up at me.

I make a face. "Does it get me my answers?"

"No," he answers mildly.

"Then no, still not on board," I say irritably.

James chuckles. He's supposed to be studying something too, but he has long since closed his fingers around his book and taken to staring at the canopy over his head instead.

I turn my frustration on him. "I'm glad Sophie's possible demise is amusing to you," I snap.

He pushes himself onto his elbows and raises an eyebrow. "'Demise'? Don't you think that's a tad dramatic?"

"She's stuck in Lyria with the group of people that I've been assured are *the* most evil here. And, with a day and a half left to go get her, still no decision has been made. And you think I'm being dramatic?"

Now he sits upright. "I *know* you're being dramatic," he corrects. "Cara, believe it or not things like this have happened before. We know what we're doing. Don't you trust us by now?"

"That's not the problem. I'm not leaving my sister's life in other people's hands!" I fall back onto the pillows and throw an arm over my eyes.

"Like I said," I hear James murmur. "Dramatic."

I open my eyes to glare at him, which in return earns me an impish grin.

But the smile fades quickly. "We need you to believe in us," James says seriously. "Nothing here is ever going to work if you don't believe in us, Cara. You don't have to trust everyone all the time, but please, trust Crispin and me. We know what Sophie means to you, we do, and she means something to us too. If she's here, we're not going to let her get hurt."

To my annoyance, I feel a lump form in my throat. "How am I supposed to fulfill a world-saving prophecy for you guys, when I couldn't even keep my own sister safe?" I whisper.

James exhales. "That's what you're worried about?" He's sitting close enough to me that he can reach over and place a reassuring hand on my arm, which he does. Heat crawls up my neck at his familiar touch. I force it away. "Cara, no matter how powerful you might come to be someday, even you can't be in two worlds at once."

Using all the graciousness I can muster, I decide not to point out that I could have gone back to Earth any time after I'd arrived here, and my disability to be in two worlds at once wouldn't matter. "We only have a day left," I say instead. "One day, out of the three we were given to retrieve her. You all better be coming up with a really good plan."

Crispin rolls his eyes and mutters something unintelligible. I scowl at him.

They're saved from the sharp remark I'm about to make by a knock at the door. Neither of the boys make a move to get it. "Please, don't everyone get up at once. *I'll* get the door," I mutter grumpily.

I swing my feet off the bed and pull the door open, expecting Sasha. Instead I see the king standing in my doorway. He is dressed in his fur-lined robe and his six-pointed crown is settled on the center of his head.

"King Rennar," I say, surprised. "W-What can I do for you?" *You're here. Outside my room. Why?*

He nods acknowledgment to Crispin and James before turning his green eyes on me. "With everything that has happened lately, Lady Cara, you and I have never had the opportunity to talk."

About what? I want to ask, but I hold my tongue.

"So, boys, if you will excuse us, Lady Cara and I are going to take a walk," he continues.

I blink and move my wide-eyed gaze to Crispin and James. I don't think the king knows how ominous he just made that statement sound. But the boys are wearing identical, reassuring smiles, so I clear my face of any and all anxiety before looking at Rennar once more. He opens the door wider for me to exit. I have a feeling I shouldn't refuse.

When my bedroom door swings shut behind us, Rennar takes the lead. We walk down the stairs to the main entrance and out the door in complete silence. I don't know if I'm supposed to speak first, but since he doesn't give me a sign that I should, I keep my mouth shut.

We walk down the wide stone path that leads to the front gate. He veers left before we reach the gate to the city, however, toward a staircase which I hadn't noticed before because it is set flush against the castle wall. The battlements it leads to are wide, with no second railing on their back side, and set about five feet below the top of the wall. It makes me feel awfully short when I step up to peer over at the sprawling city below.

It's so beautiful here. It's hard to imagine everything that's happening in such a peaceful-looking place. Clouds are beginning to roll in from the distance as the sun sets, darkening the hills below. The townspeople, whom I have yet to meet, glance at the sky as they mill about, probably determining how much time they have left before the weather will force them back indoors.

When I remember that the king is standing here with me, I blush and spin quickly to look at him. I forget James' one-time instruction not to look the king or queen in the eyes unless directed.

Rennar's face softens into a smile as he notes my discomfort. "There's no need to stand on courtesy at the moment, dear girl. We're alone." Apparently with nothing more he wants to say, he folds his arms on the top of the wall and leans into them, looking out over his city.

Finally, I can't stand the silence any longer. "Have you ever been to my world, sir?" I blurt out.

He turns his head to regard me. "Yes, Lady. Once. When we first heard the tear had opened again. As the king, it was my job to see where it had opened to."

"And it took you to Kansas? How long did you stay?"

But he shakes his head. "The first place we ended up was in a state called New York."

My eyebrows shoot up. "You were in New York? How? And, wait...does that mean the tear moved then?"

King Rennar chuckles softly. I cringe inwardly, realizing who it is I'm talking to. To my relief he doesn't seem at all offended by my rapid questions. "Yes, Cara. In the Otherworld, as there is so little magic, we have found that the tear moves depending on where the most magic is concentrated. This time around, we think the tear has been moving with you."

"But..." I struggle to recall everything I've learned here. "Logue. Didn't he say the tear opened twenty-five years ago? I wasn't even born twenty-five years ago. My parents weren't even married twenty-five years ago."

He nods, obviously having already thought of this. "Either—and this is unlikely—another Otherworlder with a capacity for magic was in New York at the time the tear opened. Or the tear knew something we didn't. There is so much about magic that even we do not understand, Lady. But, in all the years before you were born, the tear did not move, not once. And it seems that until you first moved away from your childhood home, it too stayed. The day we jumped the tear and found ourselves somewhere new must have been at the same time your family moved to a new state."

"So that's why Crispin was so interested the day he learned all the places I'd lived," I murmur.

"It must be," the king agrees.

"Sir, you said 'in the Otherworld' the tear moves. So then it stays put here in Lyria?" I ask after another beat of silence.

Rennar looks at me appraisingly. "Well caught, Lady Cara. Yes, it does." His brow furrows slightly. "Have you and Verne gone over nothing?" he asks.

Uh oh. I don't want Verne to be in any trouble. "There hasn't really been any time," I'm quick to say. "My first morning in the castle, I was supposed to be part of a tutoring session, but we ended up in the treasury instead." I pull off my ring, as if it's proof that I'm telling the truth.

He takes it from my hand. "Queen Layla's ring," he states quietly.

"Her, I did learn about," I say, matching his stance and looking out over Geler again. "They told me about the war and the Krelans and everything. So I suppose we *have* gone over *something*." I hesitate, recognizing that now is the opportune time to explain what we learned. I didn't count on having to have this talk on my own though; I thought Crispin or James or maybe Verne or Sasha would be at my side.

But I take a deep breath before I can change my mind and say, "King Rennar, when I was seven, my Uncle Amos brought a Navite guest to my birthday party. And that Navite gave me this ring before he left. I never saw him again. When we were in the treasury the other day Crispin did some kind of cast that showed us who took Layla's ring from its slot and replaced it with a fake. And it was my uncle. I don't know what all that means, but everyone else seems to have an idea."

I pause, long enough that the king asks: "Do you have a question for me, Cara?"

"Well I've been thinking about it, and...I'm just so confused, sir. Sasha said that, in order to have access to the treasury, Amos must have been part of the court here. That there isn't any way he could have sneaked in or anything. But Crispin told me that the only Otherworlder besides myself to jump the tear was the man who wrote your prophecies. So, sir, I guess I'm asking if you knew Amos. And if he ever told you he was from Earth."

King Rennar turns my ring over in his fingers as he considers an answer. He's quiet for so long that I'm afraid he isn't going to reply. Finally though, he does. "About one year after we learned the tear between our worlds had opened, a Demesnian man came stumbling into Geler, with no memory, but dressed in noble clothing."

I unconsciously rest my chin on my crossed arms while I listen to him. "He seemed to have a general understanding of the way our court worked, so much so that it seemed he must have come from a noble family. And he stayed here, in the castle, learning quickly, and he soon earned his way onto the council. It only took him three years. A man we knew next to nothing about, who knew nothing about himself, was brilliant and shrewd enough to earn himself a council position. He never became a chief member, however he did remain on the council for years. He kept to himself; we attributed his privacy to his lost memory.

"Almost as soon as Crispin and Sasha were born, the man moved away from the castle. Though he was still a vital member of our council, he built a home on the outskirts of Geler, and he spent a good deal of his time traveling. We never pressed him for information about where he went. But his journeys seemed to tire him; every week he was a bit more exhausted, a bit more introverted. Then, almost ten years ago, he vanished. For months we were afraid he had run to another kingdom, and with all the knowledge he held about the inner workings of the Demesnian court, we were afraid for our secrets. But he never did turn up, and none of our secrets ever were exposed. We never found out what happened to him; we assumed, eventually, he had been killed."

When I feel Rennar turn his gaze on me, I lift my eyes from the people in the city below and look at him. He says: "Verne and I have talked; he already told me about your findings the day in the treasury. And the more I consider the possibilities, the more likely it seems that this man was your uncle."

"How?" I ask forcefully. "How could my uncle and some Navite know that this"—I gesture at the castle—"was my future, when even no one here did?"

Rennar takes one of my hands and presses Layla's—my—ring into my palm. "I believe, my lady, that is a question we are all curious about. It seems much more than we ever thought has been at play to orchestrate your arrival here."

I frown at the stone wall beneath my fingers, trying to process everything he's told me.

His voice startles me out of my thoughts. "I'm afraid you must have formed a rather unpleasant opinion of our world since you've come."

Much of Crispin's looks have come from this man. They share the same square jaw and angled nose, the same kind emerald eyes and unruly hair. That is probably why my response is in such a familiar tone of voice, and spoken so honestly.

"I don't know what you want me to say," I sigh. "I could love it here. Sometimes I come really close. I love the people. I like the things I've learned, as well as all the things that are hidden around the corner waiting to be found out. But too much has happened for me to be able to honestly say I have a high opinion of this world. Just when I think things may make sense, my life here starts to unravel again. It's very disorienting."

"And no doubt you feel a little betrayed by the people," the king continues for me, "for keeping you out of the loop as we have."

I agree. "You all know so much more than I do, but you only give the information to me pieces at a time. And now I'm not even being included in the meetings to decide what course of action to take with Sophie's capture!"

I whirl around, and the king follows suit more slowly, when a voice behind us says, "You wanted to see me, sir?"

I don't know why I feel guilty about what I've just said when I see James standing there, but I do. He doesn't look particularly insulted (and neither does Rennar, when I risk a glance at his expression), but he gives me a curious look before turning his eyes on his king.

"Yes, my boy," King Rennar tells him. "I was rather hoping the rest of your afternoon was open. We've kept Lady Cara cooped up in her room for long enough. I was thinking now might be as good a time as any to take her to the training grounds and let her work off some of the nervous energy that must be building."

What I want to say is that after such a serious talk with the king of Demesne, running off to have my first training session isn't high on my list of priorities, nervous energy buildup or not. But I figure, no matter how kindly it's phrased, that it would be unwise to voice this thought.

"Unless, that is..." Rennar looks to me once more. "Is there anything you'd like to talk about, Cara?"

I see James blink in surprise when the king addresses me by name. I think about it. Of course there are other things I want to talk about. When else will I have the opportunity to speak in private to the king? When else will he be so willing to answer my queries?

But I settle for one final question. "The house my uncle built, here, in Geler. Is it still here? Unoccupied?"

Slightly curious at my choice of topic, Rennar nods. "We thought more than once about selling it, about allowing other residents to move in. But it has stayed as he left it all those years ago."

Rising Calm

"I'd like to be taken there sometime," I say.

Somewhat sadly, the king smiles at me. "I am sure that can be arranged."

With a nod at each of us, which James and I return with a bow and a curtsy, King Rennar moves along the battlements and back down the stairs we came from.

James eyes me for a long moment after the king disappears. I pretend not to notice, instead using the time to slide my ring back on my finger and study the incoming clouds.

"Good talk?" he finally says. He's changed clothes since the king and I left; he's no longer in his dark vest, but only a loose white shirt, black pants and boots, and sword hanging from his hip. I'm surprised to find it looks...right. Unlike all the other guards I've seen in the castle, James never seems to be armed. This is the first time I've seen him with anything more than a knife.

I raise an eyebrow at his weak attempt to play off what he heard me say. "It was...enlightening," I reply vaguely.

He presses his lips together, but says nothing more about it. "Shall we go?"

I fall in step beside him as we walk in the opposite direction the king took. "So. The training grounds, huh?" I ask. "How much 'nervous energy' does he think I've built up?"

"Cara, you've been stuck in another world for almost a week now, and you've ventured outside the walls of the castle exactly once, only to hear there's a chance Sophie was taken by a band of marauders. We all think you have some nervous energy to let loose."

"So you're telling me that I *haven't* been hiding it very well?"

The corner of James' mouth quirks. "Yes. That's what I'm telling you."

I grimace a little, because he and the king are right. I might explode from all the pent-up energy I've got. But I'm not sure I'm going to want to let off steam in a way that has been predetermined for me.

James and I walk in silence; I admire Geler spread below us as we go. After a couple minutes, we come to a second staircase which I assume directly mirrors the first (though I can't tell for sure because we are now on the parallel wall and the castle hides it from my sight).

We then walk along a well-worn dirt path. It is directly beneath the battlements and set to run alongside the castle wall. It eventually leads to a wooden side door which, when opened, takes us to a wide stone path. James closes and locks the door behind us.

We're sort of behind the city now, though there are some homes and corrals and what seem to be storehouses back here. And still James leads me forward. Finally we come to an expanse of yellow grass, probably dying from all the times it seems to have been trampled down.

"This is one of the places the soldiers train." James breaks our easy silence. At the end of the field—if it can be called that—there are wooden posts, each about five feet tall and set ten or so feet apart.

James motions for me to follow him as he enters a large wooden shed. It's dark inside, and getting darker still as the clouds continue to cross the sky outside, so I can make little out. But I can see enough to know that one wall of shelves and racks holds a variety of weapons, and the opposite side houses row upon row of things that resemble scarecrows.

James pulls a lantern from somewhere and lights it, illuminating the swords, shields, arrows and daggers hanging in front of us. He hands the lantern off to me. "I want you to pick one. Either a sword or a knife should do it. You can leave your overdress hanging over there"—he points to a corner of the shed—"as it will only hinder you, and then meet me back on the field." With those curt instructions, James swings one of the scarecrows over his shoulders and exits.

I look after him a little incredulously. But I'm quick to turn my attention to the weapons, because keeping him waiting when he's only doing the king's bidding is probably not a good idea. I heft a couple of the swords in my hands, but they feel awkward and unusual and I hardly know how to begin swinging them. So I shelve them again, having no idea what I'm getting into.

The daggers I pick up feel too small, too light, so I finally settle for a long knife, about the length of my forearm. It is curved slightly and comes to a wicked-looking point. The golden hilt seems to fit my hand well.

I shrug off my overdress before leaving the shed with the knife in my hand. James has set the scarecrow on one of the wooden posts. As I walk toward them, I note that it is covered in something like leather.

"So. Are you going to teach me what to do?"

James shakes his head. "I don't want you focusing on technique. Not now."

I wave the knife in the air. "Then how am I supposed to know what to do with this?" I ask.

He eyes my weapon for an instant and judges my choice before finally explaining. "You have had to deal with more than we had any right to ask of you." I blink at the unexpected statement. "And we continue to deny your requests to leave. And things continue to become harder. I know you're hurt and afraid and overwhelmed, and you probably like it here less every day."

"That's not true," I tell him quickly. I know that he heard what I said to Rennar earlier. "I like it here more than I should. I just don't understand it here."

"Well, either way," he says. "This is what a lot of us do to clear our heads. The king used to do it, and he passed it on to his sons and then, eventually, to me. And we don't know anyone who needs a clear head more than you."

I study the leather-clad scarecrow momentarily before giving James my attention once more. "What is it that you're going to have me do?"

In one easy movement, James draws the sword hanging at his side. Slowly and smoothly, making sure I watch the action, he swings his sword and it comes to rest against the neck of the mannequin. "I want you to tear this dummy to shreds. Swing, stab, whatever it takes, but I want you to take the misplaced anger you have mustered against this world and its people and I want you to take it out on this." He taps the dummy with the tip of his sword.

I'm aware that my expression is stricken. I didn't know he knew how much anger I had built up. I don't know who told him. "I don't know how to do that," I say aloud. "No one's ever taught me how to fight."

"This isn't something you're taught," he tells me gently. "This is something you're born with the knowledge to do. This is attacking with no holds barred. This is instinctual. This is you, taking whatever you're feeling, and putting it into action. Into blows."

James sheathes his weapon. He turns me so I'm facing the dummy head-on, steps up behind me, and moves me a few steps forward. "Feet shoulder-width apart," he instructs. "Knife at the ready. Be ready to shift your weight."

I stop his list of instructions. "James. I don't know what to do, instinctual or not. I don't just swing a knife around when I'm angry."

He sighs. "Close your eyes."

"Because that will only make this go better for me," I mutter. When he doesn't say a word in response. I reluctantly let my eyes shut.

James places a hand low on my back and pushes me gently half a step forward. "Keep your eyes closed," he says quietly. How he knows I'm about to open them is beyond me because he's still standing behind me.

"Stretch your arm out in front of you." I do as he asks and raise my right arm from where it's hanging at my side. Before my arm is straight, the point of the knife comes in contact with the dummy. "That's how far away the dummy is, okay? Remember that." James says.

It's hard not to open my eyes, just to see how close he is standing to me. His hand is still on my back. "Now, come on, Cara. I know how you feel. You've been dragged away from home, told you can't go back. You've been told your future has been mapped out for you since before you were born. You do nothing but worry about Sophie and then, after days, when you finally get some news about her, it's only to hear that she has been captured. And now you aren't even being involved in the meetings about her fate. Everything you know is being turned upside down. Now, Cara, just swing."

And I do. Without knowing what has come over me, only recognizing that his voice in my ear has slowly become lower, more insistent, and has been repeating everything I've been thinking and feeling these last few days, in one smooth motion and without opening my eyes I slice the knife across the space in front of me where I know the dummy to be. And the knife makes contact, glancing across the leather surface.

I'm so shocked that my eyes fly open, and I draw the knife back before the swing is finished. I turn toward James, but he catches my wrist before I've spun all the way around. My knife is still held away from my body. I would have nicked him with it had he not noticed.

But he doesn't look worried. He grins, an easy smile that contrasts with the serious tone he'd been using seconds before. "See?" he says, all solemnity gone. "Instinctual." He moves around me and releases my arm to inspect the shallow scrape on the dummy's torso. "Not bad." He looks me in the eye, a challenge dancing in his own stormy gaze. "Let's see if you can do better."

James moves to stand behind the dummy; it's about half a foot shorter than he is. "Every time you think of something you're mad about, swing."

Now that the first kick of adrenaline is gone, I'm feeling foolish about the whole endeavor. I tell him so.

"You're fighting, Cara. There's nothing to be self-conscious about."

"I'm fighting a dummy, in an empty field," I point out. *With only you around to watch.*

"Your point?"

"If it's so easy, you do it," I grumble.

After a moment, he shrugs. "Fine." I watch as he disappears into the shed, and reemerges holding another dummy over one shoulder and a knife in his hand. When he reaches me, he drops the knife onto the ground, sets the dummy up so it's the same as mine, and then he unfastens his sword belt and sets it to the side as he picks the knife back up.

"I thought this exercise was all about releasing anger," I say as he works.

James waits until he's finished setting up to look over at me and raise an eyebrow. "Who says I don't have any anger that needs to be released?"

"Oh." I study him momentarily, like that will give me any of the answers I'm searching for, until he clears his throat and rakes a hand through his disheveled black hair.

"We'll just go back and forth, okay? Name something that's been eating at you, that really pisses you off, take the swing, and then I'll go."

I must still look pretty dubious about the whole arrangement, because James chuckles. "You know," he says conversationally. "Normal people would jump at the chance to grab a weapon and take their feelings out on an inanimate object."

"Well," I reply, trying for the same voice but sounding rather bitter, "if there's one thing we've learned of late it's that I can hardly be considered normal."

James winks, and his bitter smile matches mine. "Join the club, Lady Cara." He points to the dummies with the tip of his blade. "And I think we've just found the motivation behind our first swings."

After seeing him do the same, I take the stance he just showed me. In a lightning-fast motion that could be considered graceful, James takes a step with his left foot, and all his weight shifts forward as his right hand comes up to slice diagonally down the dummy's front. His left hand mirrors his right, as though he has a knife in both hands rather than just one, and the force behind the swing is enough to leave a sizable gash in the leather.

He catches me watching and forces a grin. "You're up."

Trying not to feel silly, I do my best to mimic his action. I'm not quite as fast or quite as strong, but I don't miss, and that's what I'm most concerned about. And, though the frustration at the thought of not being normal anymore doesn't leave me, the drive to do something about it does.

James nods approvingly. "What else?"

"Sophie."

"Swing."

This time, instead of matching my diagonal cut, I step forward with my right foot and slash my knife horizontally. My entire torso swivels to continue the slice.

I flash my eyes to James and turn his question on him. "What else?"

His lips form a hard line. I stare him down until he says, "My answers are staying up here." He taps the side of his head with the point of the knife.

I scowl. "Then so are mine." I'm not voicing my fears if he won't.

"Do what you want," he says with a shrug. His next swing has a bit more force behind it.

Before his motion has come to a stop I've swung again. *No one will let me save my sister.*

James moves again, burying his knife hilt-deep in the dummy's stomach.

Saladin and Logue have decided to hate me for something I never asked to happen. I cut the dummy across his throat.

James swings.

I have to go to a feast and pretend everything is okay. The dummy gets a slice taken out of his arm.

James swings.

I'm not allowed to tell anyone at home that Lyria exists. I slice an X onto the dummy's chest.

James swings.

My uncle knew what my future held, and he never came back to tell me.

He left me for ten years to find out on my own.

My life was decided for me before I ever had a choice.

James swings.

I want to go home.

And I find out James is right. There is nothing to be self-conscious about. I'm slicing the leather scarecrow to shreds, and it's the best thing I've done in days. Long after my hair comes loose from its knot, long after sweat trickles down my forehead to sting my eyes, long after my arms start aching with the effort of swinging the knife, and my feet stumble with the rhythm of stepping back and forth with the blows, I finally stop. I thrust the knife into the dummy's shoulder and lean my head against its torn chest and close my eyes and breathe.

I move only to pull my hair back out of my face, and then I see James watching me with a neutral expression.

"Feel any better?" he asks.

I'm more tired than I could have guessed the exercise would make me. But the constant itch I've had to move, to do something, anything, has faded. "A bit."

"Good." I follow his gaze as he glances to the sky. The dark clouds have rolled in as I trained, and they look fit to burst open at any time. Night has officially fallen. "I should get you back inside."

I don't protest. James lifts the two dummies from their posts and carries them back over to the shed. I scoop his knife from the grass where he's dropped it and gather his sword belt before I trail in after him. He's depositing the dummies with a pile of others in the back corner.

When I move to replace my knife amongst the others, James stops me. "You might as well keep it. These are just extra. And now that you know how that one feels in your hand, it will be easier to use."

So I slip it in my boot. I hand James his belt and he straps it on while I go and get my overdress from where I left it. James shuts the shed door and we begin the trek back to the castle.

When we reach the side door we used earlier, James hesitates. He looks to the sky, seems to listen for a moment (because when I start to speak he shushes me), and then frowns. "It's later than I thought."

"So?"

"*So*, I think the patrols around the castle walls have already started. We were supposed to be back inside before then," he says without opening the door.

"James, it's you and me. Once they see us, they'll know we're not trying to take over the castle," I sigh.

"They take their jobs seriously," he tells me. "There's no real chance that the castle will be attacked, but they're on guard anyway."

"Yes, but once they see us—"

"They'll shoot first and ask questions later," he says flatly, cutting me off.

I roll my eyes. "You have got to be kidding me right now."

James just looks at me. Then he says, "We can sneak in. I know their rotation; I can avoid them. Or we can walk around to the front and hope it isn't Logue on duty at the gate because he's liable not to let us in even if he does recognize us."

I weigh the options and grimace. We're on the back end of the castle, and the entrance to our rooms is closest to this side. And I don't want to risk running into Logue, especially if we're really supposed to be inside by this time. I can only imagine him not letting us through the front gate. "Fine, James, if you can get us in without being seen..."

He grins in anticipation. This is the answer he was hoping for. "The rain will help keep us hidden," he promises, easing the wooden door open. "Just stay close. And stay quiet."

I salute crisply. "Yes, sir," I whisper.

He shakes his head in amusement and beckons me forward.

I wonder what it is about living in a castle that makes you an expert at sneaking around. First Sasha, and now James' plan goes off without a hitch. Almost. When we've just about made it to the inner courtyard, one guard shouts something to another, and running feet come toward where we're standing.

James is quick to grab my hand and pull me down a less-used pathway of the courtyard. The footsteps continue behind us, so James mutters something under his breath and eventually pushes us behind some bushes where there is a neat little niche set low in the wall that keeps us completely dry from the rain that's been picking up. We're also successfully hidden from view, because the guards run right past us. I don't think they were chasing us in the first place, but it's nice to know we're not about to be caught.

I can still here the guards shouting, but the sound is moving off now.

Our nook really isn't all that roomy. I end up leaning lightly against James with my legs tucked under me, and his knees are pulled to his chest. I'm consciously aware of his closeness, the smell of him, pine and rain, his lean body tense with anticipation.

Finally the voices of the guards die down, and the only sound left is our own breath in our ears.

James smiles crookedly down at me. "That was a close one, huh? Can you imagine the humiliation? The castle waking up tomorrow only to find that our warrior and the crown prince's right hand had to be escorted to bed because they weren't clever enough to stay hidden or quick enough to escape?"

I chuckle because he's absolutely right. Saladin and Logue would have a field day. "Our reputations would be ruined! All respect for us would be lost."

We both laugh quietly for a moment, and, though it is probably time we find a way back inside, neither of us move. I close my eyes and listen to the wind rustle through the leaves and the rain pattering down. I imagine the past I've been told about, where someone could call the elements to them and direct them as they please.

"Thank you," I say to James after a time. "For the training. For being patient with the training. I didn't even know how much energy I had to get out until we started, but I needed that."

"It was my pleasure," James says easily. "Though if you hadn't been so enthusiastic, we might not be in this situation..."

I elbow him halfheartedly. "Next time I'll try to reign in my enthusiasm," I say dryly. "Besides, you were the one 'training' me. Which means you were supposed to be the teacher, showing me how to do these things because I don't know how yet. Telling me when curfew's coming so we don't accidentally get shot by our own guards."

"All right," James says. "Our next lesson is sneaking into our rooms before someone finds us out here and mistakes us for enemy soldiers."

"Because we're so fearsome, hidden craftily under the bush," I mutter. But, with a small sigh I slide out from our hiding place. It's pouring rain now. For a moment I stay underneath the cover of the castle wall. But then the wind whips raindrops at me, getting me wet anyway, and I'm sweaty and tired from my one-sided knife fight, and there's nothing I want more right this second that to have all of that washed off of me.

So, without a second thought, I step into the downpour.

The cold of it is a shock, because the day had been fairly warm, but I stand my ground against the chill and turn my face to the sky. I spin in slow circles, trying and failing to keep the rain from my eyes so I can watch as it comes down. The rain quickly soaks my hair and dress. I shiver with delight, mouth open to catch the drops like I would do if I were with Sophie.

Eventually I remember James is standing by, so I drop my arms to my sides and turn to face him. I can't hide my wide smile.

Clearly, James hasn't had the same reaction to the rain I have. He's just standing there, letting the rain run over him, plastering his black hair to his head. His dark, serious eyes are the same color as the cloud-covered sky, and they are trained on me. I feel the grin fade slowly from my face as I look at him. My heart starts to pound, but I don't look away. I can't. His white shirt is stuck to his chest, outlining the muscles of his stomach and arms; his eyes are unreadable.

Part of me wishes he would turn and lead the way inside, but the other part is praying for him not to. I finally raise my shoulders in a long shrug, wondering what it is he's waiting for.

James closes the gap between us, slowly, until we're mere inches apart. Hesitantly, he reaches up one hand and brushes my wet hair back from my cheek, behind my ear, leaving a trail of fire along my cold skin. He leaves his hand there, twined in my hair, and looks down at me.

He's so close that our breath mingles in the cool night air, and I shiver from something other than the cold. James is looking at me intensely, curiosity and desire plain on his face. My breath catches. The longing I feel to reach out and touch him takes me by surprise; to trace his defined cheekbones, his strong jaw, the long lashes framing his dark eyes, his collarbone and the scar there that's visible at the base of his neck because, as usual, he's failed to fully lace up his shirt.

Neither of us speak; we just stand there together.

"James." His name slips from my mouth before I can stop it. I try to think of something to follow it with, but every coherent thought has flown from my head. He doesn't seem to mind. With a soft exhale that I can barely hear over the drumming rain, James leans down and presses his lips to mine.

For a moment, I am too startled to move. But then I feel my heart fly to my throat and heat rush to my face. My arms slide around his neck of their own accord, like they have been aching to do. I pull myself up to meet him. James kisses me firmly, urgent but sweet, holding me tight against him. His fingers are wound in my hair; my mouth yields to his. My heart is singing, and his is keeping perfect time with it.

I wonder if he knows how often I've thought about this. What it would be like to be in his arms, to see him look at me the same way I'm sure I look at him.

His urgency tells me that he feels the same way. James parts my willing mouth with his own, his tongue tracing my bottom lip and making me gasp. My hands are knotted in the fabric of his shirt and I'm standing on my toes, arched into him.

The rain pours down on us while we stand there. My heart beats faster as I feel him smile against my mouth, so I press closer against him.

I have no idea how long James and I stand in the courtyard, but a clap of thunder eventually causes me to break away. James' chest is rising and falling rapidly, and I know mine is too. He manages to smile his wonderfully crooked smile at me before taking my hand and pulling me along until we reach the kitchen door and slip inside. When James closes the door quietly behind him, he reaches for me, draws me to him once more, and kisses me gently and swiftly. Then we race up to our rooms, and I smile the whole way there.

****

Once I get back to my chamber, I spend a long time standing in the middle of my floor, afraid that if I move the bubble of happiness surrounding me will disappear.

James had seemed reluctant to leave me when he dropped me off in front of my door. And I hadn't wanted him to go. I wanted to feel his hands on my face again, his arms around me, and his lips against mine. And I wanted him to keep looking at me the way he was tonight—that wonderful mixture of longing and disbelief and elation.

Somewhere in the back of my mind I wonder what everyone else will think in the morning when they all inevitably find out. But then I think about him again, and I remember that I don't care what the rest of the world thinks, just like I haven't cared since we arrived. Why should that change?

As I finally crawl into bed, I think that the only thing wrong with the night is that I know James still has a secret that he has yet to share with me. *But I can't be mad at him for that*, I think, tracing my lips lightly with a finger. *Not tonight.*

21

Sasha doesn't barge into my room in the morning. Instead she knocks on the door once, loudly.

"What?" I call out without opening my eyes, as I bury myself farther under my covers. "Just come in."

The door doesn't open.

"Sasha?" I ask. No answer.

Grumbling, I slip a dressing gown on over my nightdress, don't bother tying it, and shuffle to the door to swing it open. "Sasha, I—"

But it's not Sasha. James—barefoot, shirt un-tucked, hair mussed up—is leaning against the doorjamb. Memories of last night are still vivid, so my heart beats a little faster at the sight of him. But I can't stop the smile that creeps across my face. To my relief, I see a similar grin cross his.

I know I must look like a mess—after all, I just woke up—but James is gazing at me like I'm...well, quite honestly, like I'm beautiful. I blush fiercely.

James takes this as an invitation to step in and kick the door shut behind him. Taking both my hands in his, he presses his lips to my forehead. I close my eyes and let him. After a long moment, he pulls back slightly and murmurs, "Good morning."

I smile up at him. "Morning."

"How did you sleep?" he asks.

"Brilliantly, as a matter of fact," I reply. It feels mundane, awkward almost, to be standing here with him after kissing in the rain the night before.

James must be thinking along the same lines, because his eyes darken slightly as he looks me over. His hands are still holding mine, but soon he slides them up my arms to my neck. He's hesitant, gentle, like he's ready for me to pull away at any moment.

I'm wide-awake now, frozen in place. I think I might be holding my breath.

Just when I think he'll lean down and kiss me, he lets me go. I try not to let my disappointment show, but he must see. Amusement is dancing in his eyes as he walks over to sit on the edge of my bed. "I should probably let you get ready. You're going to be part of the council meeting we're having in an hour or so."

I blink. "Really? To talk about Sophie?"

James just nods without a word.

"I didn't think they were going to let me be a part of that." I'm still standing in the middle of the room.

"They didn't think they could keep you away," James replies.

Then I snap out of it. I move to the wardrobe in a lame attempt to do something besides stare at him. "So then," I try for a normal conversation. "What does one wear to a council meeting?"

"How should I know?" James asks.

I roll my eyes without facing him. "Well, I had assumed you've been to one before," I respond dryly. "And that you generally had to wear some type of clothing to these kinds of things. So I was rather hoping you could base your answer off of that."

I sense rather than see him smile. "Nothing as formal as what you would wear to dinner with the royals, but nicer than what you'd wear to a tutoring session."

Now I do glance at him over my shoulder, to flash him a smirk. "Was that so hard?"

"Harder than you know," he mutters, still grinning.

I'm quick to pull appropriate clothing from my wardrobe—a white underdress and a simple, emerald green overdress—then I splash water from my washbasin on my face and run a brush through my hair. I'm completely self-conscious while I do all this, as I am well aware that James' eyes are on me the entire time. I'm almost grateful when I step into my washroom and close the door to change.

It's just James, I try to tell myself. *It's only James, same as always.*

But it's not even kind of the same as always.

I change clothes quickly, trying not to dwell on the thought that last night could have been some kind of fluke. That he might regret it. That he's sitting in my bedroom *right now*.

I have worked myself into such a state that I yank the door open with more force than is probably necessary. James glances up in surprise from his new position, lying on his back on the bed and holding an open book straight above his head. His feet are hanging off the edge.

"Have you found this at all interesting?" he asks mildly, waving the book in the air for me to see.

I try to command my heart to calm down as I make my way toward him to see what he's reading. I have to take the book from his hands and sit next to him to actually read the cover. It's *Wars of Our Ages*. "Oh," I say. "No. I got about halfway through that first chapter Verne told me to read, then I quit."

James, unmoved, chuckles. I look down at him. "Comfy?" I ask.

He grins. "Extremely." Then he moves anyway, sitting up, slipping one hand softly around my waist, and gathering me into his arms. I don't know how he can tell, but this is exactly what I need, what I want. Shyly at first, I sink into his chest as his second hand slides into my hair and holds my head where it rests against his neck. I let my hands curl into his shirt and close my eyes.

"I'm so afraid the council is going to say no," I admit into his shoulder. I breathe in his outdoorsy scent.

His thumb caresses soft circles at my waist. "I know." His mouth moves against my hair.

I can't believe he likes me too. The unbidden but honest thought pushes past all the others to the front of my mind. Though there is no way he could guess what I'm thinking, I blush and start to pull away.

James lets me go easily, shifting his hands to my shoulders and ducking to look me in the eye. "Hey," he says, misreading the way I won't meet his gaze. "It's going to be okay, Cara. The council knows what they're doing. So does the king, so does the Crown Prince, and no one is going to ignore your opinion either. It'll be all right."

He tilts my chin up with the crook of his finger and brushes a swift kiss against my bottom lip. "Now I have to get ready too." He gestures to his clothing with his free hand. "This isn't exactly meeting-appropriate attire." He doesn't move away, just brushes a stray lock of hair out of my face.

"So you *do* know what's appropriate to wear at council meetings," is all I can think of to say, working to keep my expression stern.

The corner of his mouth quirks.

James drops his hand seconds before Sasha bursts into the room, just like every morning. I should request a lock. She takes us in with a glance, raising her eyebrows, but says nothing.

James and I slide slightly apart.

"Did you sleep here?" Sasha finally asks James as she looks between us.

"Of course he didn't," I chide her. For the first time though, I notice that James does look suspiciously disheveled. Like he hadn't even gone to bed the night before. "Did you get any sleep at all?" I ask him.

Smiling slightly at his own private joke, James shakes his head.

"Why not?" I ask.

Still smiling, he says, "I think you can guess."

I blush crimson, and Sasha is looking between us, her expression suggesting she's read more into James' response than was actually there.

"I take it you're feeling better about the whole thing with your sister?" Sasha asks me.

My heart sinks a little. "No. Not better. I'm calmer about it, but I'm not better."

James stands up. The warning look he flashes Sasha is gone when he turns to me once more. "I'll see you in the meeting room. In an hour. Don't forget to eat breakfast before you come." He opens his mouth as if to say more, closes it again, and then tears his gaze from mine to nod to Sasha and exit the room.

Sasha closes the door behind him and turns slowly to face me, leaning against it, a grin growing on her face. "You and James? It's about time!"

She seems absurdly pleased, and, while I can feel a blush spreading across my face, I smile too. "What does that mean?"

"Oh, come on. I thought you had started...dating—that's the word, right?—in the Otherworld. I mean, the way you two act? Crispin had to tell me your first night here that there was nothing going on."

"Oh, stop," I laugh.

She shrugs, still grinning. "He's crazy protective of you, always around you. I just assumed..."

I shake my head. "Well, I guess you were ahead of us on that one. Sorry it took so long for the two of us to catch up."

Sasha pushes off the door and starts hunting for accessories for me, which I think are unnecessary but she doesn't. "I'm glad someone finally had the sense to grab him up. I mean, I understand that he isn't Demesnian and that he—" She breaks off suddenly, and then she skips past the thought as though she hadn't mentioned it. "—but he already seems lighter, happier, and goodness knows he deserves that. I would have thought about him myself, but he's *James*, and it never would have worked."

She says his name like she would say "Crispin" or "Branshire", and I get it. She and James together would be like her dating a brother or a cousin—someone you could never think of in that way.

"Who *have* you thought about, then? I mean, I know, Blaine, but has there ever been anyone else? Anyone serious?" I ask. *And, if so, some advice?*

"Oh no. There have been a few suitors, but nothing serious. And I still have half a year before I turn eighteen and really have to start looking for a husband."

I wait a beat before responding, to judge if she's joking or not. "You have to find a husband in a year?" Sasha is too carefree, too restless to possibly get married any time soon. "And what do you mean 'there have been a few suitors'?"

"Just a couple nobles from around Lyria coming over for my father's consideration. They weren't important."

"Sasha, are you saying you're going to have an arranged marriage?"

She shrugs and glances at me. "Don't worry, Crispin already explained that where you're from you guys don't really have marriages arranged for you. And 'arranged' is the wrong word. More like 'pre-approved by my parents'. Royal marriages are important; they set the tone for agreements between kingdoms and help keep trading and peace alive. Special circumstances can be accounted for"—

here she pauses momentarily as her mind wanders—"but my mother and father will have a voice in choosing my husband," she finishes.

I absorb that tidbit of information silently. "So then Crispin...?"

"Oh, no doubt he'll have more of a say than the rest of us in his spouse, but ultimately my parents have the final say. He'll have a marriage arranged for him, too."

"Hmm." For the first time in a long time, thoughts of Jade come to me unbidden: her talking to me about the two hot new boys at school, and how, according to her, Crispin was exactly her type. *Poor Jade, it'll never work out now.* The reminder of her is both welcome and painful.

Sasha passes me a few golden clips to hold while she pins back my hair. "Colonel Blaine... he's really nothing more than wishful thinking," she continues.

"Well, he seems like a good wish," I tell her. I can't relate to her situation, but I'm sympathetic toward it. *What would Sasha be like if she were from Earth?* I wonder. *If she could choose her own life, her own husband?*

Sasha moves in front of me and grabs my shoulders. "You are going to have to tell me everything that happens in that meeting," she says seriously, sky-blue eyes flashing. "*Everything.*"

I crack a smile. *If she were from Earth, she'd get anything she wanted.* And, though she is a princess here, part of me wishes she could know what it's like to have power over her own life.

****

The realization that I'm about to be part of a discussion full of high-ranking Lyrians about the fate of my nine-year-old sister has been coming to me in waves throughout the morning. I haven't been much of a breakfast companion to Sasha, but she talked enough for the both of us, doing her best to prepare me for what I'm about to experience. As half of what she's said has gone in one ear and out the other, I'm only feeling kind of ready.

Now she leads me down the hall from the throne room into a part of the castle I've never been in. Here the hallways are a little more dimly lit and armed guards stand at regular intervals. It takes me a moment to realize that Sasha has stopped talking. In fact, she's stopped walking altogether.

I glance up from the floor I've been studying just in time to meet the eyes of General Logue. Blaine is standing just behind him.

"Princess Sasha," Logue says, inclining his head to her. I am offered no such courtesy from him, but Blaine catches my gaze and grimaces apologetically. "We can escort the lady from here. You have come far enough."

So Sasha isn't even allowed to be near the council meeting. Her bitterness about not being included looks to be justifiable.

Despite Sasha's higher ranking, she does as the general says. She whispers, "Good luck," to me before disappearing down the hall again.

I fall in step behind Logue and Blaine without a word after watching her go.

"How are you this morning, Lady Cara?" Blaine asks me.

I remember James, and I hide a smile. But then I remember how unprepared I am for the meeting we're headed for, and I am sobered immediately. "I'm not sure," I tell him honestly.

He recognizes that some of my anxiety stems from the unknown meeting ahead. "You have to start somewhere, Lady. Soon I would guess you will partake in more of these meetings than you'll care for. And you have to know what you're getting into. What better way to begin than to enter in on a meeting where you at least understand the topic at hand? Where you have an invested opinion to share?"

"I don't know what I'm supposed to do," I admit quietly so Logue can't hear.

Blaine examines me kindly. "The wonderful thing about this being your first council meeting is that you don't have to know."

But it's my sister we're talking about. So I can't mess this up. But I manage to flash him a small, grateful smile for the effort he's making to reassure me.

The two of them usher me through a nondescript wooden door with the same tree symbol carved into it as on the doors to the throne room. We enter a room that is much smaller than I had expected. After being told the meeting wasn't being held in the same room my arrival had been announced to the council in, I had been anticipating another large room with a similar U-shaped table for the members of the council to sit around. What I am met with is a plain circular room. There is a large map of Lyria dominating one wall, and an oval table set in the middle of the floor with seven chairs on either long side and one at either end.

"The first lone seat is for the king," Blaine explains as I look around. We're the first to arrive. "The second is for the queen, if she chooses to attend the meetings. And, unless the circumstances are dire, she generally does not. So it stands empty."

"But none of that will affect you," Logue interjects. He points to one of the seats. "You will sit here to observe the meeting."

I raise an eyebrow. "Observe?" I ask coolly. "Why do you think I'll merely 'observe' the meeting?"

"Because, Lady, I fail to see what insight you could offer us into what has happened, untrained and immature as you are. No offense meant," he adds, almost as an afterthought.

I scowl. "Oh no, don't worry, it *sounded* like a compliment," I grumble.

When two soldiers enter the room and Blaine moves to speak to them, I take a moment to look at Logue. "What did I do to make you dislike me?" I ask softly, not letting my voice carry past the two of us.

Logue looks taken aback, but only for a moment. His expression is smoothly composed when he answers shortly. "More than only one thing, most of which you can't even understand at this point. Suffice to say that we've been waiting too long for a warrior for you to be her."

Though the comment shouldn't sting, it does. "Everyone else is willing to believe in me, General. Why aren't you?"

Now his expression hardens. "I have been King Rennar's general for near fifteen years now."

"Congratulations," I mumble sarcastically under my breath. I can't help it.

He continues as if I haven't spoken, which is probably for the best. "I have been in small skirmishes, led men into battle, planned more than one raid, and trained hundreds of soldiers. So I like to think I have a good eye when it comes to finding the people that will help us win our battles. And you?" Now he looks me over, making me fidget under his icy gaze. "An Otherworlder with no training, no experience, and a young girl to boot? How is it that you expect to lead an army? How is it that you expect to change the course of our world?"

I don't say anything for a long time. Then I just shrug. "That's precisely what I'm here to find out."

I'm saved from his sure-to-be sharp response by the entrance of King Rennar, Crispin, James, and the soldier I recognize as Rorck. I give them a small wave.

"Lady Cara," Rennar says with a nod at me.

The council members, all dressed in dark green shirts, file in and take their seats, all along one side of the oval table. While King Rennar takes his seat at the head with Rorck at his right, Logue, Crispin, James, and I take seats opposite the council. I'm next to James, and Crispin is only a seat down from me, in the center of our side.

A balding council member with wispy blond hair and watery eyes begins to speak. But before he gets very far in to what I imagine is going to be a very well-rehearsed speech, Blaine—who has yet to take his seat—finishes his side conversation with the soldiers.

"One quick matter before the meeting comes to a head," Blaine says. "There are more whispers of Malachi. To the east. Nothing definite, nothing we can work from, no sightings or details. Just the same name being thrown about in the same manner as always."

Most of the room looks stunned. I don't. "Who?" I ask.

King Rennar takes the explanation, which is so unexpected that I pay immediate attention. "For nearly as long as the marauders have been active, there have been murmurs of a name: Malachi. It is only ever said in fear, or in reverence. He seems to be behind every plot against Demesne, but no one has seen him nor can they tell us a single thing about him. We'd begun to think he was no more than a name; that the name is being used for others to hide behind and that there is no one man actually in control of these plans. As the whispers have become more frequent, we've started to wonder if we are right in our assumption that no such man exists."

I think the rest of the room is surprised to hear their king admit he may be wrong, but Rennar isn't paying attention to them. He's watching me. Gauging my reaction. "It has been more than a month since any new rumors of him have spread. But if everything we have heard is in fact true, than this man holds a great deal of power. And he seems to enjoy wielding it against my kingdom."

I don't know if it's my place to speak, particularly directly to the king, but I do so as Blaine takes the empty seat next to me. "Whatever followers or power he has, he never uses against the other kingdoms?"

Logue answers my question. "Attacks like those we have been faced with are not lightly shared with the other kingdoms. That would be admitting weakness, vulnerability. They do not share their mishaps with us, nor we with them."

"But why?" I press. "If they are enduring the same attacks, wouldn't it be best for everyone to know?"

"And if they weren't? Demesne would have revealed a difficulty without receiving anything in return," the general counters.

Crispin catches my eye, and the look he's giving me asks me to let it go. So I allow the argument to drop and ignore the expression of triumph on Logue's face, as though he has bested me.

"When this meeting has concluded," King Rennar says directly to Blaine, "I should like to speak to the men who brought you the information. But for now, we have a deadline approaching, and so another matter to discuss." *Sophie*.

Blaine bobs his head sharply in agreement, and the man with thinning hair resumes his speech.

For some reason which escapes me, he recaps the events of the other night for us all: the marauders and their declaration that Sophie is in Sheik hands. I listen for a time as those around me talk about patrols along the Sheik border, the believability of the marauder's claim, and how likely it could be that no one heard of the Sheiks or marauders making a trip to the Otherworld.

"There haven't even been whispers of an Otherworld visit?" King Rennar asks Logue.

The general shakes his head. "We sent messages to both the Navites and Cairnes with immediate response, and to the Sheiks, to no avail. And even from them we have heard no such thing."

"No response, even from Malloc?" Crispin asks. He looks disappointed but not necessarily surprised when Logue shakes his head. The name sounds familiar, but I don't interrupt to ask who Malloc is.

Logue then continues his report to the king: "Our patrols have not noticed any shift in the Sheiks movements, either. Nothing to suggest they've made the journey or are at all anxious about what they have done." For the first time, Logue looks at me without any distaste in his expression. "There is nothing happening across Sheik borders that would make us think they have your sister."

Most of the room is looking at me rather expectantly; I take this as my cue to speak again, though it takes me just a minute to find my voice this time. "I don't understand why that man, that marauder, would lie about the Sheiks having Sophie. What purpose would it serve him?"

"Their plan gets you alone and unguarded across—for lack of a better word—enemy lines. They want to get you away from us. If you're our warrior, then you're the most valuable person in this world right now," Crispin explains.

I blink. "I...I'm the most valuable person in the world? That can't be true." I've spent so much time thinking about what it means to the Demesnian royal family that I might fulfill their prophecy that I've given hardly any thought to what I mean to the rest of Lyria. My mind races with everything I know, everything I've learned.

"Of course you're the most valuable person," Crispin is saying, but I wave him off, silencing him, much to the surprise of everyone but James.

"The prophecy," I finally say, looking around the room at everyone. "What's the last stanza?" I struggle to remember, knowing it's important.

A council member with graying hair speaks the words: "She has the power to choose her side/ if with light she fights it will change the tide/ But if this savior answers Warlord's call/ then evil will ensnare us all."

I start to think out loud, and everyone lets me. "So you mean to tell me that all this warrior stuff, this savior stuff... It's not just with you all? You want it to be, but I have to *choose*? There's a possibility I could fight for either side in this war?" *Then evil will ensnare us all.* "People in Lyria think I could, what, fight for the Sheiks? Fight for the people holding—"

"Possibly holding," Logue corrects.

"—possibly holding my little sister captive? The Sheiks think that by getting me alone, they can make me fight for them? That's their plan? Get me away from you all, and convince me to choose their side."

King Rennar is looking at me, seemingly curious. "We think that is their plan, yes."

I frown and fight to lower my voice, which had gotten louder than I intended. "Don't they realize I would just say no?"

"Cara, if you say no the most likely scenario is they would kill you for refusing. That way no one else could have you either," Crispin tells me.

There he goes, the Crown Prince throwing yet another piece of rubble onto the already crumbled ruins of my life.

It's war we're going toward here, I've known that since day one, but death is another thing entirely. "Oh," I breathe.

James' fumbling hand finds mine under the table, and he laces our fingers together wordlessly.

I clench my other hand in the fabric of my dress to steady myself. "Regardless of that possibility, I cannot sit in this castle knowing my sister is out there."

"Lady, the purpose of this meeting is to determine whether your sister truly is 'out there', as you put it." Another member of the council is speaking, gazing at me with an expression that is carefully controlled. His hair is short and pale blond while his eyes are deep blue. He's in the middle of his side of the table, across from Crispin, so he's probably a big deal.

That doesn't stop me from narrowing my eyes at him, though. "You all will have to offer up some serious proof that she isn't here before you can get me to believe that marauder was lying."

"For one," the same man says, "we in Demesne would know if anyone had jumped the tear between worlds from our forest."

"Is there more than one location for these tears, or is the one in Demesne the only one?" I ask, a question I had been wondering about anyway.

"There is at least one in every kingdom. But, like General Logue pointed out, we have received messages from the Cairne and the Navite people, and no activity from their tears has been noticed either," he tells me.

"But, like the good general also said, you didn't get any replies from the Sheiks," I am quick to counter. "And, as it seems possible the Sheiks have been giving refuge to the marauders, or at the very least are in league with them, the most obvious answer would be that the tear in Sheik was used."

"What makes you say that the Sheiks have been giving refuge to the marauders?" Blaine asks me. Everyone had been watching the council member and me talk, their eyes flashing back and forth like we were a particularly interesting tennis match, but now Blaine's dark blue eyes are trained only on me.

I shrug. "It just seems likely," I start to say hesitantly. "I have a hard time believing that gang has enough luck to operate on Demesnian land for ten years without a single sighting. So if you guys can't cross kingdom borders and they are working with the Sheiks to some greater goal, is it not possible they've been spending their downtime in Sheik?"

"The Sheiks are not our allies, it's true, and the tension between our kingdoms grows now more than ever, but surely even they would not be so foolish as to spend a decade concealing our enemies?" another councilman—this one older and more broadly built than the one I'd been speaking to—says.

They kidnapped an Otherworld nine-year-old, I want to say. *I don't think the Sheiks' sense of morality is real top notch.*

"Cara," Crispin speaks now. "I've been giving this a lot of thought." *I should hope so.* "And Panus is the only Sheik who has even seen you. He doesn't know your name, cannot possibly know where you live or he would have accosted you there rather in The Village"—I start slightly, hearing the name of somewhere from my home tossed around in the Lyrian meeting room. "So how would they have found Sophie? How would they all have found your home, taken your sister? I can't make sense of it."

"How would they have known about Sophie if they *hadn't* seen her, hadn't found her? Crispin, by that same logic they shouldn't even know Sophie exists, let alone that she is the one person I care about more than anyone in life! That she is the one guaranteed way to get to me." James tightens his grip on my hand when my voice gets shrill. I quiet back down.

"There is always the possibility we were followed through the woods or to Kayyar, though we saw no one, or even that there is an information leak in the council reporting what you say to the Sheiks or the marauders. Anyone could have heard you talking about your sister at one time or another, and then passed the information along. And either of those possibilities is more likely than anyone having actually taken Sophie from your home," Crispin says.

I frown, hit with an idea so obvious that I cannot believe I didn't think of it before. "Why didn't we just send someone, me even to return to Earth and check after we heard she'd been taken? See if she was home or not?" I ask. The question is directed at the entire room, but my eyes are still locked on the Crown Prince.

So he answers, clearly having considered this question already: "Two reasons. One, even journeying to the tear would prove that Sophie means as much to you as they hope. We have no doubt that they have people watching the tear to see if we go to it. And we don't want to hint that your little sister is the perfect leverage against you. Two, if we go to the Otherworld, to your home, we run the risk of leading them there. As we believe that they do not know where you live, it is in our and your best interest to keep that a secret as long as possible."

Everyone besides me is wearing the same calm expression, bordering on tedium, apparently not strangers to Crispin's explanation to me. And then something clicks: this is all for show. This meeting, including me, telling me everything they've thought and talked about and considered... They knew their decision long before they opened that door to let me in.

They aren't going to go after Sophie. They've decided she isn't here.

I can't decide whether to scream in fury or burst into tears at the absolute unfairness of the situation. Luckily, I do neither. *I am supposed to be "the most valuable person" in this freaking world!* And they are all taking the decisions, which I have every right to make, right out of my hands.

"Why am I here?" My voice is commanding, steady. *Thank the Lord*.

A few people look surprised. Others look wary, as they well should. "What do you mean, Lady—?"

"I mean *why*," I interrupt, "did anyone bother to extend me an invitation at all if my opinions were going to be tossed carelessly aside in favor of whatever you had already come up with? Because it seems to me this has been a waste of what might have otherwise been a good morning." I'm radiating vehemence. My older sister protective instincts have kicked in.

Logue, not at all put off by my intensity, appears to relish the chance to enlighten me in front of an audience. "The entire purpose behind the establishment of the council, Lady Cara, was to ensure that no one voice in the kingdom, royal or not, had the final say in any decision made. That it would be a group decision, majority rules, unless the case is extreme. No matter how high a stake you think you have in this, unfortunately it is not your choice. We decided to gather once more today to hear your opinion and see if any of ours had changed. But it does not appear they have. So, yes, a decision has been made, and it is this: we will not risk the loss of our potential warrior in order to save a girl we don't believe to even be here."

It is clear by the way Rorck and a few of the council members flinch that my already angry expression has shifted to downright murderous.

Trying to regain her composure, a councilwoman blinks rapidly and tries to appease me in a shaky voice. "Perhaps we could send someone to validate the information? Someone the Sheiks wouldn't be likely to recognize. James could leave the Crown Prince in another's care and shift—"

James chooses that moment to clear his throat far more loudly than is polite, cutting the council member off mid speech.

In the silence that follows, you could hear a pin drop. James looks mutinous, the council member who had been talking looks even meeker than she did a second ago, Crispin is watching James warily, and the king's eye is roaming over the council warningly.

"Why would James be the one to check the information?" I ask. My voice carries strong and clear across the room. Expecting an answer, I let my gaze trail over everyone. But when no one offers one I turn to James himself. "Why would you be sent to check?"

The moment his dark eyes snap to mine, the rest of the room melts away until I'm only aware of the two of us.

"I can't tell you that, Cara." His voice is even, too even. It doesn't match the expression in his eyes.

I pull my hand out of his. "Why not?" No response. "You can't continue to keep secrets from me!" *Not after last night.* "How am I supposed to save a world that won't even share everything they know with me?" I cry, pounding my fist against the table in a fit of frustration. It hurts, much more than I thought it was going to, but I ignore the pain for now, choosing not to draw attention to my poor decision.

"It doesn't matter," he says forcefully, in a tone that suggests it actually matters quite a bit.

"If it could save Sophie—"

"It couldn't. That plan wouldn't work. The Sheiks would see it coming, and they wouldn't allow any of us to cross." By the way he says "us", I assume he doesn't mean the others in the room, but another group entirely.

"But—"

Again, James cuts me off before I can finish. "No."

I think the sharp word is meant for me, but when I remember that the council is still present and pull my gaze from James' face, I see that Logue has his mouth open as if to speak. "It's not your place to tell her," James continues. To my surprise, Logue snaps his mouth shut. "It's no one's place but mine."

"And you're not going to," I finish James' thought for him.

Finally, he looks a little pained, a little guilty. "Cara, look, I—"

I don't mean to stand up, but I find myself doing so. "Well, it appears you all have more to consider," I say to the room in a tight, angry voice, "and I wouldn't want to make you speak in riddles on my account. So, not that this meeting hasn't been wildly successful, I'm going to leave. Thank you all for your help."

And, before anyone has recovered enough to stop me, I sweep out of the room. The heavy wooden door slams with a satisfying thud behind me as I start for my bedroom. Biting sarcasm is probably not the best method to use to get through to the governing parties of Demesne, but for the moment I imagine it has gotten my point across.

Suddenly, I veer off in a different direction, as a new, horribly ill-advised idea has begun to form in my head.

I haven't made it more than a dozen steps before someone catches my wrist in an iron hold. I'm spun around to face James, and I glare at him with all the anger I can muster, which is quite a lot. "What?" I snarl, somewhat shocked and infinitely pleased with how well my irritation comes across in the lone word.

"Cara, just let me explain—"

"What are you going to explain? Because unless you are about to launch into a detailed description of whatever it is you're making everyone hide from me, I don't want to hear it!"

"I can't tell you. I just can't." His voice is hard, flat. Final.

I glower. "You *won't*. There's a difference."

"Fine then! I won't tell you. Happy now?"

"No."

"Look, you don't need—" he starts, but I cut him off this time.

"No, you know what, just shut up and listen to me for a second." I wrench my wrist out of his grasp. I don't know if he's startled into letting go, or if I'm stronger than I thought, but he releases me without much resistance.

"Well, only because you're being so polite," he growls. "Why are you being so irritable about this?"

"Because this is ridiculous, James!" I shout. "I'm sorry that you've got some horrible secret that apparently isn't so secret because everyone seems to know about it! I'm sorry that you get treated differently because of it! I'm sorry that, whatever it is, it makes you think badly of yourself. I'm sorry you seem to think that, if you tell me, you won't be the same person I know you to be! I'm sorry, okay? I'm just sorry, but there's nothing I can do about it unless you let me! But instead, you block me at every turn! Surely your one secret can't be worse than everything else that's happening."

"It is though, Cara. It is worse, and I don't want you to be in on this secret."

I imagine this is about what it feels like to be punched in the gut. The breath I've just taken whooshes out between my teeth before I can call it back, so I'm left speechless, bewildered, angry, and hurt. He doesn't *want* to share his secrets with me, though everyone else can know. I'm being kept out of the loop again, and it is his decision to keep me there this time.

I do the only thing I feel is left to me in my current condition. I turn on my heel and stride off without looking back, to let James go back to his meeting.

22

Now that the council has finally called the meeting to a close, James pads silently up the stairs of the library to the third level where he knows he'll find Cara. That's where she's been spending her free time, even though she denies it, because few people think to look for her up there.

The only light in the library at this time comes from the few lanterns hung from the railing between the first and second floors, but it is more than enough light for James to find his way around.

When he does reach Cara, he waits in the shadows and watches her for a moment. She didn't hear him approach—no one ever does unless he wants them to—so she doesn't look up from her book. James recognizes the look on her face. Her eyes are not skimming the page; they are locked in place. She is lost in her own world.

Suddenly loath to disturb her, James leans comfortably against the wall,. He wistfully studies the furrow that appears between her eyebrows only when she is too deep in thought to notice it, the slight tilt of her head as she contemplates, and the loose hairs that always manage to escape the knot at the base of her neck. He wonders if she knows that she bites her bottom lip when she's thinking.

Something must alert her to his presence. Cara snaps out of her reverie, and her eyes focus on a spot in the gloom not far from where he's hidden. James sighs silently and takes the few steps that bring him into the light.

Cara's curious face clears, and she slits her eyes angrily as she regards him. Her lips come together to make a hard line. James supposes the expression would actually be intimidating were it not so endearing. She doesn't shift her position on the chair as she waits for him to speak. He doesn't say a word. So eventually, though he can tell she considers breaking the silence herself, Cara turns her head and continues to read her book.

James finds himself smiling at her stubbornness, but he hides it so she cannot see. He waits.

As he expected, Cara's eyes do not stay on her book for long. They flit up to his face, gauging his reaction to her silence, and when she sees he has not moved, she scowls again and quickly averts her gaze.

Her legs are tucked underneath her, and she is settled low in her chair. James strides over to her. Before she can react, he has arranged his expression into one somewhere between frustration and indifference and braced a hand on either arm of her chair. He leans toward her, and she shrinks back slightly as she tries but fails to hold her ground. Their faces are mere inches apart. James ignores the way his heart kicks into high gear with the knowledge that a slight shift on either of their parts would allow him to sink his lips into hers again.

His breath stirs her hair, wafting up the scents that James has come to associate with Cara: old books and ivory soap and grass. He does not allow his expression to change.

Cara is not so composed. She has to fight to bring the glare back to her wide brown eyes. Her hands tighten on her book, and her back stiffens. Finally she speaks. "Can I help you with something?" she growls.

James adopts the same tone. "Yes. I would like you to stop pretending I don't exist."

Expectancy flashes across her face as she studies his own. But she speaks in the same voice. "Fine. Tell me whatever it is that you aren't telling me."

James raises an eyebrow. "Did you really think it would be that easy?" He shakes his head slightly.

Her eyes become unreadable. "Then I guess we don't have much to talk about, James. So if you'll excuse me..." Cara lowers her eyes back to her still open book. James watches her, and is pleased to see her pulse is jumping in her throat.

"Have you ever thought I might have a perfectly good reason for not telling you?" he asks her seriously.

Cara glances back up to meet his eyes. Her voice is softer now. "Of course I've thought that," she says, "but that doesn't mean I don't deserve to know."

James cannot stop the chuckle that escapes him, though it's devoid of humor. Cara looks puzzled. "I never said you don't deserve to know, Cara. I said I didn't want to tell you."

"Well, that's just as bad," she replies. But this time she doesn't drop his gaze. "I wish you didn't think so poorly of me," she admits quietly, after a pause.

"Think poorly of you?" James repeats in surprise. Cara is miserably waiting for his response. He can see that she regrets saying it, but she doesn't try to take it back. "Think poorly of you? Cara, there are very few people that I think more highly of than you," he tells her.

Cara starts to shake her head, but James lifts a hand to her face to catch her chin. "You don't believe me?" he asks.

"Why am I the only one who can't know?" she asks in reply. She does not try to pull away from him, which James takes as a good sign.

He takes time to answer, and he can see her growing impatient as she waits. "How can I say this so you'll understand?" he murmurs. James absentmindedly traces her jaw with his fingers as he thinks, and he feels her cheek heat under his fingers. "I don't want to tell you, because I love the fact that you don't know." Cara still looks unsatisfied so James tries to explain further. "This... secret. It's not a secret, not around here. It's one of those things that changes how people see you, one of those things that people are unable to look around. But, with you, I get to feel like myself. Because you don't know, I know that however you feel about me is truly because of me. Only me. And I don't want you to see me any other way. Which you will, if I tell you."

James, thankfully, does not see any pity in Cara's eyes. Only resolve. And he knows what she'll say before she speaks. "After all this you don't really think one more secret could change the way I think of you, do you?"

"That," James says, leaning even closer to her, "is exactly what I think."

"Well that's just silly," she tells him.

"Hmm..." he says softly. "Is it? Need I remind you that you don't even know what the secret is?" James cannot help the way his eyes trace her face, from her curious brown eyes down to her lips, where they linger before moving up again. Being this close to her is intoxicating. And he can feel the slight shiver that courses through her, which suggests she thinks the same thing about him.

Without thinking, James reaches over to tug her hair gently from its pins. Her lips part in mild surprise.

"James, I can't do this. Not if you're going to keep things from me," Cara whispers.

"Do what?" James asks with a slight smile.

He can see Cara barely hold back from rolling her eyes. Almost, it seems, without realizing she's doing it, Cara places a hand lightly on his chest. She doesn't push him away, doesn't pull him closer; her hand simply rests there. She watches that hand as she answers, "Don't pretend you don't know." She fingers the fabric of his shirt.

James shrugs slightly, his chest alight with her touch. He moves his hand to her hair, his other hand still braced against the chair. "Do you want me to leave?"

Cara's eyes are on his mouth as she begins to nod her head, without conviction. James slowly closes the gap between them anyway, drawing her to him. He lets his mouth skim lightly across her jaw up her cheek, to her temple, her nose, and then, with a sharp intake of breath that sends James' heart into overdrive, Cara closes her eyes and turns her head to find his lips with her own.

James feels her hand tighten against his chest and she slides her other hand around the back of his neck, using it to pull herself up to meet him. A small sound escapes from the back of his throat when she uncurls her legs and one of her ankles wraps around his own, moving him closer to her still. Her book falls from her lap; James hardly notices as it hits the floor.

"I'm trying to learn, stop distracting me," I finally say with a smile.

I'm sitting on the floor with James now, and I'm leaning into his chest. He's been telling me how surprised Logue had been with how well I'd handled the meeting—until my outburst, that is.

"You should have seen his face when you stormed out." He slides away from me so he can turn to face me. "What are you studying up here, anyway?" he asks.

I grab a book from the floor. Not the one I was reading, but I hope he doesn't realize that.

He doesn't seem to. James slips it from my hands and thumbs through it—a book of maps, detailed maps, of Demesne. I don't tell him that I've already flipped through that one twice and have long since moved on.

"Crispin and Sasha I are getting ready to have dinner. We thought you might like to join us," James tells me, as though he's only just remembered the reason he came to find me. I can tell by the way he's eyeing me that he is assessing me and judging if I'm about to fly off the handle again. I plaster a soft smile onto my face to convince him that I'm not. I think he buys it.

"I'll meet you down there. I want to finish this first."

James' brow furrows a bit as I take the book back. "Why?"

"Because if I stop now I'll never pick it up again, and these are the things I'm going to need to know someday."

A pause. "Okay. You think you can find your way to the dining room? The one we ate in the first night you got here?"

I nod. "Of course I can. Do you know how much time I've spent wandering this castle in the last two days? I'm becoming somewhat of an expert."

"Remind us to show you the secret passages sometime," James says as he stands up. "Then you'll be as knowledgeable as anyone here." He brushes himself off and gazes down at me. "Are you sure you want me to leave?"

I laugh. "Yes. No offense, but I'm far too easily sidetracked with you nearby."

"No offense taken. In fact, I take that as quite the compliment."

"Good. I'll see you in a few minutes." I wave him away and watch until he's disappeared down the stairs. Then I grab the book I was actually reading. I almost had the cast I need figured out, but then he'd come up here. Thank goodness he hadn't caught me practicing. Then he would have *known* something was up.

The book I'd dropped at his arrival was one on "locational casts", which I've found means anything from determining where you are, to where you most want to go, to the direction you should travel in. I'm trying to teach myself a cast that illuminates the cardinal directions.

I am doing everything I can to come up with a haphazard plan to go and get Sophie—by myself—which means I have to learn the geography of the land between Demesne and Sheik, how long it will take to get there, and make sure I don't get lost on the way because I don't have that kind of time to waste.

The cast had looked easy enough at first glance, but teaching it to myself is proving harder. I want to practice the boulder-moving spell, just to recall the feeling that comes with casting, but it seems a bit difficult to use in a library, and I don't know how I would practice it outside without anyone seeing. So I'm stuck.

Supposedly, if I stand facing one direction, the four points will glow on the ground around me, three in a kind of yellow light, and north in red. I need to travel due south, to the river that acts as a border between Sheik and Demesnian territory, and then follow it east to where it is shallowest in order to most easily cross into Sheik. And I have to do this fast, in the next ten hours or so. So I am going to steal a horse.

This I feel guilty about, but there is no way in the *worlds* I will be fast enough on foot.

Unfortunately, once I'd learned the cast, I was planning on leaving. I hadn't counted on dinner. And, now that James has reminded me, I'm hungry. I skipped lunch to study up here. But I don't have much time to waste before the marauders' deadline.

I get up, brush myself off, and move to stand in the center of the floor where there is space. I close my eyes. I have to get it right this time.

I concentrate on the place in my chest, next to my heart, where my magic is supposed to be. I'm going to make it work; it has to work. If I can't get this, then I don't have a chance of finding Sophie on my own. *All I have to do is splay my fingers, palms to the ground, and keep my arms straight at my sides.*

I don't know how, but through sheer use of force I succeed. The space in my chest tightens, compresses, and then suddenly all the pressure releases at once and heat floods through my body. It courses down my arms and through my fingers. Though I know before I open my eyes that I was successful, I still get a certain sense of delight to find that there is a short yellow line stretching from my feet, one more at either of my sides, and, when I turn around, a dark red line is stretching away behind me.

It takes a certain amount of restraint for me not to crow with pride, but I don't. When I close my hands into fists, the lines vanish as if they had never been there.

I have a knapsack hidden under one of the armchairs; I slide it out and add—to the extra clothing, food, and knife—the book of maps. I stack the rest of the books on a side table for someone else to put away, sling the pack over my shoulder, and take it downstairs with me. There I hide it behind a row of dusty books. Then I take off for the small dining hall before James comes looking for me again.

When I arrive (after only two accidental detours), the other three are already seated at the far end of the long table. Crispin is at the head with Sasha and James on either side of him, and I can see the tip of Nelma's tail at his feet. I take the seat next to James. I think I see Sasha smile, but I refuse to look at her, so I can't be sure. James I do glance at, and he is grinning.

"Why are you having dinner in here? Why not with your parents?" I ask Crispin and Sasha as I load up my plate.

"We were still in the meeting during lunch, but Sasha and my mother said you didn't show up to eat. And we guessed you weren't dying to have another official dinner with all the royals after the way this morning went. So instead we decided it would be best to have a smaller dinner with just us," Crispin tells me. He never once elaborates on who "we" is.

"Are you allowed to do that? Skip out on family dinner?" I ask, trying to avoid any talk of Sophie or the council meeting.

"For you," Crispin says sincerely, "there is very little we're not allowed to do."

I hide a small frown and start eating, not sure what to say to that. I haven't done anything to earn the respect I'm being shown from most people, and I'm about to do something that will probably make them wish they hadn't shown me so much respect in the first place. I'm no expert, but I'm pretty sure running away falls under the things-not-to-do-when-your-friend's-kingdom-is-trying-to-keep-you-safe category.

We eat in relative silence. I'm too preoccupied with my own thoughts and nerves to carry on a real conversation, and the other three seem to be slightly apprehensive around me, as though I'm liable to start shouting the way I did in the meeting this morning.

"I meant to ask you," I begin after a few minutes of nothing but the sounds of silverware clinking against plates. All three look up, grateful, it appears, that I've chosen to break the silence. "The whole curfew and armed patrols around the castle deal. What time does that start? How late are you allowed to be out?" It's James I'm asking, because he's the one who knows what I'm talking about.

He seems both amused and slightly uncomfortable with the question. "About that—"

"What 'curfew and armed patrols deal'?" Sasha interrupts, straightening up in her seat, suddenly interested. Crispin is looking at James and me with a certain amount of interest too.

An annoyingly familiar feeling of delayed understanding sweeps over me. And when I look James in the eye, I know what he was about to say. "You made it up?" I ask accusingly.

He shrugs and looks away to poke at his food. "I wanted to see how well you could follow me, and how quiet you could be while you did so. I didn't make it up completely; the guards *are* more wary at night. But they wouldn't have attacked us on sight."

"What did you tell her?" Crispin asks James. He sounds irritatingly entertained by James' lie. I listen with a scowl while James tells the story, leaving out the kiss. Sasha seems a little disappointed by this.

"And you believed him?" Crispin says to me when James finishes.

I tactfully choose not to respond to this, as there are servants in the room helping clear plates, and I've noticed that I receive some odd looks when I argue with the Crown Prince. I settle for sticking out my tongue when no one else is looking. Childish, but effective. He rolls his eyes and focuses on his food.

I didn't know until this moment that time was capable of speeding by, while at the exact same time inching along. Each slow second of dinner is agony, is a moment longer that Sophie is lost and alone, is time I should be spending going to find her. But before I've had enough time to think, enough time to dwell, enough time to perfect my plan, the last of the dishes are being cleared and my friends are standing to leave.

Apprehension knots my stomach. Surely I can't pull this off? Surely I can't sneak past the castle guards, past the royal family, past James who is watching me cautiously even now?

But I have to. I have to because no one else will do it for me.

The three start to say something about visiting a portrait gallery now that we've eaten, but I shake my head before I even know what it is I'm refusing. "I'm going to grab a book from the library and head to my room," I lie in a voice that can't possibly belong to me. It is far too even, far too believable to be coming out of my mouth when inside I am a bundle of nervous energy.

They don't seem to think my statement is unreasonable. In fact, as we walk out the dining hall door, they look as though they rather expected it.

"Will you be okay on your own?" Crispin asks, placing a hand on my shoulder. The expression of worry in his emerald eyes is mirrored in Nelma's mint-green ones. It leaves me wondering, not for the first time, if there is more to her than there seems.

"Oh, of course I will," I bluster. "It's been a long day, and I just want to sleep."

He nods, squeezes my shoulder comfortingly, and then Sasha discreetly leads him down the hall. Now I'm left with James.

"Does Crispin not know?" I say, looking at James with raised eyebrows.

He blinks at me before understanding dawns. "About last night? No, I haven't quite told him. Today has been busy enough that it hasn't come up."

I nod. There is a beat of silence. "Well, goodnight then," I say lamely, turning away in a sudden rush to be off before anything they do can convince me I should stay.

James loops a hand around my elbow and brings me swinging back to face him. I very nearly collide with his chest in the process.

I glower up at him, not because I don't want to talk to him, but because I need to leave. Now. Before I have more time to think, to talk myself out of it, or to give my plan away.

He looks bemused by my expression. "Chill, Cara. Look, I just wanted to say that I hope you know if there was any part of us that truly thought Sophie could be here, in Lyria, we'd be going after her. You know that, right? We'd never leave her to get hurt."

His gaze is pleading as he searches my face and continues holding me close to him.

I move my free arm to rest my hand in the middle of his chest. "Of course I know that," I tell him softly, trying not to let my guilt show. "I know," I repeat. *But just because you think she's not here doesn't mean I agree.*

The worry lifts from his expression, fueling my guilty conscience. He slips a hand around the back of my neck and kisses my cheek. "Goodnight, then. Sleep well. We'll see you tomorrow."

The full weight of my plan hits me now because, if I do this, he won't see me tomorrow. If I go and offer to take Sophie's place, I'll be stuck in Sheik. I can't fight my way out. And from all I've heard, I can't imagine they plan on ever letting me go once they have me.

This could be the last time I walk through the castle. That could have been the last Demesnian meal I'll ever eat. My eyes find Crispin and Sasha watching James and me from where they stand, and I know I might not see them after this.

Then I look to James. I soak up every inch of him with my gaze to commit him to memory. I didn't know someone could mean so much to me after knowing them for so little a time. And despite everything, this secretive, protective boy does mean a lot to me. And it almost hurts to know I have him, and that I have to let him go.

I think something changes in my face, because a line appears between James' eyebrows. "Are you sure you're okay?" he asks.

I loop my arms around his neck and stand on my toes to kiss him, hard. He holds me, more out of surprise at the unexpected gesture than anything, but by the time he relaxes enough to respond, I'm already pulling away.

And I lie one more time. "I'll see you in the morning."

Then I'm gone, off to grab my hastily packed things, and I don't look back.

****

I wait outside of the stable for what feels like an eternity, but in reality is probably only two minutes. It took an unexpectedly long time to cross the castle lawn without being seen, as I had to pause every few seconds to make sure the noises I'd heard were not guards. Turns out they weren't. Now it's dusk, and I'm hiding in the same patch of grass and weeds Sasha and I had used only days ago to avoid being seen. I'm listening for any sound to suggest someone is within.

No noise besides the soft sounds of the horses inside the stable reaches me, so I fumble my way in. Luckily, a few lit lanterns still stand at intervals. They are set up high and secure against the walls. But, to my dismay, this light shows me that none of the horses are tacked. Which means I'm going to have to do it myself. Which is going to take ages.

I move along the stalls until I find Misty. She looks content, sleepy, and I feel bad for making her join me on this suicide mission. But I don't want to take someone else's horse, nor do I want to do this with a horse I've never ridden before. So that leaves me with Misty.

The blanket and heavy saddle I slide onto her back with relatively little difficulty, and I pull the straps tight and adjust the stirrups so they'll hang right for me. The bridle proves to be more difficult. Misty is quite awake now, and I don't think she's happy with me. I try giving her an apple from my pack to calm her down, but it only wakes her up more. Now when I attempt to put her bridle on she shifts her head to nudge me for more treats.

"No. No, Misty, stop. I need you to stop. I need you to cooperate. *Misty*." But she isn't listening to me anymore, if she ever was.

I whirl around when I hear a muffled laugh behind me. "She isn't going to do what you say if you talk to her like that." Talit is standing there, along with a younger, dark-blond haired, green-eyed boy whom I've never seen before.

"Then how am I supposed to talk to her?" I ask him, trying to act as at ease as I can.

"You have to calm her down with your voice. Stop trying to bridle her, just stroke her and murmur to her until she stops pulling away. Then try again," Talit tells me.

The other boy pipes up, "Like this." And, though Talit reaches out a hand to stop him, the boy steps up next to me and demonstrates.

"Koda," Talit begins, but I shake my head to let him know it's fine, I don't mind. "This is my younger brother," Talit explains to me instead.

Koda is probably three or four years younger than I am, and apparently he could not care less that I'm supposed to be some kind of celebrity. "See?" he says as Misty settles under his touch. "She just needed a second."

I nod. "Yeah, I see. Thanks." I can't hide a smile, and when I glance over I see that Talit is concealing one too.

"Hey, Koda, I'll finish up in here. Tell Blaine I'll be out in just a few minutes."

Koda looks like he wants to argue, but his older brother shoots him the same listen-to-me-now look that I often use on Sophie. So Koda bobs his head in my direction. "Nice to meet you, Lady Cara," he says quickly, and then he dashes out of the stable.

"Nice to meet you too," I murmur as he leaves. I tilt my head to regard Talit. "I didn't know you had a brother," I say.

He steps up by my side, where Koda just was, and takes the bridle from my hands to start fastening it around Misty's nose. "Two. I have two brothers. Koda and Blaine."

"You're related to Blaine?"

He gestures to his tall, lanky frame, which is nothing like Blaine's broader build. "I bet you never would have guessed that. But yes, my brother is the Colonel. And my other brother is a stable hand. And I'm...whatever I am."

I grin at the reference to all the odd jobs he seems to do, and we are both quiet for a moment.

When Talit finishes putting the bridle on, he checks my work on the saddle and pats Misty's rump. He turns his blue eyes on me and studies me curiously. "You're sneaking off?" he asks finally.

I've been wondering if he guessed. I know there's no use denying it. "I have to, Talit. No one else is doing it for me." It's the same argument I've been using with myself.

"But, what if something happens to you? We need you, Lady Cara."

I fight back the guilt rising in me. "I know you think you do. But Talit, this is my little sister we're talking about. If there is even a chance she's here, caught, because of me? I have to go." He still looks anxious about letting me go. I put a hand on his arm. "If it were your little sister, alone and helpless? What if it were Koda? Or even Blaine? What would you do?" I'm looking at him pleadingly now. "What would you do?" I repeat, more steadily.

He doesn't answer, so I know what I've said is hitting home. "Talit, I have to do this. I cannot risk Sophie's life on the chance that the Sheiks were lying."

"I could go with you," he begins, but I shake my head.

"I have to do this by myself. They said I needed to come alone. And you can't tell anyone, Talit. I need whatever head start I have before they notice I'm gone."

He doesn't look sold on my idea, and I don't think I'll ever convince him. I take Misty's reigns from his hands and he doesn't stop me, but he walks beside me as I start to lead Misty out of the stables.

"I can't just let you go," he says without conviction.

I continue walking, offering no response. We make it all the way to the door in the side of castle wall before Talit speaks again. "I have to tell someone." His voice is no more than a whisper.

I open the door, and then turn to look him in the eye. *I'm the most valuable person in Lyria? Let's see if that's true.* "I'm telling you that you can't, Talit. I'm ordering you not to."

Talit looks stunned at my commanding tone. I am a bit too.

I don't give him time to find his voice. Pulling Misty after me, I step through the door and shut it behind me. I think I remember the path Sasha and I took to get out of the city without being spotted, and I do my best to follow it quickly, not knowing if Talit will actually obey my order. I don't really have any authority, after all. *I'll have to ask Crispin to teach me that cast from the treasury room*, I think as I move through town. Then I could sense the way Sasha and

I went and eliminate all the backtracking I'm having to do in the city streets. I bite my lip when I remember that I probably won't get the chance to talk to him again.

Since it's later than it was when Sasha and I sneaked out, I don't see a single soul on the streets. And then I'm outside the city limits with my heart pounding. I expect to get caught at every turn.

Though I'm not a completely proficient horseback rider, once I exit town and mount up I urge Misty into a gallop, and I ride until the castle is no more than a spot in the distance. Time is not on my side. I only have until morning to find Sophie in the first place, but now I can't guarantee I'm not going to be followed.

When Geler fades out of sight behind me, I slide off Misty's back. Casting is easier this time than any before. I splay my fingers, and the cardinal directions light up around my feet. I grin, make sure I'm still on the right track to the river, and hop back on my horse to take off again.

I travel like this for hours: gallop, stop, cast, mount, repeat. I am a horrible judge of distance, so it is impossible for me to know how many miles I've traveled or how far I still have to go. The repetitive motion stops me from thinking too much about where I'm headed.

It must be at least three o'clock in the morning by the time Misty and I reach the river. I dismount and rub her nose gratefully. We both take a break. She wanders a few feet away while I take a roll and my canteen from my pack and sit next to the roaring water.

The river is so blue in the dark that it's almost black, and the moonlight is reflecting off the rapids. I'm proud to say I was correct in guessing that I would not be able to cross the river here; it's both too wide and moves too swiftly to be safe.

As much as I miss home, I'm going to miss it here too. The rolling green hills and the warm rainy weather. And the people. I'm definitely going to miss the people. But I am swift to shake that line of thinking out of my head.

After a few minutes of rest, I pack up my things and mount Misty again. I ride within feet of the riverbank. The sky is lightening subtly by the time the forest comes into view. True to the maps I poured over earlier, here the river starts to curve left into Demesnian territory.

I'm close. I'm so close. My palms begin to sweat; I wipe them on my skirt even though there is no one around besides me to notice. When I realize I'm trembling, I am quick to hop off Misty. My dismount is somewhat wobbly, and I begin walking next to her to steady myself. The movement helps.

For a full minute I can't remember what I'm doing on this journey. Fear is pushing everything else from my mind. My mouth is dry, so I take another swig from my canteen. And then I grit my teeth and press on.

Before I reach the line of trees, I drop Misty's reigns and smack her rump to send her cantering away in the direction we came from. I wish I'd had time to learn the cast Sasha used, to ensure her horse made it home safely. As it is, all I can do is hope Misty will be okay, because she's been a good horse to me. The two times I've ridden her. I watch her disappear into the distance, feeling a pang of regret as I do. Two times or not, Misty was the last living, breathing connection I had to the things I care about in Geler. And now she's gone. And I'm officially and completely alone.

On the other side of the river, rose, apricot, and amethyst hues are brightening the sky.

"*Damn,*" I mutter as I enter the trees without stopping to admire the view. I don't have much time left until the deadline.

Even though day is breaking, it is still dark in the cover of the forest. I keep next to the water and walk until it grows calmer, shallower, and eventually is no more than fifteen or so feet in width. I pull my book of maps out, check to make sure where I'm about to cross will take me into Sheik land, and then I hesitate.

It's the hesitation that does it. Before I can make myself remove my overdress and step into the water, something knocks me over the head, and I'm unconscious before I hit the ground.

****

I wake up to an intense pounding in my skull and an uncomfortable ache in my arms that I can't explain. I'm unable to hold back the groan that escapes from between my lips. My back is stiff, and my legs are cramped and curled up underneath me. It is another moment before I can open my eyes, but I finally wrench my eyelids apart only to be confronted by blinding daylight.

Eventually my mind and my body catch up to one another, and I realize my arms have gone numb, and that the scraping against my back is a tree trunk. The throbbing in my head originates from one spot behind my ear. And when my eyes adjust to the light, I can see more trees towering above me, surrounding me.

Every part of me hurts, and I'm cold, and I have no idea where I am. I soon find that my arms are numb because they're tied behind me, around the tree. I struggle to stretch my legs out in front of me, working out the pins and needles that have developed since I've been stuck here.

Wherever here is.

Some kind of weird instinct takes over when my head clears a bit, so despite the pain I'm in, I know to figure out as much as I can about where I am without attracting attention to myself. I refrain from struggling or calling out, though that's my initial thought. Instead I lean my head back, close my eyes, and try desperately to remember what happened to get me here.

It hurts to think; the harder I try to remember, the worse my headache gets. *The meeting...I sneaked out...*

Sophie. Sophie, Sophie, Sophie. It takes everything in me not to cry out her name. I open my eyes again. There's not another soul nearby.

How did I screw up so badly? Am I across the river? Am I in Sheik? Did they find me before I could find them? And if so, why keep me tied up in a forest?

I struggle—twisting in my bonds and ignoring the major rope burns I'm receiving. This was not part of the plan. I had envisioned marching into Sheik with my head held high to turn myself in willingly. To watch Sophie go home and to know I was the reason why that was possible.

My struggling is useless. After ten painful minutes, the ropes haven't loosened an inch. Whoever tied me up knew what they were doing. With a rush, I remember that I can cast, but that hope is quickly snuffed out when I note that my hands are tied just as tightly as the rest of me. And I only know two casts. I don't think my ability to throw boulders and illuminate north is going to be much use at the moment.

I must spend hours working against the rope while trying desperately to think of ways to free myself, but it's all to no avail. I'm just as stuck as ever. So I do the only thing left. I let the pain overtake me, and I sink into a fitful sleep.

****

I come to again when the snapping of a branch nearby startles me out of my light slumber. I squint around as it's dark once again, and I search for the source of the noise when a sudden light blazes up before me. A yelp escapes me before I can stop it, and I have to blink away the brightness as my eyes adjust all over again.

"Note to self," I say out loud, trying to hide my fear. "When confronted with an enemy in the dark, quickly shine a light in their eyes. Remove said light. Repeat. Keep them blinded. However, if that enemy is tied to a tree... Well then it doesn't matter much if they can see or not."

"You can stop with the act, girl," a rough voice sounds from the other side of the light—a torch, now that I can look at it. "Didn't your boy ever tell you? Fear has a distinctive scent." Someone, I assume the man talking, takes a deep breath through his nose, exhaling contentedly. "And you, my dear, are positively covered in the smell."

My boy? I don't have a boy. "Well, that's just uncalled for," I say bravely, calling images of James and Crispin to mind. I try to picture how they would act in this situation. Be bold, I suppose. "I only bathed this morning," I continue. "Or, I believe it was this morning. Hard to tell how long you've been unconscious and kept tied to a tree in a dark forest."

The torch holder tosses the flame over his shoulder. For a wild moment I think that it will land in the grass and set the forest on fire, but it lands neatly on a pile of wood that starts to smoke and ignite. As it does, my surroundings again become clear. They've changed through the course of the day. Or I was much less observant earlier than I thought.

Off to one side, far to my right, are the outskirts of a campsite. Blankets, articles of clothing, and other odds and ends are scattered about. No tents though, I note. I'm tied to a tree on the edge of a small clearing, so the sky is easy to see. The forest stretches around me on all sides.

But it is what's between the trees that make me catch my breath. I'm not surrounded by Sheik. Instead, a few dozen wolves are prowling toward me and baring their teeth. Once I've spotted them they begin to snarl and snap. I can't help but push myself back a little more into the unyielding tree, as if it will protect me.

With a sharp bark, one wolf silences the others.

"My second," the now torchless man says airily, as though this explains everything.

It doesn't. "Your second what?" I ask.

He sneers at me, so I glower at him. "Second in command," he tells me.

I know how blank my expression is, but I can't do anything about it. I tear my eyes from the man in front of me and look to the wolves again. "How'd you get to be in charge of...?" I start to ask, but then it dawns on me. Crispin's explanation of magical creatures. Granite the dwarf. James' list of creatures he gave me my first day in the castle. I blink. "You're a werewolf."

The man is tall, broad, clearly muscled, and the firelight is casting shadows over his strong face. His dark blue eyes glint with positively feral light when he grins. It sends a chill down my spine. He spreads his arms out, as if to encompass the entire wolf pack. "Sweetheart, we all are."

The pack growls in unison, a deep, rumbling sound that echoes deep in my chest, like the bass from music that's being played just a touch too loudly. I think they're laughing.

I'm lashed to a tree, surrounded by a pack of werewolves, and no one knows that I'm here. Fear races through me. "I didn't come here to find you. It wasn't your place to stop me." My voice comes out as no more than a whisper, so I clear my throat and try again. "I'm going to find my sister. Untie me," I say, more firmly.

The man lets out a throaty chuckle and crouches down in front of me. "Ah, your sister," he says conversationally. He reaches out a hand to hold my chin, which forces me to look at him, though how he could know I'm dying to look away is beyond me. A common reaction to him, perhaps?

"Your sister," he repeats slowly as his eyes rake over me. "Between you and me, sweetheart, that was one of our better plans. For what kind of cold-hearted, selfish girl would you have to be to leave your younger sister in the hands of a gang of marauders? We knew you'd find a way to go after her." His sneer stays on his face as he continues. "Of course, it was purely luck that you chose to come and get her alone. With no soldiers, no backup, not even your darling prince by your side. You couldn't have made this easier if you'd tried."

The wolves are in on this too? Why does everything in this world seem to be working against me? "Where is she?" I growl, albeit somewhat shakily. I refuse to try and pull away from his grip. I know it won't do me any good.

"You haven't figured it out yet?" he asked, amusement flitting across his features. He seems pleased by the idea of explaining it to me. He leans in closer to me until his face is only inches from mine. I stare him down and fight my suddenly increased heartbeat because I know he'll notice it. "Your sister," he says once more, "is safe at home with your precious parents. They are all still blissfully unaware of Lyria's existence."

The man, a smile still curling the corners of his mouth, is waiting for my reaction.

The news should shock me, should send me reeling. I sneaked out of the castle, left everyone who could have helped me behind, all to rescue Sophie, who it turns out wasn't even here in the first place. I risked my life and the trust of the Demesnian people on what was nothing more than a hoax.

I don't realize that every muscle in me is tense until I relax in sudden, overwhelming relief. *She's safe. She's safe. She's safe.*

The man couldn't have been more surprised if I'd broken my bonds and punched him in the stomach—*which is still a viable option*, I remind myself. He expected me to be devastated. He'd just made my night. *My baby sister is okay!* Suddenly everything else in my life, everything that Sophie's "capture" had overshadowed, snaps back into focus.

"Well," I say finally, as cheerily as I can manage with his fingers still digging into my jaw. "Isn't that just the best news?" I look around the clearing at the other wolves, to include them in the conversation. "Isn't it?" I'm so giddy I hardly care that I'm probably being suicidal.

The man's hand tightens painfully; I suck in a sharp breath. I keep talking though. "So how did you all manage to get those marauders to say such a thing? Wait." A thought hits me. "Are *you* the marauders?"

The man chuckles again. I really hate that sound when it's not coming from me. "What need would we have to raid Demesne? And the royals' palace pet would have sensed us long ago if we were the ones stealing supplies."

I blink at him, at a loss once again, having no idea what he's talking about. *So no?*

"Maybe we should start with an easier question," I say, when it becomes clear that what I've asked is not going to get a more straightforward response. "Who are you?"

Finally the man releases his hold on me. I roll my jaw around once he's let go, and I can feel the imprint of each of his fingers. I'll probably have bruises there now. *Add them to the injury list.*

"I," the man says as he straightens, "am Kerr, alpha wolf of this pack."

I look past him and feign disinterest in his answer. I can tell it irks him. I instead glance over the rest of the wolves. "Is there an alpha female?" I ask curiously, the first question that comes to mind.

One snow-white wolf straightens haughtily, even as Kerr replies: "No."

"Hmm..." I know I should keep him talking, but I don't have much else to say. "What are the odds of you untying me, just a little bit?" I ask eventually.

Kerr shakes his head, most likely at my foolish question. Well, it was worth asking. "You, sweetheart, are a prize," he tells me as he leans down to pat my cheek. This time I do flinch away from his touch. "We won't be giving you up lightly. Not now that we've got you."

"That's nice to hear," I mutter.

"We do, however, have to decide exactly what it is we want to do with you." Some of the wolves stiffen in apparent dissent. "So, until then, you may want to consider getting some rest."

"Like that's even a possibility," I say under my breath.

Kerr has begun walking away from me, but apparently he can hear what I've said anyway. "With all these wolves around?" he grins, turning partially back to look me in the eye. "You'll want to be at your sharpest."

He disappears into the shadows of the forest. Two of the wolves back into the trees, and two men replace them seconds later to put out the fire. I can't tell if these men are the wolves or merely humans, but it doesn't really matter. The rest of the pack fixes their glowing eyes on me until the firelight dies. Though I can hardly see a thing in the dim moonlight, I can tell when they all follow Kerr and vanish from the clearing.

I shut my eyes and let loose the moan I've been holding back. "Ouch," I whisper to the night. Everything hurts. And then, cursing the fact that my captor was right—I need to have all my wits about me in this situation—I lean my head back gingerly and get as comfortable as possible in my current position. And then I surprise myself by drifting off to sleep.

23

"Do you really expect Orrick to share a single coin of that reward with the pack? He would never give any of the credit for the capture to the werewolves." Kerr's voice is quiet, growling.

A second voice is slightly more whining. "We cannot possibly cross King Orrick. Would you risk breaking an alliance with the Sheiks over this?"

"To gain an even stronger alliance with Malachi?"

"Or to walk away with nothing? We don't even know where he is! How would we deliver her?"

Whatever position I fell asleep in is exceedingly uncomfortable, and it takes a heroic amount of effort not to move a muscle. I keep my breathing as even as possible. Kerr and the other man must be standing only yards from where I'm tied up, and I'm well aware that they are only speaking so close to me because they believe me to be sound asleep.

"We could send a message with one of his men," Kerr is saying.

"Which of his men has a stronger union to us than to King Orrick?"

I can hear Kerr's smirk when he speaks again. "Any of them. Once they're turned."

Now I can't help the way my eyes fly open. *Turned? That can't mean what I think it means.* But, judging by Kerr's expression, it means exactly that. *Holy crap. He's going to turn someone into a werewolf? Just to earn their allegiance?*

The other wolves are prowling around. They are far enough from Kerr that his conversation is private, but close enough to make me nervous, and close enough to keep an eye on me.

Kerr and the tall, stocky man next to him notice my slight movement, and they turn their eyes on me and shut their mouths. I blink sleepily, doing my best to look as though I've just woken up while keeping my pulse under control and praying they don't guess what I've heard.

"And the warrior awakens," Kerr smirks.

I grimace in response. "How long are you going to keep me here?" I shrug my shoulders—one of the few moves I can actually make—to draw attention to my bonds. I wouldn't have thought it possible, but my rope burns and aching muscles actually hurt *more* today. Only a week ago, this pain would probably have had me in tears, if only because somehow crying makes things feel a little better. But that isn't an option here; I don't even consider it.

I put on my best brave face and hold Kerr's dark blue eyes. He seems entertained by me. A good thing, I hope.

He crosses his arms over his broad chest as he regards me. "My pack and I still have to decide what to do with you. Until then, you'll remain right there."

I nod mockingly, pretending to understand more than I do. "Would you care to hear what I have to say?" I ask politely.

"No."

"*I think,*" I press on, "that tying me up here is a poor idea. You see, you'd have to be in league with both the Sheiks *and* the marauders in order to have captured me, right?"

Humoring me, Kerr inclines his head in acknowledgment of my true statement and allows me to continue.

"Which means they knew you were going to capture me, and they know you're holding me. So your pack may not have as much time to decide as you think." I try to act nonchalant. "You see, it turns out that I'm pretty dang important. So what makes you think everyone else will stand by and wait for you to make your decision?"

"The Sheiks can't cross the border. And those marauders know nothing. They do only what they are told, when they are told. The real power lies elsewhere."

I know it's a gamble, it is infinitely dangerous, but I need answers. "Does it lie with Malachi?"

Every wolf within earshot stops what they are doing. I swallow, hard, as each of their glowing eyes fixes on me.

"What do you know about Malachi?" Kerr says. His voice is calm, dangerously so.

I tell the truth in a weak voice. "Very little... His name."

Kerr spends a time eyeing me. I don't believe he knows if I'm telling him the truth or not. Finally what he says is, "Allow me to be the first to tell you. Malachi is waiting for you. He is waiting for someone to bring you to him. And you're going to help him when he gets you."

I raise my eyebrows. "When did I decide that? And why did no one inform me that I made such a momentous decision?"

A flicker of annoyance crosses Kerr's composed face. I almost smile. Though it may not be my proudest accomplishment, it gives me a certain thrill to know I can get under the skin of the alpha werewolf.

"I think you'll find him...persuasive, once you meet him," Kerr smirks.

I glower. "He thinks he can just use me, doesn't he? Does everyone in this stupid world think they can use me to get to their own ends? Like I don't have a mind of my own? Like I won't notice?" I struggle to sit up a little straighter, trying to look less pathetic than I know I do now. "Well I'm not having it, do you hear me? Tell *that* to Malachi. See how he likes it."

To my chagrin, after gazing at me for a long, silent moment, Kerr's mouth breaks into a smile. "Oh, he is going to like you."

I scowl.

"Unfortunately, I don't have the same patience with smart mouths." He snaps his fingers, and, before I have a chance to tell him what an overused gesture that is, a small woman with dark blonde hair comes to my side and kneels down to force a gag in my mouth. My words of protestation are cut off as she yanks it tighter, knocking my head against the tree. My eyes water, but I glare at her anyway.

She smiles sweetly and ties it even more tightly. It's disgusting; I'll never be able to wash the foul taste of dirt and sweat from my mouth. And it hurts—she's tied it right over the knot I have behind my ear, probably on purpose.

Kerr looks on, irritatingly smug, until the woman stands up and backs away. "That's better."

I roll my eyes, determined not to let him see how humiliating this is for me. For the first real time since my adventure in Lyria began, I understand why everyone insists that I be taught and be trained. Maybe, if I knew something about werewolves and the geography of the forest, I could escape. Maybe, if I could fight or cast, I could power my way past them. Maybe I wouldn't have gotten caught in the first place.

He must see the fight drain out of me, because Kerr relaxes almost imperceptibly.

"Of course Malachi wants to use you," Kerr hisses, crouching in front of me like he did before. "And when he gets you, he will be indebted to the one who brought you to him. So you will stay here, we will *keep* you here, until we find a way to get you to him."

I glare at him. I'm unwilling to try and speak as I know he's waiting for it, and I know I won't be able to. But he's putting all the pieces of the once-elusive puzzle into place for me. The wolves, the marauders, and the Sheiks are working with—or, more likely, *for*—Malachi. Who is real, just as the Demesnians feared. And I'm somewhat safe here, for now, because the wolves can't hurt me if they're trying to sell me off. I feel both insulted and relieved.

Kerr stands and walks away from me abruptly, barking demands to his pack. I wonder idly how long I've been here. And as soon as I think that, I realize I'm starving and dehydrated, and I don't see my knapsack anywhere. I am mildly surprised to find I can still be hungry in a situation like this.

For hours, the pack moves about without sparing me a glance. Kerr has disappeared. As a matter of fact, I have yet to see any human apart from myself appear from between the trees this evening.

The sun is setting again. *How on earth—in Lyria, I mean—are these days passing so quickly?* Then one of the wolves howls at another, and a dull throb shoots through my head and causes me to wince. *I think I have a concussion.*

I groan through my gag. I've never had a concussion before, but I know what they're supposed to be like. They're supposed to be like this. And being held captive is not what the doctor ordered. Which makes my bad predicament even worse.

I watch the pack work while I wait for something to happen. A group of three wolves, patched multiple hues of gray, seem to be hunters. At regular intervals, teeth stained red, they drag meat into the clearing for the rest of the pack, who fall on it ravenously. I try not to look to closely at that. Other wolves move in and out of the trees. They only communicate in yips and snarls, so there is no way for me to understand what is going on. But they all seem determined. In fact, they all seem on edge.

I sit here until dusk, waiting for something, waiting for them to remember me, resolved not to give in to my headache and fall asleep again because who knows what I would miss.

So moments later I'm wide awake as a chocolate-brown wolf hauls a limp form into the clearing and drops it right in front of me. Kerr follows in his human shape, muddy and bloodstained. But it isn't his blood. The limp form on the grass is an injured man, an injured *Sheik*, and Kerr appears to have made him this way.

The man's head is turned so that he is staring directly at me where he fell, confusion and pain the only emotions in his black eyes.

I hold his gaze. I don't know if I should be angry with him for the lies his people had a part in telling me, or if I should be sympathetic about the fact that he is seriously injured and stuck here with me. So I settle for a blank expression as I watch him watching me.

Neither of us look away, even as the wolf pack slowly emerges from the trees to surround us. The man has no escape, just like me.

"Any of them. Once they're turned." I have no doubt that this is the man Kerr means to turn into a werewolf, just to send a message. A very clear message, but still.

Kerr breaks the heavy silence that has fallen on the clearing. His words are for his entire pack, but his eyes constantly flicker to me. I want to tell him what a wonderful show he's putting on, but my gag is restricting me, as gags often do.

"This," Kerr announces, "is Lord Wile, of King Orrick's court. Wile is privy to the more heavily guarded information of the court, to the types of secrets that are usually kept under lock and key. Information such as how King Orrick has been maintaining contact with Malachi. Unfortunately for us, Lord Wile is a devoted member of the court, and as such does not willingly divulge his king's secrets."

As I refuse to look away from Lord Wile's pain-laced eyes, I sense, but do not see, Kerr's self-confident sneer.

"Unfortunately for *him*, it was my job in this well-laid plan to decide on the deadline to give this girl"—here he jerks a thumb at me—"to 'rescue' her sister. And I planned for all possibilities."

Here I am pleased to find that, gagged or not, I can still scoff loudly enough to cause Kerr to falter and the rest of the pack to hear. He is one cocky alpha male. But he soon continues as though I've made no sound. "I knew it might come to this. We are at a point where our pack is not receiving the respect we should be, especially considering how vital we were to this plan being successful. We are being underestimated. I recognized the Sheiks' false promises for what they were, and have taken matters into my own hands as I thought I might have to. Which is why I timed this girl's capture to the night of the full moon. So that if information were needed from the Sheik court, we would have a means to get it.

"By midnight there will be a new wolf in our pack, one whose loyalty is to us, to me. His knowledge will become ours, and he will be sent, with an escort, of course, to give Malachi this message: If he wants his warrior, he will have to deal directly with us to get her."

And then, for the first time, I see someone shift. Kerr's face elongates, his ears stretch and become pointed. His back legs seem to shorten as his feet lengthen. His hands morph into clawed paws, he falls but does not shrink to his hands and knees, and sandy fur covers every inch of him.

A wolf snarls where Kerr had been standing only seconds before. And I watch, wide-eyed, as this wolf leaps forward, buries his teeth in Lord Wile's side, and causes the man to cry out in pain.

Though earlier it seemed that not all the werewolves in his pack had been happy with Kerr's decision, they all howl in agreement now. Their harmonized call fills the air and makes my hair stand on end. It's synchronized, perfected...eerie.

Wile is shaking, whether in pain, fear, the effects of turning, or even all three, I can't tell. But I do know that Kerr is looking only at me now. He ignores his pack yowling around him and watches for the reaction he's been trying to elicit.

I finally meet his eyes, which are the same shade of blue as when he's human, and I raise my eyebrows. My expression says, "You expect me to be impressed? You'll have to do better than that." Inside, I am not ashamed to admit I'm quaking. From what I understood, Kerr's plan does in fact sound fairly foolproof. He seems to have taken precautions to ensure he is awarded the power he feels he deserves. And I no longer think that the marauders or the Sheiks know where it is I'm being held, so I can't expect any kind of appearance from them.

Kerr seems to know he has gotten to me, for he bares his teeth in what must pass for a wolfy grin, his mouth red. I remember what he said about fear having a scent, and I know it must be rolling off of me right now. No matter how set my expression is, there is little I can do about my emotions.

And then the pack stops howling. They don't fade out; they cut off. Leaving a silence so absolute my ears start ringing, every wolf in the clearing freezes. Hackles raise, lips pull back in soundless snarls, each pair of glowing eyes locks on something behind me. The wolves that had just stood in a circle around Kerr, Wile, and me, draw together to form a huddle of large furry bodies facing whatever this new player to the game is.

With growing apprehension, I try and turn my head to look. The restraints around my torso won't allow me to do more than attempt a quick, painful glance over my shoulder. This problem is solved for me when the source of the new tension, a large, lean, jet-black wolf, pads into the clearing. All eyes follow him.

He's not bigger than Kerr, doesn't have a pack behind him, but his commanding presence makes up for it. If it is possible for a wolf to emit indifference, this wolf is doing it.

Finally, Kerr breaks the silence with a snapping growl. None of his pack relaxes their defensive stances.

The new wolf casts a glance at me. Fear spikes through me. If his presence alone is enough to agitate the pack, then he's not with them. But that doesn't mean he's on my side either. And, with a jolt, I realize he's positioned himself precisely between Kerr and me.

When the black wolf makes no move to respond to Kerr's barked declaration, Kerr growls. It sounds like a warning.

Kerr suddenly relaxes his posture and shakes his ruff. Now the black wolf, for the first time, tenses; the fur on his shoulders stands on end. With a huff of breath, Kerr strides into the darkness of the trees. When he reappears seconds later, he's fastening a pair of pants, having shed his wolf form. He snaps an order at his pack, and they slowly lower their bellies to the grass. Each of them looks ready to leap up at a moment's notice.

I haven't seen him without a shirt before; Kerr's bare chest is as broad and muscled as it seemed. Scars pepper his back and chest. One large scar on his forearm catches my eye—a bite mark.

Heart pounding, I flash to my first day in Lyria—a lifetime ago—treating James' wounds and brushing the scar at the base of his neck. The scar that I see every time his loose shirt reveals the slope of his shoulder. The scar that he's never explained to me.

"Let's talk, my boy," Kerr is saying to the black wolf, his arms spread wide in a false show of welcome. And, when the black wolf turns to look at me before padding into the shadows of the forest, I know. Long before James steps back into the moonlit clearing wearing nothing more than a pair of dark cloth pants, I know.

James Sable is a werewolf.

The realization rocks me.

James flashes a swift glance at me, his eyes filled with so many emotions I can't even begin to interpret them before he's looked away.

My heart is in my throat as I watch him take a few cautious steps toward Kerr. He plants himself between the two of us once more with his arms crossed. He doesn't flinch away from the hard, mocking glance Kerr fixes him with.

"Decide to come crawling back to us, did you?" Kerr sneers.

Though I can't see his face, I know James is stung by the words when the muscles in his back and arms tense. "You know that's not what I'm here for," he replies. His voice is cold, tight. Poorly concealed anger is bubbling beneath his calm façade.

"We wondered if the king and his son would send their palace pet to retrieve the girl." Kerr waves a hand toward me.

It's hard to pay attention to what they're saying when my mind is whirling. Everything I didn't understand, everything no one would explain to me—all of it finally makes sense. Why the Demesnians avoid him and watch him out of the corner of their eyes. His silence, the way he fades into the background, how he doesn't open up around anyone but Crispin and Sasha. And now me. His distaste for any talk associated with magical creatures. Why he'd be the Crown Prince's only guard. Why he could be sent to check information across kingdom borders.

But for as many questions as this finally answers, it introduces many more. Most namely why Kerr is watching him warily with such venom in his eyes. *Why isn't James part of the pack?*

But I think I know the answer. By choice. He hates talking about magical creatures because he's doing everything in his power not to be one.

"No one sent me," James is telling Kerr. "Believe it or not, I am capable of acting on my own orders. I don't have to be told what to do. I'm not some blind follower of yours any longer."

"That you aren't," Kerr agrees, looking him over.

The haughty white wolf I'd seen yips; the quiet sound is like a gunshot in the silence. Kerr's hard glare falls on her and stays there for a long time. The instant he looks away, she stands and moves into the trees. And it takes only moments for her to reappear in her human form.

Both Kerr and James watch her stride toward them. She's thrown on a loose white dress—it's sleeveless and hangs below her knees, and it somehow manages to show off her curvy frame rather than hide it. Her blonde hair is loose and wavy. She'd be beautiful, if she hadn't been part of the wolf pack that tied me to a tree and gagged me.

"James," she practically purrs through white teeth and full lips. "I seem to remember you claiming you'd never set foot in this stretch of the forest again." She arches her eyebrows slightly. "Did something change your mind?" I would guess her to be in her early twenties, but she is eying James in the way some of the more forward girls at Shawnee Mission East High had: adoring gazes that beg to be returned.

James expression is carefully blank when he meets her eyes to reply, "This is a...special circumstance. One that I didn't know was in the realm of possibilities when I made that claim."

She takes a step closer to him—too close, I think. There are mere inches of space between them. She's still smiling. "What is it that makes this so *special*?"

When James doesn't answer—doesn't even move—she laughs lightly. My stomach knots when she reaches out and gently runs her fingers down his arm. "Maybe you've finally realized where you belong? Here? With us?" She says "us" like she means "me".

James removes her hand. His voice sounds a little too tight when he says, "You and I both know that's not the case."

"Do we?" she asks. She trails her hand along his chest, walking around him as she studies him. The pleasant grin drops from her face when she flashes her eyes to me. In pain and scared as I am, I feel my expression twist to match hers, though I imagine mine to be more effective because all I want to do is leap up and tear her arm away from James. I think she knows too, because her glare turns to a smirk. But she continues talking in the same sultry tone.

"Face it, James, palace life isn't for you. The rules, being constantly under watch, being so restricted. We all know the way you're treated in the cities. The looks you get." She is standing in front of him again, walking her fingers up his chest.

It's making me sick to my stomach. *Be a little more obvious, please.* I probably would have said it aloud, but the gag is making me unable to do so. I can only watch.

James isn't pushing her away, which makes me anxious. He can't actually be listening to her, can he? But she's *still* talking.

And they gagged me. I wonder how much more peaceful it would be if I tore the gag off and wrapped it around *her* mouth instead. I imagine everyone would thank me.

"You belong here, James," she says in a low voice. Then she flashes a sultry smile, which makes me roll my eyes. "So tell me, what exactly is keeping you in Geler?"

Kerr, who has been observing from the sidelines, finally steps back in the conversation. "I have a better question for the boy, Rose." To James: "Did you really expect to waltz in here and have the pack just hand the girl over to you?" He's sneering again, probably a bad sign. "For the powerful wolf you pretend to be, that doesn't seem like much of a plan."

James takes a step back from them both. As if he can't help it, he turns his gaze on me. This isn't a quick glance to make sure I'm still securely in place. This time his dark eyes linger on my face as he begins to speak, as though he's wondering what my reaction will be to his words. "No, Kerr. If the pack refuses to give her to me, my plan is to fight for control of the pack."

Not the answer they were expecting. The carefully controlled expressions of Rose and Kerr drop as astonishment steals over them, if only for a moment.

I hate being gagged. I don't know what's going on, and there's no way for me to find out. I widen my eyes, still holding James' eyes, and shake my head. He looks away to the wolves sitting behind their leader.

And then something pulls against my bonds.

I freeze. Did James bring backup? Is this part of his plan? Or is this some new enemy of mine (as I seem to have an alarming surplus of them)? If they're with James then I don't want to bring any attention to the fact that they seem to be attempting to free me. But, if this is some third party coming to join the action, I want everyone else to know it.

Acting on impulse, I do one of the few things I know how to do. I willingly close my eyes against everything that's happening in front of me, and I stretch my magic out from me as far as I can. It goes forward first, because I don't quite know how to stop it, and I connect to the entire wolf pack.

James' magic makes sense now. All the other wolves feel the same way: a slow dark mix of magic that finally has an explanation. Werewolf.

With considerable effort, I expand my "magic feelers" farther back behind me. And I'm hit with a wall of magic so strong I know it can only be Crispin. I think I let out a choked noise of relief, but no one hears it. I don't even have time to be afraid for the danger he, as the Crown Prince, is putting himself in by being here. All I know is that I'm not alone anymore.

But I can't draw attention to him or to the bonds I can feel loosening around my wrists. So I open my eyes and look to James again.

Things are coming to a head between him and Kerr. Kerr had seemed amused by James' declaration moments ago. Now his features have darkened into a scowl. "This pack would never follow you," he spits.

James doesn't flinch. He looks pointedly at Rose before flitting his eyes back to Kerr, as if to say, "Some of them would."

I know the look means nothing, but it still makes my heart clench.

"You would do all this, take back by force everything you've worked so hard to give up, all for one girl?" Kerr asks him, smirking like he knows something James doesn't. "You would die for *this* girl?"

James' response is curt, tight, and his eyes find mine momentarily. "Yes."

I blink rapidly and shake my head, hoping he'll walk away, hoping he'll leave. Hoping he doesn't do something that could end in his death. But he has already looked away.

"Interesting," Kerr breathes. He turns to look at me, his back to James for the first time. James tenses.

Kerr's blue eyes bore into me as I bravely hold his gaze. He reassesses me and tries to determine what he missed the first time.

Nothing, I want to tell him. *You didn't miss a thing. I am all there is, and if you kill the first boyfriend I've ever had, I will hunt you down and hang your furry pelt on the castle wall.* I'm not sure how much of that actually gets across to him in my stony glare, but enough seems to.

He narrows his eyes at me. "Well then," he says to James. "Let's see if you are still the same wolf who left so many years ago." And without any more warning, Kerr shifts before my eyes and turns to lunge at James.

I try to cry out a warning through my gag, but James has already moved, ducking and rolling away from Kerr's teeth and claws before leaping to his feet and shifting himself.

In a single second, the boy I've come to care so much for has been replaced by the jet-black wolf whose teeth are bared in a blood-chilling snarl and who flies at Kerr without a moment's hesitation.

From my reading (if Earth fantasy novels count as applicable Lyrian reading) I've learned enough to know that in order to take control of a pack, another wolf has to defeat—has to kill—the current leader. So it doesn't surprise me when Rose steps out of range of the fight, or when none of the other werewolves move to help their alpha. It isn't their place.

Fear for my own life is immediately and painfully replaced by fear for James. I know he's strong and quick and clever, but Kerr is bigger and he's fighting to save his own skin.

All eyes, human and wolf, are on James and Kerr. James, even as a werewolf, is surprisingly silent. Few growls or snaps escape between his bared teeth. Instead I can see the same quiet concentration he has always emitted as a human. He seems to be on defense more than offense, though whether this is his strategy or because Kerr is overpowering him, I can't tell. He moves as fast as he ever has, dodging swipes that could cause serious injury while giving as good as he gets.

I wish I could call out to him. I wish I could offer some encouragement. But whatever Crispin is doing is taking forever, so I am still bound.

"Hello, Lady Cara," a voice murmurs next to my ear.

I'm grateful for my bonds and gag for the first time, as they stop me from leaping up with a shriek and calling attention to myself and Talit, who has appeared by my side. He is still hidden from the pack by the tree's massive trunk. I stare at him with wide eyes.

He smiles. "Keep your eyes on the fight please. They'll notice if you aren't watching."

I do as he says, wincing with every blow the two wolves strike.

"I came over here to tell you that, in the name of stealth, Crown Prince Crispin's plan to get you out of this rope is going more slowly than expected. I believe that having Blaine standing over him telling him what to do is only adding to the time it's taking."

Intent as I am on James and Kerr, and overcome by the thought that Kerr doesn't seem to be tiring or giving any ground, Talit's humor very nearly startles a smile out of me. I didn't know he had it in him. But he seems cool and unruffled by the situation.

Then Kerr lets loose a chilling snarl as his teeth latch onto James shoulder. James bucks and twists to escape from the grasp. I can see red staining Kerr's mouth when he's finally forced to let go. I don't know if Talit is still talking, I can't find it in me to care. Both wolves are on their hind legs, wrestling to get their huge front claws around the other's neck to push him to the ground.

The rest of the pack has begun to bark and howl as they watch the fight progress. My heart is in my throat and blood is roaring in my ears because I still can't move, can't help, and James is good, but is he good enough to win?

When I risk looking over my shoulder, Talit has vanished from my side. I can still feel the tug on my bonds that suggests Crispin is still working. *Please hurry,* I want to say. *Please work faster. Can't you see James is in danger? Can't you see he's fighting for me, and it's killing me?*

As if my silent plea has spurred Crispin on, the rope finally falls free. And in that same instant, Crispin's voice is calling at me to *move*, and that draws the attention of every wolf in the clearing. Crispin is moving his hands rapidly in a cast, and Blaine is throwing me a knife, and Rose is a pure white wolf again. She lunges for me with rage in her blue eyes, and I have to fling myself to the side. I scramble out of the way and have no time to catch the weapon Blaine has tossed to me. She misses me by a foot. And now she is between the knife and me.

I hardly have time to realize how weak I am before I have to roll away again as Rose pounces with exposed teeth exactly where I had fallen seconds ago. Crispin is somehow holding the other wolves at bay, but it must be taking all his concentration to do so because he doesn't see me. And Blaine is now battling two men with swords, and Talit is rushing to his aid.

Every time I move my head throbs, like someone is beating my skull with a bag of bricks from the inside. I think the feeling is going to make me sick. I still manage to twist out of Rose's path once more, and now I'm facing James. Despite the fact that Kerr is still coiled to spring at him, he is watching me with a human expression of horror shining from his gray-blue eyes.

This time I can't move fast enough. This time Rose's entire weight lands on top of me, and I am left gasping for air as her claws rake my stomach and her teeth find my arm.

I scream as blinding pain rips through me. I have the sense to struggle, to try and get out from under her, but it only seems to incite her anger. Her snowy muzzle is dripping red when she releases my arm and growls down at me. The hole she's just gouged into my stomach is on fire.

Then she's gone. I don't have it in me to move any more, but my head lolls to the side. I see that James has come to my rescue and is now fighting both her and Kerr at once. And he must have been holding back in his previous fight, because he turns and strikes and dodges with more speed and grace than either of the other two.

I'm still afraid for him, but the realization hits me, deep in my gut, that I'm not scared *of* him. That he's a werewolf, and I don't care. I just want him to be okay.

Crispin has abandoned his cast and is fighting alongside Blaine; Talit is no longer in sight. And I'm still lying on the ground. Every movement is agony, but I force myself to my knees and crawl to the knife lying in the grass a few feet away. A brown wolf breaks away from Crispin and Blaine to come at me, and as he leaps I hold the knife in front of me. His last second adjustment does not stop the knife from burying into his flank. He howls and drops to the ground, tearing the knife—my only weapon—from my grip.

I have one more idea, because I know the five of us cannot take on an entire pack of werewolves and win. I know what I have to do. Clutching my stomach as if that will stop the pain, I get to my feet, somewhat wobbly, brace my back against the tree I'd been tied to, and, in a voice so shrill it can't possibly be mine I shout, "Crispin, Blaine, James, move!" I give them mere seconds to do so. And then I cast.

I vaguely remember James telling me something about being able to cast with both hands, so with all the energy I have left, I move my fingers in the fashion the boys showed me that day in the woods. When I shove my hands away from me, leaves, branches, and every wolf in my path are sent flying.

Then I do something completely unexpected. Before I have time to assess the damage I've done, I faint.

24

It takes time for me to float into consciousness, but the moment I come to my eyes fly open. I immediately snap them shut again when I'm met with blinding white light. I groan.

"She's awake! She's awake. Cara. Cara, come on. Open your eyes."

"James, back up."

"Give her space."

I don't realize until they're removed that rough hands are resting on my arm.

Someone's cool, dry hand presses against my forehead. "Lady Cara, are you awake?"

My throat is dry and sore; I don't trust myself to speak so I only nod.

"Good, good." I recognize the voice to be Prince Elik's. "First thing, I need you to open your eyes, all right?"

I nod again, but it takes me a few moments and a couple of tries to actually accomplish the task. When the brightness no longer causes me to tear up, I glance around to find that I'm in a long, airy room. One wall is lined with large windows. Beds that I'm sure match the one I'm lying on are set at equal intervals on both sides of the room—four poster beds with the hangings pulled back.

Prince Elik is leaning over me; his pale blue eyes are scrutinizing my face. "Still okay?" he asks.

I nod for a third time. I can see the pattern of sunlight falling through a window behind my bed onto my white sheets. It's probably the reason it had been so hard for me to see. James and Crispin are standing anxiously at the foot of my bed. I manage a small smile at them both but only Crispin returns it.

Elik takes something from my bedside table. He slips an arm under my shoulders to lift me slightly from where I've been lying down. Pain shoots through me at the movement; what had been a dull ache throughout my body is now a throbbing hurt. I have to bite my lip to keep from crying out.

If he notices, Elik doesn't mention it. He simply tells me: "Here, drink this," and presses a wooden cup to my lips. I do as he says without complaint.

I'm slowly becoming more aware. Details are swimming into focus: the worried lines on Elik's forehead, James' injuries, Crispin's disheveled appearance. There are tight bandages around my torso, some around my right bicep, and both my arms hurt like hell. And judging by my ridiculous headache, I'm also pretty sure that knot on my head is the size of a softball.

As I take slow sips of whatever sweet liquid is in the cup, warmth spreads through me. It doesn't relieve the pain, but it dulls it, and my aching muscles loosen. Elik lets me drain the whole thing. Then he eases me back down. I sink into the pillows gratefully.

"Will you be okay if I leave for a moment?" Elik asks.

Normally I would laugh. I'm lying in a sickbed, completely out of commission; *yeah, I'll be fine*. But I'm slowly recalling the events of the night before—*was it the night before?* I have no idea how long I've been out—and each memory is a little more frightening than the last. So I nod at him yet again, and he exits with a bow, which despite everything makes me blush. He's a prince. He shouldn't be bowing to me.

The moment the door shuts behind Elik, James moves to sit in a chair to the side of my bed, and Crispin stands next to me.

"How are you?" Crispin asks.

I shake my head. "Fine," I croak, feeling anything but. I need to talk to them about everything. Everything I learned in my short time with the pack, everything that's become clear to me. They need to know all that I do. I'm about to try and speak again, when I realize how big what I have to say really is.

"I have to talk to the king," I rasp, pushing past my discomfort to sit up. "And Verne. And possibly"—though I hate to admit it—"General Logue."

James shoots me a quizzical look, like he can't understand why I won't lie down and rest. So I glance pleadingly to Crispin.

He looks me over, nods curtly, and turns to leave the room without a word.

I turn my eyes to James when Crispin is gone. His expression is stony. I reach out to take his hand and try to bring some life back into him. I try to get him to look at me, but the second our fingers brush he pulls away and stands up.

"James," I start to say, but he shakes his head roughly.

"Don't, Cara," he says quietly, an edge to his voice.

I sit up a bit straighter. "Don't what?"

"Don't act like nothing has changed!" He's standing at the foot of the bed again facing me, and his hands are gripping the footboard so tightly that his knuckles are turning white.

I glower at him. "Nothing *has* changed," I tell him seriously. He just rolls his eyes.

"I know that as soon as you can, you're going to ask about what I am. You're probably not going to ask me, maybe Crispin or Sasha instead, and knowing them, they'll answer you. But I also know they won't tell you everything out of loyalty to me. So let me give you the rundown. Werewolves are... Cara, they're monsters. They don't make alliances; they don't honor rules or treaties. They've claimed their own territory, which they guard above everything else. They think they're horribly underappreciated by everyone, and they're hell-bent on strengthening their pack, nothing more. They're never afraid to attack, or to kill.

"And I'm one of them." Raw pain enters his voice as he speaks, and I swear his voice would have broken had he not stopped talking.

Irritated now, despite the fact that I can see his conflicting emotions on his face I say, "Stop feeling sorry for yourself! You are *not* one of them, James. I don't care what you, or anyone else in this world thinks. You are not a monster. You're not any of the things you just described." James looks away, the muscle in his jaw twitching, but I continue before he can speak, needing him to understand the things that I've come to realize.

"This is not your fault! This isn't something you planned, is it? So the werewolves you know are monstrous. So what, James? You aren't! Do you think I would like you like I do if you were some evil wolf like you're trying to say you are? Do you think you would like me like I think you do if you were 'hell-bent' on all things wicked?"

I'm ranting now, but I can't seem to stop. Because I knew he would do this. From the moment he changed forms and stepped into that clearing, I knew this was the secret that he had gone to such lengths to keep from me. And I knew it was because he was ashamed of it. "People around here love you. They trust you. Just because everyone else doesn't isn't any reason to think you're something you're not.

"James, I don't care. I don't care what you are, or what you think you are. I know you. You said once that you didn't want me to look at you and see anything other than *you*, as you are. And I'm not. I'm looking you in the eye right now, and you're the same boy I got an unexplainable crush on that first day in photography, who made sarcastic comments and kept me out of trouble, and who was much better looking than anyone I had ever seen. You're still him, and nothing you say can change that for me."

Finally, I stop. I'm out of breath and out of things to say, so I drop my hands to my sides and wait for his reaction.

"Are you done?" he asks evenly.

"I think I am, thanks for asking," I reply in the same tone.

James sits down lightly at the foot of the bed, and drops his head into his hands. "Why do you refuse to ever see things the way they really are?"

I scoff. "You mean the way you see them?"

"Cara, why can't you react like a normal person?"

"What do you want me to do?"

James sighs. "I would like you to be appropriately worried about the situation we're now in," he eventually says.

"Oh, God, no!" I say sarcastically, pretending to swoon. "Anything but a werewolf. The horror!" James does not appear to find this funny. He turns his head to glare at me.

I try to look suitably apologetic. And then I shrug. "Why aren't you more pleased about this?" I ask. "Shouldn't you be glad that I'm *not* reacting like everyone else has?"

Now, finally, he smiles slightly. "Yes. I should be."

"But...?" I prompt.

"But, there's no way this reaction lasts. One day you're going to wake up, and it's going to hit you that the boy who likes you is a wolf. And I don't want to have to sit around and wait for that day to come."

I stare at him, until he raises a questioning eyebrow. Somehow, through all the thoughts pounding in my head, I manage to say, "You don't know me very well if that's what you think."

He bursts out abruptly, "Do you know how badly you could have been hurt? What could have happened? We might not have gotten there in time, and—" He stops and takes a shuddering breath. His head is down, his hair falling in his face.

Ignoring my protesting muscles, I struggle to reach over to take his hand. "But nothing did happen," I say. "James, I'm okay, you did get there in time. I'm okay."

He moves both his hands to encase mine instead of pulling away, and he stares down at them silently. I can see he's thinking, so I let him.

"If we hadn't gotten you back to Elik when we did, Rose's biting you would have caused you to turn. Werewolf bites only cause the recipient to turn when the moon is full. You have to be bitten that same day, that same night, to have the bite take any effect. So naturally, the time you'd be caught by a werewolf pack would fall under the one time this month you could be turned."

That fits with what I heard, though I'm still a little shaken to hear that had things gone differently, I could be sitting here as a werewolf too. "Kerr said something like that," I tell James. "He didn't exactly offer that same explanation, but whatever deal he cut with those marauders and the Sheiks left him in charge of choosing the Sophie deadline. He wanted it to correspond with the full moon. But I don't think he did that so he could turn me."

James' hands have tightened around my own. "No, I don't think he did either. That would cause unrest with all four kingdoms and give us all a common enemy. Kerr wouldn't want that. I'm sure he only wanted the option available."

"I'm sure he did. After all, the man thinks of everything."

There is so much sarcasm poured into that phrase that James can't seem to help letting a slow, weak smile start across his face. He stands and walks over to me hesitantly. I think my breath catches in my throat, but I find myself unable to do anything about it as James takes my face carefully in his hands and kisses me once softly before pulling back to rest his forehead against mine.

"You can be so infuriating," he breathes.

I make a face. "Right back at you."

James makes a show of straightening my covers and refluffing my pillows before moving to sit on the chair again.

I consider him for a moment and mentally compare him to the rest of the werewolves I so recently met. I wonder how he ended up here when he obviously lived with the pack before. I wonder why the other wolves dislike him so much and what made James leave them, for I still believe it was his choice to do so.

"Who's Rose?" I ask.

James grimaces. "Oh. Rose." He sighs. "I wondered if you'd ask about her."

"That's not an answer," I feel compelled to point out when he pauses.

"I know... Rose used to be a Demesnian royal before she was bitten by Kerr." That explains her superior attitude. "Once she declared her allegiance to the pack instead of to Demesne, her land was taken from her. So ever since then, she's been looking for a way back to the top. In order for her to be in charge of anything again, she'd have to be the alpha of the wolf pack, or at least the mate to the alpha. And it seemed for a while that I was going to be Kerr's second, which means I would take over the pack after him. So she—" He stops and exhales again. His head is lowered, so when he looks at me it is through his dark eyelashes.

Uncomfortable with the topic of his ex-girlfriends (though I had asked the question), I ask, "How long were you with Kerr?"

James shakes his head. "Can we not talk about this right now? Please?"

The "right now"—because it means we can talk about it someday—makes me fall silent for a moment. "For the record," I say eventually, "I'm glad you're not the leader of a werewolf pack. I'm glad you didn't have the time to finish that fight."

"It was never my intention to win that fight," James says. "I only did it to keep Kerr and his pack diverted so Crispin could act. I don't want to lead them any more than Kerr wants me to. He was right, they'd never follow me."

"Wouldn't they have to?"

James' expression closes off and his jaw stiffens. When it takes him too long to respond, I reach over and lay my palm against his cheek. "I'm sorry," I say softly. "Never mind. It doesn't matter."

"I don't want to force anyone to follow me, to respect me. I don't want to earn it like that."

"I know." His face clears a bit. "I know." Then, though I know it's a silly request, needing a change of topic, I can't help asking, "Will you sit by me, before everyone else gets here? So I won't have to go through this soon-to-be-interrogation alone?"

James, looking infinitely more pleased than my question warrants, grins widely and says: "Of course I will."

I ignore my protesting muscles and scoot over as best I can to make room for him. I had thought it would be awkward around James. Not only because I ran away and put my life in jeopardy after being explicitly told how important my safety was, but also because relationships are a completely new thing to me and I was afraid I had messed this one up terribly.

But it is surprisingly easy to move to being more than just his friend. It's easy to talk to him, to reach for his hand when he's uncomfortable, and to allow myself to be wrapped in his arms. But more than that, it's natural. Despite the fact that I'm confined to a hospital bed in a world I'm supposed to save, spending my time with a boyfriend who happens to be a werewolf, it feels...right.

When I tell James this, he grins crookedly and plants a swift kiss on my forehead. "It feels right to have you in Lyria with us, too," he tells me.

I blush at his honesty.

When he's settled down on the bed next to me, James links his arms around me, and I sink into him. I feel him bury his face in my hair.

"Do you have any idea how glad I am that you're safe?" he murmurs. I don't respond; he doesn't mean for me to.

We stay in this position until the others arrive.

Crispin, thank goodness, has the courtesy to knock before he reenters, giving James and me just enough time to compose ourselves. But to my surprise (and to everyone else's, when they see him), James, who is usually careful not to show more public affection than necessary, doesn't move away from me. He simply settles his arm on the headboard behind me and leans back, still so close to me that our legs brush.

Crispin hides a small smile when he sees us. Rennar accepts it without a word, Logue scowls, and Verne simply raises an eyebrow.

Though these are the only people I've asked for, Blaine and Elik soon follow them all. My face flushes when I see their amused expressions. Blaine takes his position just behind Logue, while Elik immediately begins to tend to me again, checking bandages and pressing medicine into my hands. I take it without complaint as everyone else gathers at the foot of my bed. Except for Crispin. He takes the chair at my bedside that James had occupied earlier.

This is slightly awkward, I think, not having anticipated the crowd.

"You have something to share, Lady Cara?" Logue is the first to speak, of course. "Something *other* than what the Crown Prince has already explained to us?" He seems to be expecting the answer to be no.

Refusing to rise to his condescending tone, I only nod. I fix my eyes on King Rennar. He's watching me impassively, but I see a flicker of concern for me cross his face when I try to sit forward and wince when pain shoots through me.

James shifts quickly to help me sit up straighter; he has one arm around my back and his other hand resting lightly on my shoulder. For the first time, I don't blush at his proximity. I have more important things to worry about.

"Your majesty, I realize that Crispin and James must have told you all about what happened in the woods. And I know that what I did, leaving like that, seems inexcusable to you. So for that I apologize. But the boys weren't there the whole time, and I...I heard some things. Things I don't necessarily understand, but that I believe you'll need to know.

"Kerr and his pack said the reason they caught me was to deliver me to King Orrick. The marauders were all part of the plan. They knew I would never leave Sophie in their hands. They expected me to come after her.

"But Kerr and his second were arguing about what to do with me when they thought I wasn't listening." James and Crispin look as intent on my story as the others do; this is the first time they haven't known everything I do, the first time we all haven't been on the same page. "Orrick wants me so he can deliver me to someone else. And the pack was trying to decide if they should deliver me themselves, to get the whole reward."

It's still eating at me that there is a price on me, like I could be sold to the highest bidder. The way James' hands tighten around me suggests he feels the same. That knowledge fills me with a rush of warmth and steadies me so I can get to the point.

"Those rumors," I say, "The ones about Malachi. The ones you were talking about in the council meeting I attended. They're true. They're all true. The marauders, the raids, they're a cover. A smokescreen to keep him hidden. But he's out there." I pause, taking a shuddering breath. "That's who Kerr captured me for. Malachi wants *me*."

Thick, pressing silence fills the room, as if everyone simultaneously has caught their breath. "Lady Cara, are you absolutely sure that's what you've heard?" Verne asks slowly, as though he's giving me time to consider.

I don't hesitate. "Yes. They were talking about someone named Malachi. I know what I heard."

"Well then, this situation has just become much more serious," King Rennar says.

I nod. I know. I've played over the foggy conversation I heard in my head more than once in the hopes that I missed something or that I misheard, but I know with crushing certainty that I didn't.

Everyone begins talking at once, allowing me to stay silent and fall back into James. He's stiff, quiet, and clearly as shocked by the news as everyone else seems to be. He, Crispin, and I are the only ones not saying a word. We exchange long looks. I know how shell-shocked my expression must be after everything. Crispin just looks tired. There are dark circles under his eyes and his posture is defeated, but he manages to flash me a comforting smile nonetheless. I don't even look at James, I just lean against him and let his arms wrap around me.

"Tell us everything you heard," Rennar finally says to me.

"It's not much," I tell him. "I was..." I reach up and gingerly touch the bump behind my ear. "It was soon after I got this." I feel James tense, as I knew he would at the reminder of my injuries. "So I was just coming-to again when I heard them talking. And they stopped when they realized I was waking up. So I was groggy, and I only heard pieces."

I explain about overhearing Kerr and his second talking about what to do with me, the short piece of the conversation I managed to listen to. And when Logue asks how I know the marauders are a plot to keep attention diverted, I tell him that I asked the head werewolf.

James inhales sharply. "You did what?" he says in my ear.

I shrug it off. "I got the information I needed," I mutter back. "It's fine."

"It's not even kind of fine," he hisses, but he lets the conversation lay for now.

"Kerr told me that the orders for the marauders don't come from within their gang. And when I asked if they come from Malachi, he got all defensive," I tell them.

"That's hardly proof," Logue sneers.

I glare at him. I mean *really* glare at him. My carefully concealed fury and pain and fear overflow into that one expression. Logue actually looks taken aback, but only for a moment. "Next time I'm tied to a tree, in the middle of a forest, in a world I've spent only a week in, surrounded by a pack of werewolves who are trying to decide who to sell me to, I'll be sure to ask them for more detailed information about their secret plot," I growl through gritted teeth. "Until that time, I guess you're just going to have to take my word for it."

I try to soften my expression as I turn to face Rennar again, as glaring at the king might be a poor decision. I'm not entirely sure I succeed, but he doesn't seem to mind. "I know I'm right," I say firmly. "I don't know much around here, but I know I'm right."

Rennar and I hold eye contact for a long moment. And I finally see that he believes me. So I close my eyes gratefully and lean my head against James' shoulder. He slips his hands around my waist and holds me close.

I hear the rest of them murmuring to each other, some kind of plan being made for a council meeting, and then I hear the crowd filing out of the infirmary. I wait to open my eyes until their voices have disappeared down the hall.

Crispin and James and I are the only ones here; even Elik has left, and the rest of the infirmary is empty.

None of us speak for a moment. And it's Crispin who breaks the silence first. "So... you two are together now?"

I laugh breathlessly and painfully, for it hurts my wounded stomach to do so. And though what he's said isn't really funny at all, I find myself unable to stop. After all that's happened, this is the conversation my friend, the Crown Prince, wants to have. I think it's ridiculous, and it makes me happier than I've been in a while to realize I can still think that way. That I haven't gotten over the crazy situation I'm in, but that I can find it amusing, and even normal, instead of overwhelming.

When I'm finally able to stop and catch my breath, I say: "Thanks, Cris. You have no idea how much I needed that."

He smiles at me. "That's the first time you've ever shortened my name."

"What?"

"You called me 'Cris'."

"So?"

Crispin shrugs, but it means something to him.

"You've never shortened *my* name," James says then, pretending to be offended.

I grin, craning my neck to look at him. "How do you suggest I shorten the name 'James'?" I ask.

"I don't know. 'J', perhaps?"

I snort. "You really want me to call you 'J'?"

"No. No I do not."

I roll my eyes.

"There's really a price out on you?" Crispin asks eventually.

James tenses once more at the thought, and I pat his arm reassuringly as I answer, "Yeah. It seems that way."

"Well that's no good," Crispin says.

"A bit of an understatement," I tell him, "but no, it's not good."

"So what do we do?" James asks quietly.

When Sasha flings the infirmary door open, Crispin and I no longer need to respond to James' question. "Cara! You're okay!" She rushes to hug me, but James holds a hand out to stop her when I flinch back into him in anticipation of the pain. She looks slightly crestfallen.

I lean forward as best I can and hold out my arms. "Gently, please," I plead, knowing it's going to hurt anyway.

It does, but she seems happier as she lets me go and sits on the end of my bed. That doesn't stop her from fixing me with her best princess glare, though.

"What did you think you were doing?" she asks me seriously. She looks simultaneously angry and relieved and scared and concerned, and I realize she means a lot to me too and that I'm so happy to see her. And to be here, even in the hospital of the castle I thought I was leaving behind.

Sudden and unwelcome tears prick the back of my eyes. I haven't cried yet about what I've been through. And I don't want to. I want to be—I need to be—stronger than that. My voice is raw when I say to them all: "I am truly sorry for what I did. But I hope you can understand why I did it."

James kisses the top of my head, Crispin reaches for my hand, and Sasha looks like she might cry too. I shake my head at her. "I didn't think. I couldn't, because if I had thought about it then I couldn't have done it. But Sophie wasn't here." Now I glance at the boys. "You guys were right, she wasn't ever here. I'm sorry for not believing you."

Crispin is shaking his head. "We shouldn't have risked it, Cara. We know what she means to you, and we never should have let the council vote against going for her."

"Cris and I told them we wanted to go look for Sophie," James says, "in the previous meetings. We said to assume the Sheiks had her and to go after her. I just want you to know that. If it had been our decision, we would have gone and made sure she was safe."

I don't know why hearing them say those things make this seem better, but it does. Somehow it helps. *They were on my side the whole time.* I close my eyes, because now I really am in danger of crying. "Oh, thank you," I breathe.

James slips a hand under my blanket-covered legs and gently shifts me so that I'm curled against his chest and my tears are hidden in his shirt. "You need to sleep," he murmurs. "Sleep. We'll be here when you wake up."

I breathe in his pine and rain and musk smell, keep my eyes closed tight, and allow myself to drift off (I assume with a little help from Elik's medicines) by remembering that I'll be safe when I wake up.

****

Prince Elik seems to be indispensable to the castle's infirmary. I don't know whether he is in charge because he is the best, or because he is the prince, but either way the nurses and healers answer to him. They come to him with problems or requests during the time he spends at my bedside, and they usually accept his answers. Occasionally they argue or protest, and sometimes they change his mind. But they don't act like he's their prince when he is in here. They simply see him as a respected leader.

"How did you get them to stop treating you like royalty?" I ask Elik, when he finishes yet another discussion with one of the nurses. "Everywhere else you go, you're a prince. Why not in here?"

Elik takes a rare moment to sit next to me and give me a small smile. "I didn't let them. When I found out that my magic was meant for healing, I did nothing more than ask for a position here. The first thing the nurses did was offer to show me around and explain how the infirmary ran. But I told them that wasn't what I wanted. I asked for an internship, to be taught as any other would be. And it took them some time to stop seeing me as their prince. But we all worked at it, and now they know me as their equal. Because I know things they don't, and because they are continually teaching me."

In a way that I am quickly coming to recognize that only Elik does, he alone understands exactly why I'm asking and gets straight to the heart of the matter. "It will take time for you too, Lady Cara. But the more time you spend making everyone understand you don't want special treatment, and the more time you spend treating everyone around you as equal to you, the sooner they will understand how to act toward you. You have already become equals with both a Crown Prince and a guard, and it seems you are well on your way to doing the same with Princess Sasha and myself. I imagine it will not take long for you to do this with the others in my world too."

I'm sitting up today, surrounded by pillows to prop me up, and I tilt my head to regard him. He's different than the rest of his siblings, but a good different. A comforting, untroubled kind of different. He doesn't care much about ruling, which I've learned is the reason he has no wife and still lives in the castle instead of on his own land. He cares for his work, and for the people who work with and under him, and in what he does he is always searching for improvement. Elik doesn't look for more than that in his life. And this simplicity makes me enjoy his company and truly appreciate him.

Elik brushes his too-long hair out of his pale blue eyes. "You should take a break," I tell him. "You've been here with me all day, and you look exhausted." Evening is falling now, which makes it time for dinner anyway.

"I am exhausted," he agrees. "But it is resulting in your healing, which makes it worthwhile."

I relax into my pillows. "Thank you, Prince Elik. For everything you do for me."

He merely waves off my gratitude and stands to join his other nurses. But he truly has done much for me. Elik has been acting as my personal physician since I arrived. Not only did he save me from Rose's werewolf bite, he patched my stomach where Rose clawed it to shreds and—though he won't allow me to see the injury—he assures me it is healing as well as can be expected. Whatever meds he's giving me keep the pain dulled, which I am grateful for. I can still remember how it felt to have her claws tearing into me, and I have no wish to relive that feeling.

The bandages have been removed from my arm where the bite mark has scabbed over and is already beginning to fade. It matches the one on James' shoulder. He unwillingly admitted to me that it will scar, that I will always bear the mark of having been bitten. But after considering it, I don't mind. It's a reminder, not that I need one, so I don't forget anytime soon what I did, or what was done for me. It's explaining the scar to friends and family on Earth that I'm worried about.

Tonight when Elik leaves for dinner, it is James who brings food up to me from the dining hall some time later. The first evening it had been Crispin, the next Sasha.

"What have you brought me?" I ask as he sets food out.

"Tonight," he says in a very good impression of an Earth waiter. "Our special is roast pork with Frale's secret sauce, a side of vegetable soup, a pile of dinner rolls and a too-large helping of apple butter, which I will be assisting you in finishing, and, of course, to top it all off you will be receiving a slice of some kind of chocolate cake, which Frale has made specially for you. I think she believes you to be wasting away up here."

I haven't eaten since breakfast this morning, at Elik's request, and I get hungrier with every word he says. "Frale is too good to me," I sigh.

"That she is," James says, taking a seat at the foot of my bed, cross-legged, to face me. "When I'm injured all I get is hospital food and whatever Crispin sneaks me. You practically get a buffet. It's hardly fair."

I smirk and dig into my chocolate cake first. "When you are saddled with a world-saving prophecy"—I point my fork at him—"then I am sure you can demand any food you would like."

James launches into a list of all the food he *would* demand, given the chance. I study him as he speaks. I know he didn't want to tell me his werewolf secret, but now that it's out it is as though a weight has been lifted from him. His secret, his life, really is a burden to him, and he seems so light without it weighing him down in my presence.

"It's because of the way you reacted," Sasha had told me the day before, when I'd tried explaining this to her. "It's the way people take the news that burdens him, not the secret itself."

I hope that's true. Maybe if they realize I can handle things, people here will stop trying to shield me from the truth.

"Are you even listening?" James is peering at me curiously. "Did you not hear any of my demands for apple butter?"

Grinning, I toss him a roll from my pile and pass the dish of butter to him. "I would never ignore your need for apple butter."

"You get so lost in your head sometimes," James murmurs unexpectedly, eyes dark. "I wish I could follow you there."

I close my eyes briefly and sigh. "My head isn't always my favorite place to be," I tell him. "There's a lot going on in there."

"Then come back out," he urges. "I'm out here, you know."

Now I chuckle. "Trust me, James. You're in there too."

The wide, genuine smile he flashes makes me glad I said it out loud.

25

"This is a horrible idea." I fidget while Sasha continues to carefully wind my hair into a knot at the nape of my neck. When she doesn't reply I add. "A *really* horrible idea. I can't even dance on Earth, when no one is watching. Now I have to dance in Lyria, injured, with everyone watching?"

"No one is going to force you to dance," Sasha sighs. "They'll just be expecting you to."

"Same thing," I mutter.

"Yeah, pretty much," Sasha agrees.

When I feel her finish I stand up and glance in the mirror.

"Good?" Sasha asks.

"Perfect," I reply, "as always." She parted my hair off to one side, and French-braided the front of the larger part before tangling it all in a curly knot that's set off-center at the back of my neck.

Now that I've been released from the infirmary, Sasha's feast plan is a go. I have been declared concussion-free, my arm no longer hurts with every move, and, as long as I make no sudden movements, my stomach wounds will be fine. So though it's a bit behind schedule, Demesnian nobles have been arriving throughout the day to attend the king and queen's feast.

Sasha is eyeing my hair critically. "Hang on," she decides. "I want to add something."

"Sasha, it looks wonderful. You can leave it as is."

She chuckles. "Not now that I've got a better idea I can't." She's pulled a length of thin, dark blue ribbon and a few strands of something that looks like gold tinsel from the pile of accessories she brought across the hall. After pressing a few extra pins into my hand, Sasha walks me back to the bed to sit down.

I let her work in silence and hand her pins when she asks for them.

"Finished!" she sings. "Now, it's perfect."

To my chagrin, she's right. She's threaded the color through my braid and pinned the ends in with the rest of my hair in the back.

"You look very Demesnian," Sasha says. "You know, except for your hair and eye color and everything."

I laugh. "So not Demesnian at all?"

"As close as you can without dying your hair," she amends.

"Good enough for me." I look out my windows at the evening light. "How much time do we have left?" I ask her.

"Oh, probably not much," Sasha says, unconcerned as she begins styling her own hair. "But we can be late."

I shake my head. Being fashionably late isn't only an Earth idea apparently. "Then can I at least see my dress now?" I ask her. "I might as well change while you do that."

"It's been in your wardrobe all day," Sasha says, giving me a look. "You haven't seen it yet?"

"Why didn't you tell me?" I cry, rushing over to pull the doors open.

The dress is hanging front and center, over all my other clothes. I catch my breath when I see it. "Sasha, I can't wear this."

Sasha comes over to join me, still pinning sections of her hair up. "Why not?" she asks, scrutinizing it.

"It's...Sasha, it's too much."

It's beautiful—absolutely stunning—and it would give Saladin all the ammo he needs to claim my pretentiousness in front of everyone. The fabric of the overdress is soft and pale gold in color. In shape, it's much like the overdress I wore on my first day here a lifetime ago: a similar v-neck with a few buttons down to my waist and a wide triangle at the front of the skirt for another color to show though (a popular style for Demesnian dresses). The golden skirt is so long that it will trail behind me, and the fabric seems to shimmer in the light.

Under this, there is a midnight blue underdress whose hem will just brush the ground. Sleeveless, with a scooping neck, this fabric is thicker under my touch. Strappy gold sandals are set for me under the ensemble.

Sasha huffs at my reaction. "You're wearing it, Cara. I had too much fun helping the tailors design it to let it go to waste."

"Then you wear it," I mumble as she walks away.

She hears me. "Me? Can't. I already have an outfit."

I pull the dress out of the wardrobe and gently lay it across the bed. "Sasha, are you sure about this?" Part of me is hoping she'll change her mind and I'll avoid all the attention the dress is sure to bring, but another part of me really wants to put it on.

"Cara. Just get dressed."

I retrieve my Earth undergarments; I still haven't come around to all Lyrian clothes. The deep blue underdress fits me closely and hugs every curve I have before brushing the floor. I quickly figure out how to put on the sandals before sliding the gold dress over it all. Its long sleeves loosen at my elbows and fall just past my wrists. I button it up, straighten out the wrinkles, and brace myself to look into the mirror with Sasha.

She's grinning broadly. "I knew it would look beautiful."

It does.

"No accessories for me this time?" I ask her.

"Nothing besides your ring. Oh! And this." She pulls a short gold chain from a bag. From it dangles a good-sized emerald.

I take it from her carefully and study the jewel. The same tree that is engraved on the throne room doors is carved into the otherwise flawless surface of the gem, and its lines are painted gold.

Sasha is watching me. "It's the Demesnian symbol," she explains, sounding nervous. "I know you don't think you're who we think you are, but if you were...Cara, would you fight with us?"

I meet her worried eyes, wait a time before answering, and try to figure how to respond. "If I thought I could actually make a difference in the outcome of this impending war?" I eventually clarify. I pause again, then, "Yes, Sasha. I think I would fight for Demesne."

She immediately relaxes. "Then wearing this will say that to everyone else tonight."

I'm hesitant to wear it. I don't want to give anyone at the feast some kind of false hope, but after gazing at the necklace for long moment, I clasp it around my neck all the same.

Sasha beckons me down the hall to her room so she can change. Her underdress is embroidered white and gold, while her overdress is velvety and bright green. A sky blue sash wraps around her waist, ties at the back, and trails down behind her with the rest of the dress. She wears a pair of gold sandals that are identical to the ones she gave me.

She settles her crown on her head and her multitude of rings around her fingers. The collar of her dress is high around her neck, so she doesn't wear any necklaces tonight.

"Are you ready for this?" Sasha asks me.

I study myself once more in her mirror. "I think I have to be," I reply.

She links her arm through mine reassuringly. "You'll love it, I know you will."

Just as we reach the door to leave, it opens.

"Divia!" Sasha cries, throwing herself into the arms of the slender blonde woman who has entered my room. "Cara, Lady Cara, this is my sister, Duchess Divia of Kenstral. Divia, this is—"

"I can guess who this is, Sasha," Divia says with a soft smile as she looks me up and down.

Divia looks like her mother. She's tall, elegant, and carries herself in the way royals do. But there's something kind in her eyes which makes me think she may not be as proper as she seems.

"Duchess," I say, nodding at her. I think it might be customary to curtsy to royalty, but by the time I realize this Divia has already nodded back, leaving us on equal footing.

"It is an honor to meet you, Lady Cara," Divia says, "and I don't mean to rush you. But Sasha, the guests are expecting an entrance from the royal family, which means we need you in the courtyard."

That sounds like exactly the kind of thing I'd prefer to avoid, but I trail obediently out the door when the sisters beckon me. As we near the courtyard and the sounds of a party, I halt. "Could I watch your entrance from the sidelines?" I ask Sasha. "And is there maybe a back way I could enter from?"

Sasha rolls her eyes at me. "The feast is for you, Cara. You're allowed to make an entrance."

"I don't want to make an entrance. Please, Sasha?"

Divia rescues me. "Down that hall is a door that leads to the garden. You can come in to the courtyard through a door in the wall, and you'll find yourself on the edge of the party. Is that what you want?"

I smile at her. "That's exactly what I want."

"It's the second door on your right."

So as they hurry together down one hall, I turn down another. When I make it to the garden I stand still for a moment, breathing the night in. I can hear the guests from here, their voices floating over the stone wall that separates this from the courtyard. I can hear their applause as the royal family makes their entrance, and the short silence as they probably wonder where I am.

I take the time to steel myself against the unwanted attention I'm sure to receive as the night goes on. I take comfort in the darkness and solitude of the garden while it lasts. Then I find the wooden door to my right, and hesitantly, I step through it into the immense courtyard where the feast is being held. And for a moment, all I can do is stand in awe.

Lanterns shine in every available space. They are hanging from the archways, resting along the tables, and there are even some scattered in the bushes and trees. They don't only glow yellow; some magician—Verne or Crispin, I'm sure—has the flames within them pulsing slowly with different colors, shades of pink and green and blue.

There is laughter and the clinking of glasses, and floating over the noise is beautiful music, foreign to me.

And the people. Not a soul I can see is downcast tonight. They sway and twirl and mingle, and they wear colors that are brighter than any I have seen since my arrival. They dance and clap and seem to shimmer when they move.

Above it all, the stars gleam in a deep blue sky. The trees rustle in the breeze and the tan walls of the castle rise high around us.

And it's all for me.

I continue to look around as I skirt the edges of the crowd and stay in the shadows. I am afraid of being recognized, even though I'll have to be eventually. I'm afraid of the people here finding out that I don't know what I'm doing.

Finally I find them. Crispin grins broadly at me when I catch his eye, and he looks immensely pleased to see me. Then he leans over and nudges James, whose back is to me. James' face lights up when he sees me standing there. Though I had wanted nothing more than to see them both, suddenly I feel self-conscious. Blushing, I look down.

So they come to my side. Crispin is in dark brown pants and boots, and his crisp white shirt is almost completely obscured by the emerald, long-sleeved, long-tailed jacket with golden hems and polished golden buttons he has over it.

But as he always seems to, even against Crispin's brightness James draws my eyes. His outfit is of the same style as the other guards I see scattered about the crowd, but his is a touch nicer. He wears black pants and a sword at his side, but his deep blue jacket is trimmed in gold like Crispin's. He is smiling like a guest to the feast, not a guard on duty.

Both he and Crispin bow to me. "Lady Cara," James murmurs, close to my ear. "You look stunning."

I kiss him on the cheek and, planning to use them as a kind of shield, before I lose my nerve I link one of my arms with him and the other with Crown Prince Crispin, and I step into the sight of the crowd.

At first, only the people nearest us notice, and even then they see and bow to Crispin first. But then their eyes sweep over me. Surprise, awe, and even reverence can be seen in their expressions. And as they stop to stare, so do those around them, and those around *them*, until I seem to be the focus of everyone's attention.

Crispin pulls me forward, to the guests nearest us, and he begins to make introductions as if that was his plan all along. I meet more dukes and duchesses and lords and ladies than I can possibly keep straight, but I manage to curtsy and smile at them all. Some comment on my dress and my necklace, others on my hair and eyes; all say how honored they are to finally be meeting me, and how long they have been waiting for this moment. I hardly know what to say at these proclamations, but they all accept my murmured thanks.

We make our way through the courtyard slowly. I let the boys lead the way. One of the women we stop to talk to has black hair, but eyes that match Sasha's. Neither of the boys comment on it, so I hide my surprise at her dark hair and politely introduce myself. When she turns to speak to Crispin I take the chance to glance around the party again. Now that I'm paying attention, I see that there are a few men and women around who have black hair or too-dark skin to be Demesnian. When the woman walks away I look at James curiously. "What happened to Demesnians having blonde hair?" I ask.

"Nobles sometimes marry between kingdoms," he explains quietly as we continue moving through the crowd. "She, for instance, is the daughter of a Demesnian duke who married a Navite noble. Crispin has a brother in Sheik, as well as a sister in Nava and one in Cairne. When their kids reach sixteen however, they can choose whether to stay in the same kingdom as their parents or move where they might better fit in. Lady Iris"—he gestures to the woman walking away—"could have moved to Nava. Most do move. She chose to stay."

I ponder this quietly, trying to decide what I think about this system.

Just when I think I don't want to meet any more people, Crispin leans toward me to whisper, "These last two I think you're going to like."

Before I can ask what he means, we've stopped in front of two young men with matching mops of sandy hair and twinkling blue eyes. It takes me a moment to notice subtle differences between them: one has an emerald stud in his left earlobe, the other has a faint scar over his eyebrow, and his hair is more evenly trimmed.

"Lady Cara," Crispin says, grinning broadly. "These are Dukes Arlin and Aldim, my older brothers."

The twins bow to me in unison. Their smiles match Crispin's when they straighten up and I curtsy, and soon Cris has released my arm to hug his brothers.

"Lady Cara," the one with the piercing—Aldim, if Crispin's vague gesture during the introduction can be believed—begins. "I have no doubt that you have been getting this all night, but..." I'm ready for another comment on my appearance, but he grabs my hand and what he says is, "How did you manage to steal a Demesnian ring without anyone noticing? Fantastic!"

I'm startled into a grin.

"You and I both know *she* didn't steal it," Arlin tuts. "I'm sure she magicked a guard into doing it for her." He raises an eyebrow at James, whose arm is still linked with mine. "You'll have to teach us the trick," Arlin winks.

"I'm not sure the two of you would be able to use quite the same kind of magic she does to persuade me," James tells them as he tightens his hold on me. When I look up at him, he's grinning along with the rest of them.

Aldim pretends to be shocked. "Has our own James Sable lost his heart at last?"

I'm pulled away from James' side by Arlin, who spins me around before I have a mind to stop him and makes a show of examining me. "What do you think, Aldim? Is she worthy of our young guard?"

Aldim spends time thinking about the question. "Hmm..." He grabs my hands and holds me at arm's length. I try not to giggle at his serious expression as looks me over. "Young, pretty, powerful...I would say James here has excellent taste. But can she dance?"

Arlin bows and takes my hands from his twin. "Let's find out. The dance floor is right this way."

I feel as though I should protest, but James does so for me. His hand closes around my uninjured arm, tugging me from Arlin's grasp. "Gentlemen, I think I should be the judge of her dancing, don't you?"

The twins smile like they were expecting this response. "Good luck with this one, Lady," Aldim says. "We'll see you later in the evening."

"Save me a dance," Arlin says with a wink. And then, pulling an amused Crispin after them, they disappear into the crowd.

Unable to wipe the smile from my face, I turn to look at James. "Them, I like," I tell him.

"They and their families visit the castle all the time. I'm sure you'll see more of them," James says. He links his fingers with mine and, keeping me close to his side, leads me to the dance floor.

My nerves evaporated sometime during the conversation with the dukes; my smile is no longer forced when someone stops me to introduce themselves. And, though many people are wary with James around, I never remove my hand from his so they are forced to acknowledge him. And the longer they talk to me, the more comfortable they seem with James standing there.

It's not much by way of getting him accepted, but these *are* the nobles of the kingdom. So it's a start.

If James can tell what I'm trying to do, he doesn't comment on it. And eventually, even with all the introductions made on the way, we reach the dance floor. During my stay in the infirmary someone has constructed a slightly raised, silver platform in the middle of the courtyard, on which dozens of couples are dancing. A kind of orchestra, made up of both familiar instruments and instruments I've never seen before, plays off to the side.

"I tried to tell Sasha earlier," I murmur, "I can't dance. Especially not ballroom dancing. I don't know how, James."

"It's not hard," he says in my ear. "I promise. And people will be expecting you to dance. Just follow my lead." And before I know what's happening, James has fitted my right hand lightly in one of his. I have just enough time to place my other hand on his shoulder before he's whirled me onto the dance floor.

The mass of people is overwhelming; for a moment I can't find the rhythm. The unfamiliar music is daunting. I stare at my feet and try to match my movements with James'. But then he uses our twined hands to lift my face so he can meet my eyes.

"Relax, Cara," he says to me. I can tell he's at ease, despite the impenetrability of his expression. James holds me closer to himself, with his hand firmly on the small of my back.

And so I move with him. I force myself not to focus on anything except his face and his body against mine. I study his dark hair, the tips of which glow silver in the moonlight. His gray-blue eyes flit around the dance floor as he weaves us expertly between the other couples, but they always come back to rest on my face again.

I'm far too aware of every move he makes—of my arm resting on his, our hands tight together, the shifts of his feet and waist that tell me without words where to go next.

"You're doing great," he murmurs. The song fades into another. This new one slow paced, so James only draws me closer until his chin is brushing the top of my head, and my eyes are level with his shoulder. We're too close now for me to raise my head and look at him, so I lightly rest my cheek on his chest.

His content sigh ruffles my hair and makes my heart flutter in my throat. "See, Cara? I know you haven't experienced much of it, but it can be good here sometimes too."

I'm about to reply when he draws back from me. My heart sinks a little when I see why. Saladin is standing behind him, clearly waiting to cut in. I frown. "And then that good moment has to end."

James looks none too pleased about giving me up either, but with people watching and Saladin being a prince, he doesn't really have a choice. So he bows to me, kisses the back of hand, and lets me go. He steps off the dance floor, but keeps me in sight.

Saladin looks about as happy as I do with the arrangement. "This is my parent's idea," he grumbles. "Not mine."

"Noted."

We keep about a foot of space between us as we dance; it's nowhere near as easy as dancing with James; Saladin seems less inclined to show me what moves to make.

After about a minute of strained and awkward silence, I say, "I'm curious. What made your parents think this dance would fix anything between us? Because I've got to say, I don't think it's working."

Saladin glowers, but I keep my expression composed. Eventually he mutters: "I'm supposed to be apologizing."

"Ah. And how is that going for you?" I can't help but ask.

"They think it might earn me an apology from you for hitting me," he continues like I haven't spoken.

I almost halt in the middle of the dance floor, but Saladin seems to sense it and he keeps pulling me along, out of the way of the other couples. Which I suppose I'm grateful for, but it's annoying.

"Well I hate to be the one to tell you this, but I'm not even kind of sorry for punching you because you completely deserved it. A forced apology from your parents is not going to get you an apology in return," I inform him.

He looks disgruntled, and I realize that I don't want his apology. He meant the things he said. In its own weird way, the fact that he doesn't like me, and that he's going to be waiting for me to mess up makes me want to prove him wrong. I decide that I'll only accept an apology from Prince Saladin when I've earned it.

"You know what, Sal?" I ask, shortening his name just to irritate him. I see that it works. "Don't bother. Tell your parents things are peachy between us if you want, but don't apologize, because I'm not going to."

Saladin looks like he thinks I might be tricking him. The song we've been dancing to ends then, and I step back and curtsy to him. "Fake apology accepted. Now if you'll excuse me, there are people here who actually want to dance with me."

Very nearly amused by me, he shakes his head. I pretend not to notice. "Mother and father will be thrilled," he says, bowing. And then he steps off the dance floor and walks away.

James is at my side the second Saladin is gone, and I wrap my arms around him. I'm happy to have him next to me again. He draws me off to the side as the next song begins. "What did Saladin want?" he asks.

"We just needed to talk. Clear the air and whatnot," I sigh.

"So, what, you're going to get along now?"

I scoff. "Yeah right. Not even kind of."

James laughs lightly, an arm around my waist so he can lead me away from the dancers and the rest of the crowd. We're in the shadows now, finally hidden again from the sight of everyone else.

"I feel I should point out that the party is actually that way..." I don't mind at all that we're not going the right direction; a break is exactly what I need. But someone has to break the silence, and James apparently is not going to be that someone.

The corner of his mouth tugs up in a grin. "I know." I give him a minute to say more, and he does. "I just need a second."

I frown slightly, but allow the quiet to continue.

Eventually, about halfway down a courtyard path, with the sounds of the feast fading behind us, James catches my wrist and draws me to a stop. "Okay," he says. "I've got it now."

"Got what?" I ask, confused.

He shakes his head. "I want to tell you that...I'm sorry."

I blink. Part of me wants to ask how it took him this whole walk to come up with that. But the other part of me is too surprised by the unexpected apology to bother. So I settle for: "Why?"

As always, I've amused him. James chuckles. "Because of everything you've had to deal with since you've gotten here. I'm sorry about your magic, your ring, your prophecy. I'm sorry you have to worry about meetings with royalty and council members. I'm sorry you had to learn about werewolves the hard way, and that you're injured because of it. I'm sorry you haven't been able to go home."

I cover my face with my hand for a moment. "Oh, James," I breathe. "I'm not." And I mean it. "I mean it." I have to say it aloud. I need him to know it too. I remove my hand from over my eyes and look up at him. "I'm not sorry for any of it. And it scares me that I'm not, that I'm okay with everything that's happened, that's happening, but I am. I'm okay with it." Not my most eloquent moment, but there it is.

He steps forward and rakes his fingers through Sasha's carefully constructed hairdo. I'm struck, as he gazes down at me, at how far we've come. James Sable used to be a stranger to me. He was just a good-looking boy in one of my classes, someone I could gossip about with Jade and dream about having actual conversations with. And now I'm standing alone with him, in the dark, in the middle of another world's courtyard, with the moon shining in his hair and the stars in his eyes. He's leaning down to kiss me, and our friends—the princes and princesses of Demesne—are somewhere behind us, at a party being held for me.

I simultaneously laugh and tear up, because it's so much, and I'm part of it, and I love it.

Ever conscious of my injuries, James doesn't move his hands from my hair. So I rest mine on his waist as the kiss deepens, until he pulls back just enough to smile. "We need to get back," he whispers.

I make a noncommittal noise and don't move away. He exhales softly, apparently trying not to laugh, and takes my hand to lead me back the way we came.

"What do we have to go back for?" I ask, falling in step.

James shrugs. "I think they have a presentation for you or something."

His grip on my hand is what makes me continue forward, even though my feet would like to stop. "I'm sorry, a presentation?"

"It was supposed to be a surprise," he admits.

"Surprise," I mutter at the stone path.

I know James is smiling even though I don't look up to see it. He squeezes my fingers. "You're going to love it, I know you are."

"You can't just, I don't know, tell me what it is?" I ask, smiling up at him hopefully.

He chuckles at my lame attempt. "Not a chance."

I fall silent and contemplate the horrors that could be awaiting me at the other end of the courtyard. I have had enough surprises to last anyone two or three lifetimes. I don't really want another one. *But it seems I'm doomed to get it.*

Soon, too soon, James and I are again at the fringes of the crowd. He leads me around everyone and toward the front, which heightens my anxiety. The music has stopped, as have the dancers. "So a private presentation isn't really a possibility here?" I ask. James doesn't answer me.

"And there she is!"

I freeze momentarily as every eye in the courtyard turns to find me. James—the jerk—lets me go and fades into the crowd so that I am alone. Everyone parts to make a path for me to the raised center table, where Crispin is standing and evidently making some kind of speech. He smiles broadly at me. I return the grin a little more weakly.

"Lady Cara, would you mind joining me up here?" Crispin asks.

I take a few stumbling steps forward until my feet remember how to work properly. Sensing my discomfort, Crispin meets me halfway and leads me back to where he was standing. He turns to face his captivated audience again. I shoot swift glances at the king and queen, who are seated at a table that is apparently reserved for the royal family. I see Arlin and Aldim, Divia, and seated with them are people I assume are their spouses and children. Rennar and Andromeda smile kindly at me and gesture at me to look at the crowd.

I do so. Crispin puts a steadying hand on my elbow when I draw in a quiet, shaky breath. Being in front of a sea of strangers is high on my list of things I don't like. Right under being told I have to save the world.

"My family and I have been trying to decide how to best show Lady Cara how much she means to us. So far, in her time here, she has been told a multitude of unbelievable things, shown even more, thought her younger sister from Earth had been brought here and held captive in Sheik territory, and been captured by and rescued from a pack of werewolves," Crispin announces.

"Thank you, Crown Prince, for that lovely reminder," I say. Only those closest to us hear what I said, but they all let out unsure smiles, as if they can't decide whether laughing at a joke made at their Crown Prince's expense is appropriate. I nod at them, and hope they'll understand that it's fine, and I appreciate it. The majority of them nod back.

"Anytime, Lady," he replies with a grin. Then he continues more loudly, "But she's still here. She is still doing everything in her power to understand and to be part of our kingdom, of our world, and for that we are more than grateful.

"Now, we recognize that there is no real way to know if Lady Cara is who we have been waiting for, and it seems too much to ask that after just more than a week here, she accept our prophecy fully. But we would like her to know that if this is the path her life takes her down..." Crispin turns to me now, taking one of my hands in both of his own. His words are spoken for the benefit of the crowd, but they are meant for me. "Then she has our full support, and we want her to know that we will stand behind her one hundred percent."

I blush. Both the crowd and the royal family applaud. I catch James' eye as he moves to stand to the side of the center table—ever watchful of his prince—and his smile shows that he seconds everything Crispin is saying.

Crispin is not finished yet. "In Lyria, we have almost nothing that is a greater symbol of power than our rings. We have signet rings, rings to show rank, and rings to symbolize family members. So after a talk with a dwarf who has been serving Demesne by making our royal rings for almost thirty years, we created a new ring. One for Lady Cara alone. A ring to show everyone who sees it who she is to us. Granite?"

Our cheerful friend the dwarf steps up onto the raised platform as Crispin moves to make room for him. Granite stands right in front of me and holds out a small, simple box made of dark wood. After a go-ahead look from Crispin, I take it.

Curious despite myself, I flip the lid of the box open. Inside is nestled a thick, gold ring with five stones set in a row across its face. An emerald is settled in the center of the row. It is flanked on one side by a sapphire and a ruby, and on the other by citrine and an onyx stone.

Crispin has moved to stand behind me and is looking over my shoulder. "There's a gemstone there for every kingdom, even a ruby for Krela. The emerald, if you haven't guessed, represents Demesne, the sapphire is for

Nava, the citrine for Cairne, and the onyx for Sheik. Since you're important to all of us, we thought it was only fair you should have something from each of the kingdoms."

It's beautifully made, simple but perfect. I look to Granite and hand him the box. A bit bemused behind his tangled beard, he takes it. "Which finger do I wear it on?" I ask him quietly.

Granite's beady black eyes study me for a moment. Then he takes my left hand, and he slides the new ring on my middle finger. "Tha' one," he says gruffly.

I smile at him gratefully. "Thank you," I murmur. Then I look at Crispin and his family. "Thank you all. This is beautiful."

Granite beats a hasty retreat off the raised platform as the entire royal family stands and comes over to me. One at a time, they each take my hand and bow over it as the crowd applauds. I blush fiercely. I wish James could stand here with me to help steady me, but I know this is something I have to bear on my own. And when I look out over the crowd again, they're still clapping. For me. Like they really believe I could be the one who saves them.

Crispin draws me to a seat at the royal table by his side—which means James is at my other side, thankfully—as King Rennar and Queen Andromeda begin their own speech to the crowd. Marveling at my new ring, I examine it. I don't have nearly as many rings as Cris, but it looks like I'm on my way.

"Here." Crispin leans over and places another ring in my palm. "The Demesnian signet ring. I'm not sure how often you'll get to use it, but we decided we wanted you to have one, just in case."

Signet rings are used to put the royal family's official seal on proclamations and charters, and I'm surprised to receive one. The seal is the Demesnian tree, intricately carved into the penny-sized surface, with seven stars curved around below it. The band and the seal are gold.

"It goes on your left pinkie," James says helpfully.

I nod and put it on. Three. I have three rings to James' one and Crispin's... "How many rings do you have, Cris?" I ask quietly. The king and queen are still addressing their guests, so I try not to draw attention to us.

The table we're sitting at has a crisp white tablecloth spread over it, and empty plates, bowls, and glasses are set before us. Crispin pushes his plate out of the way and splays his fingers on the table. His signet ring—like James' and mine—sits by itself on his left pinkie. His royal ring is joined on his right ring finger by another. It has two thin strips of gold twined together with a single emerald in the center and one small diamond set at its side. There are two plain gold bands on his index, middle, and pinkie fingers of his right hand, all of varying widths. On his left hand, there are two simple silver bands on his left thumb, and two more on his left index finger, also of different thicknesses. On Crispin's left middle finger—where my new ring is placed on my own hand—is a wide gold ring inlaid with seven emeralds.

I pull that hand closer to me, to study the ring.

"It's because I'm a seventh son," Cris explains, wiggling the finger.

"And the rest?"

"The plain bands are for my siblings; the gold rings are for my brothers, the silver for sisters. This one"—he taps the one above his royal ring—"represents my parents. The diamond means my mother is the one with royal blood. My wedding band will go where yours do on Earth, my left ring finger, and then I'll get more rings, to represent my wife and any kids."

"Wow." I stare at his hand a moment longer before allowing him to have it back.

We sit in silence until the king and queen finish their speech. As they take their seats and the audience applauds them, servants emerge from the shadows. Some carry tables and chairs, other plates and cups, and in seconds the tables are set, tablecloths are thrown over them, and places are arranged. Each guest seems to know where to sit. They do so as the servants back away.

And then the kitchen staff, dressed in white and loaded down with trays of food, comes out. They serve the royal table first. I follow Crispin and James' leads, taking what I want from the trays that pass by and piling it all on the plates in front of me. It's more food than I've eaten since my stay in the infirmary, and frankly I don't think I'll be able to finish it all. But I want to try it; it all looks delicious.

We are seated on one side of the long table, facing the crowd below who are sitting at round tables. Every so often the guests shoot fleeting glances at the royals, but otherwise they seem comfortable conversing with one another.

Crispin and James keep me entertained throughout dinner with family anecdotes and stories from when they were children. Apparently the two have been friends since James arrived at the Demesnian castle, though when that was they don't tell me. I don't ask. I don't want to spoil dinner with questions they don't want to answer, but I'm tired of the mysteries.

When dinner is over and the party resumed, Crispin stands and offers his hand to me. "I think it's my turn for a dance," he smiles.

For the rest of the evening, I alternate between dance partners: the twin dukes, Crispin, Branshire, Elik, and even Blaine, Rennar, and Sasha take their turns. I laugh and twirl and accept the compliments I'm given by complete strangers, and, overall, I have more fun at this feast than I've had in all my time in Lyria.

In the early hours of the morning, when we finally say goodnight to the last guest and I make it to my bedroom perfectly happy, I fall asleep smiling. *I could get used to this.*

26

I know I'm dreaming because I'm holding a sword—that's what clues me in. Usually in my dreams, it all feels real until I wake up. But not this time. This time I know immediately that none of this can be true.

The sword feels right in my hand. The hilt fits like it was made to sit in my palm, and, though in reality I'm clueless about weapons, I know the sword's balance is perfect. I'm holding it out in front me as though I'm waiting for something to jump out of the shadows.

It's dark, wherever I am. It's rainy; the storm clouds obscure the sky. But somehow, despite the darkness and the unfamiliarity of the landscape, I'm not afraid. Something about the rain comforts me.

When I glance to my left, there is an immense black wolf prowling at my side. Both dream-me and real-me feel a rush of relief. *James.* When I look ahead, the tip of Nelma's silver tail is just visible through the downpour. And, when something compels me to fix my eyes skyward, there is a large, tawny and white bird, like a falcon or an eagle, soaring above my head.

All of these things mean nothing to real-me, but they ready dream-me for whatever lies ahead.

Suddenly any sense of well-being I have vanishes, as does the rain. James, Nelma, the bird, and I stop together. The rain is replaced immediately by ridiculous, suffocating heat. It's so thick, so humid, that it's hard to breathe. I no longer hold my sword at the ready but drop it to my side.

The landscape surrounding me is still hidden, though the rain is gone. Now heavy, dark smoke is filling the air. Dream-me is filled with a rush of fear. I turn in a slow circle and the animals match me move for move.

"This is just a taste, little warrior. A small glimpse into what you can expect if you continue down this path." A low, smooth voice echoes around me. I continue to spin, looking for its source, but it fills the very air, coming from nowhere in particular.

"Who are you?" real-me asks. Dream-me already knows, but she doesn't share the information.

Small flames lick up from the ground. No matter where I turn, fire is there. I send up a fervent prayer for the rain to come back, but it goes unanswered.

"Who am I?" the voice laughs. *"You and I, Lady Cara, we're going to meet soon enough. The less you know for now, the better. For both of us. No, I just thought we should...chat."*

"About what?" I call bravely.

"About us. About you. About your future."

"What could you possibly know about my future?"

"Oh, naïve girl, I am your future. I am written on every page of your life from this moment on."

That sounds ominous. Real-me cringes. Dream-me doesn't flinch.

The flames roar higher when I don't reply. *"Out of things to say already? I expected more from you, warrior."*

"Sorry to disappoint," I mutter.

Wherever he is, the man behind the voice can hear me no matter how quietly I speak. *"So there is some fight in you after all,"* he chuckles. *"Good. Some strong opposition will be welcome. I'm surrounded by only lesser minds."*

I find my voice and call: "What makes you think I'm not a lesser mind?"

"I know of your stunt with the werewolves, the cast you used. No 'lesser mind' could have done such a thing, little warrior. I'm eager to see what you can do after you've been trained. I look forward to the time we meet."

Apparently I'm not in control of my own dream. I want to ask him more questions; I want to wake up. Instead, as the man's laughter grows louder, the flames start to lick the sky. James, Nelma, and the bird have disappeared. My sword grows red-hot in my hand and I drop it immediately. The inferno begins to rage around me. I can't escape. The flames flicker around my feet; I start to feel real pain through my shoes as the heat burns their soles. I gasp for air through the smoke.

I wake up panting, my eyes wide, and I'm suddenly too hot under my covers. I throw them off and stumble to the window. Opening it, I lean out to breathe in the cool morning air. It takes me far too long to catch my breath. *It's just a nightmare. It was only dream.* I repeat the words over and over, though I'm not sure they're true. It felt too real, unlike any dream I've had before. I've never had a dream so vivid; I've never been scared of a figment of my imagination.

Steering clear of my fireplace, and feeling foolish as I watch the still-warm coals out of the corner of my eye, I walk to the washroom to splash water on my face. I curl my fingers around the edges of the washbasin and stare down at the floor. I don't want to start having nightmares. On top of everything else that has happened to me, I don't want to start being afraid of falling asleep.

The sun is rising outside. The castle will soon begin to wake up, if it hasn't already. Shaken, knowing I'm not going to go back to bed this morning, I move to change into a simple green dress.

On an impulse, I slip out of my room before I've made the conscious decision to do so. I let my feet carry me where they will. Which is why, minutes later, I'm opening the door to the prophecy room.

Nothing has changed since I was last here. The same lantern is lit on the same table. The bed has remained untouched. I step forward and run my fingers along the carved words of the prophecy. One by one, I trace each and every letter. Despite the gloomy message the prophecy portends, the deliberate action of moving my hands over the words is calming.

My legs crossed and my skirts spread around me, I'm sitting on the floor of the room in front of the prophecy when Verne finds me. I can't say I don't welcome the intrusion to my thoughts.

I don't speak for a long time; he doesn't either.

"Something's changed in you, my dear," he finally tells me, looking me over carefully.

I nod. I think so too. "I've been doing a lot of thinking," I say. "And reading, in the library. Researching."

Verne takes a seat in the wooden chair that I myself used the first time I was in here. "About anything in particular?" he asks.

"Well the prophecy has been pretty front and center in my thoughts," I reply dryly.

Verne doesn't respond to the sarcasm; I didn't really think he would. I can't shake the voice of the man from my dream out of my head, which prompts me to say, "That magic I can do; teaching myself that cast, how strong that boulder thing I used on the wolf pack was. That... It's big, isn't it? Even by Lyrian standards. I know you guys always tell me how powerful I 'feel', but I really am, aren't I? Powerful, I mean. This is the kind of magic you've been waiting for. And I haven't even been trained yet."

"The boys did tell me what you did to the wolf pack," Verne tells me. "They said it was impressive. Much bigger than they expected. You either knocked out or scared every wolf in the clearing, which is what gave you all the time to get away. I know that Prince Crispin and James came to rescue you, but, in the end, dear, you saved yourself."

I didn't know that; neither of the boys told me exactly how we got away, only that we did. And I hadn't asked for more details.

He continues, "So in answer to your question, yes, you really are powerful."

I nod, turning the information over in my head. "I haven't really believed all this prophecy stuff before now, before these last few days. I kept thinking maybe there was something someone was missing. Maybe you all were wrong, but I could fake my way around it all until you realized it. But now... Now I don't know what to think." I don't know what I want to think.

Verne is watching me impassively.

"I have a whole life at home, you know," I say suddenly, facing the prophecy once more. He doesn't say a word, so I keep talking. "I have Sophie. I have these amazing friends that I technically just met but that I feel like I've known my whole life. I have a job in this one incredible bookstore, and a house, and a school that I go to everyday." I've knitted my fingers together and placed them in my lap. I study them momentarily, my rings and their familiarity, before I finally turn around to meet Verne's eyes, which are still carefully trained on me. "I have a whole life," I repeat, as though he didn't hear me the first time.

"I see," Verne says simply. He nods, very slightly, which I take as a gesture to continue.

So I do. "And I can't be away from all that forever. I can't put that life on hold to sit here and wait around for some war that could be years and years and years down the line. I can't do it, Verne."

He watches calmly as I hold my head in my hands. When it's apparent I'm done, all he asks is, "Who said you had to?"

"Everyone," I say softly. "That's what everyone seems to expect I'll do."

Verne thinks for a time, and this time I stay silent. "You can't because you don't want to? Or you *can't*?"

"I want to," I whisper, surprising myself. "This is the kind of thing I've always wanted." I pause, trying to decide how best to word what I'm thinking. I find myself reading the prophecy—my prophecy—as I answer. "I know it's a common feeling, at least on Earth, to expect more from your life than what you've been given, to want more. I feel like I've been waiting on the sidelines of my own life for something extraordinary to finally happen to me. And I've spent so much time wrapped up in books, feeling like I was living somebody else's life, that, though this is unbelievable, I can believe it. I want to believe it. So far, it's just been a matter of putting aside everything that I've been taught is true and replacing it with everything that I've just found actually is. So yeah, I *want* to be here. I like it here more than I ever thought I could. I just can't."

"Cara," Verne says kindly. "No one, *no one*, is going to make you stay here. There are certainly those who'd prefer you were in Lyria, to train and to learn all you can. But if it is the wish of our warrior to go home for a time, I have no doubt that can be arranged."

"Why would you want *me*?" I ask him quietly, seriously. "Of anyone, in any world, why would you want to put your hope in me? There has to be someone better. There has to be someone else who would at least know what they should do."

Verne gazes at me, a twinkle in his eye but sympathy in his expression. "You can't feel it yet, you haven't been here long enough, but the peace we have here in Lyria is reaching a tipping point. And no one knows which way it will fall. The marauders, the Sheiks' involvement, the rumors"—he corrects himself at my expression—"the *information* about Malachi, this all is new to us as well. This calm that we have here, it is...rising. It's peaceful now, but soon it is going to hit a crescendo and the heavens are going to open up on us. And that's when we're going to need you.

"Not knowing what to do, Cara, that's understandable. Despite what everyone else thinks, you don't have to have it all figured out yet. You have been offered a tremendous burden to carry. But I believe it is *yours* to carry. So the question becomes not what do you want to do, nor, what can you do, but rather, dear, what would you do if you were not afraid?" Of course he isn't fooled by my bravado, not in the slightest. Only Verne could look at me and see how truly my refusals stem from my fear.

Though I continue to gaze at the prophecy for a long moment after he speaks, I know the answer to his question as soon as he asks it. If I were not afraid, if I were not *terrified*, I would be accepting the challenge. I would be thrilled at the possibility that my life was bigger than I'd ever dared hope it could be. I would be doing my best with what I had been shown, with what I had been offered.

When I finally do meet Verne's eyes, I see that he is smiling knowingly. "So what are you waiting for, my dear? This is your time."

I feel ridiculous tears welling up in my eyes. Tears of fear, tears of disbelief, but, also tears of acceptance. Because I have finally, *finally*, made my decision.

Verne pulls me to my feet and wraps me tightly in his big, strong embrace. He wipes the tears from my face, and tells me, "I think you have some young men who would be delighted to hear the news."

I laugh because he's right, and I hop up to dash out of the room and find Crispin and James. But before I leave I turn back to look at Verne. He's watching me with pride in his gaze, just as a father would look at his daughter.

"How did you get to be so smart?" I ask him.

He shrugs modestly. "Well, it was a long road. And I tripped a lot along the way."

I smile gratefully at him once more before I sprint down the corridors to search for the two boys who will be prouder than anyone that I have finally chosen my own fate.

****

"I tried to work up the courage to tell you guys 'no' so many times. I knew that if I refused, if I came to you one day and said I really did want to go home, then you'd have no choice but to find someone else. And I think part of you guys wanted me to. But whenever I got close, it hit me that refusing meant someone else would take my place. I would think about someone sitting in the library with Verne, or joking with Crispin over his dedication to his studies, or...sitting here, in the garden, with you... And, I couldn't stand it. So instead of trying to imagine what it would be like if I said no, I tried to imagine my life if I agreed."

I'm sitting with James in the castle courtyard, in the shade of one of the trees down a lesser-used path. I hadn't known whether I should go to Crispin or James first—part of me had hoped they'd be together—but my feet had led me to seek out James, who had been wandering the castle grounds. And it felt right to talk to him first.

So now I glance up at him through my lashes and try to gauge his reaction before I continue speaking. James is watching me calmly with his storm-colored eyes. I know him well enough to recognize the rigidity in his posture though.

I take a deep breath before I continue. "And I talked to Verne just now, and, in true Verne fashion, he made me think about everything in a new way. I don't know how, and I don't know why, but I do think this is what I'm supposed to do. It feels right to be in Lyria. It's where I'm supposed to be."

"This isn't Jade talking through you with her whole universe idea, is it?" he asks finally. I still can't read his expression. He isn't disappointed, he isn't angry, but I don't think I could go so far as to say he's pleased either.

I close my eyes and turn my face to the sun streaming through the tree branches. "It probably is," I sigh. I'm surprised he remembers Jade said that. He only heard us talking about it once, weeks ago. "I'm sure Jade had no idea just how applicable that simple statement would be to my life."

"Cara." I open my eyes to meet James'. "Are you agreeing to this because you want to? Or because we've made you feel like you have to?"

I twist a blade of grass around my fingers. "I want to."

He doesn't look convinced. "You still don't sound completely happy. And I don't want you to make this decision because we pressured you into it."

I blow air out of my cheeks at his reaction. All this time, he's certain that I'm Lyria's warrior. And now that I think so too, *now* he's having second thoughts. It's unhelpful. I scoot back a couple feet behind him and wrap my arms around him. I bury my face between his shoulder blades and breathe him in. "Why can't you be happy for me?" I murmur.

He relaxes against me and places his hands over mine. "I am. I want you to be too. And you're not yet. What's bothering you about your decision?"

I stay silent, eyes closed. Finally, softly, I admit: "I don't want to screw this up. And I don't know how to be your warrior."

James sighs now. "But you're going to try," he says, apparently coming to terms with my decision then and there. "And that's all we need, Cara. That's all we need."

I don't know how long we sit there, but I'm the first to move. "Where's Cris? I want to tell him too."

"Training with some of the soldiers, I think," James replies. He pulls away from me to stand and then pulls me up with him. He wraps an arm around my waist and kisses the top of my head. "You, Lady Cara, might be the bravest girl I've ever met."

I flush at the compliment. "I don't feel like the bravest," I murmur.

"You may not feel like it yet," he says. "But you are."

Now his eyes are glowing with pride. That's like I was waiting for, and it makes my decision easier to accept. *I'm never going to be alone*, I realize. *I'm never going to have to do any of this by myself*. And it's a relief to know that.

James holds my hand and leads me to the same field I once shredded a dummy in. This time it is full of soldiers. Only a few organized drills are actually being run. For the most part, the men are cheering and shouting and standing in a circle around something. They part for James and me but don't disperse. I stay close to James side.

Crispin is in the middle of this circle, sword fighting with a man twice his size. Both he and his opponent are smiling, and when I listen, I hear the men around me betting on the outcome. Crown Prince Crispin seems to be the favorite. It's not hard to see why.

He is fast on his feet. Though he and the other man are holding heavy shields, Crispin is quick, dodging as many blows as he blocks. They must have been at this for some time to have amassed such a crowd. They are dripping sweat and circling one another.

James voice calls over the rest of the men's, "Finish up, would you two? Lady Cara's got some news for you, Cris!"

Crispin's emerald eyes find us in the crowd; he grins at his guard's interruption. But he does as James says. With a few swift blows that knock the other man's shield from his hands, Crispin's sword is at his throat.

The man drops his weapon in surrender and shakes his head at his prince. "I wish you would not go so easy on me. I was starting to think I might have the upper hand."

Crispin lowers his blade and claps the man on the shoulder. They are both short of breath. "As always, you were a more than worthy opponent, Nox. I look forward to next time."

Money passes hands as the soldiers who had been watching the sparring start to walk away. None of them appear surprised by the outcome. Crispin exchanges a few more words with the men around him before coming over to us. His hair is damp with sweat, and I duck away laughing when he flicks his head in my direction.

"What's the news?" he asks. We follow him as he walks to the shed that houses the weapons and passes his sword and shield off to the man inside.

"I think it is me, Cris," I answer simply. "The one in the prophecy. Your warrior. I really think I could be her. And I'm still not entirely sure how it can be true, but I believe it is."

I'm not quick enough to dodge his sweaty hug. Crispin sweeps me into his arms, then drops me and holds me at arms length. "I can't believe I'm looking at our warrior," he breathes.

I remember how long they have been waiting for this. James and Crispin have spent the better part of their lives on Earth trying to find me, and now that job is done. I'm here.

"You're going to be great, Cara. And we're going to be with you through all of this. Everyone here is." He pauses, and then adds: "Thank you."

I laugh a little incredulously. "For what?"

"For trusting us. For saving us."

I don't know how to respond.

****

"Rise and shine, Lady Cara!" Sasha sings, waltzing into my room. "It's time for you to go home."

I've been awake for hours. After admitting my acceptance of the prophecy to Crispin and James and

Verne, I'd had an immediate meeting with the king, queen, and other royals in the throne room. Now that they know I will come back, now that I've told them I *want* to return, King Rennar and Queen Andromeda have decided to let me leave, though not without Crispin and James. I can't say I mind having the boys go back with me. I don't know that I'd be able to handle the return alone.

Nerves have been clawing at my stomach all night. I shouldn't be afraid of my family and friends, but I am. What do you say to the people you love when you've disappeared without explanation for two weeks? How can I make them understand that it was necessary? I'm not exactly supposed to tell them about Lyria. And what will I do when it's time for me to come back here? How will I explain leaving again?

Sasha joins me where I'm standing at the window. My pack of Earth clothes and Demesnian books (Verne wants me to study while I'm away) is already slung over one of my shoulders, and I'm dressed in my riding clothes from Kayyar.

"How long do you think it will be before you can return here?" she asks.

I shrug. "I doubt anyone at home is very happy with me right now. I don't know how long it will take before they calm down."

"Have you decided how you're going to explain your absence?"

I twist my royal ring around my finger. "I think I'm going to tell my parents that I was looking for my uncle. I won't tell them why, but maybe if they think I'd run away from home to find him, then they'll talk to Amos themselves. Maybe then I'll get to see him again, and he can explain why he didn't stick around to tell me about Lyria in the first place."

Sasha nods. "Do you think everyone on Earth will believe that?"

"No. I just need to be convincing enough that they don't ask too many questions." My parents might let the matter drop eventually, but I don't think that Sophie will, or that Jade will. "Besides, it's not my 'why I was away' story that I'm most worried about. It's what I should say when it's time for me to come back."

We're both silent for a moment as we watch the guards patrol the grounds below us.

"I wish I was going with you," Sasha admits. "Now that Crispin and James found you, now that you're here, I wish you could stay."

"I wish you were coming with us, too," I tell her. "Showing you around Earth would be fun. And it would make me feel less alone. But we still have the rest of the day together." Sasha has talked her parents into letting her travel to the tear with Crispin, James, and me. As long as at least one of her guards goes with us so she won't be alone on the return journey.

Finally Sasha pushes away from the window sill. "Well come on, then. The boys are probably already down at the stables."

I cast one long, last look around my bedroom. My clothes, the accessories loaned to me from the princess, the tapestry I'd seen in the hall one day and said I'd liked, so Crispin had ordered it hanged in my room... This place is as much mine as my room back on Earth. And, as I shut the door behind us, I know I'm coming back to it.

Crispin and James are indeed already waiting for us. Tumble and Misty (who did make it home the night I was captured, thankfully) are tacked and ready. And Talit hands Sasha the reigns to a third horse, the one the two of us rode to the outpost. I glance around, expecting to see James' horse, but there isn't another one in sight.

"Why are we short a horse?" I ask.

James, who is leaning against one of the stall doors, answers: "I only ride when I have to. Horses don't much care for me, and frankly I'm faster on my own."

I raise an eyebrow. "Really? You're going to run all the way to the tear?"

"Cara, it's been weeks since I got a good run in. I don't tire as quickly as you think. And, now that you're in on the secret, I don't see why I should bother with a horse."

"I was not aware that your wolfiness came with superpowers like speed and endurance," I tell him.

He almost smiles. "Don't forget heightened senses."

That makes sense. His eyesight and especially his hearing are remarkable. But I still make a face at his tone.

As the four of us exit the stables, we see Blaine and Koda making their way across the lawn. They are each carrying a small knapsack. When they reach us, one of the packs is handed to Crispin, and the other is passed to me.

"Frale sends her best." Talit has followed us, and he passes a pack of his own to me, then moves to join his brothers. I don't need to look inside to know it's delicious food she's sending with us.

"Give her our thanks," Crispin tells them, and they all nod.

Blaine steps in front of me as Talit moves back. "King Rennar, General Logue, Verne, and I agree that you should have this with you, just in case," he says, handing me a cloth-covered bundle.

I take it, unwrap it, and from inside the folds of fabric I pull out the golden-hilted knife I used with James that day on the training grounds. "I thought I'd lost this!" I exclaim. "I thought the wolves took it from me. How did you find it?"

"Talit and I took back the Demesnian trinkets from the werewolf pack the night we rescued you. We recognized the knife as ours, and James later recognized it as yours. I think we'd all feel better if you had it with you on Earth."

"I'd feel better too," I say, turning it over in my hands, "but I'm not really allowed to take knives most places I go on Earth. And this one is a little conspicuous."

James takes it from my hands and settles it in the knapsack of my things that I've tied to Misty's saddle. "You can at least keep it in your house, or in your bookstore. Have it on hand, just in case."

I smile at Colonel Blaine. "Thanks," I say.

"We just want you safe."

"I'll do my best to stay out of trouble," I promise the three of them.

One by one, the brothers bow to Crispin and Sasha, nod to James, and kiss the back of my hand. Then, with a wave and calls that they'll see us soon, they walk back the way they came. Talit goes with them.

I watch them go. Probably to see if he can catch the colonel by surprise, Koda leaps onto Blaine's back when he thinks his brother isn't looking,. But Blaine is ready for him; he sweeps him away with a long arm and sends him sprawling. Koda, up in an instant, laughs and moves to attack Talit instead.

I'm in charge of keeping them safe. It's not just a few kingdoms I have to worry about; it's the people in them whose lives I'm now in charge of protecting.

Feeling more than a little queasy at the revelation, I ask Crispin if we can go, just so I can move.

The rest of the royal family meets us at the castle gate. Aldim, Arlin, and Divia left the night of the feast, so only the king and queen, Branshire, Elik, and Saladin are present to see me off. Everyone but Sal seems sad to see me go.

To my surprise, against formality, Branshire and Elik hug me swiftly. I blush, pleased by the gesture. To Saladin I merely nod, but even that is a step up from where our relationship used to be. The king and queen bow and curtsy to me, and I do the same to them.

"We'll be seeing you soon, Lady Cara," the king says.

"Yes," I reply. "You will." We had said almost everything that needed saying during out meeting the previous day.

And then Verne comes hurrying out of the castle. He was worried he'd missed us, and he sweeps me up in his embrace when he sees he hasn't. *Everyone is acting like I'm leaving forever.* I wonder if they're still afraid I won't return. I decide they must be.

While Crispin says goodbye to his parents, Verne takes the opportunity to pass me a scroll. "A copy of the prophecy," he says. "It's not a secret, you're allowed to have one, but I can't help thinking the boys might be a little upset at the idea of you dwelling on it in your world. I just didn't want you to be without it. And who knows? You might notice something in the words that we haven't." He looks down at me kindly. "Be careful, my dear. We need you back in one piece."

Finally the castle gate is opened: our cue to leave. Sasha's guard and Crispin's sparring partner, Sergeant Nox, comes out from the stables with his own mount, and he takes the lead in our little group.

"Keep her safe!" Verne calls to Crispin and James as the gate swings closed behind us.

We walk our horses straight down the main, cobbled road.

"When you come back," James tells me when he sees me trying to take the city in, "we'll bring you into town. It's about time you saw it and met some of its people."

I stop craning my neck to peer in every shop window. The villagers clear a path for us, bowing in respect to the Crown Prince and his twin. When they catch my eye, I nod, and receive many in return. Little kids are running about, darting between people, alleys, and merchants' stalls to catch a glimpse of royalty. They all wave frantically at us, and I can't help waving in response.

And then we're out of the main part of town and on toward houses near the end of the city. Crispin starts to slow and gestures for Nox to do the same. He pulls Tumble to a halt in order to point at a small house at the edge of town. Few residences are left out here, only farms. "That's Amos' old home."

I follow the line of his finger to a house with little land around it. It's a one-story stone cottage with an unkempt garden and a thatched roof. Though it isn't in disrepair, the house has an obvious feel of being abandoned. Even had I not known my uncle no longer lived there, I would be able to tell.

"My father said you wanted to visit it," Crispin is saying.

I stare at the house. For a brief moment, I wonder what's inside. I wonder what questions entering that house could answer, and if Amos left anything behind for me to find.

But I'm still angry with him for leaving me to discover Lyria alone and for not sharing the secrets he knew. While I might venture inside it someday, today I just want to go home, and I don't want Amos to be the reason we delay our journey.

So I step past Crispin and tug Misty along after me. "I do," I tell him. "Want to visit. But not now."

Cris doesn't argue, he only falls in step next to me.

James waits until we are out of sight of the city to shift into a black wolf. It's quicker than Kerr's shift had been, leaving me wondering if Kerr had purposely shifted slowly, to show off.

James tilts his head to look at me when the transformation is complete. Even as a wolf, I think he's wondering if he's frightened me. I don't know how many times I'll have to reassure him that he isn't going to scare me away, but I'll tell him as many times as it takes.

Hesitantly, curiously, unsure how he'll react, I sink to my knees in the tall grass and hold out my hands questioningly. Crispin leads Misty and Tumble a few yards away and makes a show of conversing with Nox and pointing out something in the distance. Sasha graciously joins them.

James understands what I'm asking. He takes two steps forward and slowly presses his nose to my palm.

Taking this as an invitation, I bury my fingers in his thick fur. It's the weirdest feeling, knowing the large wolf in front of me is also the boy I'm dating. This jet-black creature is also the dark-haired guard with gray-blue eyes that I've fallen for. My hands trace his snout, his pointed ears, the bones of his shoulder and spine. He still smells like James, like fresh rain and pine trees, and his intelligent eyes stay locked on mine the entire time.

When the other three start to make their way over to us, James backs away and I stand up.

"Thank you," I murmur, hoping his wolf hearing will pick up the quiet words.

With that, Crispin helps me mount Misty, Nox does the same with Princess Sasha, and then the two swing onto their own horses and we all race away, leaving Geler in the dust.

James easily keeps pace with the cantering horses. His strides match theirs. *He's as good-looking a wolf as he is a boy*, I note with pride. He's big enough that his shoulders brush my feet as I ride, and his black fur glints hues of blue and gold in the sunlight.

The hours of riding blur together in a mass of hills and sky and swaying grass. Nothing but the sounds of hooves and the calls of birds penetrate the silence. Maybe because I'm wishing it would take just a little bit longer, our arrival in Kayyar seems to happen in no time.

James disappears around a building and returns moments later as a boy again, fully clothed. Raffin is there to greet us like he was before. This time, Nox deals with him and leaves the rest of us to talk without supervision for the last time today. James agrees to shift again once we leave Kayyar. That way, we can stable Tumble and Misty but ride Sasha and Nox's mounts to the tear and considerably reduce our travel time.

So, once Raffin is paid, we walk through the main streets of the city. Sasha points out her favorite shops, the people she knows, and the places she's visited. She seems proud of the time she has spent in the small town outside the castle walls.

And then, after too short a time, we've reached the dirt path that leads out of the city to the forest where the tear is located. Crispin and I mount Sasha's horse, while the princess joins her guard on his own. James again shifts into a large wolf, then we're off.

"How do you guys do it?" I ask Crispin. I'm trying to ask all the questions I can in the short time we have remaining. "How does no one on Earth notice your absences and returns? How do you explain where you've been?"

Crispin holds up a finger to halt my questions. "My magic is strong enough that I have a unique ability to sense magic in others, to an extent. It doesn't take the same amount of concentration for me as it does for everyone else. But, it takes more magic. That is to say, the way I sense magic is a kind of cast in itself."

He seems to be taking his sweet time getting to the point; this seems to have little to do with the question I asked. "What are you trying to tell me, Cris?" I try to hurry him along.

"I'm trying to say that I can feel magic nearby, but I can't always pinpoint it on Earth without casting. And as we've told you, we try to avoid casting because of the interference it has with technology. I'm trying to explain that every time James and I went through the tear to Earth, I could tell if you were around. All these years, that's how we've been keeping track of you. And when the day came in each of those states that I couldn't feel you, it meant you had moved homes again. And, therefore, the tear was going to change locations too. So when that happened James and I would come to Lyria and wait, to give the tear time to find you again."

James takes the lead as the horses splash across the river. He's scouting ahead the way he had weeks ago, but this time I understand and appreciate the precaution. Now I know some people around here really are after me. I'm pleased that I have fewer questions than I used to (though, don't get me wrong, I have plenty of them). I'm proud of how much I've learned.

I wait for Crispin to continue. I know he has a point, but I wish he would just make it already. "We never had to explain our absence, Cara, because we never went back to a place once we had left it. We didn't leave friends or family behind; we started fresh everywhere we went. This will be our very first time returning to the same city we left. This will be the first time that we'll have to explain where we've been."

I sum it all up for him: "You mean to say that you two don't know what you're doing either?"

Crispin grins at the simplicity of my statement and nods. "That's what I mean. I think it will be easier for James and me when we get back. All we have to do is follow your story when we're with your family and friends. But we don't live with people we have to answer to. We won't have to stick by the story every moment of the day. You will."

I'm seated in front of Crispin on the horse, and I lean back tiredly into his chest as we ride. "I have to pretend to be something no matter what world I'm in. Cris, I don't know how well I'll be able to keep this ruse up."

"By the time we have to come back here, you, James, and I will have had plenty of time to come up with something to tell your family," he assures me. "We'll make it believable. I don't think this will be as hard as you're imagining."

I tilt my head to look at him with raised eyebrows. "Says the boy who, for once, has no idea what he's talking about. I don't want them to hate me for disappearing like I did."

"They love you, Cara. No matter how much they may want to, they could never hate you."

"That's the least reassuring thing I've ever heard," I inform him.

He laughs lightly in my ear.

I hardly recognize the place we finally stop at. My only memories of this stretch of forest are vague, blurs of green and brown and confusion and fear. But Crispin assures me that the tear is here. "It's just as magical as you and me; you can reach for it like you would a person. That's how you can find it." He dismounts and then helps me do the same. "You should try it."

"Ever the teacher," Sasha mutters with a smile.

James has disappeared into the trees to change.

"Seriously. Close your eyes, ignore all of us, and see if you can feel the tear without us telling you where it is," Crispin says.

I wonder briefly if Crispin will ever run out of things to teach me. *No. No chance. "ever the teacher" is right.* I start to close my eyes, doing as he says, but before I have shut them completely I snap them open again. "I can feel it already," I tell him.

He looks at me appraisingly. "You're getting faster."

I shake my head. "No, no, no. Without doing the 'magic feelers' thing. The tear is right there." I point without knowing what I'm pointing to.

Nox and Sasha look to where I'm gesturing; Crispin is eying me with a small frown.

James comes out of the trees to my side to join us. "What's up?"

"Cara can sense the tear," Crispin answers.

"So? You can too. *I* can too."

"No, not like that. Without all that."

"Really?" Now James looks at me curiously too.

I crack a smile at how quickly they just spoke. Then, sensing that it is in fact my turn to talk now, I say: "Yeah, really. Apparently."

Sasha skips up to my side. "That is so neat!" she exclaims.

"I'm glad you think so," I say to her. "I'm guessing we can add this to the list of things that set me apart from everyone?" Despite their surprise, I can feel the tear, though if Crispin hadn't said anything I doubt I would have figured out what the feeling meant. There is a constant flow of heavy energy pulsing from the air only yards away. When I don't focus on it, the feeling fades into the back of my mind, but without any kind of concentration I can pull the feeling to the front.

"I wonder how," Crispin is musing. "Is it because you are from the Otherworld, maybe? Or simply because your magic is stronger? Or because your home is directly on the other side? Or—?"

"Oh my gosh, Cris, we don't have time for this," James hushes him.

Crispin falls silent, but he continues to look at me as though I am one of the books he has been waiting to study.

Suddenly, Sasha throws her arms around me. "I'm going to miss you," she says in my ear. "With you gone, my only company is Saladin and whatever lady-in-waiting I coerce away from her daily chores to talk."

I return the embrace. "I won't be gone long. With everything happening to me, I'm not sure I can afford to be."

"I know." It takes her a long moment to let me go and step back. She hugs Crispin and James before taking her horse's reigns from Nox. He's been standing patiently off to the side this whole time.

While Sasha mounts and Crispin collects our bags, James' warm, rough hand slides into mine. I blink up at him, smiling softly at the content expression in his storm-colored eyes. "You'll see her soon," he tells me. "You know, she reminds me a little of Jade."

"I wonder how they would get along," I say quietly. I wonder if I'll ever get the chance to find out.

Sasha straightens her crown, sweeps her gaze over the boys and me one more time, and then she and Nox trot away into the trees.

I watch them until they are out of sight and the sound of their horses' hooves have faded into the forest. And then I turn to take a long look at the two boys in front of me. Only days ago, had I been asked how close I was to them, without thinking I would have answered, "Oh, not too close We just met, really." But that isn't true. Not anymore. I know, in some deep, instinctive part of me, that Crispin and James and I know each other better than anyone else, in any world. They had led me to the ends of the Earth, literally, and they had pulled me past it. They're willingly putting their lives in my hands.

Crispin holds out his hand for me to take so we can all jump together. "Ready to go home?" he asks.

I grin widely. "As long as you promise we'll be back in time for my training. I'm going to need it."

The boys' pleased laughter is the last thing I hear as Lyria fades into darkness.

****

I stand outside the crooked brick building that is The Scarlet Letter as I try desperately to think of a good way to explain my absence. Mr. Pelegro is the last person I want to lie to; he has been nothing but kind and understanding toward me for as long as I've known him. And I don't think the story the boys and I came up with is quite going to cut it with him. He's shrewd enough to see right through it.

I close my eyes and take deep breaths in an attempt to slow my heart, which is doing it's best to leap out of my chest. *What to do, what to do, what to do,* it seems to beat out rapidly. I have the presence of mind to laugh at myself. When deciding to save a fantasy land, I remain calm. But realizing I have to lie to a nice old man? Instantly terrifying.

"You can walk away," James breathes suddenly, standing so close behind me I can feel his breath on my neck. "Cara, it's just a job. You can walk away."

I open my eyes and stare wistfully at my little shop. Because it *is* mine. It was the place that made me feel like I belonged in this city. The first place in Kansas that I had felt completely at home in as soon as the door swung shut behind me. I remember how Mr. Pelegro never asked too much of me and never thought too little of me. I remember how he gave me advice even when I didn't ask for it. How he'd welcomed my friends and me into his store and his life the moment we'd entered. How he had wasted no time offering me a job.

I remember the smell of the old books and the teetering shelves and the afternoons I'd spent curled up in the armchairs because business was slow and I didn't have to worry about being found or disturbed. And I know I need the job, not for the money, but for the comfort it provides.

For the stability it will give me in my now upside-down world.

Something must shift in my gaze or in my stance, because James sighs behind me, his breath stirring my hair. I turn to smile at him, and find his face closer than I expect. He looks charmingly exasperated.

I then realize I had never considered using the word "charming" to describe anything about James.

"It's not just a job to me," I tell him.

"Of course it's not. We can't have anything so simple in Cara's World. Where jobs are always more than they appear..." His tone is mocking, but his eyes tell me he understands.

Some of my tension evaporates at that look of his, and I grin appreciatively. Then I push open the door to my shop.

The small bell above the door chimes softly as I enter, James still at my heels. When I look over, no one is at the counter. When I stand and listen, I don't hear any telltale mutters or creaking that would suggest customers are in the shop.

My fingers trail lightly along the spines of the nearest shelf, and I wonder how often I will see them after this.

I know the spots on the floor I should avoid to keep my steps quiet. For the first time I walk with less noise than James as we make for the office in the back of the store.

Mr. Pelegro meets us at the end of the aisle, and seems unsurprised at my appearance, even after such a long absence. He doesn't look angry, but he doesn't smile. One bushy eyebrow rises above the rim of his glasses.

I search frantically for the right words. I can't find them. "Mr. Pelegro," I begin, and then I falter.

James, who until this point had been pretending to scan the shelves nearby, slides his hand into mine and links our fingers.

"What would you say if I told you I had been on an adventure?" I ask Mr. Pelegro suddenly. I decide to get straight to the point. He looks at James' hand in mine pointedly. "No," I say. "Not that kind of adventure. Well, not only that kind," I amend.

Finally, Mr. Pelegro smiles his easy smile, and I am struck by a similarity to Crispin at that moment. I can see, only for a fleeting instant, what Crispin will be like when he grows old, and simultaneously what Mr. Pelegro must've been like when he was young. And, relieved, I know he understands me perfectly, just as Cris always seems to. I immediately feel more at ease. James senses it, so he untangles our hands and slips a book from its shelf. He pads over to the chair I often occupy and begins reading.

I watch him sitting there, one leg slung over the arm of the chair, elbow resting on his knee, looking completely comfortable, and I know he knows what I'm going to do.

I turn back to face Mr. Pelegro, who has been watching James too. My smile now matches his, my eyebrows now raised questioningly. He has yet to answer my initial question, and he knows it.

Steadily meeting my eyes, he looks just as he does when he is telling me about a book he is waiting to read. "I would tell you," he says, "that it sounds as though you have a story to tell me."

ABOUT THE AUTHOR

Haley Fisher was born, lives, and is a student in Kansas City, Kansas, where she currently goes to Johnson County Community College. She has worked a number of odd jobs over the last few years including childcare, kennel staff in a veterinary clinic, and is now employed at a local restaurant as she tries—and often only succeeds through late nights and early mornings—to find the time to write. She has always loved reading, so it seemed only natural that writing should follow. *Rising Calm* and its sequels are her first novels. When she isn't reading or writing or working (which is rare), she spends her time with friends and family, catching up on her favorite TV shows, on vacation—or at least wishing she was—and buying books for her never-ending collection. For more information about the series or Haley, visit www.haleyfisherbooks.com.

Made in the USA
Lexington, KY
28 February 2013